WESTERN STARS

Song of the West

and

The Law is a Lady

ANTHOLOGIES

WESTERN STARS

Song of the West

and

The Law is a Lady

TWO NOVELS IN ONE

NORA ROBERTS

St. Martin's Paperbacks

This is a work of fiction. All of the characters, organizations, and events portrayed in this book are either products of the author's imagination or are used fictitiously.

First published in the United States by St. Martin's Paperbacks, an imprint of St. Martin's Publishing Group.

WESTERN STARS: SONG OF THE WEST copyright © 1982 by Nora Roberts and THE LAW IS A LADY copyright © 1992 by Nora Roberts.

For information, address St. Martin's Publishing Group, 120 Broadway, New York, NY 10271.

www.stmartins.com

ISBN: 978-1-250-78375-2

Our books may be purchased in bulk for promotional, educational, or business use. Please contact your local bookseller or the Macmillan Corporate and Premium Sales Department at 1-800-221-7945, ext. 5442, or by email at MacmillanSpecialMarkets@macmillan.com.

Printed in the United States of America

St. Martin's Paperbacks edition 2021

10 9 8 7 6 5 4 3 2 1

Song of the West

CHAPTER 1

The land in southeast Wyoming is a magnificent paradox. Spreading plains and rolling hills coexist with rocky mountains and thick velvet pines. From the kitchen window, the view was astounding, and Samantha Evans halted in her duties for a moment to drink it in.

The Rockies dominated the vast curtain of sky, their peaks laced with snow, though it was late March.

Samantha wondered if she would still be in Wyoming the following winter. She dreamed of long walks with the air biting and sharp on her cheeks, or wild rides on a spirited mount with hooves kicking up a flurry of white. But none of that could happen until her sister was well enough to be left alone.

A frown creased her smooth brow. Sabrina was her reason for being in Wyoming, with its majestic mountains and quiet plains, rather than in the more familiar surroundings of Philadelphia's tall buildings and traffic-choked streets.

The two sisters had always been close, with that special, magical intimacy that twins share. They were not identical. Though they were the same in height and build, Samantha's eyes were a dark cornflower blue, widely set, with thick, spiky lashes, while Sabrina's eyes were a light gray. Both faces were oval set with small, straight noses and well-shaped mouths, but while Samantha's rich brown hair, with its highlights of gold, was shoulder length with a fringe of bangs, Sabrina's ash blond was short, framing her face with delicate curls. The bond between them was strong and enduring. Even when Sabrina had married Dan Lomax and moved so many miles away to settle on his ranch in the Laramie Basin, their devotion had remained constant and unwavering.

They kept in touch by phone and letter, which helped to mitigate Samantha's aching loneliness. And she was happy in her sister's delight in the coming baby. The two women had laughed and planned together over the phone. But that was before Dan's call. Samantha had been aroused from a deep predawn sleep by the shrill ringing of the phone. She reached groggily for it, but was instantly alerted by the anxious tone of her brother-in-law's voice. "Sam," he said without any pre-amble, "Bree's been very ill. We did manage to save the baby, but she has to be very careful for a while now. She will have to stay in bed and have constant round-the-clock care. We are trying to find someone to—"

Samantha had only one thought—her sister, the person she loved best in the world. "Don't worry, Dan, I will come immediately."

She was on the plane to Wyoming less than twenty-four hours later. . . .

The whistle of the kettle brought Samantha back to the present. She began to brew the herbal tea, placing delicate floral cups on a silver tray.

"Teatime," she called as she entered the living room. Sabrina was propped up with pillows and comforters on the long wood-edged sofa. Though her smile was warm, her cheeks still retained a delicate pallor.

"Just like the movies," Sabrina commented as her sister set a tray on the pine table. "But the role of Camille is getting to be a bore."

"I imagine so." Samantha poured the fragrant tea into cups. "But you may as well get used to it, Bree, you've got the part for a month's run." She transferred a large gray-striped cat from Sabrina's lap to her own, offered Sabrina a steaming cup and sat on the rug. "Has Shylock been keeping you company?"

"He's a terrible snob." With a wry smile, Sabrina sipped at her tea. "He did graciously allow me to scratch his ears. I have to admit, I'm glad you brought him with you, he's my biggest entertainment." She sighed and lay back against the pillows, regarding her sister seriously. "I'm ashamed to be lying here feeling sorry for myself. I'm lucky." She rested her hand on her stomach in a protective gesture. "I shall have my baby, and I sit here moaning about you waiting on me."

"You're entitled to moan a bit, Bree," said Samantha, immediately sympathetic. "You're used to being active and busy."

"I've no right to complain. You gave up your job and left home to come out here and take care of me." Another deep sigh escaped, and her gray eyes were dangerously moist. "If Dan had told me what you were planning to do, I would never have allowed it."

"You couldn't have stopped me." Samantha attempted to lighten the mood. "That's what older sisters are for."

"You never forget those seven minutes, do you?"

Sabrina's eyes cleared, and a reluctant smile curved her generous mouth.

"Nope, it gives me seniority."

"But your job, Sam."

"Don't worry." Samantha made another dismissive gesture. "I'll get another job in the fall. There's more than one high school in the country, and they all have gym teachers. Besides, I needed a vacation."

"Vacation!" Sabrina exclaimed. "Cleaning, cooking, caring for an invalid. You call that a vacation?"

"My dear Sabrina, have you ever tried to teach an overweight, totally uncoordinated teenager the intricacies of the parallel bars? Well, the stories I could tell you about vacations."

"Sam, what a pair we are. You with your teenagers and me with my preadolescent Mozarts. Lord knows how many times I cleaned peanut butter off the keys of that old Wurlitzer before Dan came along and took me away from scales and infant prodigies. Do you think Mom expected us to come to this when she dragged us to all those lessons?"

"Ah, but we're well-rounded." Samantha's grin was faintly wicked. "Aren't you grateful? She always told us we'd be grateful one day for the ballet and the piano lessons."

"The voice lessons and the riding lessons," Sabrina continued, ticking them off on her fingers.

"Gymnastics and swimming lessons," Sabrina concluded with a giggle.

"Poor Mom." Samantha shifted Shylock to a more comfortable position. "I think she expected one of us to marry the president, and she wanted us to be prepared."

"We shouldn't make fun." Sabrina wiped her eyes with a tissue. "The lessons did give us our living."

"True. And I can still whip up a mean spinach soufflé.

"Ugh." Sabrina grimaced, and Samantha lifted her brows.

"Exactly."

"You have your medals," Sabrina reminded her. Her smile warmed with pride and a trace of awe.

"Yes, I have the medals and the memories. Sometimes, it feels like yesterday instead of nearly ten years ago."

Sabrina smiled. "I can still remember my terrified excitement when you first swung onto the uneven bars. Even though I'd watched the routine countless times, I couldn't quite believe it was you. When they put that first Olympic medal around your neck, it was one of the happiest moments of my life."

"I remember thinking just before that competition, after I'd botched the balance beam so badly, that I couldn't do it. My legs felt like petroleum jelly, and I was mortally afraid I was going to be sick and disgrace myself. Then I saw Mom in the stands, and it ran through my mind how much she'd sacrificed. Not the money. The bending of those rather strange values of hers to allow me those years of training and those few heady moments of competition. I had to prove it was justified, I had to pay her back with something, even though I knew she'd never be able to say she was proud of me."

"You proved it was justified." Sabrina gave her twin a soft smile. "Even if you hadn't won on the bars and the floor exercises, you'd proved it by just being there. And she was proud of you, even if she didn't say it."

"You've always understood. So get over the idea I'm doing you a favor coming here. I want to be here. I *belong* here."

"Sam." Sabrina held out a hand. "I don't know what I'd do without you. I don't know what I *ever* would have done without you."

"You'd manage," Samantha returned, giving the frail hand a squeeze. "You have Dan."

"Yeah, I do." The smile became soft. "This is the time of day that I miss him most. He should be home soon." Her gaze wandered to the glass-domed anniversary clock on the mantel above the fire.

"He said something about checking fences today. I can't quite get away from the image of him chasing rustlers or fighting off renegade Native Americans."

With a light laugh, Sabrina settled back among the cushions. "City slicker. You know, Sam, sometimes I can't even remember what Philadelphia looks like. Jake Tanner was riding along with Dan today to make sure the boundary fences were in good repair."

"Jake Tanner?" Samantha's question was idle.

"Oh, that's right, you haven't met him yet. The northwest corner of the ranch borders his. Of course, the Lazy L would fit into one corner of his ranch. He owns half the county."

"Ah, a land baron," Samantha concluded.

"A very apt description," Sabrina agreed. "The Double T, his ranch, is the most impressive I've seen. He runs it like clockwork, super efficient. Dan says he's not only an incredible rancher, but a very crafty businessman."

"Sounds like a bore," Samantha commented, wrinkling her nose. "Steel-gray hair around a leathered face, a handlebar mustache drooping over his mouth and a generous belly hanging over his belt . . ."

Sabrina's laughter rang out, high and sweet.

"You're about as far off the mark as you can get.

Jake Tanner is anything but a bore, and speaking from the safety of marital bliss, he's a fascinating man to look at. And, being rich, successful and unattached, all the females under forty buzz around him like bees around honey."

"Sounds like a good catch," Samantha said dryly. "Mom would love him."

"Absolutely," Sabrina agreed. "But Jake has eluded capture so far. Though from what Dan says, he does enjoy the chase."

"Now he sounds like a conceited bore." Samantha tickled Shylock's smooth belly.

"You can hardly blame him for taking what's offered." Sabrina defended the absent Jake Tanner with a vague movement of her shoulders. "I imagine he'll settle down soon. Lesley Marshall—her father's ranch borders the other side of the Double T—has her sights set on him. She's a very determined woman, as well as being more than a little spoiled, and dreadfully rich."

"Sounds like a perfect match."

"Mmm, maybe," Sabrina murmured. Her face creased in a small frown. "Lesley's nice enough when it suits her, and it's about time Jake had a wife and family. I'm fond of Jake. I'd like to see him set up with someone with more warmth."

"Listen to the old married woman." Samantha addressed a dozing and unconcerned Shylock. "A year of nuptial bliss, and she can't stand to see anyone unattached."

"True. I'm going to start on you next."

"Thanks for the warning."

"Wyoming's full of good-looking cowboys and handsome ranchers." Sabrina continued to smile as her sister grimaced. "You could find a worse place to settle down."

"I have no objection to settling here, Bree. I've become quite attached to the wide open spaces. But"—she paused significantly—"cowboys and ranchers are not among my immediate plans for the future." She rose from the floor in a fluid motion. "I've got to check on that roast. Here." She handed her sister the novel that rested on the table. "Read your love stories, you incurable romantic."

"You won't be so cynical when you fall in love," Sabrina predicted with the wisdom of experience.

"Sure." Samantha's grin was indulgent.

"There'll be bells ringing and fireworks shooting and trumpets blaring." She patted her sister's hand and strolled from the room, calling over her shoulder. "Angels singing, flames leaping . . ."

"Just you wait," Sabrina shouted after her.

Samantha busied herself preparing vegetables for the evening meal, clucking her tongue at her sister's nonsense. *Love,* she sniffed derisively. Her only experience with that complex emotion had been fending off unwanted attentions from eager males. Not once had any man lit an answering spark in her. But whatever this love was, it worked for Bree. The younger twin had always been more delicate, softer and more dependent. And though Sabrina was trying to be brave and strong, her sister knew the fear of miscarriage still lurked in the back of her mind. She needed Dan's support and love, and right now, she needed to feel his arms around her.

Like the answer to a prayer, Samantha spotted two

figures on horseback approaching from the lower pasture. Grabbing her heavy jacket from the hook by the back door, she scurried out of the kitchen and into the cold March air.

As Dan and his companion drew closer, Samantha greeted him with a smile and a wave. She had noticed, even at a distance, Dan's expression of concern. But a smile relaxed his features when he spotted Samantha.

"Sabrina's all right?" he asked as he reined in next to her.

"She's fine," Samantha assured him. "Just a trifle restless, and tremendously lonely for her husband."

"Did she eat better today?"

Samantha's smile warmed, lighting her face with a quick flash of astonishing beauty.

"Her appetite was much better. She's trying very hard." Samantha lifted a hand to stroke the smooth flank of the gelding he rode. "What she needs now is you."

"I'll be in as soon as I stable my horse."

"Oh, Dan, for heaven's sake. Let your hand do it, or I'll do it myself. Bree needs you."

"But . . ."

"'S all right, boss," the other horseman interrupted, and Samantha spared him a brief glance. "I'll tend to your horse. You go on and see the missus."

Dan flashed his companion a wide grin and dismounted. "Thanks," he said simply as he handed over the reins and turned to Samantha. "Coming in?"

"No." She shook her head and hunched her shoulders in the confines of her jacket. "You two could use some time alone, and I'd like some air."

"Thanks, Sam." He pinched her cheek with brotherly affection and moved off toward the house.

Waiting until the door closed behind him, Samantha walked over and dropped wearily onto the stump used for splitting wood. Resting her back against the fence, she breathed deeply, devouring the brisk, cold air. The strain of caring for her sister in addition to running the house and cooking the meals, including, over his objection, Dan's predawn breakfast, had taken its toll.

"A few more days," she whispered as she closed her eyes. "A few more days and I'll have adjusted to the routine and feel more like myself." The heavy corded jacket insulated her from the bite of the cold, and she tilted back her head, allowing the air to play on her cheeks as her mind drifted on the edge of exhaustion.

F unny place to take a nap."
        Samantha sat up with a jerk, confused and disoriented by sleep. Her eyes traveled up to the speaker's face. It was a lean face, skin bronzed by the sun and stretched tightly over cheekbones, all lines and shadows, hollows and angles. The eyes were arresting, deep-set and heavily lashed. But it was their color, a deep, pure jade that caught and held her attention. His dusky gold hair curled from under a well-battered Stetson.

"Evening, ma'am." Though he touched the brim of his hat with due respect, his extraordinary eyes were faintly mocking.

"Good evening," she returned, struggling for dignity.

"Person could catch a bad chill sitting out too long after the sun's low. Wind's picking up, too." His speech was slow and thickly drawled. His weight was distributed evenly on both legs, hands deep in pockets. "Oughtn't to be out without a hat." His comment was accompanied by a fractional movement of his head toward her unadorned one. "Hat helps keep the heat in."

"I'm not cold." She feared for a moment her teeth would chatter and betray her. "I was . . . I was just getting some air."

"Yes, ma'am." He nodded in agreement, glancing behind her at the last, dying brilliance of sun as it slipped behind circling peaks. "Fine evening for setting out and watching the sunset."

Her eyes flashed at the teasing. She was embarrassed to have been caught sleeping. He smiled a slow, careless smile that crept unhurried across his face. The movement of his lips caused the hollows to deepen, the shadows to shift. Unable to resist, Samantha's lips curved in response.

"All right, I confess. You caught me napping. I don't suppose you'd believe I was just resting my eyes."

"No, ma'am." His answer was grave, with just a hint of apology.

"Well." She rose from her seat and was dismayed at how far she still had to look up to meet his eyes. "If you keep quiet about it, I'll see to it that you get a piece of the apple pie I baked for dinner."

"That's a mighty tempting offer." He considered it with a long-fingered hand reaching up to stroke his chin. "I'm partial to apple pie. Only one or two things I'm more partial to." His eyes roamed over her in a thorough and intense study that caused her heart to pound with unaccustomed speed.

There was something different about this man, she thought swiftly, something unique, a vitality at odds with lazy words and careless smiles. He pushed his hat back farther on his head, revealing more disorderly curls. "You've got yourself a deal." He held out his hand to confirm the agreement, and she placed her small hand in his.

"Thanks." The single word was breathless, as she found her speech hampered by the currents running up her arm. Abruptly, she pulled her hand away, wondering what it was about him that disturbed her equilibrium. "I'm sorry if I was short before, about Dan's horse." She spoke now in a rush, to conceal a reaction she could not understand.

"No need to apologize," he assured her, and the new soft texture in his tone both warmed and unnerved her. "We're all fond of Mrs. Lomax."

"Yes, well, I . . ." she stammered, suddenly needing to put a safe distance between herself and this slow-talking man. "I'd better go inside. Dan must be hungry." She looked past him and spotted his horse, still saddled, waiting patiently. "You didn't stable your horse. Aren't you finished for the day?" Hearing the concern in her own voice, she marveled at it. Really, she thought, annoyed, why should I care?

"Oh, yes, ma'am, I'm finished." There was laughter in his voice now, but Samantha failed to notice. She began to study the mount with care.

It was a magnificent animal, dark, gleaming chestnut, at least sixteen hands, she estimated, classic lines, fully flowing mane and proud, dished face. Arabian. Samantha knew horses and she recognized a full-blooded Arabian stallion when she saw one. What in the world . . . ? "That's an Arabian." Her words interrupted her thoughts.

"Yes, ma'am," he agreed easily, entirely too easily. Her eyes narrowed with suspicion as she turned to him.

"No ranch hand is going to be riding around on a

horse that's worth six months' pay." She stared at him
and he returned the steady survey with a bland poker
face. "Who are you?"

"Jake Tanner, ma'am." The slow grin appeared
again, widening, deepening, then settling as he lifted
the brim of his hat at the introduction. "Pleased to
meet you."

The land baron with the women at his feet, Samantha's brain flashed. Anger darkened her eyes.

"Why didn't you say so?"

"Just did," he pointed out.

"Oh." She tossed back her thick fall of hair. "You
know very well what I mean. I thought you were one
of Dan's men."

"Yes, ma'am." He nodded.

"Stop *ma'aming* me," she commanded. "What a
mean trick! All you had to do was open your mouth
and say who you were. I would have stabled Dan's
horse myself."

"I didn't mind." His expression became annoyingly
agreeable. "It wasn't any trouble, and you had a nice
rest."

"Well, Mr. Tanner, you had a fine laugh at my ex-
pense. I hope you enjoyed it," she said coldly.

"Yes, ma'am." The grin widened without seeming
to move at all. "I did."

"I told you to stop . . ." She halted, biting her lip
with frustration. "Oh, forget it." Tossing her head, she
took a few steps toward the house, then turned back
crossly. "I notice your accent has modified quite a bit,
Mr. Tanner."

He did not reply, but continued to stand negligently,
his hands in his pockets, his face darkened by the late-
afternoon shadows. Samantha spun back around and
stomped toward the house.

"Hey," he called out, and she turned toward him before she could halt the reflex. "Do I still get that pie?"

She answered his question with a glare. His laughter, deep and rich, followed her into the house.

CHAPTER 2

The sound of the slamming door reverberated through the ranch house as Samantha struggled out of her jacket and marched into the living room. At the sight of her sister's face Sabrina slipped down into the pillows, picked up the novel lying on her lap and buried her nose in its pages. Dan, however, did not recognize the storm warning in his sister-in-law's blue eyes and flushed cheeks. He greeted her with a friendly, ingenuous smile.

"Where's Jake?" His gaze slid past her. "Don't tell me he went home without a cup of coffee?"

"He can go straight to the devil without his coffee."

"I expect he wanted to get home before dark," Dan concluded. His nod was sober, but his eyes were brilliant with merriment.

"Don't play innocent with me, Dan Lomax." Samantha advanced on him. "That was a rotten trick, letting me think he was one of your hands, and . . ." A giggle escaped from behind the paperback. "I'm glad you think it's amusing that your sister's been made a fool of."

"Oh, Sam, I'm sorry." Warily, Sabrina lowered the book. "It's just hard to believe anyone could mistake Jake Tanner for a ranch hand." She burst out laughing, and Samantha was torn between the pleasure of seeing her sister laugh and irritation at being the brunt of the joke.

"Well, really, what makes him so special?" she demanded. "He dresses like every other cowboy I've seen around here, and that hat of his has certainly seen better days." But, she remembered, there *had* been something special about him that she had not quite been able to define. She firmly dismissed this disquieting thought. "The nerve of him." She rounded on Don again. "Calling you boss, and ma'aming me in that exaggerated drawl."

"Reckon he was just being polite," Dan suggested. His smile was amiable and pure. Samantha sent him the look that terrified her students.

"Men." Raising her eyes, she searched the ceiling in hopes of finding the answer there. "You're all alike, and you all stick together." She bent and scooped up the sleeping Shylock and marched into the kitchen.

Time at the ranch passed quickly. Though her days were full and busy, Samantha fretted for some of the physical outlet that had so long been part of her life. At times, the confinement of the house was suffocating. Years of training and discipline had left her with an inherent need for activity.

Unconsciously, she separated her life into three categories: the pre-Olympic years, the Olympic years and the post-Olympic years.

The pre-Olympic years were a blur of lessons, piano teachers, dance instructors, her mother's gentle but inescapable admonishments to "be a lady." Then, the first time she had gripped the lower bar of the un-evens, the new chapter had begun.

By the time she was twelve years old, she had re-markable promise. The gymnastics instructor had informed her mother, who was more distressed than pleased at the praise. Though her mother had objected to more intense training, Samantha had ultimately pre-vailed.

The hours of training became months, county meets became state meets, and national competitions became international competitions. When Samantha was picked for the Olympic team, it was just another step down a road she was determined to follow. Weari-ness and aching muscles were accepted without hesita-tion.

Then it was over, and at fifteen she had found it necessary to alter what had become a way of life. Col-lege had to be considered, and earning a living. The years passed into the post-Olympic period, and she remembered her days of athletic competitions as a dream. Now her life was shifting again, though she was unsure as to the direction. The mountains and plains were calling to her, inviting her to explore, but she buried her desires, remaining indoors to see to her sister's needs. Dan is a busy man, she thought as she prepared lunch, and Bree needs someone within call-ing distance during this critical period. When she's better, there will be plenty of time to see the country.

She arched her back and rubbed a small spot of ten-sion at the base of her neck. The kitchen door opened and Dan burst in, accompanied by Jake Tanner. Sa-mantha met the amused green eyes levelly, though once more she felt treacherously at a disadvantage.

Her hair had been carelessly scooped on the top of

her head that morning, and now, with their usual aban-
donment, stray locks were beginning to escape confinement. She was dressed in a black ribbed sweater
that had seen too many washings and ancient jeans,
splattered, faded, patched and too tight. She resisted
the urge to raise her hand to her tumbling hair, forced
a smile and turned to her brother-in-law.

"Hello, Dan. What are you doing home this time of
day?" Purposefully, she ignored the tall figure beside
him.

"Wasn't too far out," Dan explained. Slipping off
his jacket and hat, he tossed both over the hooks provided. "Jake was giving me a hand, so I figured it was
only neighborly to bring him back for lunch."

"Hope I'm not imposing, ma'am." The slow smile
spread, once more rearranging the angles of his face.

"No imposition, Mr. Tanner. But you'll have to
settle for potluck."

"My favorite dish"—he paused, giving her a cheeky
wink—"next to apple pie."

Samantha sent him a withering glance and turned
away to warm the previous evening's stew.

"I'll just go tell Sabrina I'm home," Dan announced
to the room in general, and strode away. Samantha
did her best to ignore Jake's disturbing presence. She
stirred the stew busily.

"Smells good." Jake moved over to the stove and
lounged against it. Samantha went to the cupboard to
get the bowls.

When she turned back to place them on the round
kitchen table, she noticed that he had shed his outdoor
clothing. The slim-fitting jeans, snug and low on narrow hips, accentuated his leanness. His flannel shirt
fitted over his broad shoulders and hard chest before
tapering down to a narrow waist. The athlete in her

immediately responded to the firm, well-proportioned body; there was not an ounce of spare flesh on him.

"Don't talk much, do you?" The drawl was there again, the exaggerated twang of the previous evening. Samantha turned her head, prepared to freeze him with her eyes.

His face was barely inches from hers as he slouched by the stove. For a moment, her mind ceased to function.

"I really have nothing to say to you, Mr. Tanner." She struggled to keep her voice cold and detached, but she could feel the blood rush to her face.

"Well, now, we'll have to see if we can change that." He spoke with easy confidence as he straightened to his full height. "We're not much on formalities around here. Just make it Jake." Though his words were spoken with his usual lazy delivery, there was an undertone of command. Samantha's chin rose in defense.

"Maybe I prefer to keep things formal between us, Mr. Tanner."

His lips were curved in his careless smile, but in his eyes she now recognized that special something that separated him from an ordinary ranch hand. *Power.* She wondered how she had missed it at their first meeting.

"I don't think there's much chance of that." He paused and tugged at a loose lock of his hair before adding with irritating emphasis, "Ma'am. Nope, I don't think there's much chance of that at all."

Samantha was saved from coming up with a suitable rebuttal by Dan's reappearance. She began to spoon the stew into ceramic bowls, noting to her dismay that her hands were not altogether steady. This man was infuriating her with his arrogantly lazy confidence. I have never met a more irritating male, she thought. He thinks he can switch on that rugged cowboy charm and women will drop in droves at his feet. Well, maybe some do, but not this one.

"Okay, Sam?" Dan's voice shattered the electric silence.

"What? I'm sorry, I wasn't listening."

"You'll keep Jake company over lunch, won't you? I'll have mine in the living room with Sabrina."

She swore silently. "Of course," she answered with an impersonal smile.

Within a short time, Samantha found herself sitting across from the man she wanted most to avoid.

"You've a fine hand with dumplings, Sam." Her brows rose involuntarily at his easy use of her nickname, but she kept her voice even.

"Thank you, Mr. Tanner. It's just one of my many talents."

"I'm sure it is," he agreed with an inclination of his head.

"You haven't changed much from the girl in the picture in Sabrina's parlor." Samantha was astonished.

"You'd have been about fifteen," he continued. "A bit skinnier than you are now, but your hair was the same, not quite willing to stay bundled on top of your head." Samantha's blank expression had turned to a frown at the word skinnier. She remembered the photo clearly.

"You'd just finished winning your second medal." She had indeed been fifteen. The picture had been snapped at the moment she had completed her floor routine. It had captured the look of stunned triumph, for she had known in that instant that a medal was hers.

"Sabrina's just about as proud of you as you are

worried about her." Samantha said nothing, only staring into the lean, handsome features. His brows rose ever so slightly, a movement that would have gone unnoticed had she not been so intent on his face. For a moment, she forgot the thread of the conversation, caught up suddenly in a series of small, irrelevant details: the curling gold which spilled over his brow, the tiny white scar on his jawline, the thickness of his long lashes. Confused, she dropped her eyes to her bowl and struggled to bring her thoughts to order.

"I'd forgotten Bree had that picture," she said. "It was a long time ago."

"So now you teach. You don't look like any gym teacher I ever knew."

"Oh, really?"

"No, ma'am." He shook his head slowly and considered her through another mouthful of stew. "Don't look strong enough or old enough."

"I assure you, Jake, I'm both strong enough and old enough for my profession."

"What made you become a gym teacher?" His sudden question caught her off balance, and she stared at him.

"Well, I . . ." Her shoulders moved restlessly. "Our mother was a fanatic on lessons when Bree and I were growing up." She smiled in spite of herself. "We took lessons in everything, Mom's theory on being well-rounded. Anyway, Bree found her talent in music and I developed a knack for the physical. For a while, I focused on gymnastics, then, when the time came to work, it seemed natural. Bree taught little people to play the classics, and I teach bigger people to tumble."

"Do you like your work? Are you happy with it?"

"As a matter of fact, I do," she retorted. "I like the activity, I like being involved in a physical type of work. It can be frustrating at times, of course. Some of the girls I teach would rather be flirting with their boyfriends than learning gymnastics, I suspect."

"And you yourself are more interested in calisthenics than men?" The question was delivered with a broad masculine smile.

"That's hardly relevant," she snapped, annoyed that she had lowered her guard.

"You don't think so?"

Samantha scraped back her chair and moved to the stove. "Coffee?"

"Yes, ma'am, black." It was unnecessary to turn around; she felt the slow grin crease his face as clearly as if she had witnessed it with her eyes. She set the cup down on the table with a bang. Before she could spin back to pour her own, her hand was captured in a firm grip. There was nothing soft about the hand. It was hard and masculine.

Completely outmatched in the short battle that ensued, Samantha discovered that under the lean, lanky exterior lay an amazing strength. Deciding that it was undignified to grapple in her sister's kitchen, she allowed her hand to rest quietly in his, meeting his laughing eyes with a resentful glare. Her heart began to pound uncomfortably against her ribs.

"What do you want?" Her voice came out in a husky whisper. His eyes left hers to travel slowly down to the generous curve of her mouth, lingering until she could taste the heat on her lips, as real as a kiss. Taking his time, he moved his gaze back to her eyes.

"You're jumpy." His observation was laconic, as if none of the heat had touched him, though she herself was beginning to suffocate. "Powerful strong for such a little bit of a thing."

"I'm not little," she retorted. "You're just so big."

She began to tug at her hand again, feeling a near desperate urgency to shake off the contact that was infusing her with an unexplained weakness around the knees.

"Your eyes are fabulous when you're angry, Sam." His tone was conversational. "Temper agrees with you. You grow beautiful with it." He laughed and pulled her closer.

"You're insufferable," she said, still struggling to escape his grasp.

"For telling you you're beautiful? I was just stating the obvious. I'm sure it's been mentioned to you once or twice before."

"You men are all the same." She ceased her struggles long enough to aim a lethal glare. "Always grabbing and groping."

"I don't grope, Samantha." His drawl was feather-soft. For an instant, the cocky cowboy vanished, and she glimpsed the man, shrewd and ruthless, beneath. Here was a man who not only expected to have his own way, but would. "And the next time I grab you, it won't only be to hold your hand." Releasing her, he leaned back in his chair. "You have been warned."

Later, as Sabrina napped and the house grew still around her, Samantha found herself staring blankly at the pages of a novel. Scowling, she tossed it aside and rose from the sofa to pace to the window. What an infuriating man. Obviously, he considers himself irresistible. She began to wander the room, attempting to block out the effect his blatant virility had had on her.

It was too bad, she decided on her fourth circle, that all those good looks, all that strength and appeal, had to belong to such a rude, arrogant man.

Deciding that a brisk walk was just what she needed to get Jake Tanner out of her mind, she stopped her pacing and grabbed a warm jacket. Moments later she was out the door, gazing around her in delight at the beauty of the starlit Wyoming night. Her breath puffed out in thin white mists as she moved. The air, tinged with frost, carried the aroma of pine, and she drank it in greedily, enjoying the mixed scent of hay and horses and aged wood. She could hear the lonely sound of a coyote calling to the full silver moon. And suddenly she realized that she had fallen in love with Wyoming. The spell of the mountains and plains was on her, and she was inexplicably glad she had come.

Goodness, you were out a long time," her sister commented as Samantha plopped down in a wingback chair in front of the fire a few minutes later. "You must be frozen."

"No." Samantha stretched out her legs and sighed. "I love it out there. It's fantastic! I never realized how big the sky was before, and I don't think I'll ever get used to the space, the openness."

She turned her attention to the powerfully built man sitting next to her sister on the sofa. "I wonder if you appreciate it, Dan, living here all of your life. Even your letters, Bree, didn't do justice to that world out there." Running her fingers through her hair, she made a small sound of pleasure. "To someone used to traffic-choked streets and huge buildings, all this . . ." Her hands moved in an inadequate gesture.

"You haven't had much of a chance to see anything since you've been here," Dan observed. "You've been with us a month and you haven't gone a quarter mile away from the house. And that's been mostly to fetch the mail in the mornings."

"I'll have plenty of time to explore later. I'll be around through the summer."

"Just the same, we're not having you tied to the house while you're here, Sam," Dan announced, and sat back against the cushions. "Even the most devoted sister is entitled to a day off."

"Don't be silly. You make it sound as though I were slaving from dawn to dusk. Half the time I'm not doing anything."

"We know how hard you're working, Sam," Sabrina said quietly, glancing up at Dan before returning her gaze to her twin. "And I know the lack of activity is harder on you than the work. I also know how you disrupted your life to come out here and take care of me."

"Oh, Bree, for heaven's sake," Samantha began, shifting uncomfortably. "I never would have found out how much I love Wyoming if I hadn't come."

"Don't try to shrug if off, Sam." Dan grinned at the embarrassed motion of her shoulders. "We're grateful, and you'll just have to get used to us telling you so. But tomorrow, we're going to show we're grateful instead of just talking about it. We're kicking you out for the day."

"Huh?" Blankly, Sam blinked at the bland smile before shifting her gaze to Sabrina's serene one.

"That's right." His grin widened as she drew her brows together. "Tomorrow's Sunday, and I'm staying home with my wife. And you . . ." He pointed a warning finger at his sister-in-law. "You're going to have your pick of the horses and take off."

Samantha sprung up from her slouched position.

"Do you mean it?" Her face was glowing with pleasure, and Dan's smile warmed with affection.

"Yes, little sister, I mean it. It should be more."

"The dapple-gray gelding," she began in a rush, ignoring the last part of his comment. "Can I take him?"

"Already inspected the stock, and it appears you know your horses." Dan chuckled and shook his head. "Spook's a good mount. A little frisky, but from what Sabrina's told me, you can handle him."

"Oh, I can, and I promise I'll be careful with him." She sprang from her chair and crossed the room, flinging her arms around his neck. "Thanks, Dan. You are absolutely my favorite brother-in-law, bar none."

"I think she likes the idea, Sabrina," Dan commented as he met his wife's eyes over Samantha's head. "In fact, I'd say she's downright pleased about it."

"And I thought I hid my emotions so effectively." She gave his cheek a loud, smacking kiss.

"You be ready to start out about nine." He patted Samantha's slim shoulder. "Jake'll be around then."

"Jake?" Samantha repeated. Her smile froze.

"Yeah, he'll be riding out with you. Actually," Dan continued, "he suggested the idea this afternoon. He thought it would do you good to get out of the house for a while." He sighed and scratched his dark head, managing to appear sheepish, for all his size. "I'm ashamed I didn't think of it first. I guess I've been a bit preoccupied and didn't notice you were looking a littled tired and hemmed in."

"I'm not tired," she denied automatically.

"Hemmed in?" Sabrina offered with a knowing smile.

"A little, maybe, but I'm hardly in the last stages of cabin fever. I'm sure it's very kind of Mr. Tanner to be so concerned about my welfare." She managed to say his name in a normal voice. "But there's certainly no need for him to go with me. I know he has hundreds of more important things to do with his Sunday."

"Well, now, he didn't seem to think so," Dan said. "It was his suggestion, and he seemed keen on the idea, too."

"I don't know why he would be," she muttered. "Besides, I don't want to impose on him. We're practically strangers. I can just go by myself."

"Nonsense." Dan's refusal was good-natured but firm. "I couldn't possibly let you ride out by yourself just yet, no matter how good you are on a horse. You don't know the country, and it's easy to get lost. There's always the possibility of an accident. Besides," he added, and his grin was expansive, "you're part of the family, and I grew up with Jake, so you're not strangers. If anyone knows his way around this part of Wyoming, he does." He shrugged and rested his back against the cushions. "He owns half of it, anyway." Samantha glanced at her sister for help. Sabrina, however, appeared to be engrossed in her needlepoint.

Frowning at the lack of support, Samantha stewed over her predicament. If she refused Jake's company, she would not only forfeit the opportunity to ride the Wyoming countryside, but she would spoil Sabrina and Dan's plans for a day alone together. She shrugged in resignation and offered a smile.

"I'll be ready at nine." She added to herself, if Jake Tanner can stand a day in my company, I guess I can stand a day in his.

CHAPTER 3

Sunday dawned with a sky as cold and clear as sapphire. The sun offered thin light and little warmth. To her annoyance, Samantha had overslept. Hurriedly, she showered and dressed in forest-green cords and a chunky beige pullover.

Her riding boots clattered on the parquet floor as she hurried from her room and down the hall to the kitchen. She frowned as she reached the doorway. Jake was sitting at the table, enjoying a cup of coffee with the air of one very much at home.

He was, she noted with illogical irritation, every bit as attractive as she remembered.

"Oh, you're here." Her greeting was hardly welcoming, but he returned it with his slow smile.

"Morning, ma'am."

"Don't start ma'aming me again," she said.

He remained silent as she clattered the cups in the cupboard and filled one with the steaming liquid from the pot on the stove.

"Sorry." She popped a piece of bread in the toaster

and turned with a peace-offering smile. "My! I over-slept. I hope you haven't been waiting long."

"I've got all day," he answered, leaning back in his chair as if to emphasize his words.

She drew a slab of bacon and a carton of eggs from the refrigerator. "Have you eaten?" she asked in invitation.

"Yeah, thanks." He rose, poured himself another cup of coffee and resumed his position at the table. "Dan's already seen to breakfast for himself and Sabrina. They're having it in their room."

"Oh." She replaced the items and pulled out the butter.

"Aren't you going to eat?"

"Toast and coffee. I'm not much on breakfast."

"If you always eat like that," he observed over the rim of his cup, "it's no wonder you never grew any bigger."

"For goodness' sake." She whirled around, brandishing the butter knife. "I'm hardly a midget. I'm five-four, that's tall enough for anybody."

He held up his hands in mock surrender. "I never argue with an armed woman."

"Ready?" He rose when she had finished both the toast and another cup of coffee.

When she mumbled her assent, he plucked her jacket from its hook, holding it out so that she had no choice but to allow him to help her into it. She stiffened as his hands touched her shoulders and turned her to face him. Her pulse responded immediately. As if he were aware of her reaction, he began to do up her leather buttons with slow care. She jerked back, but his hold on the front of her coat prevented her from a clean escape.

"You're a pretty little thing," he drawled, completing his task with his eyes directly on hers. "Can't have you catching cold." He reached out and plucked Sabrina's dark wide-brimmed hat from a peg and placed it neatly on her head. "This'll keep your head warm."

"Thanks." She pushed the hat firmly in place.

"Anytime, Sam." His face was unperturbed as he pulled his own sheepskin jacket over his flannel shirt and jeans.

On the way to the stables, Samantha increased her pace to a trot to keep up with Jake's long, careless stride. Despite herself, she admired the confident, loose-limbed grace of his movement. He took his time, she noted, deciding he probably did nothing quickly, and more than likely still finished ahead of everyone else.

The dapple gray had been saddled and led outside by a smiling ranch hand.

"Howdy, ma'am. Dan said to have Spook ready for you."

"Thanks." She returned his friendly smile and patted the gelding's neck. "But I could have done it. I don't like to give you extra work."

"No trouble, ma'am. Dan said you weren't to do a lick of work today. You just go and have yourself a good time, and I'll rub old Spook down when you get back."

Samantha vaulted easily onto the horse's back, happy to feel a mount beneath her again. Riding was an old pleasure, to be enjoyed only when finances allowed.

"Now, you take good care of Miss Evans, Jake," the cowboy admonished with a conspirator's wink Samantha failed to catch. "Dan sets great store by this little lady."

Little again, Samantha thought.

"Don't you worry about Miss Evans, Lon." Jake mounted his stallion with a fluid motion. Again Samantha noticed that he wasted no time on superfluous movement. "I intend to keep a close eye on her."

Samantha acknowledged Jake's statement with a wrinkled nose, then, following the direction his hand indicated, set off in a brisk canter.

As the neat cluster of ranch buildings was left behind, her irritation vanished. The rushing air was exciting, filling her lungs and whipping roses into her cheeks. She had almost forgotten the sense of liberation riding gave her. It was the same sensation that she had experienced many times when flying from top to bottom or springing high in a double twist.

They rode in silence for a quarter of an hour. Jake allowed her to fill her being with the thrill of movement and the beauty of the countryside. Wild peaks jutted arrogantly into the sky. The rolling plains below were yellow-green with winter. They rode by Herefords, white-faced and sleek, who noted their passing with a lazy turn of the head before resuming their grazing.

A shape darted across an open field, and Samantha slowed her horse to a walk and pointed. "What's that?"

"Antelope," Jake answered, narrowing his eyes against the sun.

"Oh!" She halted her mount and watched the animal's graceful, bounding progress until it streaked over a hill and out of her view. "It must be marvelous to run like that, graceful and free." She turned her unguarded face to the man beside her and found him regarding her intently. His eyes held an expression she did not understand. A strange tingling raced along her spine, like warm fingers on cold skin. The tingling increased, the sensation spreading to settle somewhere in her stomach. Suddenly, his expression changed. The shadows of his face shifted as his lips moved into a smile.

"Someday you will be caught, little antelope."

She blinked at him, totally disoriented, trying to remember what they had been talking about. His grin increased. He pointed to a large, bare-limbed tree a quarter of a mile away.

"Race you." There was challenge under the lazy dare.

Her eyes brightened with excitement. "Fine chance I'd have against a horse like that. What handicap do I get?"

Jake pushed his hat back as if to view her more completely. "From the look of you, I'd say you've got a good fifty-pound advantage. That should balance the odds some."

"No head start?"

"No, ma'am."

She pouted for a moment, then grinned. "All right, Jake Tanner, I'll give you a run for your money."

"Whenever you say, Sam." He pulled the brim of his hat low over his forehead.

"Now!"

She met the gelding's sides with her heels and spurted forward in a gallop. The quiet morning air vibrated with the thunder of hooves. Samantha, her hair flowing behind her, gave herself over to the thrill of the race. She reached the finish just ahead of her competitor and reined in, filling the morning with dusty, breathless laughter.

"Oh, that was wonderful, absolutely wonderful."

"Any time you want to give up teaching, Sam, you can work for me. I can use a hand who rides like you."

"I'll keep that in mind, even though I know you let me beat you."

"Now what makes you think that?" He leaned his arm on the horn of his saddle and watched her thoughtfully.

"I'm not stupid." Her grin was good-natured and friendly. "I couldn't beat that Arabian in a million years. You, maybe," she added with a touch of arrogance, "but not that horse."

"Pretty sharp, aren't you?" he returned, answering her grin.

"As a tack," she agreed. "And," she continued, brushing her hair from her shoulders, "I am not a weak female who needs to be placated. With my background, I know how to compete, I know how to lose, and"—she grinned and lifted her brows—"I know how to win."

"Point taken." He tilted his head as if to view her from a different angle. "From now on, Sam, we play head-to-head." He smiled, and she was no longer sure they were talking about the same thing. "I know how to win, too," he added slowly. They continued at a leisurely pace for a time, crossing a narrow branch of the Medicine Bow River. They paused there for the horses to quench their thirst in the icy water that forced its way over shining rocks with hisses and whispers. At Samantha's request, Jake began to identify the surrounding mountains.

Pointing to the long fingers of peaks at the south, the Laramie Range, he told her they extended from eastern Colorado. The middle section was the Medicine Bow Range, and the Sierra Madre loomed to the west. The vast ranges were separated by broad tongues of the Wyoming Basin. Silver-blue, they gleamed in the sunlight, lacings of snow trembling from their summits.

She had reined in without being aware of her action. "I can never look at them long enough. I suppose you're used to them."

"No." There was no laughter or mockery in his tone. "You never get used to them."

She smiled a bit uncertainly, not at all sure she could deal with this side of him.

"Are there bears up there?" she asked.

He glanced up at the mountains, smiled, then looked back at her. "Black bear and grizzly," he informed her. "Elk, coyotes, mountain lions . . ."

"'Mountain lions'?" she repeated, a little nervously.

"You're not likely to run into one down here," he returned with an indulgent smile.

She ignored the mockery in his voice and looked around her, again awed by the miles of open space. "I wonder if this looked the same a century ago."

"Some of it. Those don't change much." He indicated the Rockies with an inclination of his head. "The Native Americans are gone," he continued, as if thinking aloud. "There were Arapaho, Sioux, Cheyenne, Crow, Shoshone, all roaming free over the state before the first white man set foot here. Then trappers came, trading with them, dressing like them, living like them, and the beaver was nearly driven into extinction." He turned back to her, as if suddenly remembering she was there. "You're the teacher." His smile appeared. "You should be telling me."

Samantha shook her head in mock despair. "My knowledge of Wyoming's history is limited to late-night westerns." They were walking their horses slowly, side by side. She had completely forgotten her aversion to the man beside her. "It's impossible to believe the killing and cruelty that must have gone on here. It's so serene, and so vast. It seems there would have been room enough for everyone."

This time it was Jake who shook his head. "In 1841 more than a hundred and fifty thousand people crossed the South Pass going west, and a few years later, fifty thousand more came through on their way to California looking for gold. This was Native American land, had been their land for generations. Game disappeared, and when people get hungry, they fight. Treaties were signed, promises made by both sides, broken by both sides." He shrugged.

"In the 1860s, they tried to open the Bozeman Pass from Fort Laramie to Montana, and open war broke out. The trail ran through the Sioux hunting ground. The fighting was of the worst kind, massacres, indiscriminate killing of women and children, butcheries by both sides. More treaties were signed, more misunderstandings, more killing, until the whites outnumbered the Native Americans, drove them away or put them on reservations."

"It doesn't seem fair," Samantha whispered, feeling a wave of sadness wash over her.

"No, it doesn't." He heard the wistful note in her voice and turned to regard her. "Life isn't always fair, though, is it, Samantha?"

"I suppose not." She sighed. "You seem to know quite a bit about what happened here. You must have had a good history teacher."

"I did." He held her curious look with a teasing half-smile on his lips. "My great-grandmother lived to be ninety-eight. She was Sioux."

Samantha lifted her brows in surprised interest. "Oh, I'd love to have met her. The things she must have seen, the changes in nearly a century of living."

"She was quite a woman." His smile faded a moment. "She taught me a lot. Among other things, she told me that the land goes on no matter who walks on it, that life moves on whether you fight against it or flow with it, that when you want something, you go after it until it's yours."

Suddenly, she felt he was leading her out of her depth, reaching for something she was not sure she possessed. She turned from the directness of his eyes to search the land.

"I'd like to have seen all this before there were any fences, before there was any fighting."

Jake pointed skyward. Glancing up, Samantha watched the graceful flight of an eagle. For a timeless moment, it soared overhead, the undisputed sovereign of the skies. They moved off again, in companionable silence. "I hope you're getting some fun out of this trip, some compensation for taking care of your sister," Jake said at last.

"I don't need any compensation for taking care of Bree. She's my sister, my . . ."

"Responsibility?"

"Well . . . yes. I've always looked out for Bree, she's more delicate, more . . . dependent than I am." She shrugged and felt uncomfortable without knowing why. "Dad always joked that I took my share of strength and half of Bree's while we were still in the womb. She needs me," she added, feeling compelled to defend what she had always taken for granted.

"She has Dan," Jake reminded her. "And she's a grown woman now—just as you are. Did it ever occur to you that you have your own life to lead now that Sabrina has a husband to care for her?"

"I'm not trying to take over for Dan," she said quickly. "Perhaps you can figure out how he could see to her needs and tend to the house and the ranch all at the same time, but I can't." She glared at him, half in anger, half in exasperation. "What do you expect me to do? Sit up in Philadelphia teaching kids to jump on a tramp while my sister needs help?"

"No, Samantha." He met her eyes with a quiet patience that was more disturbing than angry words and shouts. "What you're doing is very kind and unselfish."

"There's nothing kind or unselfish about it," she interrupted, shrugging the words away. "We're sisters. More than that, we're twins. We shared life from its beginning. You can't understand the kind of bond that creates. I'd give up a hundred jobs to help Bree if she needed me."

"No one's condemning your loyalty, Samantha. It's an admirable trait." He gave her a long, level look. "Just a word of advice. Don't become so involved that you forget who Samantha Evans is, and that she just might have the right to her own life."

Samantha drew herself up to her full height in the saddle. "I hardly need your advice on how to run my life. I've been managing nicely for some time now."

His face creased in a lazy smile. "Yes, ma'am, I'm sure you have."

CHAPTER 4

Samantha had been riding the dapple gray in stubborn silence for nearly thirty minutes when she noticed more cattle. Her guide seemed unperturbed by her silence and slowed his Arabian's gait to the gelding's meandering walk. She would never have admitted to the man at her side that his words had disturbed her peace of mind.

What business was it of his how she chose to run her life? What gave Jake Tanner the right to question her relationship with Sabrina? No one asked him for his advice. And why in heaven's name should anything he said matter in the first place?

They were approaching a large ranch house. A redwood porch skirted the building's front, graced by evergreen shrubs. A gray wisp of smoke rose in a welcoming spire from the chimney. Ranch buildings sat neat and unobtrusive in the background.

"Welcome to the Double T, ma'am."

Jake drew her eyes with the uncharacteristic formality in his tone. She turned to see him smile and touch the brim of his well-worn Stetson.

"Thank you, Mr. Tanner. I can honestly say your ranch is spectacular. But what, may I ask, are we doing here?"

"Well, now . . ." Jake shifted in the saddle to face her directly. "I don't know about you, but nearly three hours in the saddle gives me a powerful appetite. I figured here we might do a bit better than beef jerky."

"'Three hours'?" Samantha repeated, and pushed Sabrina's hat from her head so it lay against her back. "Has it really been that long?"

The angles of his face moved slowly with his grin, and she found herself once more intrigued by the process. "I'll take that to mean you were so delighted with my company, time stood still."

She answered with a toss of her head. "I hate to tread on your ego, Jake, but the credit goes to Wyoming."

"Close enough for now." Reaching over, he plopped the brimmed hat back in place on Samantha's head and urged his mount into a canter.

Samantha stared after him in exasperation, watching the confidence with which he rode the Arabian. They moved like one form rather than horse and man. Scowling, she pressed her heels to the gelding's side and raced forward to join him.

As she reached his side, he skirted the ranch house and rode toward the buildings in the rear, following the left fork on a long, hard-packed road. A large, sleepy-eyed Saint Bernard rose from his siesta and romped forward to greet them. A deep, hoarse bark emitted from his throat. Jake halted in front of the stables. He slid off the Arabian's back, running his hand through the dog's thick fur as he hit the ground.

"Wolfgang's harmless." He acknowledged the loving, wet kisses with another brief caress and moved to the gelding's side. "He's just a puppy."

"A puppy," Samantha repeated. "You don't see many hundred-and-fifty-pound puppies." Tilting her head, she gave the overgrown baby a thorough examination before she brought her leg over the saddle to dismount.

Jake gripped her waist as she made her descent, holding her off the ground a moment as if she were weightless. As her boots touched earth, she was turned around and drawn against a hard chest. She tilted her head to inform him that his assistance was unnecessary, but saw only a brief blur of his face before his lips captured hers.

Her mind whirled with the touch and scent of him. She felt as though she were falling into a deep well and her heart began to beat a mad tempo against her ribs. She clutched at his jacket in defense. Perhaps the kiss was brief. It could have lasted no more than a portion of a minute, but it felt like forever. She knew his mouth was warm and sure on hers while decades flew into centuries.

The strange sensations of timelessness and loss of control frightened her. She stiffened and began to struggle against his grasp. He released her immediately, staring down at her clouded blue eyes with a satisfied smile. The smile transformed terror into fury.

"How dare you?"

"Just testing, ma'am." His answer was complacent, as though the kiss had been no more than that, a traditional touching of lips.

"'Testing'?" she repeated, running an agitated hand through her hair. "Testing what?"

"I've always wanted to kiss a teacher." Grinning, he gave her a friendly pat on the cheek. "I think there're some holes in your education."

"I'll show you holes, you conceited, high-handed"—
her mind searched for something appropriately de-
rogatory and settled on a generality—"*man*. If I didn't
consider that kiss so insignificant, you'd be lying on
your back checking out the sky."

He surveyed her as she trembled with a mixture of
fury and wounded pride. He rubbed his chin thoughtfully. "You know, Sam, I almost believe you could
do it."

"You can bank on it," she confirmed with an arrogant toss of her head. "And the next time you . . ."
Feeling her arm sharply pulled, she glanced down to
see the sleeve of her jacket captured in the awesome
jaws of the Saint Bernard. "What'd you do, teach him
to eat unwilling females?"

"He just wants to make your acquaintance." Jake
laughed as he led the horses to the stable to turn them
over to one of his men.

Samantha was not normally timid, and her pride
refused to allow her to call Jake to untangle her from
the teeth of his puppy. She swallowed and spoke to her
canine captor.

"Hello . . . Wolfgang, wasn't it?" she muttered.
"I'm Sam. You, ah, wouldn't consider letting go of
my jacket, would you?" The dog continued to stare
with droopy, innocent eyes. "Well, that's all right,"
she said, trying out magnanimity. "It's just an old
one, anyway. I'm very fond of dogs, you know." Tentatively, she brought her free hand up to touch the fur
on his huge head. "Well, actually, I have a cat," she
admitted in apology, "but I have absolutely no prejudices."

Though his expression did not alter, she decided it
was prudent to give him time for consideration. Her

patience was rewarded when he released her sleeve and bathed her hand with his enormous tongue.

"Well, I see you two have made friends," Jake drawled, coming up behind her.

"No thanks to you," she said. "He might have eaten me alive."

"Not you, Sam," Jake disagreed, taking her hand and striding toward the house. "Too tough for Wolfgang's taste."

Jake led her to the back entrance through a paneled, tiled-floor mudroom and into the kitchen. A large square room, it was bright and cheery with tangerine curtains framing the wide windows. The pleasant-looking woman who stood by the sink smiled at Samantha. "Jake, you scoundrel, have you had this poor little lady out in the cold all this time?" Samantha met the warm brown eyes with a returning smile.

Jake grinned, unabashed. "Samantha Evans, meet Annie Holloway, my cook, housekeeper, and best girl."

"Don't you try soft-soaping me, you young devil." She brushed off his words with indulgent affection, but pleased color rose to her pudgy cheeks. "Thinks he can get around me with sweet talk. Pleased to meet you, Miss Evans." Samantha found her hand enclosed in a firm grip.

"Hello, Miss Holloway, I hope I'm not putting you out."

"Putting me out?" Annie let out a rich, full laugh, her ample bust heaving with the sound. "Isn't she the sweet one? Don't you be silly, now, and you just call me Annie like everyone else."

"Thank you, Annie." Samantha's smile warmed. "Everyone calls me Sam."

"Now that's a pretty thing," Annie commented, peering candidly into Samantha's face. "Yes, sir, a right pretty thing. You two run along," she commanded with an attempt at sternness. "Out of my kitchen. Lunch will be along, and I'll bring you in some tea to warm you up. Not you," she said with a scowl as Jake grimaced. "For the little lady. You don't need any warming up."

"Annie runs things," Jake explained as he led Samantha down a wide hall into the living room.

"I can see she does, even when she's securely wrapped around your little finger."

For a moment, his smile was so boyish and full of mischief, she nearly gave in to the urge to brush the curls from his forehead.

The paneling in the living room was light. The expanse of wood was broken by a large stone fireplace and wide windows framed with cinnamon-colored sheers. The dark gleaming furniture had been upholstered in gold, burnt sienna, and rich browns. There was a comfortable hodgepodge of Hepple-whites and Chippendales with piecrust tilt-top tables and Pembrokes, ladder-back chairs and candlestands. In the center of the hardwood floor lay a wide rug of Native American design, so obviously old and handworked, that Samantha wondered if it had been his great-grandmother's fingers that had hooked it perhaps nearly a century ago. The room reflected a quiet, understated wealth, a wealth she somehow did not associate with the rangy, brash cowboy side of Jake.

A Charles Russell painting caught her eye. She turned to study it, attempting to sort out her new impressions of this complex man. Turning back, she found him watching her reaction with unconcealed amusement.

"I have a feeling you were expecting bearskins and oilcloth."

Samantha focused her attention on the inviting fire. "I never know what to expect from you," she muttered.

"No?" He dropped his lanky form into a wingback chair and pulled out a long, thin cigar. "I thought you were pretty bright."

Samantha seated herself in the chair across from him, keeping the warmth and hiss of the fire between them. "This is a lovely room, very appealing and very warm."

"I'm glad you like it." If he noticed her blatant change of subject, he gave no sign. Lighting his cigar, he stretched out his legs and looked totally relaxed and content.

"I have a weakness for antiques," she continued, deciding the topic was safe and impersonal.

He smiled, the smoke curling lazily above his head. "There's a piece in one of the bedrooms you might like to see. A blanket chest in walnut that was brought over from the East in the 1860s."

"I'd like that very much." She returned his smile and settled back as Annie wheeled a small tea cart into the room.

"I brought you coffee," she said to Jake, and passed him a cup. "I know you won't take tea unless you douse it with bourbon. Something not quite decent about doing that to a good cup of tea."

"Tea is an old ladies' drink," he stated, ignoring her rapidly clucking tongue.

"How do you think Sabrina looks?" Samantha asked him when Annie had bustled back to the kitchen.

"I think you worry too much about her."

She bristled instinctively before replying. "Perhaps you're right," she surprised herself by admitting. "Our mother always said Bree and I were mirror images, meaning, I discovered after a while, opposites."

"Right down to Sabrina being right-handed, and you being left."

"Why, yes." She looked at him in faint surprise. "You don't miss much, do you?" He merely shook his head and gave her an enigmatic smile. "Well," she plunged on, not sure she liked his expression, a bit like a cat who already had the mouse between his paws. "I suppose the summary of my discrepancies was that I could never keep the hem in my white organdy party dress. You'd have to know my mother to understand that. She would have Bree and me all decked out in these frilly white organdy dresses and send us off to a party. Bree would come back spotless, pure and angelic. I'd come back with dirt on my frills, bloody knees and a trailing hem."

During her story, Jake's smile had widened. The coffee in his cup cooled, unattended as he watched her. "There're doers and there're watchers, Samantha. I imagine you had fun scraping up your knees."

As ridiculous as it seemed, she felt she'd just been complimented, and was both pleased and faintly embarrassed.

"I suppose you're a doer, too." She dropped her eyes. "You couldn't run a ranch like this and not be. Cattle ranching sounds romantic, but I imagine it's long hours, hot summers, and cold winters. I don't suppose it's really all that different from the way it used to be a hundred years ago."

"The range isn't open anymore," he corrected. "You don't find cowboys going off to Texas to punch cattle with a ten-dollar horse and a forty-dollar saddle." He shrugged and set his empty cup on the table beside him. "But some change slow, and I'm one who likes to take my time."

She was frowning into his smile when Annie announced lunch. It was not until they were settled in the dining room that she spoke directly to him again, pressing him for more details on how the ranch was run.

He explained how roundups, which had once been accomplished on the vast open range with only men and horses, were now aided by fences and technology. But it was still men and ponies who moved the cattle into corrals. Over a few states there were still strong-holds of riders and ropers, men who cultivated the old techniques and blended them with the new. On the Double T, Jake employed the best of both.

"If roundups aren't what they once were, they still accomplish the same end. Getting the cattle together and branding them."

"'Branding'?" Samantha interrupted, and shuddered.

"Your Philadelphia's showing, Sam." He grinned. "Take my word for it, branding is a good deal more unpleasant for the branders than the brandees."

She decided to ignore his comments and changed the subject abruptly. "Bree told me your ranch borders Dan's. This place must be huge for it to have taken us three hours to get here."

Jake's deep, rich laughter filled the room, and she decided unwillingly that she liked the sound very much. "It's a pretty big spread, Sam, but if you take the straight road north for the Lazy L, you can be here in twenty minutes on horseback. I took you on a big circle today," he explained. "Just a small taste of our part of the Laramie Basin."

They lingered over coffee, relaxed in each other's company.

"We'd better get started back," Jake said after a while. He rose and extended his hand. Her own slipped without hesitation into it as he pulled her to her feet. When she looked up at him, her smile was warm and spontaneous.

"Annie was right, that's a pretty thing." He lifted his hand and traced his fingers over the curve of her mouth. She started. "Now don't go skittish on me, Sam, I'm not going to use spurs and a whip."

His mouth lowered, gentle and persuasive. One hand held hers while the other circled the back of her neck to soothe with coaxing fingers. She had only to sway forward to feel his body against hers, had only to lift her hand to bring his mouth firmer and warmer on hers. Before the choice could be made, he drew her away and the decision was taken out of her hands.

"Sam." He shook his head as if exasperated and lightly amused. "You're enough to try a man's patience."

With this, he pulled her through to the kitchen.

"Well, so you're off again." Annie wiped one hand on her apron and wagged the other at Jake. "And don't be keeping her out in that cold too long."

"No, ma'am," Jake returned with suspicious respect.

"Thank you, Annie," Samantha broke in. "Lunch was wonderful."

"Well, now, that's fine, then." She gave Samantha a friendly pat on the cheek. "You just come back real soon, and you say hi to Sabrina for me, and that young rascal Dan, too. As soon as she's fit again, I'll be coming by to see her. Oh, Jake, I clean forgot." Annie turned to him and sighed at her absentmindedness. "Lesley Marshall called earlier, something about dinner tonight. I told her you'd give her a call, then it went straight out of my mind."

"No problem," Jake said easily. "I'll get back to her later. Ready, Sam?"

"Yes, I'm ready." She kept her smile in place, though a large black cloud seemed to have suddenly smothered the sunshine.

Lesley Marshall, she mused, automatically going through the motions of securing her hat and coat. That was the woman Bree had predicted would marry Jake when he decided to settle down. *Why should it matter to me?* She straightened her spine and accompanied Jake to the waiting horses. *I have absolutely no interest in Jake Tanner's affairs.*

He's probably had dozens of girlfriends. Well, it's no concern of mine. Vaulting into the saddle, she followed as he set off down the hard-packed road.

They spoke little on the return journey. Samantha pretended an engrossment with the scenery that she was far from feeling. Unhappily, she realized Wyoming's magic was not quite enough to lift her flagging spirits. Snow-capped peaks glistened just as brightly in the late afternoon sun, and the land still spread and beckoned, but as she surveyed them now she felt strangely depressed.

It had been an unusual day, she concluded. Jake had annoyed her, charmed her, angered her and delighted her, all in a handful of hours. His kiss had aroused excitement and a deeper feeling she could not explain.

The knowledge that he was dining with another woman that evening depressed her beyond belief. She stole a sidelong look at his lean, tanned features.

He was undeniably attractive, she admitted, pulling her eyes away from him before he could sense her study. There was a powerful aura of virility about him, which alternately intrigued her and made her wary. Perhaps it would be wise to avoid his company. He confused her, and Samantha liked to know precisely where she stood with a man. She wanted to call the shots, and she realized that this man would never allow anyone to call the shots but himself.

She would keep her distance from now on. Let him spread his charm over this Lesley Marshall, or any of the other women who were undoubtedly thirsting for his attention. Samantha Evans could get along very easily without him. As the Lazy L grew closer, she resolved to be polite and casually friendly to her escort. After all, she reflected, there was no reason to be rude. He was perfectly free to dine with whomever he chose; his life was most assuredly his own. Besides, she added to herself, if she had anything to say about it, they would be seeing very little of each other in the future.

When they reached the ranch, she dismounted, handing Spook's reins to a waiting cowboy. "I had a wonderful time, Jake." Samantha's smile was faultless in its social politeness as he walked her toward the ranch house, leading his stallion behind him. "I appreciate your time and hospitality."

Jake's mouth lifted at one corner. "It was my pleasure, ma'am."

If there was mockery in his tone, Samantha chose to ignore it. Reaching the back door, she turned to smile at him again as he stood, tall and lean, beside the gleaming chestnut.

"Would you like some coffee before you go?" she invited, determined to be polite.

"No, thanks, Sam." He continued to watch her, his eyes shaded by the brim of his hat. "I'd best be getting along."

"Well." She breathed a small sigh of relief when her hand touched the doorknob and safety was in easy reach. "Thanks again."

"Sure." He nodded briefly and turned to his horse, paused and turned back to look at her with a penetrating intensity that turned her legs to water. When he spoke, it was soft and final. "I mean to have you, you know."

Several moments of silence passed before she could summon up an answer.

"D-Do you?" Her voice was a shaky whisper, unlike the coolly flippant tone she would have wished for.

"Yes, ma'am." He vaulted onto the chestnut's back and pushed the Stetson back on his head so that she had a disturbingly clear view of his eyes. "I do," he confirmed, turning his mount and galloping away.

CHAPTER 5

Often over the next few days, Samantha told herself that her reaction to Jake's kiss had been merely a passing physical attraction. She was a normal woman, wasn't she? So why feel guilty about it?

Jake Tanner *was* a very attractive man. *Too attractive,* she added to herself. And he knew too much about charming women. The fact that Jake was abrasive, smug and irritating had nothing to do with the way she had acted. It had just been a passing fancy. *And would certainly not occur again.*

Finally Sabrina was allowed up from the confinement of her bed. Samantha decided it was safe to leave her sister for a few hours. With a light heart, she saddled Spook and set off from the ranch at a brisk canter. For a while she enjoyed the feeling of Spook's hooves pounding the hard road. The sky hung low above her, and heavy, leaden gray clouds draped the distant mountains in mysterious gloom. There was a stillness, a waiting in the air, unnoticed by Samantha in her eagerness to escape the close confines of the house.

She rode swiftly past the bored, white-faced cattle and the stretches of barbed wire, eager to explore new territory, tasting the joy of motion and freedom. The mountains, grim sentinels above her, stood stone-gray under the unbroken sky. Remembering Dan's instructions, Samantha took care to mark her route, choosing a clump of rocks, a cottonwood tree with a broken limb, and a gnarled stump as landmarks for her return trip.

She led her mount to a crest of a hill, watching as a jackrabbit, startled by her intrusion, darted across the road and out of sight.

Nearly an hour passed before the first flakes began to drift lazily from sky to earth. She stopped and watched their progress in fascination. The snow fell slowly. Lifting her face, she let it caress her cheeks and closed lids. The air was moist, coming to life around her, and she stirred herself out of her dream.

"Well, Spook, this is my first Wyoming snow. I'd like to stay here all day and watch it fall, but duty calls. We'd better head back." Patting the horse's neck, she turned back toward the ranch.

They rode slowly. Samantha was enchanted with the fairyland that was forming around her. Cotton-woods and aspens were draped in white, their branches a stark contrast to the brilliant etchings of snow. The ground was cloaked quickly. Though the beauty was breathtaking, Samantha began to feel uncomfortably alone.

She took Spook into a canter. The sound of his hooves was soft and muffled. The quiet surrounding her was unearthly, almost as though the world had ceased to breathe. She shivered, suddenly cold in the warm confines of her jacket. To her annoyance, she saw that in her preoccupation with the landscape she had taken a wrong turn, and she began to backtrack, berating herself for carelessness.

The snow increased, plunging down from a sky she could no longer see. She cursed herself for having come so far, fighting down a sudden surge of panic. "Don't be silly, Sam," she spoke aloud, wanting the reassurance of her own voice. "A little snow won't hurt you."

The cold became more intense, piercing the layers of her skin. Samantha tried to concentrate on thoughts of steaming coffee and a blazing fire as she looked around for a familiar landmark. Nothing was the same as it had been. She clamped her lips tight to still the chattering of her teeth, telling herself that it was impossible that she could be lost. But it was a lie. The trees and hills around her were strangers blanketed in white.

The snow fell thickly, a blinding white wall blocking her vision. A wind had sprung up, breaking the silence with its moans and tossing snow, hard and bitter, into her face. She was forced to slow the gelding to a walk, afraid of tangling with the sharp teeth of barbed wire she was unable to see. Her teeth savaged her lips in an effort to control a growing terror.

It's so cold, she thought as she began to shiver convulsively, so unbelievably cold.

The snow had soaked through the wool of her slacks and slipped mercilessly down the neck of her coat. She hunched her shoulders against the driving wind. Snow was everywhere, blocking her in and seeping into her clothing.

She let the reins hang limp, praying that the horse's instinct would guide him back to the warm shelter of his stables. They trudged on, the vortex of white that had begun so innocently now whirling around her. Time and direction had lost all meaning, and though she tried calling out, her voice was soundless against the fierce breath of the wind.

Now she felt the cold. Her body was numbed into submission. Her mind was following suit. The swirling snow was hypnotic, and a growing lethargy was creeping over her. In a small part of her mind, she knew her survival depended on remaining alert.

Horse and rider plodded on. There was no time, no world beyond the unbroken curtain of white. Samantha felt her eyelids growing heavy, but she willed them open with all her strength. The snow piled onto her back, weighing her down until she slumped onto the gelding's mane and clung to him. Staring down at the gelding's front hoof, she began to count each drudging step that Spook took as he continued his slow progress through the blinding storm.

Samantha's concentration on the horse's halting steps began to fade.

If I close my eyes, she thought dimly, I won't see all that white and I can sleep. Oh, how I want to sleep. . . .

The snow was talking, she mused deliriously. Well, why not? It's alive. Why should it sound like Jake? Helplessly, she began to giggle. Well, why shouldn't it? *They both play to win.*

"Samantha!" The snow was shouting at her. "Open your eyes. Stop that insane laughing and open your eyes!"

Wearily, she forced herself to obey the command. Dimly she saw the blur of Jake's features through the flurries of snow. "You would be the last thing I see before I die." With a moan, she closed her eyes again and sought the silence.

"Tell Dan we've found her," Jake shouted against the howl of the wind. "I'm taking her back to the Double T."

The darkness was comforting. Samantha gave herself over to it, feeling herself falling slowly into a hole with no bottom. She burrowed deeper into it. Her consciousness swam to the surface.

Bemused, she looked around a dimly lit room. The snow that pooled around her was not snow at all, but a bed with a thick, warm quilt. She allowed her heavy lids to close again.

"Oh, no, you don't." The lids opened fractionally, and Samantha saw Jake standing in the open doorway.

"Hello."

His mouth thinned as he advanced to the bed to tower over her. It seeped through the misty reaches of her brain that he was angry. She stared at him with lazy fascination.

"What in heaven's name were you doing out in such a storm? I've seen some dumb stunts, but taking a joyride in the middle of a blizzard tops them all."

She wanted to ask him to stop shouting at her, but lacked the energy. "Where am I?" was all she could find to say.

Sitting on the edge of the bed, he drew her head from the pillow, then held a cup to her lips. "Here, drink this first, then we'll talk."

The brandy was warm and strong, and she sputtered and gasped as he poured it down her throat. Its power spread through her, pushing back the mists of unconsciousness.

"Now, to answer your question, you're at the Double T." Jake set the empty cup aside and laid her head back on the mound of pillows.

"Oh."

"Is that all you can say?" He was shouting again. He took her shoulders as if to shake her. "Just 'Oh'? What in heaven's name were you doing out there?"

"It seems so long ago." She frowned in concentration, closing her eyes with the effort. "It wasn't snowing when I left," she said in weak defense.

"'Wasn't snowing'?" Jake repeated, incredulous. "Samantha, didn't you see the sky? Where are your brains?"

"There's no excuse for insults," she retorted with a small flash of spirit.

"'No excuse for insults'? Are you stark-raving mad? Do you realize what nearly happened to you?" His hands retreated to his pockets, as though he could barely prevent them from throttling her. "Out here in the middle of a blizzard, half-frozen and helplessly lost! It was a miracle we found you. A little longer, and you'd be lying somewhere buried in it, and no one would have found what was left until spring. Dan was half out of his mind when he got through to me and told me you'd gone out in this."

"Bree?"

"Knew nothing." He whirled to face her again. "She was taking a nap. It never occurred to her that you had gone out with a storm brewing." He laughed harshly.

The memory of the snow and the terror washed over her, and she began to shake. "I'm sorry," she managed through the tears that threatened to flow. With a brief oath, Jake ran a hand through his hair. He closed the distance between them and gathered her in his arms. "Samantha," he murmured against her hair. "What hell you put us all through."

"I'm sorry," she repeated, and she began to sob in earnest. "I was so scared, so cold."

He rocked and murmured words she could not understand, his lips brushing through her hair and over her damp cheeks until they met hers. The kiss mingled with the salt of her tears. "I've gotten your shirt all wet," she murmured after a while.

He let out a deep breath. She saw his smile begin to spread before he rested his brow against hers. "That is without doubt the worst calamity of the day."

"It's dark," she said with sudden realization. "How long . . . ?"

"Too long. What you need now is rest."

"Spook?" she began as he lay her down on the pillows.

"Is sleeping off his adventure in the stables. He looks a lot better than you, I might add."

"I want to thank you for everything." Samantha reached for his hand. In that instant, she discovered there was nothing covering her save sheets and blankets. "M-My clothes," she stammered, drawing the quilt higher in a purely feminine gesture that caused Jake's mouth to twitch.

"Soaked through, Sam." Rising, he stood, rocking gently on his heels. "It was necessary to get you warm and dry."

"Did Annie?" She managed a smile at the thought of the matronly presence of Jake's housekeeper. "I seem to have put everyone to a lot of trouble. Will you thank her for me?"

"Well, Sam, I'd like to oblige you, but Annie

left yesterday for Colorado to spend a week with her nephew." Jake's grin broadened.

"Then who—?" The question caught in her throat, and her eyes became round and impossibly dark. "Oh, no," she whispered, closing her eyes in humiliation.

"No need to be embarrassed, Sam, you have a beautiful body."

"Oh, no." With a moan, she squeezed her eyes tighter.

"Now, don't you fret." His tone took on the light insolence of the cowboy she'd met a month before in the cold March sunset. "When I took off your clothes and rubbed you down, it was strictly medical. I'd do as much for any stray." He patted her hand, and her eyes opened warily at his touch.

"Yes, of course." Moistening her lips, she attempted to see the practical side. "I, well . . . thank you."

"'S all right, don't give it a thought." He moved toward the door, then paused and turned back. "Now, the next time I get your clothes off, my purpose'll be completely different."

He strolled casually from the room, leaving a speechless Samantha.

CHAPTER 6

Samantha looked around her. She remembered with a shock that she was in Jake's house—and, worse yet, *naked* in bed. She was debating the wisdom of wrapping the quilt around her and searching for more appropriate attire when footsteps sounded down the hall outside her room. She pulled the covers to her chin as Jake strode through the open door.

"So, you're awake. How do you feel?"

"Fine." Her respiratory system behaved erratically as he continued toward her and dropped onto the bed. "I'm just fine," she repeated, then added unnecessarily, "It's still snowing."

"So it is," he agreed without taking his eyes from her face. "Slowing down, though."

"Is it?" She forced herself to look out the window.

"The worst'll be over by midday." He reached up and pried one of her hands loose from the death grip on the blankets. "Calm down, Sam, I'm not going to ravish you. I'm going to check your pulse."

"I'm fine," she repeated again.

"Far from fine, Samantha," he corrected. His fingers brushed against her cheek, as if to test its substance. "The first thing is to get some food into you." Rising, he held out a large flannel robe that he had dropped at the foot of the bed. "You'd probably feel better if you had something on." His smile was gently mocking. "Can you manage to get into this by yourself?"

"Of course." Plucking it from him, she kept a cautious grip on the blankets. "I'm not an invalid."

"You best think like one. Put that on, then get back in bed. I'll bring you some breakfast."

"I don't . . ."

"Don't argue." The two words were swift and final. He was gone before she could say another word.

He had shut the door, however, and grateful for the concession, Samantha tossed back the covers and slipped her arm into the robe. When she stood, the room swayed and spun around her. She sank back onto the bed and slipped her other arm into its sleeve, pulling the robe around her before attempting to stand again. Her limbs felt heavy and weak, and she noted with puzzlement that her ankle was throbbing lightly. Gripping one poster of the bed until the room steadied, she rolled up the sleeves of the robe several times until her hands became visible, then moved to the bathroom to study herself in the mirror.

The sight of her own face caught at her breath. Her skin seemed nearly transparent, her eyes darker and larger in contrast. The breath of color that resulted when she pinched her cheeks faded instantly. She ran a hand through her hair falling on the shoulders of the dark green robe.

It must be his, she realized, looking down at the sleeves, which swallowed her arms, and the hem, which fell nearly to her ankles. A strange sensation flowed over her as she felt the material on her skin. Turning away from the mirror, she studied the bed.

"I'm not getting in there again," she muttered, and with a small gesture of defiance belted the robe more securely. "I can eat at the table like a normal person."

After a moment, her progress down the hall seemed more of a crawl than a walk. Her legs were heavy with a weakness which infuriated her. The stillness of the house vibrated around her, playing havoc with her nerves, and the need to hear the natural, everyday movements of another human being became increasingly important. She cursed the waves of giddiness that swam around in her head, forcing her to stop time after time to rest her hand against the wall.

"This is ridiculous."

"You're right."

The harsh agreement came from behind as Jake's hands gripped her shoulders.

"What are you doing out of bed?"

"I'm all right." She swayed against his chest. He gripped her waist to support her, and she rested her hands on his arms.

"I'm just a bit wobbly, and I'm having some trouble with my ankle."

He let his gaze travel down to rest on her bare feet. "Probably turned it when you fell off the horse."

"I fell off Spook?" Her expression was incredulous.

"You were unconscious at the time. Now, get back in bed and stay there." Effortlessly, he swept her into his arms, and she laid her head against his shoulder.

"Jake, don't make me go back to bed. It's so quiet in there, and I don't feel like being alone now."

He bent and brushed lips that parted in confusion. "If you think you can sit in a chair without sliding on your face, you can come in the kitchen."

She nodded, sighed and closed her eyes. "I hate being so much trouble."

She felt him shift her in his arms before he began the journey down the hall. "I knew you were trouble the minute I set eyes on you."

"Don't tease, Jake, I'm trying to thank you."

"What for?"

She lifted a hand to his cheek, turning his face so that he would look at her. "For my life."

"Then take better care of it in the future," he suggested.

"Jake, please, I'm serious. I owe you . . ."

"Nothing, you owe me nothing." His voice had hardened with annoyance. "I don't want your gratitude." They had reached the kitchen, and he placed her in a chair at the table. "Which ankle did you hurt?" He crouched down by her feet.

"The left one. Jake, I— Ouch!"

"Sorry." He grinned up at her, then rested his hand with friendly ease on her knee. "It's not swollen."

"It still hurts," she said stubbornly.

"Keep off it, then," he advised with simple logic, and turned away to finish breakfast.

"You've got some bedside manners, Dr. Tanner," she observed sharply.

"Yes, ma'am, so I've been told." When he turned to face her, his smile was bland. "Tell me, Sam, does Sabrina have a mole on her left hip, too?"

Color flooded her face. "You . . . you . . ." she faltered, and clutched the robe tight at her throat.

"Around here, we call that locking the barn door after the cow's got loose. Have some coffee," he invited with sudden graciousness, pouring a cup and setting it on the table. "Start on this bacon," he ordered, sliding a plate in front of her. "That color didn't last long, you're pale as a ghost again. When did you eat last?"

"I . . . at breakfast yesterday, I guess."

"Toast and coffee, I imagine," he said disgustedly. "It's a wonder you can manage to sit up at all. Eat." He plucked a piece of bacon from the plate and held it out to her. "I'll have some eggs ready in a minute."

Obediently, she accepted the bacon and took a bite. "Are you going to have something?"

"In a minute," he answered absently, involved with breaking and beating eggs in a bowl.

With the first bite of bacon, Samantha realized she was ravenous. Through her preoccupation with food, she watched Jake cook with a deftness that amused and surprised her.

In a moment, he sat across from her, his plate piled high. She wondered how he could eat with such abandon and remain hard and lean.

She watched him under the cover of her lashes, and the thought came unbidden into her mind that never before had she shared a breakfast table with a man. The intimacy of their situation washed over her; the scent of bacon and coffee drifting through the air, the house quiet and empty around them, the soft flannel of his robe against her skin, the faint masculine scent of him clinging to it. It was as if they were lovers, she thought suddenly, as if they had shared the night, and now they were sharing the morning. Her face grew warm.

"I don't know what thought put roses back in those cheeks, Sam, but keep it up."

Her eyes lifted to his, and she had the uncomfortable feeling that he knew very well what road her thoughts had taken. She dropped her eyes to her plate. "I should call Bree and let her know I'm all right."

"Phones are out," he said simply, and her eyes flew back to his.

"The phones are out?" she repeated.

No telephone, her mind said again. Without a telephone, they might as well be on an island a thousand miles from anyone. Their isolation was complete, and the snow was still falling as though it would never stop.

"With a storm like this, it's not surprising to lose the phones. Power's out, too. We're on a generator. Don't worry about Sabrina, she knows you're with me." His words did nothing to erase her tension.

"When . . . when do you think I'll be able to get back?"

"Couple of days," he returned with an easy shrug, and sipped his coffee. "The roads'll have to be cleared after the storm lets up, and you're not in any shape to travel through a mess like that yet. In a day or two, you'll be more up to it."

"A couple of days?"

He leaned back comfortably in his chair, his voice smooth as a quiet river. "Of course, by then you'll be hopelessly compromised, not a scrap of your sterling reputation left. Alone with me for two or three days, without Annie to add a thread of decency to the situation." His eyes traveled down her slim figure. "Wearing my bathrobe, too." He shook his head. "Not too many years back, I'd have had to marry you."

"Thank goodness for progress," she retorted smartly.

"Oh, I don't know, Sam." His sigh was convincing. "I'm an old-fashioned sort of man."

"It's only a matter of circumstance that we're alone here in the first place." With great dignity, she folded her arms. "And I've hardly been compromised, as you so quaintly put it."

"No?" He watched her through lazily narrowed

eyes. "So far, I've undressed you, tucked you in, and fixed your breakfast. Who knows what that might lead to?"

His smile might have been lazy, but it was full of meaning. Suddenly Samantha found it difficult to swallow.

"Relax, Sam." His laugh was full of arrogant enjoyment. "I told you I mean to have you, but it's not in my plans to take on a pale child who barely has the strength to stand." He paused, lit one of his long, thin cigars and blew smoke at the ceiling. "When I make love to you, I want you to have your wits about you. I don't want you passing out in my arms."

The man's arrogance was amazing! "You conceited mule," she began. "How dare you sit there and tell me you're going to make love to me? You seem to think you're irresistible! Well, you have another think coming—"

"I'm going to remind you of that one day, Sam," Jake said mildly as he crushed out his cigar. "Now, I think you better lie down again. You're not quite up to sparring with me yet."

"I do not have to lie down. And I certainly don't need you carting me around. I can manage." She stood up, then was forced to grasp the table as the room revolved around her.

"You don't look ready to turn cartwheels, teacher," Jake observed as he took her arm.

"I'm all right." Her hand, which she had lifted to push him away, lay weakly on his chest for support. He tilted her chin, and he was no longer smiling. "Samantha, sometimes you have to be strong enough to let someone else take care of things. You're going to have to hand over the reins to me for a couple of days. If you fight it, you're only going to make it harder on yourself."

With a sigh, she allowed her head to fall against his chest, not protesting as his arms encircled her. "Do I have to like it?"

"Not necessarily." He gave a short laugh and lifted her easily and carried her back to bed.

Her small spurt of energy deserted her. With an odd feeling of contentment, she settled down under the covers. She was asleep even before his lips had lightly touched her forehead in a farewell kiss. . . .

I was beginning to think you'd sleep through the night." She turned her head quickly. Jake was sitting across the room, the smoke of his cigar spiraling upward, the flickering lights from the fire shooting specks of gold into his eyes. Samantha brushed the tousled hair from her face and struggled into a sitting position.

"It's dark," she said. "What time is it?"

He glanced at the gold watch on his wrist and took a slow drag from his cigar. "It's a bit past six."

"Six? I've slept for hours. I feel as if I've slept for weeks."

"You needed it." Tossing the stub of his cigar into the mouth of the fire, Jake rose and moved toward her. His concerned eyes roamed over her sleep-flushed cheeks and heavy eyes. Gradually, his expression lightened, the angles of his face moving into a satisfied smile. "Your color's coming back." He took her wrist, and her eyes dropped from his to study the dancing flames of the fire. "Pulse's a bit jumpy." The smile reflected in his voice. "Strong though. Hungry?"

"I shouldn't be." She forced her eyes to meet his. "I've done nothing but lie around all day, but I'm starved."

He smiled again, lifting her without comment. She felt small and vulnerable in his arms, a sensation that was both pleasant and disturbing. She found it difficult to resist the impulse to rest her head against the strong curve of his shoulder. Instead, she concentrated on the sharp, clean lines of his profile.

"I'm sure I can walk. I really feel fine."

"I doubt it." She could feel his warm breath on her face. "Besides, you seem to fit in my arms pretty well."

Finding no quick comeback to this comment, she took the journey to the kitchen in silence.

L eaning back in her chair, replete and content, Samantha sipped the cool white wine in her glass and gave Jake a nod of approval.

"You're going to make some woman a terrific husband. You're an outstanding cook."

"I think so." He nodded smugly. "My wife wouldn't have to be a gourmet cook," he added with casual consideration. "I'd demand other qualities."

"Adoration," Samantha suggested. "Obedience, unswerving loyalty, solicitude."

"That's all right for a start."

"Poor woman."

"Of course, I don't want her to be a doormat. Let's say I like a woman who knows how to think, one who doesn't pretend to be anything but who she is. Of course," he added, finishing off his wine, "I'm also partial to good looks."

"Well, so far it doesn't sound as though you're asking for much," Samantha giggled. "Just perfection."

"The woman I have in mind can handle it." He smiled broadly as he rose to pour coffee. Samantha stared at his back, feeling as though her heart had been dropped into a deep hole. *Lesley Marshall*. Her mind flashed the name like a neon sign in bright red letters.

Jake squelched her offer to do the dishes and swooped her from her chair and deposited her on the living room sofa.

"I feel useless," she muttered, helplessly cocooned by blankets and pillows. "I'm not made for lying around. I'm never sick." She gave Jake a sulky glare as if the entire matter was his fault. "I don't know how Bree has coped with this sort of thing for a month."

"Could be you got her share of strength, and she got your share of patience," he considered, then shrugged. "Of course, I could be wrong." She heard his chuckle and the quiet click of his lighter as he lit a cigar.

Well, Samantha, she chided herself, you've really done it this time. Not only are you isolated with a man who constantly confuses you, but you can't even stand on your own feet. They say people learn about each other quickly when they live together, but I think it's going to take much more than one day to learn what this man is all about. Living together, she repeated to herself, more amused than embarrassed. If Momma could see me now, we'd need a gallon of smelling salts.

CHAPTER 7

Dawn was breaking. Pink and gold streaks split the hazy blue of the sky, and light tumbled through to rest on Samantha's closed lids.

Morning? Sitting up with a start, she shook her head vigorously to dispel the last remnants of sleep. Pulling on the borrowed robe, she set her feet on the floor, took three deep breaths and stood. When both the room and her head remained stable, she let out a long sigh of relief. Her legs were weak, but they no longer felt as if they would melt from under her, and the stiffness in her ankle had disappeared.

Mobility, she thought with arrogant glee. I've never truly appreciated it until now. Coffee. One thought followed swiftly on the trail of the other, and she deserted the room with the intention of making fantasy fact. A door opened as she passed it, and with a cry of surprise, she fell against the opposite wall.

Jake stood in the doorway, rubbing a towel briskly through his damp hair, a terry-cloth robe tied loosely around his waist. "Morning, ma'am."

"You startled me." She swallowed, overpowered

by the lean, bronzed maleness that the terry cloth did little to hide. He took a step toward her, and her breath caught instinctively. "I—I'm much better." She began to babble, unconsciously cowering against the smooth paneling. "I can actually walk a straight line."

Her voice died to a whisper as he stood directly in front of her. Her eyes were on a line with the tanned column of throat revealed by the open neck of the robe. His hand lifted her chin, and she trembled.

"Relax, Sam." His laughter sounded deep in his throat. "I just want to look you over. You must have the constitution of an elephant," he concluded with unflattering candor. "You look as though you've been on vacation instead of battling blizzards. One day's rest after nearly freezing to death. Most women would have been stretched out for a week."

"I'm not most women." She pushed his hand away from her face. "I'm not fragile and delicate, and I'm not going back to bed. I'm going to fix breakfast." She nudged him out of her path and started down the hall.

"Coffee's already on," he called after her.

Samantha had breakfast under way by the time Jake joined her. Clad in the less disturbing attire of corded jeans and flannel shirt, he watched her prepare the meal as he silently sipped at his coffee at the kitchen table.

"I'm getting used to having a pretty face across from me at breakfast," he commented when she sat down to join him.

"I'm sure I'm not the first," she commented with studied indifference. Nor, she added to herself, will I be the last.

"Nope," he agreed easily, "but there's something to be said for big blue eyes first thing in the morning."

"Blue eyes are common enough," she muttered,

and lowered them to the contents of her plate. "Besides, this is hardly a long-term arrangement." He did not speak for a moment, and her fork moved restlessly among her eggs.

"We should have the road clear enough sometime tomorrow."

"Tomorrow?" she repeated. A hollow feeling spread through her stomach.

"There's a lot of snow out there, some of the drifts are small mountains. It's going to take a little time to move it."

"I see."

"Do you think you could manage on your own for a while today?"

"What? Oh, sure, I'll be fine."

"There's a lot I should see to. My foreman was in charge yesterday, but the men need all the help they can get." He was frowning. "Cattle need hay brought out to them. They haven't the sense to dig through to the grass. They'll just stand there and starve to death."

"I suppose the storm did a lot of damage."

"It's only minor from the reports I've gotten. We were hit worse a couple years ago."

"Reports?"

"One of my men came by yesterday afternoon to fill me in." Pouring more coffee in his cup, he reached for the cream. "You were asleep."

"Oh." Strange, she thought, there had been a ripple in their isolation and she had been totally unaware of it.

Lifting his cup, he studied her over the rim. "I don't like leaving you alone, especially with the phones out."

Her shoulders moved. "Don't worry about me, I'll be fine." Glancing up, she met his speculative gaze.

"I don't know how long I'll be gone."

"Jake, stop fussing. I feel fine."

He tilted his head to the side, his eyes still narrowed. "Stand up. I want to see how you feel for myself."

Before she realized his intent, his arms were around her, and his mouth was on hers. Her legs buckled.

His mouth was light, teasing, his teeth nibbling at the fullness of her bottom lip until she moaned from the exquisite agony. She gripped his shoulders as a dim light of control seeped into the darkness. Pulling away she shook her head in refusal.

"Now, Sam . . ." His voice was soft and persuasive, but the hands that descended to her hips were firm. "You wouldn't send a man out in the cold without something warm to remember, would you?"

Insistently, he brought her closer, molding her hips, exploring the soft roundness until she was pressed against him with exciting intimacy. His mouth closed over her protest, his tongue moving with slow devastation to tease hers until she felt the room spinning as wildly as it had the day before. Slowly, his hands ascended, his thumbs circling the side of her breasts while his mouth and tongue destroyed all resistance. She was straining against him, moving against him, reason forgotten. Her body heated urgently at his touch. Her sigh was a moan as his mouth descended to her throat. His lips tasted, lingered, traveled to new territories, the tip of his tongue moist and warm against her skin, erotic and devastating against her ear, until her mouth was desperate for its return to hers.

Her mouth was to go unsatisfied. He pulled her away with the same arrogance as he had pulled her to him. Dazed and limp, she could do no more than stare up at him as her body throbbed with a myriad of newly discovered desires.

"You're learning fast, Sam. That was enough to keep any man moving through a six-foot snowdrift."

Furious, and humiliated by her own response, she drew back her hand.

"Now, Sam." He caught her wrist easily, holding it aloft, ignoring her efforts to escape. "You're not strong enough yet for wrestling. Give yourself a couple more days." Turning her hand over, his lips brushed her palm, causing her struggles to cease abruptly. "I'm going to bring in Wolfgang to keep an eye on you. Take it easy today, and try to remember, you're not as tough as you'd like to think."

Ruffling her hair as though she were a child, he disappeared into the adjoing mudroom.

Later Samantha indulged in a hot, steaming shower, attempting to forget, as she soaped her skin, the feel of Jake's hands running over her. In the bedroom, she noticed her clothes piled neatly on the spoon-back chair. She slipped them on and wandered through the house in aimless exploration, the Saint Bernard lumbering at her heels.

The house abounded in small, delightful treasures, an oak rolltop desk, a wall box with Friesian carving, a Windsor cradle. With a small sigh, she wondered if the latter had rocked the baby Jake. Opening yet another door, she found Jake's library.

It smelled of leather and age, and her fingers ran over volume after volume. She pulled out a small volume of love poetry and opened the cover. Light, feminine handwriting adorned the top corner, and her mouth turned down at the inscription.

Darling Jake . . . To remind you.

Love, Lesley

Shutting the book with a snap, Samantha held it for one heat-blinded movement over the wastebasket, then, grinding her teeth, stuck it firmly back in place.

"It makes no difference to me," she informed Wolf-gang. "She can give him a hundred books of poetry, she can give him a thousand books of poetry. It's her privilege."

She nudged the big dog with her toe. "Come on, Wolfgang, let's get moving."

She returned to the living room and built up the fire, which had burned down to a hissing pile of embers. She curled up beside it.

One hour slipped into two, two slipped into three. Surely, Jake should be home by now, she told the silent clock as the hands crept past six. It was getting dark. Rising, Samantha stared out into the diminishing light.

What if something had happened to Jake? Her throat went dry, fear creeping along her skin. Nothing could happen to him, she told herself, running her hands over her arms to combat the sudden chill. He's strong and self-reliant.

But why am I so worried about him?

"Because," she said aloud, slowly, *"I love him. I've lost my mind and fallen in love with him."* Her hands lifted to cover her eyes as the weight of the knowledge crushed down on her. "Oh, how could I be so stupid? Of all the men in the world, I had to fall in love with this one."

A man, she remembered, who has chosen Lesley

Marshall to be his wife. Is that why I've felt pulled in two? Is that why I respond to him when I've never responded to anyone else? Looking out into the darkness, she shuddered. I might as well admit that I don't care about anything except his getting home. . . .

When finally the sound of the outside door slamming reached her ears, she ran into the mudroom and threw herself at an astonished, snow-covered Jake.

"Sam, what's going on?" He tried to pull her away from his cold, wet jacket.

"I was afraid something had happened to you." Her voice was muffled against his chest, her cheek oblivious to the frigid dampness.

"Nothing's happened, except I'm half-frozen and soaked to the skin." Firmly now, he took her shoulders, disentangling himself from her arms. "You're getting covered with snow." His grip was gentle. She stared up at him with huge, swimming eyes. "I'm sorry I was gone so long, but things were piled up, and it's slow working in a mess like this."

Embarrassed by her outburst, she backed away. "You must be exhausted. I'm sorry, it was stupid to go on like that. It must come from being alone in the house all day." As she babbled, she was backing purposefully toward the door. "You probably want a shower and something hot to drink. I—I've got dinner on."

"Something smells good," he commented. His eyes roamed over her flushed face, and a smile spread over his features.

"S-Spaghetti," she stammered and despised herself. "I'll go finish it up."

Retreating into the kitchen, Samantha kept her back toward him when he emerged and announced casually that he would have a hot shower before dinner. She mumbled a vague reply, pretending a complete involvement with her dinner preparation. Listening to his receding footsteps, she let out a long, pent-up breath.

"Oh, idiot that I am," she sighed, and pushed her hair from her face in an angry gesture. The type of behavior she had displayed in the mudroom would only lead to trouble. She took a solemn oath to keep her emotions on a tight leash as long as Jake Tanner was around.

Tomorrow, she remembered, with a mixture of relief and disappointment, she would be back with her sister, and avoiding Jake would be a great deal easier. She had only to get through one more evening without making a fool of herself, and then she would sort out her thinking.

She was setting the table when Jake returned.

"If that tastes as good as it smells, I'll die a happy man." He lifted the lid on the pot and gave a sigh of approval. Grinning, he disappeared for a moment, then returned with a bottle of wine just as she was placing the pot on the table.

"A nice burgundy," he said, opening the bottle and setting out two glasses.

"Samantha, this is fantastic." He broke off eating long enough to give her a smile. "Where'd you learn to cook like this?"

"More of my mother's famous lessons."

"What else can you do?"

"Well, let's see. I do a rather superb swan dive, a very graceful arabesque, I can walk on my hands as easily as some walk on their feet, whip up an incredible quiche, and waltz without counting the time."

"I am suitably impressed. How did a woman of your talents spend the day?"

She sighed and grimaced and began to toy with her spaghetti. "Sleeping, mostly."

"Hmm." His cough did not quite cover his laugh.

After dinner, Samantha insisted on seeing to the washing up herself. She wanted to avoid the intimacy of working side by side with him in the confines of the kitchen.

When the last signs of the meal had vanished, she walked down the hall to the living room. Jake was adding another log to the low, shifting blaze. As she entered, he turned to smile at her. "Want some brandy?"

"No, no, thank you." She took a deep breath and willed her legs to carry her to the sofa.

"Not in training, are you?" He moved from the hearth to join her on the sofa.

Smiling, she shook her head. "The fire's wonderful." Grasping the first topic that came to mind, she riveted her eyes on the flames. "I always wanted one in my apartment. We had one at home, and Bree and I used to pop corn over it. We'd always burn it, and . . ."

The rest of her rush of words was lost as Jake placed his finger under her chin and turned her face to his. His face moved closer, and when she jerked back in defense, his brow lifted in amusement. He bent toward her again, and again she started.

"I'm only going to kiss you, Samantha." His grip tightened on her chin. Sliding from her chin, his hand framed her face as his lips moved over hers, soft as a whisper. In spite of herself, she relaxed against him. Her lips parted, inviting him to explore, begging him to take.

"Samantha." Her name was a sigh.

"Kiss me again," she whispered slowly as she lifted her mouth to his.

With a low groan, he brought his lips down on hers. She clung to him, her body throbbing with heat, her heart desperate against his, while a part of her looked on, aghast, as she answered his kiss.

Her mouth clung, avid and sweet, to his. Dormant passion exploded into life until there remained only man and woman and the need, older than time, to love and be loved, to possess and be possessed.

He opened her shirt and claimed her breast. The first desperation mellowed into slow exploration as his fingers trailed lightly, drugging her with a new, delirious languor. His mouth moved to sample the taste of her neck, his face buried in the spreading lushness of her hair. She pressed against the rippling muscles of his back as his mouth and tongue and hands raged fire over her.

She felt rather than heard him say her name against her mouth, sensed rather than felt the tension enter his body before her lips were set free. Dimly, she heard the strident insistence of bells ringing as she groped to bring heaven back within reach.

"Hell of a time for them to fix the phones." She opened her eyes, dark as sapphires, and stared without comprehension. "There's nothing I'd like more than to ignore it, Samantha, but it might be important." Her lids fluttered in confusion. She could feel the warm raggedness of his breath against her cheek. "The phones have been out for two days, and there's a lot of damage out there."

His body left hers and took the warmth with it. She struggled to sit up, pulling her shirt closed. The hands that worked at the buttons were unsteady and, rising on weak legs, she sought the warmth of the fire. Pushing at tumbled hair, she wrapped her arms around her body and closed her eyes.

What had she done, losing herself that way? Tossing away pride like damaged goods! What if the phone hadn't rung? Her arms closed tighter. Does love always hurt? Does it always make a fool of you?

"Samantha." She whirled at the sound of her name, her arms still tight in protection. "It's Sabrina." Dropping her eyes from his, she moved into the hall.

Samantha picked up the phone and swallowed. "Hi, Bree." Her voice sounded strangely high-pitched to her ears, and her fingers gripped hard on the receiver.

"Sam, how are you?"

Taking a deep breath, she answered. "Fine. How *you* are is more important."

"Stronger every minute. I'm so glad you had the sense to head for the Double T when the snow started. The thought of you getting caught in that blizzard makes my blood turn cold."

"That's me, a steady head in a crisis." Samantha nearly choked on a gurgle of hysterical laughter.

"Are you sure you're all right? You sound strange. You aren't coming down with a cold, are you?"

"It's probably the connection."

"I thought they'd never get the phones fixed! I guess I just couldn't really relax until I'd talked to you and made sure you were safe! Of course, I know Jake would take care of you, but it's not the same as hearing your voice. I won't keep you, Sam, we'll see you tomorrow. By the way, I think Shylock misses you."

"Probably indigestion. Tell him I'll see him tomorrow." After replacing the receiver, she stared at it for a full minute.

"Samantha." She whirled again at Jake's voice, finding him watching her from the living room archway.

"I . . . ah . . . Bree seems fine." She avoided his eyes and toyed with the ink pot by the phone. She took a step backward as Jake advanced. "She said she thought Shylock misses me. That's quite an accomplishment, he's so self-sufficient and aloof."

"Samantha. Come, sit down." He held out his hand for hers. She knew if he touched her, she would be lost.

"No, no, I think I'll go to bed, I'm still not quite myself." Her color had ebbed again, leaving pale cheeks and darkened eyes.

"Still running, Sam?" The anger in his tone was well controlled.

"No, no, I . . ."

"All right, then, for the moment we seem to be at a stalemate." He captured her chin before she could avoid the gesture. "But we haven't finished by a long shot. Do you understand?"

She nodded, then broke away to flee to the sanctuary of her room.

CHAPTER 8

As each day passed, Sabrina became more cheerful. Her features took on a roundness that gave her a contented appearance. And as Samantha watched her, she wondered if Sabrina possessed more strength than she had ever given her credit for. It was a sobering experience to see her usually dreamy sister grabbing life with determination and purpose while she herself couldn't seem to stop daydreaming. Jake Tanner, she had to admit, was disturbing her days and sneaking into her dreams.

Stuffing her hands in her pockets, she scowled and continued her morning trudge to the mailbox. He meant to have her, did he? Well, Samantha Evans had no intention of being had by anyone, especially some annoying cowboy with too much charm for his own good . . . and fascinating green eyes, and that beautiful mouth. . . .

Now the days began to lengthen. The sun grew in strength. Spring began to drift over the basin,

greening the grass and teasing the crocuses to push
their heads from the earth.

Scurrying down the hall as the doorbell interrupted
her latest project—painting the nursery—Samantha
wiped a few streaks of canary yellow on her jeans and
opened the door.

The woman in the doorway smiled, her almond-
shaped dark eyes making a thorough survey. "Hello,
you must be Samantha. I'm Lesley Marshall."

The introduction was unnecessary, for with an
instinct she had been unaware of possessing, Samantha
had recognized the woman instantly. "Please, come in.
It's still rather cold, isn't it?" She smiled, refusing to
acknowledge the effort it cost her, and shut the nippy
May air outside.

"I'm so glad to meet you at last." The dark eyes
swept down, then up Samantha briefly. "I've heard so
much about you." There was light amusement in her
voice.

"Oh, really? I'm afraid I can't say the same." Her
smile was faintly apologetic. "But, of course, I've been
rather busy."

"I would have been by sooner, but I wanted to wait
until Sabrina was more up to company."

"Bree's feeling much better these days. I'm sure
she'll be glad to see you. Let me take your coat." Samantha hung the soft fur in the hall closet. Turning
back to her visitor, she needed all her willpower to
keep the social smile in place. The oatmeal slacks accentuated Lesley's sleekness; the trim cerise blouse set
off her delicately feathered ebony hair and the perfect
ivory of her skin. Desperately, Samantha wished a miracle would transform her navy sweatshirt with its Wilson High School banner and her paint-streaked jeans
into something smart and sophisticated. As usual, her

hair was escaping from its pins. She resisted the urge to bring her hand up to it and jam them in tightly.

"Bree's in the living room," she announced, knowing the pale gray eyes had studied her and found her wanting. "I was just about to make some tea."

Sabrina appeared at that moment, and Samantha gladly relinquished the role of hostess and escaped to the kitchen.

"So, she's beautiful," she grumbled to an unconcerned Shylock as she set the kettle on to boil. "So, she's smooth and sophisticated and makes me feel like a pile of dirty laundry." Turning, she lowered her face to his and scowled. "Who cares?" Shylock scowled back and went to sleep. Her thoughts wandered on. "I don't imagine he's ever laughed at her and patted her head as though she were a slow-witted child," she muttered as she gathered up the tea tray.

"Sabrina, you look wonderful," Lesley commented sometime later, sipping from a dainty china cup. "I'm sure having your sister with you must be very good for you. I don't have to tell you how concerned everyone has been."

"No, and I appreciate it. Sam's made everything so easy. I didn't have anything to do but sit and heal." She shot her sister an affectionate glance. "I don't know what we would have done without her these past two months."

Lesley followed her gaze. "Jake was telling me that you're a gym teacher, Samantha," she purred, managing to make this sound faintly disgusting.

"Physical education instructor," Samantha corrected, slipping into a vague southern drawl.

"And you were in the Olympics, as well. I'm sure it must have been fascinating. You don't look the sturdy, athletic type." The shrug of her shoulders was elegant, as was the small gesture of her hand. "I suppose one can never tell." Samantha gritted her teeth against a biting retort and was vastly relieved when, glancing at a slender gold watch, Lesley suddenly rose from her chair. "I must run now, Sabrina, I have a dinner engagement." Turning to Samantha, she offered a small smile. "So happy to have met you. I'm sure we'll be seeing each other again soon."

She left amidst a swirl of fur and the drifting scent of roses. Samantha sat back in the cushioned chair, relaxing for the first time in more than an hour.

"Well, what did you think of Lesley?" Sabrina questioned, shifting into a more comfortable position on the sofa.

"Very sophisticated."

"Come on, Sam." Sabrina grinned, her hands folding across the mound of her belly. "This is Bree."

"I don't know why I should have to comment, since you seem to be reading me so well. But"—her mouth curved into a rueful smile—"I suppose she's a bit smooth for my taste, and I didn't much care for the way she looked down that aristocratic nose at me."

"Actually, you really don't appear very sturdy." The observation was made with wide-eyed innocence. Samantha grimaced, pulling pins from her hair with a sharp tug until a cascade of golden brown tumbled in confusion about her shoulders.

"She'd have gotten her own back on that one if you hadn't sent me that 'Don't make a scene' look."

"Oh, well, Lesley can be nice enough when it suits her. Her father spoils her dreadfully. Her mother died when she was barely into her teens, and he transferred all his attention to Lesley. An overabundance of clothes, the best horses, and, as she grew older, cars and European tours and so on. Whatever Lesley wants, Lesley gets."

"Poor thing." The sarcasm caused her to feel spiteful and unjust. She sighed. "I suppose too much is as bad as too little. It was nice of her to come and see how you were getting along."

Sabrina's laughter floated through the room. "Sam, darling, I've never known you to be so slow." At her sister's puzzled expression, she continued. "Lesley didn't come to see me, she came to get a look at you."

"At me?" Finely etched brows disappeared under a fringe of bangs. "What for? I wouldn't think a lowly gym teacher from Philadelphia would interest Lesley Marshall."

"Any teacher who caught Jake Tanner's attention the way you have would interest Lesley. He wouldn't have gone out of his way to show just anyone around the ranch, you know."

A light color rose in Samantha's cheeks. "I think Miss Marshall's mind was put to rest after she got a good look." Her hand moved expressively down her sweatshirt and jeans. "She'd hardly see any danger here."

"Don't underestimate yourself, Sam."

"No false modesty." Samantha's sigh came from nowhere. "If a man's attracted to silk and champagne, cotton and beer are no competition. I'm cotton and beer, Bree," she murmured. Her voice trailed away with her thoughts. "I couldn't be anything else if I wanted to."

The following day, Samantha's continuing battle with her paints and brushes was interrupted by a more welcome visitor. Annie Holloway arrived at the ranch's kitchen door with a beaming smile and a chocolate cake.

"Hi." Samantha opened the door wide in welcome. "It's nice to see you again, and bearing gifts, too."

"Never like to come empty-handed," Annie announced, handing the thickly frosted cake to Samantha. "Dan always had a partiality for chocolate cake."

"Me, too." She eyed the cake hungrily. "He's not here right now, and I was just going to make some coffee. Do you suppose we could start without him?"

"Good idea." Setting herself comfortably in a chair, Annie waved a wide-palmed hand. "I reckon it wouldn't hurt for us to have a slice or two."

"Bree's taking a nap," Samantha explained as she put down the mugs of steaming coffee. "The doctor says she still has to lie down every day, but she's beginning to grumble about it a bit. Very quietly, of course."

"You're keeping an eye on her." Annie nodded and added two generous spoons of sugar to her coffee. "Dan says she's up to company now."

"Oh, yes, people have been dropping by now and again. Ah . . ." Samantha added cream to her own cup. "Lesley Marshall was by yesterday."

"I wondered how long it would be before Lesley hauled herself over to get a look at you."

"You sound like Bree." Sipping her coffee, Samantha shook her head. "I don't know why Lesley Marshall would want to meet me."

"Easy. Lesley's a mite stingy with her possessions, and she'd like to group Jake among them. She hasn't figured out yet that Jake is his own man, and all her daddy's money can't buy him for her. When my Jake picks his woman, he'll decide the time and place. He's always been an independent rascal. He was barely twenty when he lost his folks, you know." Samantha lifted her eyes to the warm brown ones. "It wasn't an easy time for him, they'd been close. They were a pair, Jake's folks, always squabbling and loving. You're a bit like her when she was a young thing." Annie smiled, her head tilting with it as Samantha remained silent. "Nobody's going to ride roughshod over you, at least not for long. I saw that straight off. She was stubborn as a mule with two heads, and there's times, though it's been better than ten years, I still miss her."

"It must have been hard on Jake, losing his parents and having all the responsibility of the ranch when he was still so young," Samantha murmured.

"Seemed to change from boy to man overnight, just out of college and still green. 'Course," she continued, "he'd been in the saddle since childhood and what he hadn't learned about ranching from his father and that fancy college, he learned from doing. He picked up the reins of that ranch with both hands. There's not a man who works for him wouldn't wrestle a long-horned bull if he asked them to. He can fool you with that easygoing way of his, but nobody gets the better of Jake Tanner. He runs the ranch like his life, and Lesley's going to find him a hard steer to rope and brand."

"Maybe it's more the other way around," Samantha suggested. Annie's response was prevented by the appearance at the kitchen door of the man in question.

He entered with the easy familiarity of an old friend.

"Howdy, ma'am." He broke the silence with a cocky smile, removed his battered Stetson and glanced at her attire. "Been painting?"

"Obvious, isn't it?" Samantha said sharply.

"Nice colors." He helped himself to a cup of coffee. "Are you going to part with another piece of that cake?"

"Jake Tanner!" Annie exclaimed in disgust. "You

should be ashamed, gobbling Dan's cake when you've got a perfectly good one of your own at home."

"Somebody else's always tastes better, Annie." He slipped off his jacket, tossing it over a hook, and grinned boyishly. "He won't miss it, anyway. I brought you and the cake over, didn't I? You're not going to begrudge me one little piece?"

"Don't waste those eyes on me, you young devil." Annie attempted to sniff and look indignant. "I'm not one of your fillies."

Jake's appearance had successfully shattered Samantha's peace of mind. After a reasonable period of politeness, she excused herself to Annie and Jake and went back to her job in the nursery.

Samantha's artistic talent was decidedly impressionistic. The floor, protected by plastic, was splotched and splattered, but the walls were coming to life with a joy of brilliant colors. Of the four walls, two were yellow and two were white, and each was trimmed with its opposite's color. On the one wall that was unbroken by door or windows, she had begun the construction of a wide, arching rainbow, carefully merging blues into pinks into greens.

Time passed, and in the quiet concentration of her work she forgot her preoccupation with Jake. Sitting on the ladder's top step, she paused, brushing the back of her hand across her cheek absently as she viewed the results.

"That's a mighty pretty sight."

She jolted, dropping the brush with a clatter, and would have fallen from the ladder had Jake's arms not gripped her waist and prevented the tumble.

"Sure spook easy," Jake commented, removing the dangerously sloshing paint bucket from her hand.

"You shouldn't come up behind a person like that," she complained. "I might have broken my neck." She wiped her hands on the legs of her jeans. "Where's Annie?"

"With your sister. She wanted to show Annie some things she's made for the baby." He set the bucket on the floor and straightened. "I didn't think they needed me."

"No, I'm sure they didn't. I need that paint, though, and the brush you made me drop." She glanced down, but his eyes remained on hers.

"I like the blue, especially that spot on your cheek," Jake said.

She rubbed at the offending area in annoyance. "If you'd just hand those things back to me, I could finish up."

"Green's nice, too," he said conversationally, and ran a finger over a long streak on her thigh. "Wilson High." His eyes lowered to the letters on her shirt. "Is that where you taught back east?"

"Yes." She shifted, uncomfortable that the name was prominent over her breasts. "Are you going to hand me my things?"

"What are your plans for tonight?" he countered easily, ignoring her request. She stared, completely thrown off balance by his unexpected question.

"I, ah, I have a lot of things to do." She searched her mind for something vital in her schedule.

"'Things'?" he prompted. His smile grew as his finger began to twist through a stray curl that had escaped its confines.

"Yes, things," she retorted, abandoning the attempt

to elaborate. "I'm going to be very busy, and I really want to finish this room."

"I suppose I could let you get by with that, even though we both know better. Well." He smiled and shrugged. "Come down and kiss me goodbye, then. I've got to get back to work."

"I will not kiss you goodbye. . . ." she began, the words trailing off as he gripped her waist. Her hands automatically went to his arms, and he plucked her from her perch.

He lowered her slowly, his eyes never leaving hers, and her mouth was roughly claimed before her feet could reach the floor. His hands slipped under her shirt to roam the smooth skin of her back, pressing her closer as her body betrayed her and dissolved against his. Slowly he explored her soft, firm breasts, subtly rounded hips, lean thighs.

Every time, every time, her mind murmured. Every time he kisses me, I go under deeper, and one day I'll never find my way back. His teeth moved to nip at her ear and neck, searching and finding new vulnerabilities before returning to ravage her mouth again. Without will, without choice, she rested in his arms, surrendering to forces she could never defeat.

He drew her away, breaking the intimacy, but his mouth returned to hers to linger briefly before he spoke. "About tonight, Samantha."

"What?" she murmured as his tongue traced the softness of her lips.

"I want to see you tonight."

Jerking herself back into reality, she pressed her hands against his chest, but did not manage to break away. "No, no, I'm busy. I told you."

"So you did," he acknowledged, and his eyes narrowed in speculation.

His words were cut off by the sound of Sabrina's laughter drifting down the hall. Samantha wiggled against Jake's hold. "Let me go, will you?"

"Why?" He was grinning now, enjoying the flood of color in her cheeks.

"Because . . ."

"Don't ever play poker, Sam." The warning was curt. "You'd lose your shirt."

"I . . . I . . ."

"Sabrina's due in September, right?"

The sudden question caused her to blink in confusion. "Well, yes, she . . ."

"That gives you a little breathing space, Samantha." He leaned down, and his kiss was hard and brief and to the point. "After that, don't expect to get away so lightly."

"I don't know what . . ."

"You know exactly what I mean," he said interrupting. "I told you I meant to have you, and I always get what I want."

Her eyes flashed. "If you think I'm going to let you make love to me just because you say so, then you . . ."

The suggestion she would have made died as his mouth took hers again. She went rigid telling herself she would not amuse him with a response this time. As she told herself she would not, her arms circled his neck. Her body became pliant, her lips parted with the hunger she had lived with all through the past month. As he took, she offered more; as he demanded, she gave. Her own mouth was mobile, her own hands seeking, until it seemed the month of fasting had never been.

"I want you, I don't have to tell you that, do I?"

She shook her head, trying to steady her breathing as his eyes alone caused her pulse to triple its rate.

"We'll settle this in September, unless you decide to come to me sooner." She began to shake her head again, but the fingers on the back of her neck halted the movement. "If you don't come to me, I'll wait until after the baby's born and you've got that much off your mind. I'm a patient man, Sam, but . . ." He stopped talking as Annie and Sabrina stepped into the room.

"Well." Annie shook her head at the two of them. "I can see he's been giving you a hard time." She turned to Sabrina with a half-exasperated shrug. "He's always been fresh as a new-laid egg. This is going to be a beautiful room, Sam." She glanced around at Samantha's handiwork, nodding in approval. "Let go of the little lady now, Jake, and take me back home, I've got dinner to fix."

"Sure. I've already said what I came to say." He released Samantha with a last, penetrating look and strode from the room, calling a goodbye over his shoulder.

"Fresh as a new-laid egg," Annie reiterated, and echoing his goodbye, followed him.

When the guests had departed, Samantha began to gather up paint buckets and brushes.

"Sam." Walking over, Sabrina placed a hand on her sister's arm. "I had no idea."

"No idea about what?" Bending, she banged the lid securely on rose pink.

"That you were in love with Jake." The truth she had avoided for so long was out in the open now: She had fallen hopelessly, irrevocably in love with Jake Tanner! Standing, Samantha searched in vain for words of denial.

"We know each other too well, Sam," Sabrina said before she could answer. "How bad is it?"

Samantha lifted her hands and let them fall to her sides. "Terminal."

"Well, what are you going to do about it?"

"'Do about it'?" Samantha repeated. "What can I do about it? After the baby comes, I'll go back east and try to forget about him."

"I've never known you to give up without a fight," Sabrina spoke sharply. At the unexpected tone, Samantha's brows rose.

"I'd fight for something that belonged to me, Bree, but I don't move in on someone else's territory."

"Jake's not engaged to Lesley Marshall. Nothing's official."

"I'm not interested in semantics." Samantha began to fiddle with the paint cans. "Jake wants an affair with me, but he'll marry Lesley Marshall."

"Are you afraid to compete with Lesley?" Bree asked.

Samantha whirled around, eyes flashing. "I'm not afraid of anyone," she stormed. Sabrina's lips curved in a smug smile. "Don't try your psychology on me, Sabrina! Lesley Marshall and I don't belong in the same league, but I'm not afraid of her. I *am* afraid of getting hurt, though." Her voice wavered and Sabrina's arm slipped over her shoulders.

"All right, Sam, we won't talk about it any more right now. Leave those brushes, I'll wash them out. Go take a ride. You know the only way to clear your head is to go off by yourself."

"I'm beginning to think you know me too well." With a wry smile, Samantha wiped her hands on her jeans.

"I know you, all right, Samantha." Sabrina patted her cheek and urged her from the room. "I just haven't always known what to do about you."

CHAPTER 9

During the months since their first meeting, Samantha had grown to know Jake Tanner, and to realize that when he wanted something, he made certain he got it. And she knew he wanted her.

If, when she rode out on horseback, she kept closer to the ranch than had been her habit, she told herself it was not fear of encountering Jake that prompted the action, but simply her desire to spend more of her free time with Sabrina. Now Sabrina was growing cumbersome in her pregnancy, there was a grain of truth to this, so Samantha found it easy to accept the half-truth.

Every day she fell more under the spell of Wyoming. Bare branches were now fully cloaked in green. The cattle grew sleek and fat. The land was fully awakened and rich.

"I think you may just have twins in there, Bree," Samantha commented as the two sisters took advantage of golden sun and fragrant warmth. Sabrina glanced down to where Samantha sat cross-legged on the wide front porch. "Dr. Gates thinks not." She patted the mound in question. "He says there's only one, and I'm just getting fat. One of us should have twins, though."

"I'm afraid that's going to be up to you, Bree. I think I'll revive the tradition of old-maid schoolteachers."

Sabrina was sensitive to the wistfulness in the words. "Oh, no, you'll have to get married, Sam. You can't let all those lessons go to waste."

This brought the light laugh it had intended. "I'm perfectly serious. Remember what Madame Dubois always said: 'Von must reach for ze stars.'"

"Oh, yes, Madame Dubois." Samantha smiled at the memory of their former ballet teacher. "You know, of course, that accent was a phony. She came from New Jersey."

"I'm suitably crushed. She did think she had a genuine protégé in you."

"Yes, I was magnificent." Samantha sighed with exaggerated pride.

"Let's see a few of your famous leaps now, Sam."

"Not on your life!"

"Come on, cutoffs are as good as a tutu any day. I'd join you in a pas de deux, but it would actually be a pas de trois."

Samantha rose reluctantly from her seat on the porch. "All right, I don't mind showing off a little."

With quiet dignity, Sabrina began to hum a movement from *Swan Lake,* and Samantha lowered into a purposefully dramatic body sweep before exploding with an energetic series of grand jetés, stage leaps and cabrioles. She concluded the performance with a group of pirouettes, ended by dropping in a dizzy heap on the grass.

"That's what you get," she said, closing her eyes and shaking her head at the giddiness, "when you forget to spot focus."

"Is this show open to the public?"

Samantha glanced sharply toward the sound of the all-too-familiar voice.

"Dan!" Sabrina exclaimed. "I didn't expect you back so early."

"Ran into Lesley and Jake out on the north boundary," he explained, striding over and planting a firm kiss. "I thought you and Sam might like some company."

"Hello, Lesley, Jake." Sabrina included them both in her smile. "Have a seat, I'll bring out something cool."

Samantha had been sitting, praying without result for the ground to open up and swallow her. "I'll do it, Bree." She jumped at the opportunity to escape. "Don't get up."

"I'm up," Sabrina pointed out, disappearing inside before Samantha could argue.

"Do you teach ballet, as well, Samantha?" Lesley asked. She surveyed Samantha's outfit of semiragged cutoffs and T-shirt with dark, mocking eyes.

"No, no," Samantha muttered, feeling once more desperately at a disadvantage next to the slim woman in elegantly tailored breeches and silk shirt.

"I thought it was real nice," Dan commented, innocently turning the knife.

"Samantha's just full of surprises," Jake said.

Now that he had spoken again, Samantha was forced to give Jake a portion of her attention. He looked devastatingly male, the denim shirt rolled past his elbows to expose bronzed, corded arms, the low-slung belt in his jeans accentuating his leanness. She concentrated on a spot approximately six inches to the left of his face, in order to avoid the smile that had already mastered his face.

"Yeah," she returned. "I'm just a bushel of surprises."

"Anything you can't do, Sam?"

"A few things." She attempted a cool sophistication.

"You're so energetic," Lesley commented, slipping her hand through Jake's arm. "You must be horribly strong and full of bulging muscles."

For one heady moment, Samantha considered flight. She was opening her mouth to make her excuses when Dan effectively cut off all hope.

"Sit down, Sam, I want to talk over a little idea with you and Sabrina." Sinking down on the porch steps, Samantha avoided any glimpse of Jake's face. "Do you think Sabrina's up to a little party?" Samantha looked up at Dan's question and attempted to marshal her thoughts.

"A party?" she repeated, drawing her brows together in concentration. "I suppose so. Dr. Gates says she's doing very well, but you could always ask to be sure. Did you want to go to a party?"

"I was thinking of having one," he corrected with a grin. "There're these twins I know who have this birthday in a couple of weeks." Bending over, he tugged at Samantha's loosened locks. "Seems like a good excuse for having a party."

"Oh, our birthday." Samantha's response was vague. The impending anniversary had slipped her mind.

"Did I hear someone say party?" Sabrina emerged through the screen door with a tray of iced tea.

Samantha sipped the cool, sweet tea her sister handed her and watched Sabrina's face light up with anticipation.

"A birthday party, Sam." She turned to her sister, eyes shining with excitement. "When's the last time we had one?"

"When we were twelve and Billy Darcy got sick all over Mom's new carpet." Leaning back against the porch rail, Samantha unwittingly lifted her face to Jake's.

"Well, then, it's high time for another," Dan said. "What do you say, Sam? I know it means extra work for you."

"Huh." Tearing her eyes from Jake's smile, she endeavored to pick up the threads of the conversation. "What? Oh, no, it's no trouble. It'll be fun." Concentrating on Dan's face, she blocked out the sight of Lesley lounging intimately against Jake. "How many people did you have in mind?"

"Just neighbors and friends." He reached up to rub his chin. "About thirty or forty, I'd say. What do you think, Lesley?"

The full mouth pouted a moment in thought. "If you want to keep it small, Dan," she agreed after a short deliberation. Samantha's eyes grew wide. These people definitely had a different idea of small than she did.

"Oh, Lesley, come take a look at this punch bowl I've got, see if you think we should use it." Rising, Sabrina took Dan's hand. "Come, get it down for me, Dan." Throwing her sister an innocent smile, Sabrina disappeared inside and left her alone with Jake.

"How's the painting coming?" Jake stretched both arms over the back of the swing.

"Painting? Oh, the nursery. It's finished."

That, she recalled with a frown, was just one of many times he had come upon her in a ridiculous situation. Sleeping on stumps, covered with paint, and now leaping across the lawn like some crazed ballerina. Samantha, she told herself, you have class.

"What do you want for your birthday, Sam?" He prodded her with the toe of his boot and earned a scowl.

Blowing a wisp of hair from her eyes, she moved her shoulders. "Fur, diamonds."

"No, you're not the type for furs." Taking out a cigar, he lit it and blew a lazy stream of smoke. "And diamonds wouldn't suit you."

"I suppose I'm more the quartz type." She rose, irritated.

"No, I was thinking more of sapphires." He caught her wrist. "To go with your eyes, or maybe rubies to go with your temper."

"I'll be sure to put both on my list. Now, if you'll excuse me." She glanced at her captured hand, then back at him. "I've got to go feed my cat." She gestured to where Shylock lay on the far side of the porch.

"He doesn't look very hungry."

"He's pretending to be dead," she muttered. "Shylock, let's eat."

Amber eyes opened and blinked. Then, to her pleasure, Shylock rose and padded toward her. However, upon reaching his mistress, he gave her a disinterested stare, leaped into Jake's lap, and began to purr with wicked enjoyment.

"No, ma'am." Jake glanced down at the contented cat. "He doesn't look hungry at all."

With a final glare, Samantha turned, stalked to the door, and slammed the screen smartly behind her.

The sun shone warm and friendly on the morning of the twins' birthday. Samantha carried a large parcel into the kitchen. Dumping her burden on the table where her sister was enjoying a cup of tea, she nudged Shylock away with her foot. She had not yet decided to forgive him for his treacherous advances to Jake.

"This just came, it's from the folks."

"Open it, Sam." Sabrina poked an experimental finger at the package. "Dan refuses to give me my present yet, and I've searched everywhere I can think of."

"I bet it's six books on child rearing for you, and six on etiquette for me."

"A present's a present," Sabrina stated, and tore the mailing paper from the box.

"Here's a note." After breaking the seal, Samantha produced a sheet of paper and read aloud.

"To Samantha and Sabrina:

A very happy birthday and our love to you both. Sabrina, I do hope you are taking good care of yourself. As you know, proper diet and rest are essential. I'm sure having Samantha with you during the last weeks of your confinement is a great comfort. Samantha, do look after your sister and see that she takes the necessary precautions. However, I hope you're not overlooking your own social life. As your mother, it is my duty to remind you that you are long past the marriageable age. Your father and I are looking forward to seeing you and our first grandchild in a few weeks. We will be in Wyoming the first part of September, if Dad's schedule holds true.

                                        With love,
                                        Mom and Dad

"There's a postscript for you, Bree.

"'Sabrina, doesn't Daniel know any suitable men for your sister?'"

With a sigh, Samantha folded the letter and dropped it on the table. "She never changes." Dipping into the

box, Samantha plucked out a smaller one with Sabrina's name on it and handed it to her. "'Marriageable age',"
she muttered, and shook her head.

"Did you peek in here before?" Sabrina accused, dumping out volumes on infant and child care.

"No," Samantha denied with a superior smirk. "I just know Mom." Drawing out her own package, she ripped off the concealing paper. "Good grief." She let the box drop to the table and held up a brief black lace negligee.

"I thought I knew Mom." Both sisters burst into laughter. "She must be getting desperate," Samantha concluded, holding the negligee in front of her.

"Now that's a pretty thing," Jake observed as he and Dan entered the kitchen. "But it's even prettier with something in it." Samantha bundled the garment behind her and flushed scarlet.

"Presents from Mom and Dad," Sabrina explained, indicating her stack of books.

"Very suitable." Dan grinned as he glanced through the volumes.

"Doesn't look like Sam feels the same about hers." Jake smiled. Samantha felt her already alarming color deepen. "Let's see it again."

"Don't tease, Jake." Sabrina turned to her husband. "Mom says they'll be here the first part of September."

"I'll put this stuff away." Samantha tossed the gown into the box and began to bury it under books.

"Leave that till later." Dan took her hand and pulled her away. "I need you outside for a minute."

She went willingly. Escape was escape. Imagining it had something to do with Sabrina's gift, she was surprised when Dan slowed his pace and allowed his wife to join them in their walk toward the ranch buildings. He kept her involved in a running conversation about the party until they came to a halt at the paddock fence.

"Happy birthday, Sam." Sabrina kissed her sister's cheek as Samantha's eyes focused on the golden Arabian mare.

"Oh." She could manage no more.

"She's from a good line," Dan informed her, his arm slipping around Sabrina's shoulders. "She's out of the Double T stock, no finer in Wyoming."

"But I . . ." Words faltered, and she swallowed and tried to begin again.

"What do you give someone who packs their own life away for six months without hesitation, without asking for anything in return?" Dan's free arm slipped around Samantha and pulled her to his side.

"We figured if you insisted on going back east, we'd always have a hold on you. You'd have to come visit us to ride your mare."

"I don't know how to thank you."

"Then don't," Dan ordered. "Go try her out."

"Now?"

"Now's as good a time as any." Not needing a second urging, Samantha was over the fence, stroking the mare and murmuring.

"We may convince her to stay yet," Dan commented, watching as she slipped into the saddle and took the mare around the paddock. "I could have a word with Jake."

Sabrina shook her head. "No, Sam would be furious if we interfered. She'd bolt back to Philadelphia before we could take a breath. For now, we'd better keep out of it." She lowered her voice as a beaming Samantha trotted around to them and slipped off the little mare.

"She's a real beauty," she sighed. "I don't know how I can ever bear to leave her. . . ."

Sabrina's eyes met her husband's in silent satisfaction. Perhaps it will not be necessary, their unspoken message said.

"Come, little sister," Dan said. "If you can tear yourself away from your new friend, I sure could use a cup of coffee now."

As the trio trooped back toward the house, Jake swung through the back door. "Delivery just came. It's in the living room."

"Oh," Dan murmured, looking entirely too innocent. "Come on, Sabrina, we'd best see what it is."

"Is it the piano?" Sam asked Jake, as Dan and Sabrina disappeared inside.

"Looked like one to me. I guess that's another present that'll go over big. Walk to the truck with me," Jake commanded, and captured her hand before she could protest.

"Really, Jake, I have a million things to do." She trotted to keep pace with his loose, lanky stride.

"I know, you're indispensable." Stopping by his truck, he reached in the cab and produced a package. "But this seems to be the time for gift giving. I thought I'd let you have your present now."

"You didn't have to get me anything."

"Samantha." His drawl was lazy, but his eyes narrowed in annoyance. "I never do anything unless I want to." Taking her hand from behind her back, he placed the box in it. "Open it."

Lifting the statue from its tissue bedding, she examined it in silent amazement. The alabaster was smooth and cool in her hands, carved into the shape of a horse and rider in full gallop. The artist had captured the fluid grace, the freedom of motion. She ran a hesitant finger over the delicate features.

"It looks like me." She lifted her eyes to Jake's.

"And so it should," he answered easily. "It's supposed to be you."

"But how?" She shook her head, torn between pleasure and confusion.

"A man I know does this kind of thing. I described you to him."

For the second time that day, Samantha found herself at a loss for words.

"Why?" The question was out before she could swallow it.

Slowly, a smile drifted across his face. He pushed back his hat. "Because it suits you better than furs and diamonds."

She braced herself to meet his eyes again. "Thank you."

He nodded, his face solemn. He took the box from her hands and placed it on the hood of the truck. "I think a birthday kiss is traditional."

Swallowing, she took an instinctive step in retreat, but he gripped her arms and held her still. She offered her cheek, and his laughter broke out, full and rich on the summer air. "Sam," he turned her face to his, and his eyes sparkled with humor, "you're incredible."

His lips met hers. His hands moved from her arms to her hips, drawing her firmly against the hard lines of his body. She submitted to the embrace, as long as his arms held her, as long as they were mouth to mouth, as long as the heat from his body infused hers, he owned her, and she could not run.

Finally he drew her away, bringing his hands to her shoulders while hers rested on his chest for support.

"Happy birthday, Sam."

"Thank you," she managed, still breathless from the impact of his embrace.

He lifted the box from the hood of the truck and placed it in her hands before sliding into the cab. "See you tonight." With a salute, he started the engine. The truck moved down the road, leaving her staring after it.

CHAPTER 10

Party sounds filled the house. Laughter and voices and music mingled and drifted through open windows to float on the night air.

On this evening, the twins were dramatically different in their appearance. Sabrina's pale blue gown floated around her, cunningly disguising her pregnancy. Her hair was a glinting halo around rose-tinted cheeks. Samantha's black-striped satin clung to her body, her halter neckline plunging deep to a wide, gathered waist. Her hair was free and thick around her shoulders.

As she moved and mingled with the crowd, Samantha searched for a tall, lanky form, noting with increasing despair and a gnawing jealousy that a slim, dark woman had also as yet failed to put in an appearance.

Cornered by an enthusiastic young cowboy, Samantha was feeling her attention begin to wander from a detailed account of horse breeding when her eyes met dark jade across the room.

He was standing with two men she did not recognize, and Lesley Marshall stood beside him. She was elegant in an oyster-white gown. Her fine-boned ivory hand was placed from time to time on Jake's arm, as if, Samantha thought grimly, she were flaunting her possession.

Furious with the sudden feeling of inadequacy, Samantha turned to her companion with a dazzling smile. He stammered over his lecture, his words grinding to a halt. She tucked her arm in his and used her eyes without shame.

"Howdy, Tim." Jake appeared from nowhere and placed a hand on the young man's shoulder. "I'm going to steal this little lady for a moment." He paused and smiled easily into Samantha's mutinous face. "There's a couple of people she hasn't met yet."

Without waiting for an assent, he had her unwilling hand in his, propelling her through the crowd. "Tim won't be the same for weeks," he whispered close to her ear. "A woman could get run out of town for using her eyes that way on susceptible young boys," he warned, pulling her through the sea of people.

"You don't have to drag me."

"I know a stubborn mule when I see one," he countered, without bothering to lower his voice. Her furious retort was swallowed as Jake presented her to the two men who flanked Lesley.

"Sam, I'd like you to meet George Marshall, Lesley's father." Samantha's hand was enveloped in a hearty grip. "And Jim Bailey," he continued, nodding toward the second man.

"Jim only works with cattle on paper. He's a lawyer."

"My, this is a mighty pretty girl!" George Marshall boomed. Giving Jake a sly wink, he patted his daughter's shoulder.

"You always manage to rope in the pick of the herd, don't you, Jake?"

Jake slipped his hands easily into his pockets. "I do my best. But then, roping them's one thing, getting them's another."

"Well, now, little lady," George's genial voice continued, "Les tells me you're a gym teacher."

"That's right, Mr. Marshall."

"Now, you just call me George," he instructed, squeezing her shoulder with a genial affection. "Tell me, why isn't a pretty little thing like you married and settled down instead of running around some gymnasium?"

Jake was grinning with obvious enjoyment. Samantha tossed her hair behind her back, but before she could think of a suitable answer, George's laughter boomed through the room.

"I like this girl," George announced to the group. "Looks like she has spirit. You come over to our ranch any time, little lady, any time at all."

In spite of herself, Samantha found herself liking his expansive hospitality. "If you'll excuse me now, I've got . . . got to get a tray out of the kitchen." She gave the group an all-encompassing smile and melted into the crowd.

In the kitchen, she pulled a tray from the refrigerator to give her excuse credibility and was glad she had when Jake followed her in a moment later.

"George is a good man. He has the right ideas when it comes to women." Smiling knowingly at her, he leaned against the door watching her every move.

"That's your opinion," she returned tartly, bustling around the kitchen in an attempt to ignore him.

"Sit down a minute, Sam."

She glanced up, immediately wary, then lifted the tray as a defense. "No, I've got to get back."

"Please."

Despite herself, she lowered the tray to the table and herself into a chair.

"I ran into Jack Abbot, the school principal, the other day."

"Oh?"

"He told me the girls' phys ed instructor isn't coming back next term." Leaning back in his chair, Jake studied her. "He's going to offer you the job."

"Oh," she repeated before she could stop herself.

"He wants you pretty bad. He really needs someone this fall. I told him I'd be seeing you, and that I'd mention it. He's going to call you officially, of course."

How simple, Samantha thought.

How simple it would all be if I didn't love this man. I could stay where I want to stay, work where I want to work. But now, I've got to refuse, I've got to go away.

"I appreciate your telling me, and I appreciate Mr. Abbot wanting me, but . . ."

"Don't appreciate it, Samantha, think about it."

"You don't know what you're asking me to do."

He rose to pace the room, his hands seeking the depths of his pockets. "I'm just asking you to think about it. You like it here. You've made friends. You like being near your sister. You'd still have the satisfaction of doing what you feel you're suited for. Is it so much to ask that you consider it?"

"Yes, it's quite a lot. Jake, I don't want to argue with you. There are things I have to do, the same way there are things you have to do."

"All right." He nodded, then repeated slowly, as if coming to a decision. "All right, there *are* things I have to do." Moving over, he captured her chin between his thumb and fingers.

His arms slipped around her waist to bring her close, his mouth lowering to brush her cheeks and the corners of her lips. "Come home with me now, Samantha. We can be alone there." His voice had become low and seductive, as his fingers trailed over the bare skin of her back.

"No, please don't." She turned her face away.

"I want to make love to you. I want to feel your skin under my hands, all of you. I want to hear you sigh when I touch you."

"Jake, please." She dropped her head to his chest. "It's unfair, here, like this."

"Then come home with me."

"No, I can't." She shook her head without raising it. "I won't."

"All right, Samantha." He framed her face and brought it up to his. "I said I'd give you until the baby was born. We'll stick to that. We won't argue tonight. Let's call it a truce for your birthday. Agreed?"

He kissed her once, briefly, and turned to lift the tray. "Then we'll both do what we have to do when the time comes."

Leaving her confused, Jake moved through the doorway.

Rejoining the festivities, Samantha moved from group to group, but her thoughts were only about Jake. Why was he so interested in her career choices? Why did he want her to take the job in Wyoming? Maybe he cared for her. For a brief moment, she allowed hope to shimmer. Her eyes swept the room to find him. Finally she spotted him. He was dancing with Lesley. The shining cap of her raven hair brushing his cheek, the ivory of her hand entwined with the bronze of his. Samantha winced as he threw back his head and laughed at something Lesley had said for his ears alone.

Care for me? her mind repeated in a scathing whisper. Grow up, Samantha, *caring* and *wanting* don't always mean the same thing. In a few weeks, she comforted herself, she would no longer be subjected to this constant pain. When the ache had eased, she could visit Bree again. Jake would probably be too busy with his wife to spare time for visits to the Lazy L. Samantha felt her heart contract with pain.

She turned away and bumped solidly into Jim Bailey.

"Sorry." He took her shoulders to steady her. "I didn't see you."

"It's all right," she returned, offering a smile. "Besides, I think I ran into you."

"Well, no harm done either way." She watched his eyes slide past her and focus on Jake and Lesley. "They look nice together, don't they?"

Embarrassed that he must have seen her staring at them, Samantha nodded, and looked down at her empty glass. "Come on, we better get you a refill."

A few moments later, they joined the group around the piano as Sabrina played.

"So, you're a lawyer." She smiled at Jim. "I don't think I've ever met a lawyer before."

Jim returned her smile. "And you're a gymnast."

"No, actually, I'm a gym teacher now."

He lifted his glass in a toast and drank. "I remember you. I've always been an avid fan of the Olympics. I thought you were fabulous."

"Well, that's nice to hear after a decade."

He tapped his glass to hers. "Well, Olympic star, would you like to dance?"

"I'd love to."

Samantha enjoyed Jim Bailey's easy conversation. She learned during their two dances that he was interested in getting into politics. His dark good looks and ready wit would certainly be assets, she decided.

"Sam." Sabrina motioned to her as they moved back toward the piano. "It's your turn. Union rules."

"Okay," Samantha agreed, sliding onto the bench.

She played with practiced ease, moving from one song to the next. Time slipped through her fingers. As in a dream, she was aware of the voices behind her, the faint, drifting breeze of Wyoming through the open windows.

Someone sat beside her. Recognizing the lean fingers that lifted to turn the page of her sheet music, she faltered and missed a note.

"You and Jim seem to have hit it off." Samantha heard the *click* of his lighter over the sounds of the party.

"He's a very nice man. Have you known him long?"

"Oh, only since we were about eight and I gave him a black eye and he loosened a few of my teeth."

"Sounds like a loving friendship."

Jake again turned the page before she could do so herself. "Well, after that we sort of stuck together." He pushed the curtain of hair behind her shoulder, and Samantha struggled not to break the thread of the melody. "The two of you seemed to have a lot to talk about."

"He's very charming, and we have a few mutual interests."

"Hmm." Jake shifted slightly in his seat. His thigh brushed hers, and her fingers responded by hitting three wrong notes.

"You play very well."

Was he being ironic? She turned to look at him, but found no mockery in his jade eyes.

"Pleasantly," she corrected. "I get the general melody, but the details are a bit fuzzy."

"I've noticed that you have a tendency to shrug off your own capabilities. Are you aware of that?"

"That's not true. I just know what I do well and what I don't."

"You're a very tough critic, and you're inclined to underestimate."

"Honesty," she countered, finishing the song with a flourish. "I am a totally honest person."

"Are you, Samantha?" he said softly. "That's what I plan to find out."

CHAPTER 11

The days grew hot and sultry. The skies were improbably blue, rarely softened by clouds.

Long hours in the sun had deepened the honey of Samantha's skin, teasing out the gold in her hair. As long as she was occupied, she had no time for soul searching. She could enjoy the long summer days without thinking of the fall. As Sabrina wilted like a thirsty rose in the searing heat, Samantha confined her own activities to the early morning hours. In the long, hot haze of the afternoon, Sabrina moved slowly through the house, her body clumsy. Samantha did not dare leave her. The baby was due in two weeks, and Samantha wanted to remain within calling distance of her sister as much as possible.

One particularly humid afternoon, the two women were sitting idly in the living room. Sabrina got up heavily from her chair to look out the window. "Sam," she said, "before Dan left for town, he said a storm was brewing. From the looks of the sky, I'd say he was right."

Before Samantha could answer, there was a sudden

flash of lightning. A blast of thunder rolled in on the wind, and the rain began to fall in sheets.

"It's coming down fast," Samantha agreed. "It should cool us off a bit." She looked sympathetically at her sister's bulky form.

The storm built in power. Jagged flashes of lightning illuminated the room, and an angry wind hurled the rain against the windows. The two women watched in fascination as the storm exhausted itself. Soon rain dripped tentatively from the eaves and the thunder was a mere grumble in the distance.

The sun struggled to reappear, breaking through the gloom with a hazy promise of light.

"That," Sabrina commented with an enormous sigh, "was a mean one."

Samantha turned from her place by the window and again slumped into a chair. "Remember when you used to hide in the closet whenever we had a thunderstorm?"

"All too well." She gave her sister a pained smile. "And you used to stand on the porch, loving every minute of it, until Mom dragged you in, soaking wet. On that note from the past," Sabrina announced, "I'm going to take a nap, Sam." She turned at the doorway and studied the woman slouched in the chair, bare legs and feet stretched out in unconscious grace. "I love you."

With a rather puzzled smile, Samantha watched her walk away.

Wandering out to the porch, Samantha drank in the rain-fresh air. Everything sparkled. Raindrops clung like jewels to blossoms and leaves. Though the flowers had drooped with the weight of the storm, their colors had been washed into brilliant life. A bird, flying by on a shaft of light, trilled above her. She could hear the steady dripping of the rain off the eaves above the whisper of the dying wind. Satisfied, she curled up on a porch rocker and instantly fell asleep.

She had no idea how long she had drifted in the soft twilight world when, with reluctance, she woke at the touch of a hand on her shoulder. She looked up drowsily and yawned. "Oh, Bree, I must have fallen asleep. It's so wonderfully cool out here."

"Sam, I think the baby's decided to put in an unscheduled appearance."

"Huh? Oh!" Springing to her feet, she was instantly awake. "Right now? Dan's not here, and it's not time yet. Sit down, sit," she ordered, running agitated fingers through her hair.

"I think the first thing to do is to calm down," Sabrina suggested.

"You're right. I'm not going to fall apart, it was just a shock. I wasn't expecting this for another week or two."

"Neither was I." Sabrina's smile was half amused, half apologetic.

"All right, how long have you been having contractions, and how far apart are they?"

"Only for an hour or so."

"That should give us plenty of time." Samantha patted Sabrina's hand.

"But they've been getting awfully strong, and—" Breaking off, she closed her eyes and began to breathe in a deep, methodical rhythm. "And," she continued, after a final long breath, "awfully close together."

"How close?" Samantha asked, feeling new tension at the base of her neck.

"Ten minutes."

"Ten minutes," Samantha repeated. "I'd better get you to the hospital. I'll bring the car around. Stay put," she told her sister, and raced to the garage.

Upon reaching Sabrina's compact and sliding behind the wheel, Samantha was horrified to find the engine unresponsive to the turn of the key. The little car sputtered, emitted an apologetic groan, and died.

"You can't," she insisted, and smacked the steering wheel. "We just had you fixed."

There was no use wasting more time trying to figure out what was wrong with the car. It was clearly not going to start, and Samantha hadn't the first idea of where to look for the problem.

Rushing back to the house, she picked up the phone in the kitchen. At least she could call Dr. Gates. A groan of despair was wrenched from her when she heard the dead silence on the line. Oh, no, the storm must have knocked out the phones!

Forcing herself to appear calm, she returned to the living room where Sabrina was waiting for her.

Reaching her sister again, Samantha knelt down so their eyes were level. "Bree, the car won't start. All the trucks and jeeps are out with the men, and the storm must have knocked down the phone lines."

"Looks like we've got a few problems." Sabrina took a deep breath.

"It's going to be all right." Samantha took her hand in reassurance. "I'll help you get into bed, and then I'll take a horse and ride toward the Double T. If I don't see any of the men on the way, I'll get a truck there and bring it back. Most of them have radios, and I can call ahead to the doctor."

"Sam, it's going to take time for you to get there, and to get back. I don't think I'll make it in time to get to the hospital after that. You'll have to have the doctor come here."

"Here?" Samantha repeated. Her throat closed on the word. Sabrina nodded. "All right. Don't worry, I won't be long. I'll be back as soon as I can." Samantha raced off to the stables, and without wasting the time for a saddle, she leaped on her mare's back.

The familiar landscape was a blur, as she urged more speed out of the powerful horse. The sound of her own breath was masked by the sound of thudding hooves. Every minute she took was a minute longer that Sabrina was alone. She crouched lower on the horse and dug in bare heels.

When Samantha spotted the men on horseback, she spurred the Arabian over the fence in a fluid leap. As her hooves touched earth, she met the horse's sides again. They streaked across the field, scattering annoyed cattle.

When she reached the group, she reined in sharply. The mare reared, nearly unseating her. Her breath came in gasps as she struggled to keep her seat.

"What are you trying to do, break your neck?" Furiously Jake snatched the reins from her hands. "If you're stupid enough not to care about yourself, think of your horse. What do you mean riding like a fool and jumping fences? Where's your saddle? Have you lost your mind?"

"Bree," she managed at last between giant gulps of air. "The baby's coming, and the phone's out. The car wouldn't start, and there's nobody around. Dan's in town. Bree says there's no time to get her to the hospital now, and I have to call the doctor." She felt tears of fear burning at her eyes and bit her lip.

"All right, take it easy." Twisting in the saddle, Jake called out to one of his men. "Get back to the ranch and get hold of Dr. Gates on the CB radio. Tell him Sabrina Lomax is in labor and to get to the Lazy L in a hurry." Turning back, he handed the reins to Samantha. "Let's go."

"Are you coming back with me?" Flooded with relief, she gripped tight on the leather.

"What do you think?"

Together, they sprang forward in a gallop.

Speed and thundering hooves were all Samantha
ever remembered of the ride back. There was no time
for conversation, no time for thought. She was sliding
to the ground before she came to a full stop and Jake
once more secured her reins.

"Keep your head, Samantha," he ordered, watching her bound up the steps and through the front
door.

The house was silent. Her stomach tightened as she
rushed to the master bedroom. Sabrina sat up in bed,
propped by a mound of pillows and greeted her with a
cheerful smile.

"That was quick, did you fly?"

"Just about," Samantha returned, faint with relief.

"We've sent for the doctor. Everything's under control." She sat down on the bed, taking her sister's hand.
"How are you doing?"

"Not too bad." Her hand closed over Samantha's,
as much to reassure as seeking reassurance. "I'm glad
you're back. Here comes another one."

Samantha looked on with unfamiliar helplessness.
Her fingers grew tighter over her twin's, as if to steal
some of her pain.

"We can thank Mom for that book on natural childbirth." Sabrina gave a long, shaky sigh and relaxed
against the pillows.

"Don't look so worried, I'm doing fine. Oh, hello,
Jake." Glancing at the doorway, Sabrina greeted him
with friendly cheerfulness. "I didn't know you were
here. Come in. It's not contagious."

He advanced into the room, looking tall, male

and out of place. His hands retreated to his pockets.
"How're you doing?"

"Oh, well, you've seen a cow in labor before, I
don't imagine there's much difference." The small
hand tightened on Samantha's. "Here we go again."

Samantha lifted the hand to her cheek. *Where is the
doctor?* Sabrina should be in the hospital, surrounded
by experts.

"This baby's in a big hurry," Sabrina announced
with a small moan. "I'm sorry, Sam, it's not going to
wait much longer."

I don't know anything about childbirth, Samantha
thought in a moment of terror. *What am I going to do?
What do I do first?*

Standing, she turned to Jake. "Go sterilize some
towels, lots of them, and some string and scissors."

"All right." His hand rested on her shoulder a moment. "If you need me, give a call."

Nodding, she moved into the adjoining bath and
scrubbed her hands and arms until they hurt.

"You're going to be fine," she stated as she reen-
tered the bedroom.

"Yes, I am." Sabrina lay back on the pillows and
closed her eyes. "I'm going to have this baby, Sam,
and I'm going to do a good job of it. You can't do this
for me, I have to be strong."

"You are strong." Brushing away the hair from Sabrina's cheeks, she realized with a sudden jolt that it
was true. "You're stronger than I ever knew."

Her calm had returned, and she took over the duties of midwifery with an instinct as old as time. She
wiped moisture from her sister's face, working with
her, breathing with her, uttering soothing encourage-
ments. Sabrina had not gone through all she had to

lose now, and Samantha would not allow anything to go wrong.

"All right." Wiping beads of sweat from her own brow, Samantha straightened. "I think she's going to come this time, it's almost over. You have to help."

Sabrina nodded, her face pale and composed. Her hair had darkened with dampness. She shuddered and moaned with the final pang of childbirth. A thin, shrill cry pierced the stillness of the room. Samantha held new life in her hands.

"Oh, Bree." She stared down at the tiny, wriggling form.

Dan burst into the room two steps ahead of the doctor.

Suddenly, it was all so simple, Dan standing by Sabrina's side, his large hand clutching hers, the small, fresh form swaddled in the curve of her mother's arms.

"Only one." Sabrina sighed, her eyes luminous. "You'll have to handle the twins, Sam. One at a time is enough for me."

Sometime later, Samantha shut the door behind her and walked toward the kitchen. Jake looked up at her approach.

"A girl." She lowered herself into a chair. "The doctor says she's perfect, almost seven pounds. Bree's fine." She pushed at her tumbled hair and ran a hand across her brow. "I want to thank you."

"I didn't do anything."

"You were here." She lifted her eyes, and they were young and vulnerable. "I needed to know you were here."

"Samantha." He smiled and shook his head. "You sure find a man's weak points. I'll get you a drink."

He was back in a moment with a decanter of brandy and two snifters. Sitting across from her, he filled both generously. "It's not champagne, but it'll do." Lifting his glass, he touched it solemnly to hers. "To mother and child, and to Samantha Evans." He paused, his smile fading into seriousness. "She's one hell of a woman."

Samantha folded her arms on the table, laid her head on them, and burst into tears.

"I was so scared." She found her voice muffled against his shoulder as he brought her against him. "I've never been so scared. I thought I would lose them both."

He tilted her chin as one hand rubbed the small of her back. "You're a survivor, Sam, and too stubborn to let anything happen to Sabrina or the baby."

Her forehead dropped to his chest as she struggled to stem the flow of tears.

"I always seem to fall apart in front of you."

"Don't much care for that, do you?" She felt his lips descend to her hair and allowed herself the joy of being cradled in his arms. "Most people don't look for perfection, Sam, they find it boring. You," he said, framing her face with his hands, "are never boring."

She sniffed and smiled. "I guess that was a compliment." Giving in to impulse, she leaned over and rested her cheek against his. "I don't think you're boring, either."

"Well." He stroked her hair a moment, and his voice was curiously soft. "That's about the nicest thing you've ever said to me.

"Now drink some of that." He pushed her gently away and handed her the brandy.

Obeying, she allowed the warm strength to seep into her veins and relaxed with a sigh. "Bree certainly came through this better than I did." She drank again.

Jake straddled a chair, leaning his arms on the back. "When I left her, she was lying there with the baby, looking like she'd just finished having a picnic. Dan looked like he was about to keel over, I was ready for someone to cart me away. Yet Bree lies there, glowing like a rose."

"Your sister's quite a woman."

"I know." Her eyes dropped to the surface of the table. "She said she has someone to depend on her now. I guess the time's come to stop playing big sister. She doesn't need that anymore."

"So, what will you do now?" His voice was casual.

"I'll stay around a couple of weeks, then I'll go on." She struggled, seeing only a void.

"To what?"

Her fingers tightened on her glass. "To my work, to my life." She drank, and the brandy was bitter.

"Still set on leaving?" He lifted his own glass, swirling the liquid. Amber danced under the kitchen light. "You haven't seen Wyoming in the autumn."

"No, I haven't," she answered, evading his prior question. "Maybe I'll come back next year." She stared down at her hands, knowing she never would.

"She's hungry!" Dan charged into the kitchen, his grin threatening to split his face. "Just had a baby, and she says she's hungry. Sam, I love you." Plucking her from her chair, Dan tossed her into the air. Her laughter ended on a shriek as she clutched at him on her journey down. The shriek was strangled as she was smothered by a bear hug. "I swear, if bigamy wasn't against the law, I'd marry you."

"If I was still all in one piece," she managed, turning her face and gulping for air.

"I ask you, Jake." He consulted the other man as his arms threatened to destroy the alignment of

Samantha's rib cage. "Have you ever known another like this one?"

"Can't say that I have." She heard the smile in his voice, though it was impossible in her position to see his face. "I'd say Samantha is unique. One of a kind."

Rising, he lifted his brandy and toasted them both.

CHAPTER 12

S am, you're going to spoil her."
"Impossible." Sitting in the front porch rocker
with the week-old Jennifer, Samantha smiled at her
sister. "She's much too intelligent to be spoiled. Anyway, it's an aunt's privilege."

As she continued to rock, her lips strayed to Jennifer's soft tuft of dark hair. I won't be able to do this
much longer. She looked to the massive peaks gleaming silver-blue in the afternoon sun. A light breeze
stirred the air, bringing the sweet scent of freshly
mowed grass. She breathed it in, and the soft scent of
Jennifer's talc mingled with it. A sigh escaped.

She had not realized such a small creature could
wrap her way around the heart so completely. Another
love to leave behind. In just a week, I'll have to say
goodbye to all the things that matter: Bree, Dan, Wyoming, and now Jennifer.

Dents and bruises, she thought again, but not the
open wound that comes from leaving the man. Arrogant and gentle, demanding and kind, hot-tempered
and easy; the parts that made up Jake Tanner were

complicated and many, but to Samantha, it was a simple equation of love.

Blast you, Jake Tanner, if it weren't for you, I could stay. I belong here. I felt it from the first time I saw the mountains. There's nothing for me in Philadelphia. You've left me without anything to go back to.

"Looks like Lesley's coming to pay a visit," Sabrina observed. Samantha jerked back to the present with a snap.

She watched the late-model compact winding down the drive. Ignoring the flare of impossible jealousy, she set her features in casual lines.

"Sabrina, how well you look." Lesley's greeting was obviously tinged by surprise. "It's only been a week, and you look positively . . ." She hesitated, searching for a word.

"Radiant?" Sabrina suggested, and laughed. "I just had a baby, Lesley, not open-heart surgery."

"But to go through all that here, and without a doctor." She turned to Samantha. "I heard from Jake that you were marvelous and handled everything."

Samantha shrugged, uncomfortable at hearing Jake's praise from Lesley's lips. "It was nice of him to say so, but Sabrina did all the work."

"Well, having a baby is not a prospect I look forward to." Lesley shivered delicately. "I certainly intend to put it off as long as possible." Gliding over, she bent her head over the sleeping infant. "She is quite lovely, Sabrina. Very sweet."

"Would you like to hold her?" Samantha offered.

"Oh, no." Lesley stepped back. "I'm afraid I'm not very good with babies."

As she moved, Samantha caught the glint of the large square-cut diamond on her left hand. Lesley followed her gaze, and held out her hand. "You didn't know I was engaged, did you, Sabrina?"

"No." Sabrina cast a quick glance at her sister. "We hadn't heard."

"Well, you have been rather busy." She moved her fingers, enjoying the changing lights. "And we haven't made any formal announcement yet. We're planning a bit of a party for next week. As a matter of fact, I'm just on my way into town to begin shopping for my trousseau. Of course, I'll have to make a trip into New York for some proper clothes, but I'll just have to make do locally for the time being. We've set the wedding for the end of September." She smoothed her perfectly groomed hair with a well-manicured hand. "I could have done with a bit more time, but men have no idea how difficult things are to arrange properly." She smiled again. "Well, I must fly. I have so much to do. I do hope you'll be able to make it to the wedding, Samantha."

Sabrina glanced again at her sister. "Sam won't be here in September, Lesley."

"Oh, too bad." The regret in Lesley's voice was mild. Her mind had already run ahead to her wardrobe. She opened the door of the compact and slid behind the wheel. Lifting a slim arm in farewell, she drove away.

Rising, Sabrina took the sleeping Jennifer from her sister's arms and went into the house. When she returned, she sat on the arm of the rocker and laid her hand on Samantha's shoulder.

"I knew it was going to happen," Samantha murmured. "I just didn't want to be here when it did. I didn't think it would hurt this much. Oh, Bree." She looked up at her twin with helpless, swimming eyes. "What am I going to do?"

For the first time in their relationship, their situations

were reversed, and Samantha was vulnerable, seeking comfort and advice.

"Sam, you can't go on like this. Why don't you talk to him?" Sabrina stroked the thick fall of her sister's hair. "Something is wrong here, and the two of you have to talk things out."

"No. I won't give him the opportunity to feel sorry for me."

"Pride can be a very cold companion," Sabrina murmured.

Samantha stood up. "I'm going back early, Bree. I can have everything arranged by the day after tomorrow, maybe even by tomorrow night."

"Sam, you can't run away from this."

"Just watch me."

"Mom and Dad won't be here for a few more days. They'll be disappointed."

"I'm sorry, I hate to miss them, but I can't handle this." Pausing, she repeated, the admission surprising her, "I *really* can't handle this."

"But, Sam . . ." Sabrina joined her at the porch rail. "You should at least talk to Jake. Don't you want to know how he feels? You can't just go flying off without speaking to him, without saying goodbye. Something's not right about all this. I've thought about the two of you. I've seen the way he looks at you."

Shaking her head, Samantha moved toward the door. "No, he hasn't shown his face since the baby was born, and Lesley Marshall has his ring on her finger. A diamond. He has what he wants."

Samantha spent the evening packing, while Shylock watched her in silent accusation from his habitual place in the center of her bed.

Once in bed, she spent most of the night staring at a moon-washed ceiling. When the first pale light of dawn crept into the room, she rose. The mauve shadows under her eyes were a sad tribute to the restless hours.

The house slept on, and she deserted it, making her way to the stables. She saddled her mount with quick, deft movements, then galloped over the faint mist of morning.

As the sky lightened, the air came to life with the sweet song of birds. Sadly, she listened to the song of the west, for she knew that the melody would linger forever in her heart. She watched the mountains transformed by the dawn. Ribbons of rose and gold melted into blue until the peaks were no longer silhouettes, but stood proud in the full glory of the sun. She stayed for a last look at the white-faced Herefords grazing on the short, coarse grass. She knew now that her love for this wild, free country was forever bound up with her love for Jake. In saying goodbye to one, she was saying goodbye to the other. Straightening her shoulders, she turned the little mare back to the Lazy L.

When she returned to the house, she greeted her sister with bright chatter, the meaningless words no disguise for sleep-starved eyes. Sabrina made no comment and shortly disappeared into the bedroom to tend to the baby.

Alone, Samantha wandered aimlessly from window to window. Tonight, she thought, slipping her hands into the pockets of her jeans, I'll be on a plane. And tomorrow morning, all this will just be a dream.

"Morning, ma'am."

She whirled, nearly upsetting a vase of roses with the movement. Jake leaned against the door frame, legs crossed at the ankles, as if he had been watching for some time.

"What are you doing here?"

He took a few strides into the room. "Well, now, I came to fetch you." This information was imparted in an irritatingly slow drawl.

"Fetch me? What are you talking about? I'm not a dog or a maverick calf to be fetched."

"Maverick calf sounds pretty close. You're always running off in the wrong direction." Reaching out, he took her arm. "Come on, we're going for a ride." His voice was pleasant, but the steel was there. She jerked away, angry with his arrogance, wary of his tone.

"I have no intention of going anywhere with you. Why don't you just go away and leave me alone?"

"Now, I can't do that, Sam," he returned in a reasonable tone. "We have some unfinished business to attend to. Your time's up."

The fire in her eyes flickered and died. "You can't be serious."

"I'm dead serious."

"What . . . what about Lesley?"

"She's not invited," he returned simply.

"I'm not going with you," she said, somewhere between terror and fury. "You can't make me."

Stopping, he looked down at her from his overpowering height. "Sure I can," he corrected with easy confidence. With a swift movement, he swung her over his shoulder. "See?" He walked effortlessly down the hall. "Nothing to it."

"Let me down!" Furious fists beat against his back. "This is crazy, it's illegal. I'll have you thrown in jail!"

"No kidding? Sam, you're scaring me to death."

He continued easily down the hall, as if he carried an empty sack, rather than an irate woman who was thumping against his back. Pausing, he touched the brim of his hat as Sabrina appeared in the bedroom doorway, the baby in her arms.

"Morning, Sabrina." His greeting was genial, and he cocked his head to get a better view of Jennifer. "She's a real beauty."

"Thank you, Jake. We certainly think so." She shifted the baby and smiled. "Are you two going out?"

"Thought we'd go for a little ride," Jake informed her. "We may be gone some time."

"It's a fine day for it, hardly a cloud in the sky."

"Bree." Samantha's voice was desperate. "Don't just stand there, *do* something." She pushed at the hair that hung over her face. "Don't you see what he's doing? He's kidnapping me. Call the police, call Dan." She continued to plead as Jake touched the brim of his hat once more and moved down the hall. "Bree, say something."

"Have a good time" was her sister's surprising response.

Samantha's mouth fell open in dumb astonishment. A stream of imaginative curses was hurled on Jake's unperturbed head as he took the reins of his mount from a grinning cowboy.

"Looks like you got yourself a real handful there, Jake."

"No more than I can handle," he countered, swinging into the saddle with Samantha still held over his shoulder. With a speed that defied his easygoing manner, he had her in front of him in the saddle, spurring the horse into a gallop, before she could think of escape.

"You're going to pay for this," Samantha promised, clutching the saddle horn to keep her balance. "You can't just run off with me this way!"

"I didn't see anybody try to stop me," Jake pointed out.

He followed the road for some time without decreasing his pace, then cut across an open field. At a small grove of trees, he reined in, gripping Samantha around the waist when she attempted to wiggle down.

"Now, don't do that, Sam," he warned in a friendly voice. "I'd just have to catch you, and I throw a mean lasso."

He slid from the chestnut, and before her feet could touch the ground, she was back over his shoulder. Without ceremony, she was dumped under the fragile, bending leaves of a willow while he towered over her, grinning with obvious enjoyment.

"You're going to be sorry," she predicted, smoldering with fury. "I'm going to . . ." The rest of her words slipped back down her throat as he dropped down next to her. "You—you can't do this, Jake. You're not the kind of man who forces himself on a woman."

"Who says?" Pushing her back on the soft grass, he covered her body with his.

Her body betrayed her with instant response. Her skin tingled as his mouth brushed over it. "You're not really going to do this."

"I told you once"—his mouth moved to her ear, and his words were warm and soft against it—"not to forget your own words. There are some things you just have to do."

His kiss was long and lingering.

When her mouth was free, she drew in a deep breath and spit out with all her strength, "What kind of man are you, to make love to one woman and plan to marry another?"

His eyes lazily narrowed. He propped himself on one elbow, his other arm pinning her down. Lifting his head from his elbow, he undid the top button of her blouse. "Suppose," he continued, moving down to the next button, "you tell me whom I'm supposed to marry."

His fingers trailed a slow line from her throat, down the smooth skin her open blouse revealed, and rested on the next button. The blood began to pound in her ears. His eyes alone held her still as he spread her blouse apart. Slowly, his fingers roamed up the warmth of her skin, moving with casual possession over her. Her eyes clouded with growing need as he explored.

"Tell me who I'm going to marry, Samantha." His body shifted again, molding to hers. His shirt was warm against her naked flesh.

"L-Lesley," she stammered.

"No." His mouth lowered to the curve of her throat, his tongue teasing the vulnerable skin.

She felt the waist of her jeans loosen under his hand. His finger pushed away the material and moved along her hip. With her last claim to lucidity, she pushed against his chest.

"Please stop."

"Now I just can't do that, Sam." His hands teased the curve of her hip, trailing back up to the side of her breast. "I've waited a good long time to get you where I want you."

"I'm not staying . . . Did you say you weren't marrying Lesley?"

He frowned down in consideration, winding her hair around his finger. "Seems to me I did mention that. I don't know why you're always piling your hair on top of your head when it looks so good spread all over."

"But she was wearing your ring."

"Not mine," Jake corrected, still concentrating on the hair around his finger. "Your hair's gotten lighter these past few weeks, you haven't been wearing a hat. Les has a diamond, doesn't she? I told you once diamonds don't suit you. They're cold, and they don't have much imagination. But that's Les." He shrugged and began to move his mouth over her face again. "It doesn't seem to matter to Jim."

Valiantly, Samantha attempted to follow his words. Her head shook with the effort.

"Les is engaged to Jim Bailey. I'm sure you remember Jim Bailey, you spent enough time with him at the party."

"Yes, but . . ."

"No buts," he interrupted. "Les likes to have a couple of fish on the line, and when she got it through her head I wasn't in season, she netted Jim without a struggle."

"But I thought . . ."

"I know what you thought." He cut her off again and smiled. "Running away a few days early, weren't you?"

"I wasn't running. How did you know I was leaving?"

"Sabrina told me."

"Bree?" Samantha whispered. Bree did that?

"Yeah, yesterday. She came to see me while you were packing. I like this spot right here," he stated, planting his lips against the hollow of her throat. "I've had a devil of a time putting things in order since then, so I could take time for a honeymoon. Busy time of year for a cattleman."

"Honeymoon?" Her skin was trembling where his lips continued to taste.

"I've got a good foreman," he continued, as if thinking aloud. "I reckon he can manage things for a while. I could use another day or two. I had a nice long honeymoon in mind, someplace quiet." He brought his attention back to her stunned face. "You've never been to Bora Bora, have you?"

"Are you talking about getting your ranch in order so you can take time off to marry me?" She attempted to speak slowly and clearly while her emotions whirled like a summer tornado.

"Just being practical," he explained with a bland smile.

"Why you conceited, overbearing . . . Just what makes you think I'll marry you? You sit back and make all these plans and expect me to run off to Bora Bora with you like a passive little puppy. Of all the chauvinist—"

"How about Antarctica?" he suggested, willing to be reasonable. "Not too many people there, either."

"You're crazy. I never said I'd marry you. What makes you think . . ." Her tirade was cut off effectively as his mouth coaxed her silence. When he let her breathe, her voice had lost its strength. "That's not going to help you. I'm not in love with you."

"Seems to me I recall someone telling me she was a totally honest person." His gaze was disconcertingly direct. He held her chin, preventing her face from turning away. "You want to look at me and tell me that again? You've been fighting me all along, and I think I've just about used up my patience." His lips were teasing hers again, and his hands moved over her with more urgency. "Mmm, but you have a nice body. I can't take much more of this waiting around. Six months is a long time, Sam. I've wanted you from the minute you stood there ordering Dan to have his man tend to the horses."

"Yes, you let me know very early what you wanted." She no longer struggled, but lay passive in his arms.

"Gave you something to think about. Of course,

you didn't know I wanted you to be my wife, too. It was easy to tell you I wanted you, but a bit difficult to tell you I loved you. Sam, look at me." She shook her head, but the fingers on her chin tightened in authority. "Look at me." She obeyed, her lids opening to reveal eyes veiled with tears. "You stubborn little idiot. Listen carefully, I've never said this to another woman, and I've had to wait too long to say it to you. If you don't marry me soon, I'm going to lose my mind." His mouth took hers, spinning the world into nothing. Her arms flew around him as pain evaporated into unspeakable joy. "Samantha." He buried his face in the lushness of her hair. "It's been quite a race."

"I don't understand." She brought his face back to hers, needing to see the truth in his eyes. "Why didn't you tell me before?"

"I didn't think you'd believe that a man had nearly been knocked off his feet by a picture of a girl less than half his age, then had completely lost his balance when he saw the woman she'd become. If you hadn't been so wrapped up in Sabrina those first few minutes, you'd have seen how a man looks when he gets hit by lightning."

"Just like that?" Stunned, she traced the angles of his face to assure herself she was not dreaming.

"Just like that," he agreed, bringing her palm to his lips. "Then, after I'd recovered a bit, I knew I had to work around your dedication to Sabrina until you'd figured out there was room in your life for someone else. Then you stood there telling me you were going back home as soon as the baby was born. I nearly strangled you." His fingers tightened on her hand as he brought his eyes back to hers. "How was I supposed to tell you that I loved you, that I wanted to marry you, wanted you to stay in Wyoming? The night of the party, in the kitchen, I made up my mind I wasn't letting you go, no matter what I had to do to keep you."

"But I never wanted to leave." She shook her head in brisk denial, as if he should have realized it all along. "It was just that I couldn't bear to see you married to Lesley."

"You know, things might have gotten even more complicated if Sabrina hadn't come by and laid things out for me. She's got a bit more of you in her than I had thought." Laughing, he lifted his face from hers. "She told me to sit down and listen. She'd never seen two people run around in circles so long and get nowhere."

"It's not like Bree to interfere."

"She interfered beautifully. First thing she did was ask me what business I had getting engaged to Lesley. I must have stared at her like she'd lost her mind. After I managed to tell her I was definitely not engaged to Lesley, she let me have it with both barrels. Mixed with the buckshot was the information that you were miserable about going home, and that I was a fool for not seeing it myself. Then she folded her arms, stuck out her chin exactly like someone else has a habit of doing and asked me what the devil I intended to do about it."

Samantha stared up at him and shook her head in astonishment. "I wish I could have seen that."

He smiled and lowered his mouth. "Just look in the mirror sometime." Flesh met flesh with no barriers, and with a small sound of desperation he savaged her mouth. The hard lines of his chest pressed into her breasts. "Let me hear you say it, Samantha," he murmured, unable to resist the curve of her neck. "I need to hear you say it."

"I love you." Her mouth searched for his, her arms urging him closer. "I love you. I love you." Her lips found their objective, and her silence told him again.

"I need you, Samantha." His mouth and hands continued to seek, growing wilder, possessive, demanding. "I never knew I could need anyone the way I need you. I want you for myself for a while, no distractions, no complications, just you. We've got six months of loving to make up for. I'm going to keep you fully occupied for a very long time." Lifting his face, he smiled down at her, running his hand through the hair spread over the grass. "A very long time."

She smiled back, running her hands up his chest to circle his neck. "I intend to keep you occupied, as well. Your cows are going to get very lonely." Removing his hat, she tossed it carelessly aside, then turned back to him with raised brows. "Okay, cowboy." Her arms lifted to lock around his neck, fingers tangling possessively in his hair. "Start occupying."

"Yes, ma'am." With a polite nod, he lowered his mouth and followed orders.

The Law is a Lady

To all the experts at R&R Lighting Company

CHAPTER 1

Merle T. Johnson sat on the ripped vinyl seat of a stool in Annie's Cafe, five miles north of Friendly. He lingered over a lukewarm root beer, half listening to the scratchy country number piping out from Annie's portable radio. *"A woman was born to be hurt"* was the lament of Nashville's latest hopeful. Merle didn't know enough about women to disagree.

He was on his way back to Friendly after checking out a complaint on one of the neighboring ranches. Sheep-stealing, he thought as he chugged down more root beer. Might've been exciting if there'd been anything to it. Potts was getting too old to know how many sheep he had in the first place. Sheriff knew there was nothing to it, Merle thought glumly. Sitting in the dingy little cafe with the smell of fried hamburgers and onions clinging to the air, Merle bemoaned the injustice of it.

There was nothing more exciting in Friendly, New Mexico, than hauling in old Silas when he got drunk and disorderly on Saturday nights. Merle T. Johnson had been born too late. If it had been the 1880s instead of the 1980s, he'd have had a chance to face desperados, ride in a posse, face off a gunslinger—the things deputies were supposed to do. And here he was, he told himself fatalistically, nearly twenty-four years old, and the biggest arrest he had made was pulling in the Kramer twins for busting up the local pool hall.

Merle scratched his upper lip where he was trying, without much success, to grow a respectable mustache. The best part of his life was behind him, he decided, and he'd never be more than a deputy in a forgotten little town, chasing imaginary sheep thieves.

If just *once* somebody'd rob the bank. He dreamed over this a minute, picturing himself in a high-speed chase and shoot-out. That would be something, yessiree. He'd have his picture in the paper, maybe a flesh wound in the shoulder. The idea became more appealing. He could wear a sling for a few days. Now, if the sheriff would only let him carry a gun . . .

"Merle T., you gonna pay for that drink or sit there dreaming all day?"

Merle snapped back to reality and got hastily to his feet. Annie stood watching him with her hands on her ample hips. She had small, dark eyes, florid skin and an amazing thatch of strawberry-colored hair. Merle was never at his best with women.

"Gotta get back," he muttered, fumbling for his wallet. "Sheriff needs my report."

Annie gave a quick snort and held out her hand, damp palm up. After she snatched the crumpled bill, Merle headed out without asking for his change.

The sun was blinding and brilliant. Merle automatically narrowed his eyes against it. It bounced off the road surface in waves that shimmered almost like liquid. But the day was hot and dusty. On both sides of the ribbon of road stretched nothing but rock and sand and a few tough patches of grass. There was no cloud to break the strong, hard blue of the sky or filter the streaming white light of the sun. He pulled the rim of his hat down over his brow as he headed for his car, wishing he'd had the nerve to ask Annie for his change. His shirt was damp and sticky before he reached for the door handle.

Merle saw the sun radiate off the windshield and chrome of an oncoming car. It was still a mile away, he judged idly as he watched it tool up the long, straight road. He continued to watch its progress with absent-minded interest, digging in his pocket for his keys. As it drew closer his hand remained in his pocket. His eyes grew wide.

That's some car, he thought in stunned admiration.

One of the fancy foreign jobs, all red and flashy. It whizzed by without pausing, and Merle's head whipped around to stare after it. *Oo-wee,* he thought with a grin. *Some* car. Must have been doing seventy easy. Probably has one of those fancy dashboards with—Seventy!

Springing into his car, Merle managed to get the keys out of his pocket and into the ignition. He flipped on his siren and peeled out, spitting gravel and smoking rubber. He was in heaven.

Phil had been driving more than eighty miles non-stop. During the early part of the journey, he'd held an involved conversation on the car phone with his producer in L.A. He was annoyed and tired. The dust-colored scenery and endless flat road only annoyed him further. Thus far, the trip had been a total waste. He'd checked out five different towns in southwest New Mexico, and none of them had suited his needs. If his luck didn't change, they were going to have to use a set after all. It wasn't his style. When Phillip Kincaid directed a film, he was a stickler for authenticity. Now he was looking for a tough, dusty little town that showed wear around the edges. He wanted peeling paint and some grime. He was looking for the kind of place everyone planned to leave and no one much wanted to come back to.

Phil had spent three long hot days looking, and nothing had satisfied him. True, he'd found a couple of sand-colored towns, a little faded, a little worse for wear, but they hadn't had the right feel. As a director—a highly successful director of American films— Phillip Kincaid relied on gut reaction before he settled down to refining angles. He needed a town that gave him a kick in the stomach. And he was running short on time.

Already Huffman, the producer, was getting antsy, pushing to start the studio scenes. Phil was cursing himself again for not producing the film himself when he cruised by Annie's Cafe. He had stalled Huffman for another week, but if he didn't find the right town to represent New Chance, he would have to trust his location manager to find it. Phil scowled down the endless stretch of road. He didn't trust details to anyone but himself. That, and his undeniable talent, were the reasons for his success at the age of thirty-four. He was tough, critical, and volatile, but he treated each of his films as though it were a child requiring endless care and patience. He wasn't always so understanding with his actors.

He heard the wail of the siren with mild curiosity. Glancing in the mirror, Phil saw a dirty, dented police car that might have been white at one time. It was bearing down on him enthusiastically. Phil swore, gave momentary consideration to hitting the gas and leaving the annoyance with his dust, then resignedly pulled over. The blast of heat that greeted him when he let down the window did nothing to improve his mood. Filthy place, he thought, cutting the engine. Grimy dust hole. He wished for his own lagoonlike pool and a long, cold drink.

Elated, Merle climbed out of his car, ticket book in hand. Yessiree, he thought again, this was some machine. About the fanciest piece he'd seen outside the TV. Mercedes, he noted, turning the sound of it over in his mind. French, he decided with admiration. Holy cow, he'd stopped himself a French car not two miles out of town. He'd have a story to tell over a beer that night.

The driver disappointed him a bit at first. He didn't look foreign or even rich. Merle's glance passed ignorantly over the gold Swiss watch to take in the T-shirt and jeans. Must be one of those eccentrics, he concluded. Or maybe the car was stolen. Merle's blood began to pound excitedly. He looked at the man's face.

It was lean and faintly aristocratic, with well-defined bones and a long, straight nose. The mouth was unsmiling, even bored. He was clean-shaven with the suggestion of creases in his cheeks. His hair seemed a modest brown; it was a bit long and curled over his ears. In the tanned face the eyes were an arresting clear water-blue. They were both bored and annoyed and, if Merle had been able to latch on the word, aloof. He wasn't Merle's image of a desperate foreign-car thief.

"Yes?"

The single frosty syllable brought Merle back to business. "In a hurry?" he asked, adopting what the sheriff would have called his tough-cop stance.

"Yes."

The answer made Merle shift his feet. "License

and registration," he said briskly, then leaned closer to the window as Phil reached in the glove compartment. "Glory be, look at the dash! It's got everything and then some. A phone, a phone right there in the car. Those French guys are something."

Phil sent him a mild glance. "German," he corrected, handing Merle the registration.

"German?" Merle frowned doubtfully. "You sure?"

"Yes." Slipping his license out of his wallet, Phil passed it through the open window. The heat was pouring in.

Merle accepted the registration. He was downright sure Mercedes was a French name. "This your car?" he asked suspiciously.

"As you can see by the name on the registration," Phil returned coolly, a sure sign that his temper was frayed around the edges.

Merle was reading the registration at his usual plodding speed. "You streaked by Annie's like a bat out of—" He broke off, remembering that the sheriff didn't hold with swearing on the job. "I stopped you for excessive speed. Clocked you at seventy-two. I bet this baby rides so smooth you never noticed."

"As a matter of fact, I didn't." Perhaps if he hadn't been angry to begin with, perhaps if the heat hadn't been rolling unmercifully into the car, Phil might have played his hand differently. As Merle began to write up the ticket, Phil narrowed his eyes. "Just how do I know you clocked me at all?"

"I was just coming out of Annie's when you breezed by," Merle said genially. His forehead creased as he formed the letters. "If I'd waited for my change, I wouldn't have seen you." He grinned, pleased with the hand of fate. "You just sign this," he said as he ripped the ticket from the pad. "You can stop off in town and pay the fine."

Slowly, Phil climbed out of the car. When the sun hit his hair, deep streaks of red shot through it. Merle was reminded of his mother's mahogany server. For a moment they stood eye to eye, both tall men. But one was lanky and tended to slouch, the other lean, muscular, and erect.

"No," Phil said flatly.

"No?" Merle blinked against the direct blue gaze. "No what?"

"No, I'm not signing it."

"Not signing?" Merle looked down at the ticket still in his hand. "But you have to."

"No, I don't." Phil felt a trickle of sweat roll down his back. Inexplicably it infuriated him. "I'm not signing, and I'm not paying a penny to some two-bit judge who's feeding his bank account from this speed trap."

"Speed trap!" Merle was more astonished than insulted. "Mister, you were doing better'n seventy, and the road's marked clear—fifty-five. Everybody knows you can't do more than fifty-five."

"Who says I was?"

"I clocked you."

"Your word against mine," Phil returned coolly. "Got a witness?"

Merle's mouth fell open. "Well, no, but . . ." He pushed back his hat. "Look, I don't need no witness, I'm the deputy. Just sign the ticket."

It was pure perversity. Phil hadn't the least idea how fast he'd been going and didn't particularly care. The road had been long and deserted; his mind had been in L.A. But knowing this wasn't going to make him take the cracked ballpoint the deputy offered him.

"No."

"Look, mister, I already wrote up the ticket." Merle read refusal in Phil's face and set his chin. After all, he was the law. "Then I'm going to have to take you in," he said dangerously. "The sheriff's not going to like it."

Phil gave him a quick smirk and held out his hands, wrists close. Merle stared at them a moment, then looked helplessly from car to car. Beneath the anger, Phil felt a stir of sympathy.

"You'll have to follow me in," Merle told him as he pocketed Phil's license.

"And if I refuse?"

Merle wasn't a complete fool. "Well, then," he said amiably, "I'll have to take you in and leave this fancy car sitting here. It might be all in one piece when the tow truck gets here. Then again . . ."

Phil acknowledged the point with a slight nod, then climbed back into his car. Merle sauntered to his, thinking how fine he was going to look bringing in that fancy red machine.

They drove into Friendly at a sedate pace. Merle nodded occasionally to people who stopped their business to eye the small procession. He stuck his hand out the window to signal a halt, then braked in front of the sheriff's office.

"Okay, inside." Abruptly official, Merle stood straight. "The sheriff'll want to talk to you." But the icy gleam in the man's eye kept Merle from taking his arm. Instead he opened the door and waited for his prisoner to walk through.

Phil glimpsed a small room with two cells, a bulletin board, a couple of spindly chairs, and a battered desk. An overhead fan churned the steamy air and whined. On the floor lay a large mound of mud-colored fur that turned out to be a dog. The desk was covered with books and papers and two half-filled cups of coffee. A dark-haired woman bent over all this, scratching industriously on a yellow legal pad. She glanced up as they entered.

Phil forgot his annoyance long enough to cast her in three different films. Her face was classically oval, with a hint of cheekbone under honey-toned skin. Her nose was small and delicate, her mouth just short of wide, with a fullness that was instantly sensual. Her hair was black, left to fall loosely past her shoulders in carelessly sweeping waves. Her brows arched in question. Beneath them her eyes were thickly lashed, darkly green, and faintly amused.

"Merle?"

The single syllable was full-throated, as lazy and sexy as black silk. Phil knew actresses who would kill for a voice like that one. If she didn't stiffen up in front of a camera, he thought, and if the rest of her went with the face . . . He let his eyes sweep down. Pinned to her left breast was a small tin badge. Fascinated, Phil stared at it.

"Excess of speed on Seventeen, Sheriff."

"Oh?" With a slight smile on her face, she waited for Phil's eyes to come back to hers. She had recognized the appraisal when he had first walked in, just as she recognized the suspicion now. "Didn't you have a pen, Merle?"

"A pen?" Baffled, he checked his pockets.

"I wouldn't sign the ticket." Phil walked to the desk to get a closer look at her face. "Sheriff," he added. She could be shot from any imaginable angle, he concluded, and still look wonderful. He wanted to hear her speak again.

She met his assessing stare straight on. "I see. What was his speed, Merle?"

"Seventy-two. Tory, you should see his car!" Merle exclaimed, forgetting himself.

"I imagine I will," she murmured. She held out her hand, her eyes still on Phil's. Quickly, Merle gave her the paperwork.

Phil noted that her hands were long, narrow, and elegant. The tips were painted in shell-pink. What the hell is she doing here? he wondered, more easily visualizing her in Beverly Hills.

"Well, everything seems to be in order, Mr. . . . Kincaid." Her eyes came back to his. A little mascara, he noticed, a touch of eyeliner. The color's hers. No powder, no lipstick. He wished fleetingly for a camera and a couple of hand-held lights. "The fine's forty dollars," she said lazily. "Cash."

"I'm not paying it."

Her lips pursed briefly, causing him to speculate on their taste. "Or forty days," she said without batting an eye. "I think you'd find it less . . . inconvenient to pay the fine. Our accommodations won't suit you."

The cool amusement in her tone irritated him. "I'm not paying any fine." Placing his palms on the desk, he leaned toward her, catching the faint drift of a subtle, sophisticated scent. "Do you really expect me to believe you're the sheriff? What kind of scam are you and this character running?"

Merle opened his mouth to speak, glanced at Tory, then shut it again. She rose slowly. Phil found himself surprised that she was tall and as lean as a whippet. A model's body, he thought, long and willowy—the kind that made you wonder what was underneath those clothes. This one made jeans and a plaid shirt look like a million dollars.

"I never argue with beliefs, Mr. Kincaid. You'll have to empty your pockets."

"I will not," he began furiously.

"Resisting arrest." Tory lifted a brow. "We'll have to make it sixty days." Phil said something quick and rude. Instead of being offended, Tory smiled. "Lock him up, Merle."

"Now, just a damn minute—"

"You don't want to make her mad," Merle whispered, urging Phil back toward the cells. "She can be mean as a cat."

"Unless you want us to tow your car . . . and charge you for that as well," she added, "you'll give Merle your keys." She flicked her eyes over his furious face. "Read him his rights, Merle."

"I know my rights, damn it." Contemptuously he shrugged off Merle's hand. "I want to make a phone call."

"Of course." Tory sent him another charming smile. "As soon as you give Merle your keys."

"Now, look"—Phil glanced down at her badge again—"Sheriff," he added curtly. "You don't expect me to fall for an old game. This one"—he jerked a thumb at Merle—"waits for an out-of-towner to come by, then tries to hustle him out of a quick forty bucks. There's a law against speed traps."

Tory listened with apparent interest. "Are you going to sign the ticket, Mr. Kincaid?"

Phil narrowed his eyes. "No."

"Then you'll be our guest for a while."

"You can't sentence me," Phil began heatedly. "A judge—"

"Justice of the peace," Tory interrupted, then tapped a tinted nail against a small framed certificate. Phil saw the name Victoria L. Ashton.

He gave her a long, dry look. "You?"

"Yes, handy, isn't it?" She cocked her head to the

side. "Sixty days, Mr. Kincaid, or two hundred and fifty dollars."

"Two-fifty!"

"Bail's set at five hundred. Would you care to post it?"

"The phone call," he said through clenched teeth.

"The keys," she countered affably.

Swearing under his breath, Phil pulled the keys from his pocket and tossed them to her. Tory caught them neatly. "You're entitled to one local call, Mr. Kincaid."

"It's long distance," he muttered. "I'll use my credit card."

After indicating the phone on her desk, Tory took the keys to Merle. "Two-fifty!" he said in an avid whisper. "Aren't you being a little rough on him?"

Tory gave a quick, unladylike snort. "Mr. Hollywood Kincaid needs a good kick in the ego," she mumbled. "It'll do him a world of good to stew in a cell for a while. Take the car to Bestler's Garage, Merle."

"Me? *Drive* it?" He looked down at the keys in his hand.

"Lock it up and bring back the keys," Tory added. "And don't play with any of the buttons."

"Aw, Tory."

"Aw, Merle," she responded, then sent him on his way with an affectionate look.

Phil waited impatiently as the phone rang. Someone picked up. "Answering for Sherman, Miller and Stein." He swore.

"Where the hell's Lou?" he demanded.

"Mr. Sherman is out of the office until Monday," the operator told him primly. "Would you care to leave your name?"

"This is Phillip Kincaid. You get Lou now, tell him I'm in—" He turned to cast a dark look at Tory.

"Welcome to Friendly, New Mexico," she said obligingly.

Phil's opinion was a concise four-letter word. "Friendly, New Mexico. In jail, damn it, on some trumped-up charge. Tell him to get his briefcase on a plane, pronto."

"Yes, Mr. Kincaid, I'll try to reach him."

"You reach him," he said tightly and hung up. When he started to dial again, Tory walked over and calmly disconnected him.

"One call," she reminded him.

"I got a damn answering service."

"Tough break." She gave him the dashing smile that both attracted and infuriated him. "Your room's ready, Mr. Kincaid."

Phil hung up the phone to face her squarely. "You're not putting me in that cell."

She looked up with a guileless flutter of lashes. "No?"

"No."

Tory looked confused for a moment. Her sigh was an appealingly feminine sound as she wandered around the desk. "You're making this difficult for me, Mr. Kincaid. You must know I can't manhandle you into a cell. You're bigger than I am."

Her abrupt change of tone caused him to feel more reasonable. "Ms. Ashton . . ." he began.

"Sheriff Ashton," Tory corrected and drew a .45 out of the desk drawer. Her smile never wavered as Phil gaped at the large gun in her elegant hand. "Now, un- less you want another count of resisting arrest on your record, you'll go quietly into that first cell over there. The linen's just been changed."

Phil wavered between astonishment and amusement. "You don't expect me to believe you'd use that thing."

"I told you I don't argue with beliefs." Though she kept the barrel lowered, Tory quite deliberately cocked the gun.

He studied her for one full minute. Her eyes were too direct and entirely too calm. Phil had no doubt she'd put a hole in him—in some part of his anatomy that she considered unimportant. He had a healthy respect for his body.

"I'll get you for this," he muttered as he headed for the cell.

Her laugh was rich and attractive enough to make him turn in front of the bars. Good God, he thought, he'd like to tangle with her when she didn't have a pistol in her hand. Furious with himself, Phil stalked into the cell.

"Doesn't that line go something like, 'When I break outta this joint, you're gonna get yours'?" Tory pulled the keys from a peg, then locked the cell door with a jingle and snap. Struggling not to smile, Phil paced the cell.

"Would you like a harmonica and a tin cup?"

He grinned, but luckily his back was to her. Dropping onto the bunk, he sent her a fulminating glance. "I'll take the tin cup if it has coffee in it."

"Comes with the service, Kincaid. You've got free room and board in Friendly." He watched her walk back to the desk to replace the pistol. Something in the lazy, leggy gait affected his blood pressure pleasantly. "Cream and sugar?" she asked politely.

"Black."

Tory poured the coffee, aware that his eyes were on her. She was partly amused by him, partly intrigued. She knew exactly who he was. Over her basic disdain for what she considered a spoiled, Tinseltown playboy was a trace of respect. He hadn't attempted to influence her with his name or his reputation. He'd relied on his temper. And it was his temper, she knew, that had landed him in the cell in the first place.

Too rich, she decided, too successful, too attractive. And perhaps, she mused as she poured herself a cup, too talented. His movies were undeniably brilliant. She wondered what made him tick. His movies seemed to state one image, the glossies another. With a quiet laugh she thought she might find out for herself while he was her "guest."

"Black," she stated, carrying both cups across the room. "Made to order."

He was watching the way she moved—fluidly, with just a hint of hip. It was those long legs, he decided, and some innate confidence. Under different circumstances he would have considered her quite a woman. At the moment he considered her an outrageous annoyance. Silently he unfolded himself from the bunk and went to accept the coffee she held between the bars. Their fingers brushed briefly.

"You're a beautiful woman, Victoria L. Ashton," he muttered. "And a pain in the neck."

She smiled. "Yes."

That drew a laugh from him. "What the hell are you doing here, playing sheriff?"

"What the hell are you doing here, playing criminal?"

Merle burst in the door, grinning from ear to ear. "Holy cow, Mr. Kincaid, that's *some* car!" He dropped the keys in Tory's hand, then leaned against the bars. "I swear, I could've just sat in it all day. Bestler's eyes just about popped out when I drove it in."

Making a low sound in his throat, Phil turned away

to stare through the small barred window at the rear of the cell. He scowled at his view of the town. Look at this place, he thought in frustration. Dusty little nowhere. Looks like all the color was washed away twenty years ago. Baked away, he corrected himself as sweat ran uncomfortably down his back. There seemed to be nothing but brown—dry, sparse mesa in the distance and parched sand. All the buildings, such as they were, were different dull shades of brown, all stripped bare by the unrelenting sun. Damn place still had wooden sidewalks, he mused, sipping at the strong coffee. There wasn't a coat of paint on a storefront that wasn't cracked and peeling. The whole town looked as though it had drawn one long, tired communal breath and settled down to wait until it was all over.

It was a gritty, hopeless-looking place with a sad sort of character under a film of dust and lethargy. People stayed in a town like this when they had no place else to go or nothing to do. Came back when they'd lost hope for anything better. And here he was, stuck in some steamy little cell. . . .

His mind sharpened.

Staring at the tired storefronts and sagging wood, Phil saw it all through the lens of a camera. His fingers wrapped around a window bar as he began to plot out scene after scene. If he hadn't been furious, he'd have seen it from the first moment.

This was Next Chance.

CHAPTER 2

For the next twenty minutes Tory paid little attention to her prisoner. He seemed content to stare out of the window with the coffee growing cold in his hand. After dispatching Merle, Tory settled down to work.

She was blessed with a sharp, practical, and stubborn mind. These traits had made her education extensive. Academically she'd excelled, but she hadn't always endeared herself to her instructors. *Why?* had always been her favorite question. In addition her temperament, which ranged from placid to explosive, had made her a difficult student. Some of her associates called her a tedious annoyance—usually when they were on the opposing side. At twenty-seven Victoria L. Ashton was a very shrewd, very accomplished attorney.

In Albuquerque she kept a small, unpretentious office in an enormous old house with bad plumbing. She shared it with an accountant, a real-estate broker, and a private investigator. For nearly five years she had lived on the third floor in two barnlike rooms while keeping her office below. It was a comfortable arrangement that Tory had had no inclination to alter even when she'd been able to afford to.

Professionally she liked challenges and dealing with finite details. In her personal life she was more lackadaisical. No one would call her lazy, but she saw more virtue in a nap than a brisk jog. Her energies poured out in the office or courtroom—and temporarily in her position as sheriff of Friendly, New Mexico.

She had grown up in Friendly and had been content with its yawning pace. The sense of justice she had inherited from her father had driven her to law school. Still, she had had no desire to join a swank firm on either coast, or in any big city in between. Her independence had caused her to risk starting her own practice. Fat fees were no motivation for Tory. She'd learned early how to stretch a dollar when it suited her—an ability she got from her mother. People, and the way the law could be made to work to their advantage or disadvantage, interested her.

Now Tory settled behind her desk and continued drafting out a partnership agreement for a pair of fledgling songwriters. It wasn't always simple to handle cases long distance, but she'd given her word. Absentmindedly she sipped her coffee. By fall she would be back in Albuquerque, filling her caseload again and trading her badge for a briefcase. In the meantime the weekend was looming. Payday. Tory smiled a little as she wrote. Friendly livened up a bit on Saturday nights. People tended to have an extra beer. And there was a poker game scheduled at Bestler's Garage that she wasn't supposed to know about. Tory knew when it was advantageous to look the other way. Her father would have said people need their little entertainments.

Leaning back to study what she had written, Tory

propped one booted foot on the desk and twirled a raven lock around her finger. Abruptly coming out of his reverie, Phil whirled to the door of the cell.

"I have to make a phone call!" His tone was urgent and excited. Everything he had seen from the cell window had convinced him that fate had brought him to Friendly.

Tory finished reading a paragraph, then looked up languidly. "You've had your phone call, Mr. Kincaid. Why don't you relax? Take a tip from Dynamite there," she suggested, wiggling her fingers toward the mound of dog. "Take a nap."

Phil curled his hands around the bars and shook them. "Woman, I have to use the phone. It's important."

"It always is," Tory murmured before she lowered her eyes to the paper again.

Ready to sacrifice principle for expediency, Phil growled at her. "Look, I'll sign the ticket. Just let me out of here."

"You're welcome to sign the ticket," she returned pleasantly, "but it won't get you out. There's also the charge of resisting arrest."

"Of all the phony, trumped-up—"

"I could add creating a public nuisance," she considered, then glanced over the top of her papers with a smile. He was furious. It showed in the rigid stance of his hard body, in the grim mouth and fiery eyes. Tory felt a small twinge in the nether regions of her stomach. Oh, yes, she could clearly see why his name was linked with dozens of attractive women. He was easily the most beautiful male animal she'd ever seen. It was that trace of aristocratic aloofness, she mused, coupled with the really extraordinary physique and explosive temper. He was like some sleek, undomesticated cat.

Their eyes warred with each other for a long, silent moment. His were stony; hers were calm.

"All right," he muttered, "how much?"

Tory lifted a brow. "A bribe, Kincaid?"

He knew his quarry too well by this time. "No. How much is my fine . . . Sheriff?"

"Two hundred and fifty dollars." She sent her hair over her shoulder with a quick toss of her head. "Or you can post bail for five hundred."

Scowling at her, Phil reached for his wallet. When I get out of here, he thought dangerously, I'm going to make that tasty little morsel pay for this. A glance in his wallet found him more than a hundred dollars short of bond. Phil swore, then looked back at Tory. She still had the gently patient smile on her face. He could cheerfully strangle her. Instead he tried another tack. Charm had always brought him success with women.

"I lost my temper before, Sheriff," he began, sending her the slightly off-center smile for which he was known. "I apologize. I've been on the road for several days and your deputy got under my skin." Tory went on smiling. "If I said anything out of line to you, it was because you just don't fit the image of small-town peace officer." He grinned and became boyishly appealing—Tom Sawyer caught with his hand in the sugar bowl.

Tory lifted one long, slim leg and crossed it over the other on the desk. "A little short, are you, Kincaid?"

Phil clenched his teeth on a furious retort. "I don't like to carry a lot of cash on the road."

"Very wise," she agreed with a nod. "But we don't accept credit cards."

"Damn it, I have to get out of here!"

Tory studied him dispassionately. "I can't buy claustrophobia," she said. "Not when I read you crawled into a two-foot pipe to check camera angles on *Night of Desperation*."

"It's not—" Phil broke off. His eyes narrowed. "You know who I am?"

"Oh, I make it to the movies a couple of times a year," she said blithely.

The narrowed eyes grew hard. "If this is some kind of shakedown—"

Her throaty laughter cut him off. "Your self-importance is showing." His expression grew so incredulous, she laughed again before she rose. "Kincaid, I don't care who you are or what you do for a living; you're a bad-tempered man who refused to accept the law and got obnoxious." She sauntered over to the cell. Again he caught the hint of a subtle perfume that suited French silk more than faded denim. "I'm obliged to rehabilitate you."

He forgot his anger in simple appreciation of blatant beauty. "God, you've got a face," he muttered. "I could work a whole damn film around that face."

The words surprised her. Tory was perfectly aware that she was physically attractive. She would have been a fool to think otherwise, and she'd heard men offer countless homages to her looks. This was hardly a homage. But something in his tone, in his eyes, made a tremor skip up her spine. She made no protest when he reached a hand through the bars to touch her hair. He let it fall through his fingers while his eyes stayed on hers.

Tory felt a heat to which she had thought herself immune. It flashed through her as though she had stepped into the sun from out of a cool, dim room. It was the kind of heat that buckled your knees and made you gasp out loud in astonished wonder. She stood straight and absorbed it.

A dangerous man, she concluded, surprised. A very dangerous man. She saw a flicker of desire in his eyes, then a flash of amusement. As she watched, his mouth curved up at the corners.

"Baby," he said, then grinned, "I could make you a star."

The purposely trite words dissolved the tension and made her laugh. "Oh, Mr. Kincaid," she said in a breathy whisper, "can I really have a screen test?" A startled Phil could only watch as she flung herself against the bars of the cell dramatically. "I'll wait for you, Johnny," she said huskily as tears shimmered in her eyes and her soft lips trembled. "No matter how long it takes." Reaching through the bars, she clutched at him. "I'll write you every day," she promised brokenly. "And dream of you every night. Oh, Johnny"— her lashes fluttered down—"kiss me good-bye!"

Fascinated, Phil moved to oblige her, but just before his lips brushed hers, she stepped back, laughing. "How'd I do, Hollywood? Do I get the part?"

Phil studied her in amused annoyance. It was a pity, he thought, that he hadn't at least gotten a taste of that beautiful mouth. "A little overdone," he stated with more asperity than truth. "But not bad for an amateur."

Tory chuckled and leaned companionably against the bars. "You're just mad."

"Mad?" he tossed back in exasperation. "Have you ever spent any time in one of these cages?"

"As a matter of fact I have." She gave him an easy grin. "Under less auspicious circumstances. Relax, Kincaid, your friend will come bail you out."

"The mayor," Phil said on sudden inspiration. "I want to see the mayor. I have a business proposition," he added.

"Oh." Tory mulled this over. "Well, I doubt I can oblige you on a Saturday. The mayor mostly fishes on Saturday. Want to tell me about it?"

"No."

"Okay. By the way, your last film should've taken the Oscar. It was the most beautiful movie I've ever seen."

Her sudden change of attitude disconcerted him. Cautiously, Phil studied her face but saw nothing but simple sincerity. "Thanks."

"You don't look like the type who could make a film with intelligence, integrity, and emotion."

With a half laugh he dragged a hand through his hair. "Am I supposed to thank you for that too?"

"Not necessarily. It's just that you really do look like the type who squires all those busty celebrities around. When do you find time to work?"

He shook his head. "I . . . manage," he said grimly.

"Takes a lot of stamina," Tory agreed.

He grinned. "Which? The work or the busty celebrities?"

"I guess you know the answer to that. By the way," she continued before he could formulate a reasonable response, "don't tell Merle T. you make movies." Tory gave him the swift, dashing grin. "He'll start walking like John Wayne and drive us both crazy."

When he smiled back at her, both of them studied each other in wary silence. There was an attraction on both sides that pleased neither of them.

"Sheriff," Phil said in a friendly tone, "a phone call. Remember the line about the quality of mercy?"

Her lips curved, but before she could agree, the door to the office burst in.

"Sheriff!"

"Right here, Mr. Hollister," she said mildly. Tory

glanced from the burly, irate man to the skinny, terrified teenager he pulled in with him. "What's the
problem?" Without hurry she crossed back to her desk,
stepping over the dog automatically.

"Those punks," he began, puffing with the exertion
of running. "I warned you about them!"

"The Kramer twins?" Tory sat on the corner of her
desk. Her eyes flickered down to the beefy hand that
gripped a skinny arm. "Why don't you sit down, Mr.
Hollister. You—" She looked directly at the boy. "It's
Tod, isn't it?"

He swallowed rapidly. "Yes, ma'am—Sheriff. Tod
Swanson."

"Get Mr. Hollister a glass of water, Tod. Right
through there."

"He'll be out the back door before you can spit,"
Hollister began, then took a plaid handkerchief out of
his pocket to wipe at his brow.

"No, he won't," Tory said calmly. She jerked her
head at the boy as she pulled up a chair for Hollister.
"Sit down, now, you'll make yourself sick."

"Sick!" Hollister dropped into a chair as the boy
scrambled off. "I'm already sick. Those—those
punks."

"Yes, the Kramer twins."

She waited patiently while he completed a lengthy,
sometimes incoherent dissertation on the youth of
today. Phil had the opportunity to do what he did best:
watch and absorb.

Hollister, he noticed, was a hotheaded old bigot
with a trace of fear for the younger generation. He was
sweating profusely, dabbing at his brow and the back
of his neck with the checkered handkerchief. His shirt
was wilted and patched with dark splotches. He was
flushed, overweight, and tiresome. Tory listened to

him with every appearance of respect, but Phil noticed the gentle tap of her forefinger against her knee as she sat on the edge of the desk.

The boy came in with the water, two high spots of color on his cheeks. Phil concluded he'd had a difficult time not slipping out the back door. He judged the boy to be about thirteen and scared right down to the bone. He had a smooth, attractive face, with a mop of dark hair and huge brown eyes that wanted to look everywhere at once. He was too thin; his jeans and grubby shirt were nearly in tatters. He handed Tory the water with a hand that shook. Phil saw that when she took it from him, she gave his hand a quick, reassuring squeeze. Phillip began to like her.

"Here." Tory handed Hollister the glass. "Drink this, then tell me what happened."

Hollister drained the glass in two huge gulps. "Those punks, messing around out back of my store. I've chased 'em off a dozen times. They come in and steal anything they can get their hands on. I've told you."

"Yes, Mr. Hollister. What happened this time?"

"Heaved a rock through the window." He reddened alarmingly again. "This one was with 'em. Didn't run fast enough."

"I see." She glanced at Tod, whose eyes were glued to the toes of his sneakers. "Which one threw the rock?"

"Didn't see which one, but I caught this one." Hollister rose, stuffing his damp handkerchief back in his pocket. "I'm going to press charges."

Phil saw the boy blanch. Though Tory continued to look at Hollister, she laid a hand on Tod's arm. "Go sit down in the back room, Tod." She waited until he was out of earshot. "You did the right thing to bring him in, Mr. Hollister." She smiled. "And to scare the pants off him."

"He should be locked up," the man began.

"Oh, that won't get your window fixed," she said reasonably. "And it would only make the boy look like a hero to the twins."

"In my day—"

"I guess you and my father never broke a window," she mused, smiling at him with wide eyes. Hollister blustered, then snorted.

"Now, look here, Tory . . ."

"Let me handle it, Mr. Hollister. This kid must be three years younger than the Kramer twins." She lowered her voice so that Phil strained to hear. "He could have gotten away."

Hollister shifted from foot to foot. "He didn't try," he mumbled. "Just stood there. But my window—"

"How much to replace it?"

He lowered his brows and puffed for a minute. "Twenty-five dollars should cover it."

Tory walked around the desk and opened a drawer. After counting out bills, she handed them over. "You have my word, I'll deal with him—and with the twins."

"Just like your old man," he muttered, then awkwardly patted her head. "I don't want those Kramers hanging around my store."

"I'll see to it."

With a nod he left.

Tory sat on her desk again and frowned at her left boot. She wasn't just like her old man, she thought. He'd always been sure and she was guessing. Phil heard her quiet, troubled sigh and wondered at it.

"Tod," she called, then waited for him to come to her. As he walked in his eyes darted in search of Hollister before they focused, terrified, on Tory. When he stood in front of her, she studied his white, strained face. Her heart melted, but her voice was brisk.

"I won't ask you who threw the rock." Tod opened his mouth, closed it resolutely, and shook his head. "Why didn't you run?"

"I didn't—I couldn't. . . ." He bit his lip. "I guess I was too scared."

"How old are you, Tod?" She wanted to brush at the hair that tumbled over his forehead. Instead she kept her hands loosely folded in her lap.

"Fourteen, Sheriff. Honest." His eyes darted up to hers, then flew away like a small, frightened bird. "Just last month."

"The Kramer twins are sixteen," she pointed out gently. "Don't you have friends your own age?"

He gave a shrug of his shoulders that could have meant anything.

"I'll have to take you home and talk to your father, Tod."

He'd been frightened before, but now he looked up at her with naked terror in his eyes. It wiped the lecture she had intended to give him out of her mind. "Please." It came out in a whisper, as though he could say nothing more. Even the whisper was hopeless.

"Tod, are you afraid of your father?" He swallowed and said nothing. "Does he hurt you?" He moistened his lips as his breath began to shake. "Tod." Tory's voice became very soft. "You can tell me. I'm here to help you."

"He . . ." Tod choked, then shook his head swiftly. "No, ma'am."

Frustrated, Tory looked at the plea in his eyes. "Well, then, perhaps since this is a first offense, we can keep it between us."

"M-ma'am?"

"Tod Swanson, you were detained for malicious mischief. Do you understand the charge?"

"Yes, Sheriff." His Adam's apple began to tremble.

"You owe the court twenty-five dollars in damages, which you'll work off after school and on weekends at a rate of two dollars an hour. You're sentenced to six months probation, during which time you're to keep away from loose women, hard liquor, and the Kramer twins. Once a week you're to file a report with me, as I'll be serving as your probation officer."

Tod stared at her as he tried to take it in. "You're not . . . you're not going to tell my father?"

Slowly, Tory rose. He was a few inches shorter, so that he looked up at her with his eyes full of confused hope. "No." She placed her hands on his shoulders. "Don't let me down."

His eyes brimmed with tears, which he blinked back furiously. Tory wanted badly to hold him, but knew better. "Be here tomorrow morning. I'll have some work for you."

"Yes, yes, ma'am—Sheriff." He backed away warily, waiting for her to change her mind. "I'll be here, Sheriff." He was fumbling for the doorknob, still watching her. "Thank you." Like a shot, he was out of the office, leaving Tory staring at the closed door.

"Well, Sheriff," Phil said quietly, "you're quite a lady."

Tory whirled to see Phil eyeing her oddly. For the first time she felt the full impact of the clear blue gaze. Disconcerted, she went back to her desk. "Did you enjoy seeing the wheels of justice turn, Kincaid?" she asked.

"As a matter of fact, I did." His tone was grave enough to cause her to look back at him. "You did the right thing by that boy."

Tory studied him a moment, then let out a long sigh. "Did I? We'll see, won't we? Ever seen an abused kid, Kincaid? I'd bet that fifteen-hundred-dollar watch you're wearing one just walked out of here. There isn't a damn thing I can do about it."

"There are laws," he said, fretting against the bars. Quite suddenly he wanted to touch her.

"And laws," she murmured. When the door swung open, she glanced up. "Merle. Good. Take over here. I have to run out to the Kramer place."

"The twins?"

"Who else?" Tory shot back as she plucked a black flat-brimmed hat from a peg. "I'll grab dinner while I'm out and pick up something for our guest. How do you feel about stew, Kincaid?"

"Steak, medium rare," he tossed back. "Chef's salad, oil and vinegar and a good Bordeaux."

"Don't let him intimidate you, Merle," Tory warned as she headed for the door. "He's a cream puff."

"Sheriff, the phone call!" Phil shouted after her as she started to close the door.

With a heavy sigh Tory stuck her head back in. "Merle T., let the poor guy use the phone. Once," she added firmly, then shut the door.

Ninety minutes later Tory sauntered back in with a wicker hamper over her arm. Phil was sitting on his bunk, smoking quietly. Merle sat at the desk, his feet propped up, his hat over his face. He was snoring gently.

"Is the party over?" Tory asked. Phil shot her a silent glare. Chuckling, she went to Merle and gave him a jab in the shoulder. He scrambled up like a shot, scraping his boot heels over the desk surface.

"Aw, Tory," he muttered, bending to retrieve his hat from the floor.

"Any trouble with the desperate character?" she wanted to know.

Merle gave her a blank look, then grinned sheepishly. "Come on, Tory."

"Go get something to eat. You can wander down to Hernandez's Bar and the pool hall before you go off duty."

Merle placed his hat back on his head. "Want me to check Bestler's Garage?"

"No," she said, remembering the poker game. Merle would figure it his bound duty to break it up if he happened in on it. "I checked in earlier."

"Well, okay . . ." He shuffled his feet and cast a sidelong glance at Phil. "One of us should stay here tonight."

"I'm staying." Plucking up the keys, she headed for the cell. "I've got some extra clothes in the back room."

"Yeah, but, Tory . . ." He wanted to point out that she was a woman, after all, and the prisoner had given her a couple of long looks.

"Yes?" Tory paused in front of Phil's cell.

"Nothin'," he muttered, reminded that Tory could handle herself and always had. He blushed before he headed for the door.

"Wasn't that sweet?" she murmured. "He was worried about my virtue." At Phil's snort of laughter she lifted a wry brow.

"Doesn't he know about the large gun in the desk drawer?"

"Of course he does." Tory unlocked the cell. "I told him if he played with it, I'd break all his fingers. Hungry?"

Phil gave the hamper a dubious smile. "Maybe."

"Oh, come on, cheer up," Tory ordered. "Didn't you get to make your phone call?"

She spoke, as though appeasing a little boy. It drew a reluctant grin from Phil. "Yes, I made my phone call." Because the discussion with his producer had gone well, Phil was willing to be marginally friendly. Besides, he was starving. "What's in there?"

"T-bone, medium rare, salad, roasted potato—"

"You're kidding!" He was up and dipping into the basket himself.

"I don't kid a man about food, Kincaid, I'm a humanitarian."

"I'll tell you exactly what I think you are—after I've eaten." Phil pulled foil off a plate and uncovered the steak. The scent went straight to his stomach. Dragging over a shaky wooden chair, he settled down to devour his free meal.

"You didn't specify dessert, so I went for apple pie." Tory drew a thick slice out of the hamper.

"I might just modify my opinion of you," Phil told her over a mouthful of steak.

"Don't do anything hasty," she suggested.

"Tell me something, Sheriff." He swallowed, then indicated the still-sleeping dog with his fork. "Doesn't that thing ever move?"

"Not if he can help it."

"Is it alive?"

"The last time I looked," she muttered. "Sorry about the Bordeaux," she continued. "Against regulations. I got you a Dr Pepper."

"A what?"

Tory pulled out a bottle of soda. "Take it or leave it."

After a moment's consideration Phil held out his hand. "What about the mayor?"

"I left him a message. He'll probably see you tomorrow."

Phil unscrewed the top off the bottle, frowning at

her. "You're not actually going to make me sleep in this place."

Cocking her head, Tory met his glance. "You have a strange view of the law, Kincaid. Do you think I should book you a room at the hotel?"

He washed down the steak with the soda, then grimaced. "You're a tough guy, Sheriff."

"Yeah." Grinning, she perched on the edge of the bunk. "How's your dinner?"

"It's good. Want some?"

"No. I've eaten." They studied each other with the same wary speculation. Tory spoke first. "What is Phillip C. Kincaid, boy wonder, doing in Friendly, New Mexico?"

"I was passing through," he said warily. He wasn't going to discuss his plans with her. Something warned him he would meet solid opposition.

"At seventy-two miles per hour," she reminded him.

"Maybe."

With a laugh she leaned back against the brick wall. He watched the way her hair settled lazily over her breasts. A man would be crazy to tangle with that lady, he told himself. Phillip Kincaid was perfectly sane.

"And what is Victoria L. Ashton doing wearing a badge in Friendly, New Mexico?"

She gazed past him for a moment with an odd look in her eyes. "Fulfilling an obligation," she said softly.

"You don't fit the part." Phil contemplated her over another swig from the bottle. "I'm an expert on who fits and who doesn't."

"Why not?" Lifting her knee, Tory laced her fingers around it.

"Your hands are too soft." Thoughtfully, Phil cut another bite of steak. "Not as soft as I expected when I saw that face, but too soft. You don't pamper them, but you don't work with them either."

"A sheriff doesn't work with her hands," Tory pointed out.

"A sheriff doesn't wear perfume that costs a hundred and fifty an ounce that was designed to drive men wild either."

Both brows shot up. Her full bottom lip pushed forward in thought. "Is that what it was designed for?"

"A sheriff," he went on, "doesn't usually look like she just walked off the cover of *Harper's Bazaar*, treat her deputy like he was her kid brother, or pay some boy's fine out of her own pocket."

"My, my," Tory said slowly, "you are observant." He shrugged, continuing with his meal. "Well, then, what part would you cast me in?"

"I had several in mind the minute I saw you." Phil shook his head as he finished off his steak. "Now I'm not so sure. You're no fragile desert blossom." When her smile widened, he went on. "You could be if you wanted to, but you don't. You're no glossy sophisticate either. But that's a choice too." Taking the pie, he rose to join her on the bunk. "You know, there are a number of people out in this strange world who would love to have me as a captive audience while they recited their life's story."

"At least three of four," Tory agreed dryly.

"You're rough on my ego, Sheriff." He tasted the pie, approved, then offered her the next bite. Tory opened her mouth, allowing herself to be fed. It was tangy, spicy, and still warm.

"What do you want to know?" she asked, then swallowed.

"Why you're tossing men in jail instead of breaking their hearts."

Her laugh was full of appreciation as she leaned her head back against the wall. Still, she wavered a moment. It had been so long, she mused, since she'd been able just to talk to someone—to a man. He was interesting and, she thought, at the moment harmless.

"I grew up here," she said simply.

"But you didn't stay." When she sent him a quizzical look, he fed her another bite of pie. It occurred to him that it had been a long time since he'd been with a woman who didn't want or even expect anything from him. "You've got too much polish, Victoria," he said, finding her name flowed well on his tongue. "You didn't acquire it in Friendly."

"Harvard," she told him, rounding her tones. "Law."

"Ah." Phil sent her an approving nod. "That fits. I can see you with a leather briefcase and a pin-striped suit. Why aren't you practicing?"

"I am. I have an office in Albuquerque." Her brows drew together. "A pin-striped suit?"

"Gray, very discreet. How can you practice law in Albuquerque and uphold it in Friendly?" He pushed the hair from her shoulder in a casual gesture that neither of them noticed.

"I'm not taking any new cases for a while, so my workload's fairly light." She shrugged it off. "I handle what I can on paper and make a quick trip back when I have to."

"Are you a good lawyer?"

Tory grinned. "I'm a terrific lawyer, Kincaid, but I can't represent you—unethical."

He shoved another bite of pie at her. "So what are you doing back in Friendly?"

"You really are nosy, aren't you?"

"Yes."

She laughed. "My father was sheriff here for years and years." A sadness flickered briefly into her eyes and was controlled. "I suppose in his own quiet way he held the town together—such as it is. When he died, nobody knew just what to do. It sounds strange, but in a town this size, one person can make quite a difference, and he was . . . a special kind of man."

The wound hasn't healed yet, he thought, watching her steadily. He wondered, but didn't ask, how long ago her father had died.

"Anyway, the mayor asked me to fill in until things settled down again, and since I had to stay around to straighten a few things out anyway, I agreed. Nobody wanted the job except Merle, and he's . . ." She gave a quick, warm laugh. "Well, he's not ready. I know the law, I know the town. In a few months they'll hold an election. My name won't be on the ballot." She shot him a look. "Did I satisfy your curiosity?"

Under the harsh overhead lights, her skin was flawless, her eyes sharply green. Phil found himself reaching for her hair again. "No," he murmured. Though his eyes never left hers, Tory felt as though he looked at all of her—slowly and with great care. Quite unexpectedly her mouth went dry. She rose.

"It should have," she said lightly as she began to pack up the dirty dishes. "Next time we have dinner, I'll expect your life story." When she felt his hand on her arm, she stopped. Tory glanced down at the fingers curled around her arm, then slowly lifted her eyes to his. "Kincaid," she said softly, "you're in enough trouble."

"I'm already in jail," he pointed out as he turned her to face him.

"The term of your stay can easily be lengthened."

Knowing he should resist and that he couldn't, Phil drew her into his arms. "How much time can I get for making love to the sheriff?"

"What you're going to get is a broken rib if you don't let me go." *Miscalculation*, her mind stated bluntly. This man is never harmless. On the tail of that came the thought of how wonderful it felt to be held against him. His mouth was very close and very tempting. And it simply wasn't possible to forget their positions.

"Tory," he murmured. "I like the way that sounds." Running his fingers up her spine, he caught them in her hair. With her pressed tight against him, he could feel her faint quiver of response. "I think I'm going to have to have you."

A struggle wasn't going to work, she decided, any more than threats. As her own blood began to heat, Tory knew she had to act quickly. Tilting her head back slightly, she lifted a disdainful brow. "Hasn't a woman ever turned you down before, Kincaid?"

She saw his eyes flash in anger, felt the fingers in her hair tighten. Tory forced herself to remain still and relaxed. Excitement shivered through her, and resolutely she ignored it. His thighs were pressed hard against hers; the arms wrapped around her waist were tense with muscle. The firm male feel of him appealed to her, while the temper in his eyes warned her not to miscalculate again. They remained close for one long throbbing moment.

Phil's fingers relaxed before he stepped back to measure her. "There'll be another time," he said quietly. "Another place."

With apparent calm, Tory began gathering the dishes

again. Her heart was thudding at the base of her throat. "You'll get the same answer."

"The hell I will."

Annoyed, she turned to see him watching her. With his hands in his pockets he rocked back gently on his heels. His eyes belied the casual stance. "Stick with your bubbleheaded blondes," she advised coolly. "They photograph so well, clinging to your arm."

She was angry, he realized suddenly, and much more moved by him than she had pretended. Seeing his advantage, Phil approached her again. "You ever take off that badge, Sheriff?"

Tory kept her eyes level. "Occasionally."

Phil lowered his gaze, letting it linger on the small star. "When?"

Sensing that she was being outmaneuvered, Tory answered cautiously. "That's irrelevant."

When he lifted his eyes back to hers, he was smiling. "It won't be." He touched a finger to her full bottom lip. "I'm going to spend a lot of time tasting that beautiful mouth of yours."

Disturbed, Tory stepped back. "I'm afraid you won't have the opportunity or the time."

"I'm going to find the opportunity and the time to make love with you several times"—he sent her a mocking grin—"Sheriff."

As he had anticipated, her eyes lit with fury. "You conceited fool," she said in a low voice. "You really think you're irresistible."

"Sure I do." He continued to grin maddeningly. "Don't you?"

"I think you're a spoiled, egotistical ass."

His temper rose, but Phil controlled it. If he lost it, he'd lose his advantage. He stepped closer, keeping a

bland smile on his face. "Do you? Is that a legal opinion or a personal one?"

Tory tossed back her head, fuming. "My personal
opinion is—"

He cut her off with a hard, bruising kiss.

Taken completely by surprise, Tory didn't struggle.
By the time she had gathered her wits, she was too involved to attempt it. His mouth seduced hers expertly,
parting her lips so that he could explore deeply and at
his leisure. She responded out of pure pleasure. His
mouth was hard, then soft—gentle, then demanding. He
took her on a brisk roller coaster of sensation. Before
she could recover from the first breathtaking plunge,
they were climbing again. She held on to him, waiting
for the next burst of speed.

He took his tongue lightly over hers, then withdrew
it, tempting her to follow. Recklessly, she did, learning
the secrets and dark tastes of his mouth. For a moment
he allowed her to take the lead; then, cupping the back
of her head in his hand, he crushed her lips with one
last driving force. He wanted her weak and limp and
totally conquered.

When he released her, Tory stood perfectly still,
trying to remember what had happened. The confusion in her eyes gave him enormous pleasure. "I plead
guilty, Your Honor," he drawled as he dropped back
onto the bunk. "And it was worth it."

Hot, raging fury replaced every other emotion.
Storming over to him, she grabbed him by the shirt
front. Phil didn't resist, but grinned.

"Police brutality," he reminded her. She cursed
him fluently, and with such effortless style, he was unable to conceal his admiration. "Did you learn that at
Harvard?" he asked when she paused for breath.

Tory released him with a jerk and whirled to scoop

up the hamper. The cell door shut behind her with a furious clang. Without pausing, she stormed out of the office.

Still grinning, Phil lay back on the bunk and pulled out a cigarette. She'd won round one, he told himself. But he'd taken round two. Blowing out a lazy stream of smoke, he began to speculate on the rematch.

CHAPTER 3

When the alarm shrilled, Tory knocked it off the small table impatiently. It clattered to the floor and continued to shrill. She buried her head under the pillow. She wasn't at her best in the morning. The noisy alarm vibrated against the floor until she reached down in disgust and slammed it off. After a good night's sleep she was inclined to be cranky. After a poor one she was dangerous.

Most of the past night had been spent tossing and turning. The scene with Phil had infuriated her, not only because he had won, but because she had fully enjoyed that one moment of mindless pleasure. Rolling onto her back, Tory kept the pillow over her face to block out the sunlight. The worst part was, she mused, he was going to get away with it. She couldn't in all conscience use the law to punish him for something that had been strictly personal. It had been her own fault for lowering her guard and inviting the consequences. And she had enjoyed talking with him, sparring with someone quick with words. She missed matching wits with a man.

But that was no excuse, she reminded herself. He'd made her forget her duty . . . and he'd enjoyed it. Disgusted, Tory tossed the pillow aside, then winced at the brilliant sunlight. She'd learned how to evade an advance as a teenager. What had caused her to slip up this time? She didn't want to dwell on it. Grumpily she dragged herself from the cot and prepared to dress.

Every muscle in his body ached. Phil stretched out his legs to their full length and gave a low groan. He was willing to swear Tory had put the lumps in the mattress for his benefit. Cautiously opening one eye, he stared at the man in the next cell. The man slept on, as he had from the moment Tory had dumped him on the bunk the night before. He snored outrageously. When she had dragged him in, Phil had been amused. The man was twice her weight and had been blissfully drunk. He'd called her "good old Tory," and she had cursed him halfheartedly as she had maneuvered him into the cell. Thirty minutes after hearing the steady snoring, Phil had lost his sense of humor.

She hadn't spoken a word to him. With a detached interest Phil had watched her struggle with the drunk. It had pleased him to observe that she was still fuming. She'd been in and out of the office several times before midnight, then had locked up in the same frigid silence. He'd enjoyed that, but then had made a fatal error: When she had gone into the back room to bed, he had tortured himself by watching her shadow play on the wall as she had undressed. That, combined with an impossible mattress and a snoring drunk-and-disorderly, had led to an uneasy night. He hadn't awakened in the best of moods.

Sitting up with a wince, he glared at the unconscious man in the next cell. His wide, flushed face was cherubic, ringed with a curling blond circle of hair. Ruefully, Phil rubbed a hand over his own chin and felt the rough stubble. A fastidious man, he was annoyed at not having a razor, a hot shower, or a fresh set of clothes. Rising, he determined to gain access to all three immediately.

"Tory!" His voice was curt, one of a man accustomed to being listened to. He received no response. "Damn it, Tory, get out here!" He rattled the bars, wishing belligerently that he'd kept the tin cup. He could have made enough noise with it to wake even the stuporous man in the next cell. "Tory, get out of that bed and come here." He swore, promising himself he'd never allow anyone to lock him in anything again. "When I get out . . ." he began.

Tory came shuffling in, carrying a pot of water. "Button up, Kincaid."

"You listen to me," he retorted. "I want a shower and a razor and my clothes. And if—"

"If you don't shut up until I've had my coffee, you're going to take your shower where you stand." She lifted the pot of water meaningfully. "You can get cleaned up as soon as Merle gets in." She went to the coffeepot and began to clatter.

"You're an arrogant wretch when you've got a man caged," he said darkly.

"I'm an arrogant wretch anyway. Do yourself a favor, Kincaid, don't start a fight until I've had two cups. I'm not a nice person in the morning."

"I'm warning you." His voice was as low and dangerous as his mood. "You're going to regret locking me in here."

Turning, she looked at him for the first time that

morning. His clothes and hair were disheveled. The clean lines of his aristocratic face were shadowed by the night's growth of beard. Fury was in his stance and in the cool water-blue of his eyes. He looked outrageously attractive.

"I think I'm going to regret letting you out," she muttered before she turned back to the coffee. "Do you want some of this, or are you just going to throw it at me?"

The idea was tempting, but so was the scent of the coffee. "Black," he reminded her shortly.

Tory drained half a cup, ignoring her scalded tongue before she went to Phil. "What do you want for breakfast?" she asked as she passed the cup through the bars.

He scowled at her. "A shower, and a sledgehammer for your friend over there."

Tory cast an eye in the next cell. "Silas'll wake up in an hour, fresh as a daisy." She swallowed more coffee. "Keep you up?"

"Him and the feather bed you provided."

She shrugged. "Crime doesn't pay."

"I'm going to strangle you when I get out of here," he promised over the rim of his cup. "Slowly and with great pleasure."

"That isn't the way to get your shower." She turned as the door opened and Tod came in. He stood hesitantly at the door, jamming his hands in his pockets. "Good morning." She smiled and beckoned him in. "You're early."

"You didn't say what time." He came warily, shifting his eyes from Phil to Silas and back to Phil again. "You got prisoners."

"Yes, I do." Catching her tongue between her teeth, she jerked a thumb at Phil. "This one's a nasty character."

"What's he in for?"

"Insufferable arrogance."

"He didn't kill anybody, did he?"

"Not yet," Phil muttered, then added, unable to resist the eager gleam in the boy's eyes, "I was framed."

"They all say that, don't they, Sheriff?"

"Absolutely." She lifted a hand to ruffle the boy's hair. Startled, he jerked and stared at her. Ignoring his reaction, she left her hand on his shoulder. "Well, I'll put you to work, then. There's a broom in the back room. You can start sweeping up. Have you had breakfast?"

"No, but—"

"I'll bring you something when I take care of this guy. Think you can keep an eye on things for me for a few minutes?"

His mouth fell open in astonishment. "Yes, ma'am!"

"Okay, you're in charge." She headed for the door, grabbing her hat on the way. "If Silas wakes up, you can let him out. The other guy stays where he is. Got it?"

"Sure thing, Sheriff." He sent Phil a cool look. "He won't pull nothing on me."

Stifling a laugh, Tory walked outside.

Resigned to the wait, Phil leaned against the bars and drank his coffee while the boy went to work with the broom. He worked industriously, casting furtive glances over his shoulder at Phil from time to time. He's a good-looking boy, Phil mused. He brooded over his reaction to Tory's friendly gesture, wondering how he would react to a man.

"Live in town?" Phil ventured.

Tod paused, eyeing him warily. "Outside."

"On a ranch?"

He began to sweep again, but more slowly. "Yeah."

"Got any horses?"

The boy shrugged. "Couple." He was working his way cautiously over to the cell. "You're not from around here," he said.

"No, I'm from California."

"No, kidding?" Impressed, Tod sized him up again. "You don't look like such a bad guy," he decided.

"Thanks." Phil grinned into his cup.

"How come you're in jail, then?"

Phil pondered over the answer and settled for the unvarnished truth. "I lost my temper."

Tod gave a snort of laughter and continued sweeping. "You can't go to jail for that. My pa loses his all the time."

"Sometimes you can." He studied the boy's profile. "Especially if you hurt someone."

The boy passed the broom over the floor without much regard for dust. "Did you?"

"Just myself," Phil admitted ruefully. "I got the sheriff mad at me."

"Zac Kramer said he don't hold with no woman sheriff."

Phil laughed at that, recalling how easily a woman sheriff had gotten him locked in a cell. "Zac Kramer doesn't sound very smart to me."

Tod sent Phil a swift, appealing grin. "I heard she went to their place yesterday. The twins have to wash all Old Man Hollister's windows, inside and out. For free."

Tory breezed back in with two covered plates. "Breakfast," she announced. "He give you any trouble?" she asked Tod as she set a plate on her desk.

"No, ma'am." The scent of food made his mouth water, but he bent back to his task.

"Okay, sit down and eat."

He shot her a doubtful look. "Me?"

"Yes, you." Carrying the other plate, she walked over to get the keys. "When you and Mr. Kincaid have finished, run the dishes back to the hotel." Without waiting for a response, she unlocked Phil's cell. But Phil watched the expression on Tod's face as he started at his breakfast.

"Sheriff," Phil murmured, taking her hand rather than the plate she held out to him, "you're a very classy lady." Lifting her hand, he kissed her fingers lightly.

Unable to resist, she allowed her hand to rest in his a moment. "Phil," she said on a sigh, "don't be disarming—you'll complicate things."

His brow lifted in surprise as he studied her. "You know," he said slowly, "I think it's already too late."

Tory shook her head, denying it. "Eat your breakfast," she ordered briskly. "Merle will be coming by with your clothes soon."

When she turned to leave, he held her hand another moment. "Tory," he said quietly, "you and I aren't finished yet."

Carefully she took her hand from his. "You and I never started," she corrected, then closed the door of the cell with a resolute clang. As she headed back to the coffeepot she glanced at Tod. The boy was making his way through bacon and eggs without any trouble.

"Aren't you eating?" Phil asked her as he settled down to his own breakfast.

"I'll never understand how anyone can eat at this hour," Tory muttered, fortifying herself on coffee. "Tod, the sheriff's car could use a wash. Can you handle it?"

"Sure thing, Sheriff." He was half out of the chair before Tory put a restraining hand on his shoulder.

"Eat first," she told him with a chuckle. "If you finish up the sweeping and the car, that should do it for today." She sat on the corner of the desk, enjoying his appetite. "Your parents know where you are?" she asked casually.

"I finished my chores before I left," he mumbled with a full mouth.

"Hmmm." She said nothing more, sipping instead at her coffee. When the door opened, she glanced over, expecting to see Merle. Instead she was struck dumb.

"Lou!" Phil was up and holding on to the bars. "It's about time."

"Well, Phil, you look very natural."

Lou Sherman, Tory thought, sincerely awed. One of the top attorneys in the country. She'd followed his cases, studied his style, used his precedents. He looked just as commanding in person as in any newspaper or magazine picture she'd ever seen of him. He was a huge man, six foot four, with a stocky frame and a wild thatch of white hair. His voice had resonated in courtrooms for more than forty years. He was tenacious, flamboyant, and feared. For the moment Tory could only stare at the figure striding into her office in a magnificent pearl-gray suit and baby-pink shirt.

Phil called him an uncomplimentary name, which made him laugh loudly. "You'd better have some respect if you want me to get you out of there, son." His eyes slid to Phil's half-eaten breakfast. "Finish eating," he advised, "while I talk to the sheriff." Turning, he gazed solemnly from Tory to Tod. "One of you the sheriff?"

Tory hadn't found her voice yet. Tod jerked his head at her. "She is," he stated with his mouth still full.

Lou let his eyes drift down to her badge. "Well, so she is," he said genially. "Best-looking law person I've seen . . . No offense," he added with a wide grin.

Remembering herself, Tory rose and extended her

hand. "Victoria Ashton, Mr. Sherman. It's a pleasure to meet you."

"My pleasure, Sheriff Ashton," he corrected with a great deal of charm. "Tell me, what's the kid done now?"

"Lou—" Phil began, and got an absent wave of the hand from his attorney.

"Finish your eggs," he ordered. "I gave up a perfectly good golf date to fly over here. Sheriff?" he added with a questioning lift of brow.

"Mr. Kincaid was stopped for speeding on Highway Seventeen," Tory began. "When he refused to sign the ticket, my deputy brought him in." After Lou's heavy sigh she continued. "I'm afraid Mr. Kincaid wasn't co-operative."

"Never is," Lou agreed apologetically.

"Damn it, Lou, would you just get me out of here?"

"All in good time," he promised without looking at him. "Are there any other charges, Sheriff?"

"Resisting arrest," she stated, not quite disguising a grin. "The fine is two hundred and fifty, bail set at five hundred. Mr. Kincaid, when he decided to . . . cooperate, was a bit short of funds."

Lou rubbed a hand over his chin. The large ruby on his pinky glinted dully. "Wouldn't be the first time," he mused.

Incensed at being ignored and defamed at the same time, Phil interrupted tersely. "She pulled a gun on me."

This information was met with another burst of loud laughter from his attorney. "Damn, I wish I'd been here to see his face."

"It was worth the price of a ticket," Tory admitted.

Phil started to launch into a stream of curses, remembered the boy—who was listening avidly—and ground his teeth instead. "Lou," he said slowly, "are you going to get me out or stand around exchanging small talk all day? I haven't had a shower since yesterday."

"Very fastidious," Lou told Tory. "Gets it from his father. I got him out of a tight squeeze or two as I recall. There was this little town in New Jersey . . . Ah, well, that's another story. I'd like to consult with my client, Sheriff Ashton."

"Of course." Tory retrieved the keys.

"Ashton," Lou murmured, closing his eyes for a moment. "Victoria Ashton. There's something about that name." He stroked his chin. "Been sheriff here long?"

Tory shook her head as she started to unlock Phil's cell. "No, actually I'm just filling in for a while."

"She's a lawyer," Phil said disgustedly.

"That's it!" Lou gave her a pleased look. "I knew the name was familiar. The Dunbarton case. You did a remarkable job."

"Thank you."

"Had your troubles with Judge Withers," he recalled, flipping through his memory file. "Contempt of court. What was it you called him?"

"A supercilious humbug," Tory said with a wince.

Lou chuckled delightedly. "Wonderful choice of words."

"It cost me a night in jail," she recalled.

"Still, you won the case."

"Luckily the judge didn't hold a grudge."

"Skill and hard work won you that one," Lou disagreed. "Where did you study?"

"Harvard."

"Look," Phil interrupted testily. "You two can discuss this over drinks later."

"Manners, Phil, you've always had a problem with manners." Lou smiled at Tory again. "Excuse me, Sheriff. Well, Phil, give me one of those corn muffins there and tell me your troubles."

Tory left them in privacy just as Merle walked in, carrying Phil's suitcase. Dynamite wandered in behind him, found his spot on the floor, and instantly went to sleep. "Just leave that by the desk," Tory told Merle. "After Kincaid's taken care of, I'm going out to the house for a while. You won't be able to reach me for two hours."

"Okay." He glanced at the still-snoring Silas. "Should I kick him out?"

"When he wakes up." She looked over at Tod. "Tod's going to wash my car."

Stuffing in the last bite, Tod scrambled up. "I'll do it now." He dashed out the front door.

Tory frowned after him. "Merle, what do you know about Tod's father?"

He shrugged and scratched at his mustache. "Swanson keeps to himself, raises some cattle couple miles north of town. Been in a couple of brawls but nothing important."

"His mother?"

"Quiet lady. Does some cleaning work over at the hotel now and again. You remember the older brother, don't you? He lit out a couple years ago. Never heard from him since."

Tory absorbed this with a thoughtful nod. "Keep an eye out for the boy when I'm not around, okay?"

"Sure. He in trouble?"

"I'm not certain." She frowned a moment, then her expression relaxed again. "Just keep your eyes open, Merle T.," she said, smiling at him affectionately. "Why don't you go see if the kid's found a bucket? I don't think it would take much persuasion to get him to wash your car too."

Pleased with the notion, Merle strode out again.

"Sheriff"—Tory turned back to the cell as Lou came out—"my client tells me you also serve as justice of the peace?"

"That's right, Mr. Sherman."

"In that case, I'd like to plead temporary insanity on the part of my client."

"You're cute, Lou," Phil muttered from the cell door. "Can I take that shower now?" he demanded, indicating his suitcase.

"In the back," Tory told him. "You need a shave," she added sweetly.

He picked up the case, giving her a long look. "Sheriff, when this is all over, you and I have some personal business."

Tory lifted her half-finished coffee. "Don't cut your throat, Kincaid."

Lou waited until Phil had disappeared into the back room. "He's a good boy," he said with a paternal sigh. Tory burst out laughing.

"Oh, no," she said definitely, "he's not."

"Well, it was worth a try." He shrugged it off and settled his enormous bulk into a chair. "About the charge of resisting arrest," he began. "I'd really hate for it to go on his record. A night in jail was quite a culture shock for our Phillip, Victoria."

"Agreed." She smiled. "I believe that charge could be dropped if Mr. Kincaid pays the speeding fine."

"I've advised him to do so," Lou told her, pulling out a thick cigar. "He doesn't like it, but I'm . . ." He studied the cigar like a lover. "Persuasive," he decided. He shot her an admiring look. "So are you. What kind of a gun?"

Tory folded her hands primly. "A .45."

Lou laughed heartily as he lit his cigar. "Now, tell me about the Dunbarton case, Victoria."

The horse kicked up a cloud of brown dust. Responding to Tory's command, he broke into an easy gallop. Air, as dry as the land around them, whipped by them in a warm rush. The hat Tory had worn to shield herself from the sun lay on the back of her neck, forgotten. Her movements were so attuned to the horse, she was barely conscious of his movements beneath her. Tory wanted to think, but first she wanted to clear her mind. Since childhood, riding had been her one sure way of doing so.

Sports had no appeal for her. She saw no sense in hitting or chasing a ball around some court or course. It took too much energy. She might swim a few laps now and again, but found it much more agreeable to float on a raft. Sweating in a gym was laughable. But riding was a different category. Tory didn't consider it exercise or effort. She used it now, as she had over the years, as a way to escape from her thoughts for a short time.

For thirty minutes she rode without any thought of destination. Gradually she slowed the horse to a walk, letting her hands relax on the reins. He would turn, she knew, and head back to the ranch.

Phillip Kincaid. He shot back into her brain. A nuisance, Tory decided. One that should be over. At the moment he should already be back on his way to L.A. Tory dearly hoped so. She didn't like to admit that he had gotten to her. It was unfortunate that despite their clash, despite his undeniable arrogance, she had liked him. He was interesting and funny and sharp. It was difficult to dislike someone who could laugh at himself. There would be no problem if it ended there.

Feeling the insistent beat of the sun on her head, Tory absently replaced her hat. It hadn't ended there because there had been that persistent attraction. That was strictly man to woman, and she hadn't counted on it when she had tossed him in jail. He'd outmaneuvered her once. That was annoying, but the result had been much deeper. When was the last time she had completely forgotten herself in a man's arms? When was the last time she had spent most of the night thinking about a man? Had she ever? Tory let out a deep breath, then frowned at the barren, stone-colored landscape.

No, her reaction had been too strong for comfort— and the fact that she was still thinking about him disturbed her. A woman her age didn't dwell on one kiss that way. Yet, she could still remember exactly how his mouth had molded to hers, how the dark, male taste of him had seeped into her. With no effort at all, she could feel the way his body had fit against hers, strong and hard. It didn't please her.

There were enough problems to be dealt with during her stay in Friendly, Tory reminded herself, without dwelling on a chance encounter with some bad-tempered Hollywood type. She'd promised to ease the town through its transition to a new sheriff; there was the boy, Tod, on her mind. And her mother. Tory closed her eyes for a moment. She had yet to come to terms with her mother.

So many things had been said after her father's death. So many things had been left unsaid. For a woman who was rarely confused, Tory found herself in a turmoil whenever she dealt with her mother. As long as her father had been alive, he'd been the buffer between them. Now, with him gone, they were faced

with each other. With a wry laugh Tory decided her
mother was just as baffled as she was. The strain between them wasn't lessening, and the distance was
growing. With a shake of her head she decided to let it
lie. In a few months Tory would be back in Albuquerque and that would be that. She had her life to live, her
mother had hers.

The wise thing to do, she mused, was to develop
the same attitude toward Phil Kincaid. Their paths
weren't likely to cross again. She had purposely ab-
sented herself from town for a few hours to avoid him.
Tory made a face at the admission. No, she didn't want
to see him again. He was trouble. It was entirely too
easy for him to be charming when he put his mind to
it. And she was wise enough to recognize determination when she saw it. For whatever reason—pique or
attraction—he wanted her. He wouldn't be an easy
man to handle. Under most circumstances Tory might
have enjoyed pitting her will against his, but something warned her not to press her luck.

"The sooner he's back in Tinseltown, the better,"
she muttered, then pressed her heels against the horse's
sides. They were off at a full gallop.

Phil pulled his car to a halt beside the corral and
glanced around. A short distance to the right was a
small white-framed house. It was a very simple structure, two stories high with a wide wooden porch. On
the side was a clothesline with a few things baking dry
in the sun. There were a few spots of color from flowers in pottery pots on either side of the steps. The grass
was short and parched. One of the window screens
was torn. In the background he could see a few outbuildings and what appeared to be the beginnings of

a vegetable garden. Tory's sheriff's car was parked in front, freshly washed but already coated with a thin film of dust.

Something about the place appealed to him. It was isolated and quiet. Without the car in front, it might fit into any time frame in the past century. There had been some efforts to keep it neat, but it would never be prosperous. He would consider it more a homestead than a ranch. With the right lighting, he mused, it could be very effective. Climbing out of the car, Phil moved to the right to study it from a different angle. When he heard the low drum of hoofs, he turned and watched Tory approach.

He forgot the house immediately and swore at his lack of a camera. She was perfect. Under the merciless sun she rode a palamino the shade of new gold. Nothing could have been a better contrast for a woman of her coloring. With her hat again at her back, her hair flew freely. She sat straight, her movements in perfect timing with the horse's. Phil narrowed his eyes and saw them in slow motion. That was how he would film it—with her hair lifting, holding for a moment before it fell again. The dust would hang in the air behind them. The horse's strong legs would fold and unfold so that the viewer could see each muscle work. This was strength and beauty and a mastery of rider over horse. He wished he could see her hands holding the reins.

He knew the moment she became aware of him. The rhythm never faltered, but there was a sudden tension in the set of her shoulders. It made him smile. No, we're not through yet, he thought to himself. Not nearly through. Leaning against the corral fence, he waited for her.

Tory brought the palamino to a stop with a quick tug of reins. Remaining in the saddle, she gave Phil

a long, silent look. Casually he took sunglasses out of
his pocket and slipped them on. The gesture annoyed
her. "Kincaid," she said coolly.

"Sheriff," he returned.

"Is there a problem?"

He smiled slowly. "I don't think so."

Tory tossed her hair behind her shoulder, trying to
disguise the annoyance she felt at finding him there. "I
thought you'd be halfway to L.A. by now."

"Did you?"

With a sound of impatience she dismounted. The
saddle creaked with the movement as she brought one
slim leg over it, then vaulted lightly to the ground.
Keeping the reins in her hand, she studied him a moment. "I assume your fine's been paid. You know the
other charges were dropped."

"Yes."

She tilted her head. "Well?"

"Well," he returned amiably, amused at the temper
that shot into her eyes. *Yes, I'm getting to you, Victoria, he thought, and I haven't even started yet.*

Deliberately she turned away to uncinch the saddle. "Has Mr. Sherman gone?"

"No, he's discussing flies and lures with the mayor."
Phil grinned. "Lou found a fishing soulmate."

"I see." Tory hefted the saddle from the palamino,
then set it on the fence. "Then you discussed your
business with the mayor this morning."

"We came to an amicable agreement," Phil replied,
watching as she slipped the bit from the horse's mouth.
"He'll give you the details."

Without speaking, Tory gave the horse a slap on
the flank, sending him inside the corral. The gate gave
a long creak as she shut it. She turned then to face Phil
directly. "Why should he?"

"You'll want to know the schedule and so forth before the filming starts."

Her brows drew together. "I beg your pardon."

"I came to New Mexico scouting out a location for my new movie. I needed a tired little town in the middle of nowhere."

Tory studied him for a full ten seconds. "And you found it," she said flatly.

"Thanks to you." He smiled, appreciating the irony. "We'll start next month."

Sticking her hands in her back pockets, Tory turned to walk a short distance away. "Wouldn't it be simpler to shoot in a studio or in a lot?"

"No."

At his flat answer she turned back again. "I don't like it."

"I didn't think you would." He moved over to join her. "But you're going to live with it for the better part of the summer."

"You're going to bring your cameras and your people and your confusion into town," she began angrily. "Friendly runs at its own pace. Now you want to bring in a lifestyle most of these people can't even imagine."

"We'll give very sedate orgies, Sheriff," he promised with a grin. He laughed at the fury that leaped to her eyes. "Tory, you're not a fool. We're not coming to party, we're coming to work. Keep an actor out in this sun for ten takes, he's not going to be disturbing the peace at night. He's going to be unconscious." He caught a strand of her hair and twisted it around his finger. "Or do you believe everything you read in *Inside Scoop?*"

She swiped his hand away in an irritated gesture. "I know more about Hollywood than you know about Friendly," she retorted. "I've spent some time in L.A., represented a screenwriter in an assault case. Got him off," she added wryly. "A few years ago I dated an actor, went to a few parties when I was on the coast." She shook her head, "The gossip magazines might exaggerate, Phil, but the values and lifestyle come through loud and clear."

He lifted a brow. "Judgmental, Tory?"

"Maybe," she agreed. "But this is my town. I'm responsible for the people and for the peace. If you go ahead with this, I warn you, one of your people gets out of line, he goes to jail."

His eyes narrowed. "We have our own security."

"Your security answers to me in my town," she tossed back. "Remember it."

"Not going to cooperate, are you?"

"Not any more than I have to."

For a moment they stood measuring each other in silence. Behind them the palamino paced restlessly around the corral. A fleeting, precious breeze came up to stir the heat and dust. "All right," Phil said at length, "let's say you stay out of my way, I'll stay out of yours."

"Perfect," Tory agreed, and started to walk away. Phil caught her arm.

"That's professionally," he added.

As she had in his cell, Tory gave the hand on her arm a long look before she raised her eyes to his. This time Phil smiled.

"You're not wearing your badge now, Tory." Reaching up, he drew off his sunglasses, then hooked them over the corral fence. "And we're not finished."

"Kincaid—"

"Phil," he corrected, drawing her deliberately into his arms. "I thought of you last night when I was lying in that damned cell. I promised myself something."

Tory stiffened. Her palms pressed against his chest, but she didn't struggle. Physically he was stronger, she reasoned. She had to rely on her wits. "Your thoughts and your promises aren't my problem;" she replied coolly. "Whether I'm wearing my badge or not, I'm still sheriff, and you're annoying me. I can be mean when I'm annoyed."

"I'll just bet you can be," he murmured. Even had he wanted to, he couldn't prevent his eyes from lingering on her mouth. "I'm going to have you, Victoria," he said softly. "Sooner or later." Slowly he brought his eyes back to hers. "I always keep my promises."

"I believe I have something to say about this one."

His smile was confident. "Say no," he whispered before his mouth touched hers. She started to jerk back, but he was quick. His hand cupped the back of her head and kept her still. His mouth was soft and persuasive. Long before the stiffness left her, he felt the pounding of her heart against his. Patiently he rubbed his lips over hers, teasing, nibbling. Tory let out an unsteady breath as her fingers curled into his shirt.

He smelled of soap, a fragrance that was clean and sharp. Unconsciously she breathed it in as he drew her closer. Her arms had found their way around his neck. Her body was straining against his, no longer stiff but eager. The mindless pleasure was back, and she surrendered to it. She heard his quiet moan before his lips left hers, but before she could protest, he pressed them to her throat. He was murmuring something neither of them understood as his mouth began to explore. The desperation came suddenly, as if it had been waiting to take them both unaware. His mouth was back on hers with a quick savageness that she anticipated.

She felt the scrape of his teeth and answered by

nipping into his bottom lip. The hands at her hips dragged her closer, tormenting both of them. Passion flowed between them so acutely that avid, seeking lips weren't enough. He ran his hands up her sides, letting his thumbs find their way between their clinging bodies to stroke her breasts. She responded by diving deep into his mouth and demanding more.

Tory felt everything with impossible clarity: the soft, thin material of her shirt rubbing against the straining points of her breasts as his thumbs pressed against her; the heat of his mouth as it roamed wildly over her face, then back to hers; the vibration of two heartbeats.

He hadn't expected to feel this degree of need. Attraction and challenge, but not pain. It wasn't what he had planned—it wasn't what he wanted, and yet, he couldn't stop. She was filling his mind, crowding his senses. Her hair was too soft, her scent too alluring. And her taste . . . her taste too exotic. Greedily, he devoured her while her passion drove him farther into her.

He knew he had to back away, but he lingered a moment longer. Her body was so sleek and lean, her mouth so incredibly agile. Phil allowed himself to stroke her once more, one last bruising contact of lips before he dragged himself away.

They were both shaken and both equally determined not to admit it. Tory felt her pulse hammering at every point in her body. Because her knees were trembling, she stood very straight. Phil waited a moment, wanting to be certain he could speak. Reaching over, he retrieved his sunglasses and put them back on. They were some defense; a better one was to put some distance between them until he found his control.

"You didn't say no," he commented.

Tory stared at him, warning herself not to think until later. "I didn't say yes," she countered.

He smiled. "Oh, yes," he corrected, "you did. I'll be back," he added before he strode to his car.

Driving away, he glanced in his rearview mirror to see her standing where he had left her. As he punched in his cigarette lighter he saw his hand was shaking. Round three, he thought on a long breath, was a draw.

CHAPTER 4

Tory stood exactly where she was until even the dust kicked up by Phil's tires had settled. She had thought she knew the meaning of passion, need, excitement. Suddenly the words had taken on a new meaning. For the first time in her life she had been seized by something that her mind couldn't control. The hunger had been so acute, so unexpected. It throbbed through her still, like an ache, as she stared down the long flat road, which was now deserted. How was it possible to need so badly, so quickly? And how was it, she wondered, that a woman who had always handled men with such casual ease could be completely undone by a kiss?

Tory shook her head and made herself turn away from the road Phil had taken. None of it was characteristic. It was almost as if she had been someone else for a moment—someone whose strength and weakness could be drawn out and manipulated. And yet, even now, when she had herself under control, there was something inside her fighting to be recognized. She was going to have to take some time and think about this carefully.

Hoisting the saddle, Tory carried it toward the barn. *I'll be back.* Phil's last words echoed in her ears and sent an odd thrill over her skin. Scowling, Tory pushed open the barn door. It was cooler inside, permeated with the pungent scent of animals and hay. It was a scent of her childhood, one she barely noticed even when returning after months away from it. It never occurred to her to puzzle over why she was as completely at home there as she was in a tense courtroom or at a sophisticated party. After replacing the tack, she paced the concrete floor a moment and began to dissect the problem.

Phil Kincaid was the problem; the offshoots were her strong attraction to him, his effect on her, and the fact that he was coming back. The attraction, Tory decided, was unprecedented but not astonishing. He was appealing, intelligent, fun. Even his faults had a certain charm. If they had met under different circumstances, she could imagine them getting to know each other slowly, dating perhaps, enjoying a congenial relationship. Part of the spark, she mused, was due to the way they had met, and the fact that each was determined not to be outdone by the other. That made sense, she concluded, feeling better.

And if that made sense, she went on, it followed that his effect on her was intensified by circumstances. Logic was comfortable, so Tory pursued it. There was something undeniably attractive about a man who wouldn't take no for an answer. It might be annoying, even infuriating, but it was still exciting. Beneath the sheriff's badge and behind the Harvard diploma, Tory was a woman first and last. It didn't hurt when a man knew how to kiss the way Phil Kincaid knew how to kiss, she added wryly. Unable to resist, Tory ran the tip of her tongue over her lips.

Oh, yes, she thought with a quick smile, the man was some terrific kisser.

Vaguely annoyed with herself, Tory wandered from the barn. The sun made her wince in defense as she headed for the house. Unconsciously killing time, she poked inside the henhouse. The hens were sleeping in the heat of the afternoon, their heads tucked under their wings. Tory left them alone, knowing her mother had gathered the eggs that morning.

The problem now was that he was coming back. She was going to have to deal with him—and with his own little slice of Hollywood, she added with a frown. At the moment Tory wasn't certain which disturbed her more. Damn, but she wished she'd known of Phil's plans. If she could have gotten to the mayor first . . . Tory stopped herself with a self-deprecating laugh. She would have changed absolutely nothing. As mayor, Bud Toomey would eat up the prestige of having a major film shot in his town. And as the owner of the one and only hotel, he must have heard the dollars clinking in his cash register.

Who could blame him? Tory asked herself. Her objections were probably more personal than professional in any case. The actor she had dated had been successful and slick, an experienced womanizer and hedonist. She knew too many of her prejudices lay at his feet. She'd been very young when he'd shown her Hollywood from his vantage point. But even without that, she reasoned, there was the disruption the filming would bring to Friendly, the effect on the townspeople and the very real possibility of property damage. As sheriff, all of it fell to her jurisdiction.

What would her father have done? she wondered as she stepped into the house. As always, the moment she was inside, memories of him assailed her—his big, booming voice, his laughter, his simple, man-of-the-earth logic. To Tory his presence was an intimate part of everything in the house, down to the hassock where he had habitually rested his feet after a long day.

The house was her mother's doing. There were the clean white walls in the living room, the sofa that had been re-covered again and again—this time it wore a tidy floral print. The rugs were straight and clean, the pictures carefully aligned. Even they had been chosen to blend in rather than to accent. Her mother's collection of cacti sat on the windowsill. The fragrance of a potpourri, her mother's mixture, wafted comfortably in the air. The floors and furniture were painstakingly clean, magazines neatly tucked away. A single geranium stood in a slender vase on a crocheted doily. All her mother's doing; yet, it was her father Tory thought of when she entered her childhood home. It always was.

But her father wouldn't come striding down the steps again. He wouldn't catch her to him for one of his bear hugs and noisy kisses. He'd been too young to die, Tory thought as she gazed around the room as though she were a stranger. Strokes were for old men, feeble men, not strapping men in their prime. There was no justice to it, she thought with the same impotent fury that hit her each time she came back. No justice for a man who had dedicated his life to justice. He should have had more time, might have had more time, if . . . Her thoughts broke off as she heard the quiet sounds coming from the kitchen.

Tory pushed away the pain. It was difficult enough to see her mother without remembering that last night in the hospital. She gave herself an extra moment to settle before she crossed to the kitchen.

Standing in the doorway, she watched as Helen re-lined the shelves in the kitchen cabinets. Her mother's

consistent tidiness had been a sore point between them
since Tory had been a girl. The woman she watched
was tiny and blonde, a youthful-looking fifty, with
ladylike hands and a trim pink housedress. Tory knew
the dress had been pressed and lightly starched. Her
mother would smell faintly of soap and nothing else.
Even physically Tory felt remote from her. Her looks,
her temperament, had all come from her father. Tory
could see nothing of herself in the woman who patiently lined shelves with dainty striped paper. They'd
never been more than careful strangers to each other,
more careful as the years passed. Tory kept a room at
the hotel rather than at home for the same reason she
kept her visits with her mother brief. Invariably their
encounters ended badly.

"Mother."

Surprised, Helen turned. She didn't gasp or whirl
at the intrusion, but simply faced Tory with one brow
slightly lifted. "Tory. I thought I heard a car drive away."

"It was someone else."

"I saw you ride out." Helen straightened the paper
meticulously. "There's lemonade in the refrigerator. It's
a dry day." Without speaking, Tory fetched two glasses
and added ice. "How are you, Tory?"

"Very well." She hated the stiffness but could do
nothing about it. So much stood between them. Even
as she poured the fresh lemonade from her mother's
marigold-trimmed glass pitcher, she could remember
the night of her father's death, the ugly words she had
spoken, the ugly feelings she had not quite put to rest.
They had never understood each other, never been
close, but that night had brought a gap between them
that neither knew how to bridge. It only seemed to
grow wider with time.

Needing to break the silence, Tory spoke as she

replaced the pitcher in the refrigerator. "Do you know anything about the Swansons?"

"The Swansons?" The question in Helen's voice was mild. She would never have asked directly. "They've lived outside of town for twenty years. They keep to themselves, though she's come to church a few times. I believe he has a difficult time making his ranch pay. The oldest son was a good-looking boy, about sixteen when he left." Helen replaced her everyday dishes on the shelf in tidy stacks, then closed the cupboard door. "That would have been about four years ago. The younger one seems rather sweet and painfully shy."

"Tod," Tory murmured.

"Yes." Helen read the concern but knew nothing about drawing people out, particularly her daughter. "I heard about Mr. Hollister's window."

Tory lifted her eyes briefly. Her mother's were a calm, deep brown. "The Kramer twins."

A suggestion of a smile flickered on her mother's lips. "Yes, of course."

"Do you know why the older Swanson boy left home?"

Helen picked up the drink Tory had poured her. But she didn't sit. "Rumor is that Mr. Swanson has a temper. Gossip is never reliable," she added before she drank.

"And often based in fact," Tory countered.

They fell into one of the stretches of silence that characteristically occurred during their visits. The refrigerator gave a loud click and began to hum. Helen carefully wiped away the ring of moisture her glass had made on the countertop.

"It seems Friendly is about to be immortalized on film," Tory began. At her mother's puzzled look she continued. "I had Phillip C. Kincaid in a cell overnight.

Now it appears he's going to use Friendly as one of the location shoots for his latest film."

"Kincaid," Helen repeated, searching her mind slowly. "Oh, Marshall Kincaid's son."

Tory grinned despite herself. She didn't think Phil would appreciate that sort of recognition; it occurred to her simultaneously that it was a tag he must have fought all of his professional career. "Yes," she agreed thoughtfully. "He's a very successful director," she found herself saying, almost in defense, "with an impressive string of hits. He's been nominated for an Oscar three times."

Though Helen digested this, her thoughts were still on Tory's original statement. "Did you say you had him in jail?"

Tory shook off the mood and smiled a little. "Yes, I did. Traffic violation," she added with a shrug. "It got a little complicated. . . ." Her voice trailed off as she remembered that stunning moment in his cell when his mouth had taken hers. "He's coming back," she murmured.

"To make a film?" Helen prompted, puzzled by her daughter's bemused expression.

"What? Yes," Tory said quickly. "Yes, he's going to do some filming here, I don't have the details yet. It seems he cleared it with the mayor this morning."

But not with you, Helen thought, but didn't say so. "How interesting."

"We'll see," Tory muttered. Suddenly restless, she rose to pace to the sink. The view from the window was simply a long stretch of barren ground that was somehow fascinating. Her father had loved it for what it was—stark and desolate.

Watching her daughter, Helen could remember her husband standing exactly the same way, looking out with exactly the same expression. She felt an intolerable wave of grief and controlled it. "Friendly will be buzzing about this for quite some time," she said briskly.

"It'll buzz all right," Tory muttered. But no one will think of the complications, she added to herself.

"Do you expect trouble?" her mother asked.

"I'll handle it."

"Always so sure of yourself, Tory."

Tory's shoulders stiffened automatically. "Am I, Mother?" Turning, she found her mother's eyes, calm and direct, on her. They had been just that calm, and just that direct, when she had told Tory she had requested her father's regulator be unplugged. Tory had seen no sorrow, no regret or indecision. There had been only the passive face and the matter-of-fact words. For that, more than anything else, Tory had never forgiven her.

As they watched each other in the sun-washed kitchen, each remembered clearly the garishly lit waiting room that smelled of old cigarettes and sweat. Each remembered the monotonous hum of the air conditioner and the click of feet on tile in the corridor outside . . .

"No!" Tory had whispered the word, then shouted it. "No, you can't! You can't just let him die!"

"He's already gone, Tory," Helen had said flatly. "You have to accept it."

"No!" After weeks of seeing her father lying motionless with a machine pumping oxygen into his body, Tory had been crazy with grief and fear. She had been a long, long way from acceptance. She'd watched her mother sit calmly while she had paced—watched her sip tea while her own stomach had revolted at the thought of food. *Brain-dead.* The phrase had made her violently ill. It was she who had wept uncontrollably at her father's bedside while Helen had stood dry-eyed.

"You don't care," Tory had accused. "It's easier for you this way. You can go back to your precious routine and not be disturbed."

Helen had looked at her daughter's ravaged face and nodded. "It is easier this way."

"I won't let you." Desperate, Tory had pushed her hands through her hair and tried to think. "There are ways to stop you. I'll get a court order, and—"

"It's already done," Helen had told her quietly.

All the color had drained from Tory's face, just as she had felt all the strength drain from her body. Her father was dead. At the flick of a switch he was dead. Her mother had flicked the switch. "You killed him."

Helen hadn't winced or shrunk from the words. "You know better than that, Tory."

"If you'd loved him—if you'd loved him, you couldn't have done this."

"And your kind of love would have him strapped to that machine, helpless and empty."

"Alive!" Tory had tossed back, letting hate wash over the unbearable grief. "Damn you, he was still alive."

"Gone," Helen had countered, never raising her voice. "He'd been gone for days. For weeks, really. It's time you dealt with it."

"It's so easy for you, isn't it?" Tory had forced back the tears because she had wanted—needed—to meet her mother on her own terms. "Nothing—no one—has ever managed to make you *feel*. Not even him."

"There are different kinds of love, Tory," Helen returned stiffly. "You've never understood anything but your own way."

"Love?" Tory had gripped her hands tightly together to keep from striking out. "I've never seen you show

anyone love. Now Dad's gone, but you don't cry. You
don't mourn. You'll go home and hang out the wash
because nothing—by God, nothing—can interfere
with your precious routine."

Helen's shoulders had been very straight as she
faced her daughter. "I won't apologize for being what I
am," she had said. "Any more than I expect you to defend yourself to me. But I do say you loved your father
too much, Victoria. For that I'm sorry."

Tory had wrapped her arms around herself tightly,
unconsciously rocking. "Oh, you're so cold," she had
whispered. "So cold. You have no feelings." She had
badly needed comfort then, a word, an arm around her.
But Helen was unable to offer, Tory unable to ask. "You
did this," she had said in a strained, husky voice. "You
took him from me. I'll never forgive you for it."

"No." Helen had nodded slightly. "I don't expect
you will. You're always so sure of yourself, Tory."

Now the two women watched each other across a
new grave: dry-eyed, expressionless. A man who had
been husband and father stood between them still.
Words threatened to pour out again—harsh, bitter
words. Each swallowed them.

"I have to get back to town," Tory told her. She
walked from the room and from the house. After
standing in the silence a moment, Helen turned back
to her shelves.

The pool was shaped like a crescent and its water was deep, deep blue. There were palm trees
swaying gently in the night air. The scent of flowers
was strong, almost tropical. It was a cool spot, secluded by trees, banked with blossoming bushes. A
narrow terrace outlined the pool with mosaic tile that

glimmered in the moonlight. Speakers had been craftily camouflaged so that the strains of Debussy seemed to float out of the air. A tall iced drink laced with Jamaican rum sat on a glass-topped patio table beside a telephone.

Still wet from his swim, Phil lounged on a chaise. Once again he tried to discipline his mind. He'd spent the entire day filming two key scenes in the studio. He'd had a little trouble with Sam Dressier, the leading man. It wasn't surprising. Dressier didn't have a reputation for being congenial or cooperative, just for being good. Phil wasn't looking to make a lifelong friendship, just a film. Still, when the clashes began this early in a production, it wasn't a good omen of things to come. He was going to have to use some strategy in handling Dressier.

At least, Phil mused as he absently picked up his drink, he'd have no trouble with the crew. He'd handpicked them and had worked with each and every one of them before. Bicks, his cinematographer, was the best in the business—creative enough to be innovative and practical enough not to insist on making a statement with each frame. His assistant director was a workhorse who knew the way Phil's mind worked. Phil knew his crew down to the last gaffer and grip. When they went on location . . .

Phil's thoughts drifted back to Tory, as they had insisted on doing for days. She was going to be pretty stiff-necked about having her town invaded, he reflected. She'd hang over his shoulder with that tin badge pinned to her shirt. Phil hated to admit that the idea appealed to him. With a little pre-planning, he could find a number of ways to put himself in her path. Oh, yes, he intended to spend quite a bit of time getting under Sheriff Ashton's skin.

Soft, smooth skin, Phil remembered, that smelled faintly of something that a man might find in a harem. Dark, dusky, and titillating. He could picture her in silk, something chic and vivid, with nothing underneath but that long, lean body of hers.

The quick flash of desire annoyed him enough to cause him to toss back half his drink. He intended to get under her skin, but he didn't intend for it to work the other way around. He knew women, how to please them, charm them. He also knew how to avoid the complication of *one* woman. There was safety in numbers; using that maxim, Phil had enjoyed his share of women.

He liked them not only sexually but as companions. A great many of the women whose names he had been romantically linked with were simply friends. The number of women he had been credited with conquering amused him. He could hardly have worked the kind of schedule he imposed on himself if he spent all his time in the bedroom. Still, he had enjoyed perhaps a bit more than his share of romances, always careful to keep the tone light and the rules plain. He intended to do exactly the same thing with Tory.

It might be true that she was on his mind a great deal more often than any other woman in his memory. It might be true that he had been affected more deeply by her than anyone else. But . . .

Phil frowned over the *but* a moment. But, he reaffirmed, it was just because their meeting had been unique. The memory of his night in the steamy little cell caused him to grimace. He hadn't paid her back for that yet, and he was determined to. He hadn't cared for being under someone else's control. He'd grown used to deference in his life, a respect that had come first through his parents and then through his own

talent. He never thought much about money. The fact
that he hadn't been able to buy himself out of the cell
was infuriating. Though more often than not he did
for himself, he was accustomed to servants—perhaps
more to having his word obeyed. Tory hadn't done
what he ordered, and had done what he asked only
when it had suited her.

It didn't matter that Phil was annoyed when people
fawned over him or catered to him. That was what he
was used to. Instead of fawning, Tory had been lightly
disdainful, had tossed out a compliment on his work,
then laughed at him. And had made him laugh, he remembered.

He wanted to know more about her. For days he had
toyed with the notion of having someone check into
Victoria L. Ashton, Attorney. What had stopped him
had not been a respect for privacy so much as a desire
to make the discoveries himself. Who was a woman
who had a face like a madonna, a voice like whiskey
and honey, and handled a .45? Phil was going to find
out if it took all of the dry, dusty summer. He'd find the
time, he mused, although the shooting schedule was
backbreaking.

Leaning back against the cushion of the chaise,
Phil looked up at the sky. He'd refused the invitation
to a party on the excuse that he had work and a scene
to shoot early in the morning. Now he was thinking
of Tory instead of the film, and he no longer had any
sense of time. He knew he should work her out of his
system so that he could give the film his full attention,
without distractions. He knew he wouldn't. Since he'd
returned from Friendly, he hadn't had the least inclination to pick up the phone and call any of the women
he knew. He could pacify friends and acquaintances
by using the excuse of his work schedule, but he knew.

There was only one companion he wanted at the moment, one woman. One lover.

He wanted to kiss her again to be certain he hadn't imagined the emotions he had felt. And the sense of *rightness*. Oddly, he found he didn't want to dilute the sensation with the taste or feel of another woman. It worried him but he brushed it off, telling himself that the obsession would fade once he had Tory where he wanted her. What worried him more was the fact that he wanted to talk to her. Just talk.

Vaguely disturbed, Phil rose. He was tired, that was all. And there was that new script to read before he went to bed. The house was silent when he entered through the glass terrace doors. Even the music had stopped without his noticing. He stepped down into the sunken living room, the glass still in his hand.

The room smelled very faintly of the lemon oil the maid had used that morning. The maroon floor tiles shone. On the deep, plump cushions of the sofa a dozen pillows were tossed with a carelessness that was both inviting and lush. He himself had chosen the tones of blue and green and ivory that dominated the room, as well as the Impressionist painting on the wall, the only artwork in the room. There were mirrors and large expanses of windows that gave the room openness. It held nothing of the opulence of the houses he had grown up in, yet maintained the same ambience of money and success. Phil was easy with it, as he was with his life, himself, and his views on his future.

Crossing the room, he walked toward the curving open staircase that led to the second floor. The treads were uncarpeted. His bare feet slapped the wood gently. He was thinking that he had been pleased with the rushes. He and Huffman had watched them together. Now that the filming was progressing, his producer was more amiable. There were fewer mutterings about guarantors and cost overruns. And Huffman had been pleased with the idea of shooting the bulk of the film on location. Financially the deal with Friendly had been advantageous. Nothing put a smile on a producer's face quicker, Phil thought wryly. He went to shower.

The bath was enormous. Even more than the secluded location, it had been Phil's main incentive for buying the house high in the hills. The shower ran along one wall, with the spray shooting from both sides. He switched it on, stripping out of his trunks while the bathroom grew steamy. Even as he stepped inside, he remembered the cramped little stall he had showered in that stifling morning in Friendly.

The soap had still been wet, he recalled, from Tory. It had been a curiously intimate feeling to rub the small cake along his own skin and imagine it sliding over hers. Then he had run out of hot water while he was still covered with lather. He'd cursed her fluently and wanted her outrageously. Standing between the hot crisscrossing sprays, Phil knew he still did. On impulse he reached out and grabbed the phone that hung on the wall beside the shower.

"I want to place a call to Friendly, New Mexico," he told the operator. Ignoring the time, he decided to take a chance. "The sheriff's office." Phil waited while steam rose from the shower. The phone clicked and hummed, then rang.

"Sheriff's office."

The sound of her voice made him grin. "Sheriff."

Tory frowned, setting down the coffee that was keeping her awake over the brief she was drafting. "Yes?"

"Phil Kincaid."

There was complete silence as Tory's mouth opened and closed. She felt a thrill she considered ridiculously juvenile and straightened at her desk. "Well," she said lightly, "did you forget your toothbrush?"

"No." He was at a loss for a moment, struggling to formulate a reasonable excuse for the call. He wasn't a love-struck teenager who called his girl just to hear her voice. "The shooting's on schedule," he told her, thinking fast. "We'll be in Friendly next week. I wanted to be certain there were no problems."

Tory glanced over at the cell, remembering how he had looked standing there. "Your location manager has been in touch with me and the mayor," she said, deliberately turning her eyes away from the cell. "You have all the necessary permits. The hotel's booked for you. I had to fight to keep my own room. Several people are making arrangements to rent out rooms in their homes to accommodate you." She didn't have to add that the idea didn't appeal to her. Her tone told him everything. Again he found himself grinning.

"Still afraid we're going to corrupt your town, Sheriff?"

"You and your people will stay in line, Kincaid," she returned, "or you'll have your old room back."

"It's comforting to know you have it waiting for me. Are you?"

"Waiting for you?" She gave a quick snort of laughter. "Just like the Egyptians waited for the next plague."

"Ah, Victoria, you've a unique way of putting things."

Tory frowned, listening to the odd hissing on the line. "What's that noise?"

"Noise?"

"It sounds like water running."

"It is," he told her. "I'm in the shower."

For a full ten seconds Tory said nothing, then she burst out laughing. "Phil, why did you call me from the shower?"

Something about her laughter and the way she said his name had him struggling against a fresh torrent of needs. "Because it reminded me of you."

Tory propped her feet on the desk, forgetting her brief. Something in her was softening. "Oh?" was all she said.

"I remembered running out of hot water halfway through my shower in your guest room." He pushed wet hair out of his eyes. "At the time I wasn't in the mood to lodge a formal complaint."

"I'll take it up with the management." She caught her tongue between her teeth for a moment. "I wouldn't expect deluxe accommodations in the hotel, Kincaid. There's no room service or phones in the bathroom."

"We'll survive."

"That's yet to be seen," she said dryly. "Your group may undergo culture shock when they find themselves without a Jacuzzi."

"You really think we're a soft bunch, don't you?" Annoyed, Phil switched the phone to his other hand. It nearly slid out of his wet palm. "You may learn a few things about the people in the business this summer, Victoria. I'm going to enjoy teaching you."

"There's nothing I want to learn from you," she said quietly.

"*Want* and *need* are entirely different words," he pointed out. He could almost see the flash of temper leap into her eyes. It gave him a curious pleasure.

"As long as you play by the rules, there won't be any trouble."

"There'll be a time, Tory," he murmured into the receiver, "that you and I will play by my rules. I still have a promise to keep."

Tory pulled her legs from the desk so that her boots hit the floor with a clatter. "Don't forget to wash behind your ears," she ordered, then hung up with a bang.

CHAPTER 5

Tory was in her office when they arrived. The rumble of cars outside could mean only one thing. She forced herself to complete the form she was filling out before she rose from her desk. Of course she wasn't in any hurry to see him again, but it was her duty to be certain the town remained orderly during the arrival of the people from Hollywood. Still, she hesitated a moment, absently fingering her badge. She hadn't yet resolved how she was going to handle Phil. She knew the law clearly enough, but the law wouldn't help when she had to deal with him without her badge. Tod burst through the door, his eyes wide, his face flushed.

"Tory, they're here! A whole bunch of them in front of the hotel. There're vans and cars and everything!"

Though she felt more like swearing, she had to smile at him. He only forgot himself and called her Tory when he was desperately excited. And he was such a sweet boy, she mused, so full of dreams. Crossing to him, she dropped an arm over his shoulder. He no longer cringed.

"Let's go see," she said simply.

"Tory—Sheriff," Tod corrected himself, although the words all but tumbled over each other, "do you think that guy'll let me watch him make the movie? You know, the guy you had in jail."

"I know," Tory murmured as they stepped outside. "I imagine so," she answered absentmindedly.

The scene outside was so out of place in Friendly, it almost made Tory laugh. There were several vehicles in front of the hotel, and crowds of people. The mayor stood on the sidewalk, talking to everyone at once. Several of the people from California were looking around the town with expressions of curiosity and astonishment. They were being looked over with the same expressions by people from Friendly.

Different planets, Tory mused with a slight smile. Take me to your leader. When she spotted Phil, the smile faded.

He was dressed casually, as he had been on his first visit to town—no different than the members of his crew. And yet, there was a difference. He held the authority; there was no mistaking it. Even while apparently listening to the mayor, he was giving orders. And, Tory added thoughtfully, being obeyed. There seemed to be a certain friendliness between him and his crew, as well as an underlying respect. There was some laughter and a couple of shouts as equipment was unloaded, but the procedure was meticulously orderly. He watched over every detail.

"Wow," Tod said under his breath. "Look at all that stuff. I bet they've got cameras in those boxes. Maybe I'll get a chance to look through one."

"Mmm." Tory saw Phil laugh and heard the sound of it drift to her across the street. Then he saw her.

His smile didn't fade but altered subtly. They assessed each other while his people milled and hers whispered. The assessment became a challenge with no words spoken. She stood very straight, her arm still casually draped around the boy's shoulders. Phil noticed the gesture even as he felt a stir that wasn't wholly pleasant. He ached, he discovered, baffled. Just looking at her made him ache. She looked cool, even remote, but her eyes were directed at his. He could see the small badge pinned to the gentle sweep of her breast. On the dry, sweltering day she was wine, potent and irresistible—and perhaps unwise. One of his crew addressed him twice before Phil heard him.

"What?" His eyes never left Tory's.

"Huffman's on the phone."

"I'll get back to him." Phil started across the street.

When Tory's arm stiffened, Tod glanced up at her in question. He saw that her eyes were fixed on the man walking toward them. He frowned, but when Tory's arm relaxed, so did he.

Phil stopped just short of the sidewalk so that their eyes were at the same level. "Sheriff."

"Kincaid," she said coolly.

Briefly he turned to the boy and smiled. "Hello, Tod. How are you?"

"Fine." The boy stared at him from under a thatch of tumbled hair. The fact that Phil had spoken to him, and remembered his name, made something move inside Tory. She pushed it away, reminding herself she couldn't afford too many good feelings toward Phil Kincaid. "Can I . . ." Tod began. He shifted nervously, then drew up his courage. "Do you think I could see some of that stuff?"

A grin flashed on Phil's face. "Sure. Go over and ask for Bicks. Tell him I said to show you a camera."

"Yeah?" Thrilled, he stared at Phil for a moment, then glanced up at Tory in question. When she smiled down at him, Phil watched the boy's heart leap to his eyes.

Uh-oh, he thought, seeing the slight flush creep into the boy's cheeks. Tory gave him a quick squeeze and the color deepened.

"Go ahead," she told him.

Phil watched the boy dash across the street before he turned his gaze back to Tory. "It seems you have another conquest. I have to admire his taste." When she stared at him blankly, he shook his head. "Good God, Tory, the kid's in love with you."

"Don't be ridiculous," she retorted. "He's a child."

"Not quite," he countered. "And certainly old enough to be infatuated with a beautiful woman." He grinned again, seeing her distress as her eyes darted after Tod. "I was a fourteen-year-old boy once myself."

Annoyed that he had pointed out something she'd been oblivious to, Tory glared at him. "But never as innocent as that one."

"No," he agreed easily and stepped up on the sidewalk. She had to shift the angle of her chin to keep her eyes in line with his. "It's good to see you, Sheriff."

"Is it?" she returned lazily as she studied his face.

"Yes, I wondered if I'd imagined just how beautiful you were."

"You've brought quite a group with you," she commented, ignoring his statement. "There'll be more, I imagine."

"Some. I need some footage of the town, the countryside. The actors will be here in a couple of days."

Nodding, she leaned against a post. "You'll have to store your vehicles at Bestler's. If you have any plans to use a private residence or a store for filming, you'll have to make the arrangements individually. Hernandez's Bar is open until eleven on weeknights, one on

Saturday. Consumption of alcohol on the streets is subject to a fifty-dollar fine. You're liable for any damage
to private property. Whatever alterations you make for
the filming will again have to be cleared individually.
Anyone causing a disturbance in the hotel or on the
streets after midnight will be fined and sentenced. As
this is your show, Kincaid, I'll hold you personally responsible for keeping your people in line."

He listened to her rundown of the rules with the
appearance of careful interest. "Have dinner with me."

She very nearly smiled. "Forget it." When she started
to walk by him, he took her arm.

"Neither of us is likely to do that, are we?"

Tory didn't shake off his arm. It felt too good to be
touched by him again. She did, however, give him a
long, lazy look. "Phil, both of us have a job to do. Let's
keep it simple."

"By all means." He wondered what would happen if he kissed her right then and there. It was what
he wanted, he discovered, more than anything he had
wanted in quite some time. It would also be unwise.
"What if we call it a business dinner?"

Tory laughed. "Why don't we call it what it is?"

"Because then you wouldn't come, and I do want
to talk to you."

The simplicity of his answer disconcerted her.
"About what?"

"Several things." His fingers itched to move to her
face, to feel the soft, satiny texture of her skin. He kept
them loosely hooked around her arm. "Among them,
my show and your town. Wouldn't it simplify matters
for both of us if we understood each other and came to
a few basic agreements?"

"Maybe."

"Have dinner with me in my room." When her

brow arched, he continued lazily. "It's also my office for
the time being," he reminded her. "I'd like to clear the
air regarding my film. If we're going to argue, Sheriff,
let's do it privately."

The *Sheriff* did it. It was both her title and her job.
"All right," she agreed. "Seven o'clock."

"Fine." When she started to walk away, he stopped
her. "Sheriff," he said with a quick grin, "leave the gun
in the desk, okay? It'll kill my appetite."

She gave a snort of laughter. "I can handle you
without it, Kincaid."

T ory frowned at the clothes hanging inside her closet.
Even while she had been showering, she had considered putting on work clothes—and her badge—for
her dinner with Phil. But that would have been petty,
and pettiness wasn't her style. She ran a fingertip over
an emerald-green silk dress. It was very simply cut,
narrow, with a high neck that buttoned to the waist.
Serviceable and attractive, she decided, slipping it off
the hanger. Laying it across the bed, she shrugged out
of her robe.

Outside, the streets were quiet. She hoped they
stayed that way, as she'd put Merle in charge for the evening. People would be gathered in their homes, at the
drugstore, at the bar, discussing the filming. That had
been the main topic of the town for weeks, overriding
the heat, the lack of rain, and the Kramer twins. Tory
smiled as she laced the front of her teddy. Yes, people
needed their little entertainments, and this was the biggest thing to happen in Friendly in years. She was going
to have to roll with it. To a point.

She slipped the dress over her head, feeling the
silk slither on her skin. It had been a long time, she

realized, since she had bothered about clothes. In Albuquerque she took a great deal of care about her appearance. A courtroom image was as important as an opening statement, particularly in a jury trial. People judged. Still, she was a woman who knew how to incorporate style with comfort.

The dress flattered her figure while giving her complete freedom of movement. Tory looked in the bureautop mirror to study her appearance. The mirror cut her off at just above the waist. She rose on her toes and turned to the side but was still frustrated with a partial view of herself. Well, she decided, letting her feet go flat again, it would just have to do.

She sprayed on her scent automatically, remembering too late Phil's comment on it. Tory frowned at the delicate bottle as she replaced it on the dresser. She could hardly go and scrub the perfume off now. With a shrug she sat on the bed to put on her shoes. The mattress creaked alarmingly. Handling Phil Kincaid was no problem, she told herself. That was half the reason she had agreed to have dinner with him. It was a matter of principle. She wasn't a woman to be seduced or charmed into submission, particularly by a man of Kincaid's reputation. Spoiled, she thought again, but with a tad too much affection for her liking. He'd grown up privileged, in a world of glitter and glamour. He expected everything to come his way, women included.

Tory had grown up respecting the value of a dollar in a world of ordinary people and day-to-day struggles. She, too, expected everything to come her way—after she'd arranged it. She left the room determined to come out on top in the anticipated encounter. She even began to look forward to it.

Phil's room was right next door. Though she knew he had seen to that small detail himself, Tory planned to make no mention of it. She gave a brisk knock and waited.

When he opened the door, the glib remark Phil had intended to make vanished from his brain. He remembered his own thoughts about seeing her in something silk and vivid and could only stare. *Exquisite.* It was the word that hammered inside his brain, but even that wouldn't come through his lips. He knew at that moment he'd have to have her or go through his life obsessed with the need to.

"Victoria," he managed after a long moment.

Though her pulse had begun to pound at the look in his eyes, at the husky way he had said her name, she gave him a brisk smile. "Phillip," she said very formally. "Shall I come in or eat out here?"

Phil snapped back. Stammering and staring wasn't going to get him very far. He took her hand to draw her inside, then locked the door, uncertain whether he was locking her in or the world out.

Tory glanced around the small, haphazardly furnished room. Phil had already managed to leave his mark on it. The bureau was stacked with papers. There was a notepad, scrawled in from margin to margin, a few stubby pencils and a two-way radio. The shades were drawn and the room was lit with candles. Tory lifted her brows at this, glancing toward the folding card table covered with the hotel's best linen. Two dishes were covered to keep in the heat while a bottle of wine was open. Strolling over, Tory lifted it to study the label.

"Château Haut-Brion Blanc," she murmured with a perfect accent. Still holding the bottle, she sent Phil a look. "You didn't pick this up at Mendleson's Liquors."

"I always take a few . . . amenities when I go on location."

Tilting her head, Tory set down the bottle. "And the candles?"

"Local drugstore," he told her blandly.

"Wine and candlelight," she mused. "For a business dinner?"

"Humor the director," he suggested, crossing over to pour out two glasses of wine. "We're always setting scenes. It's uncontrollable." Handing her a glass, he touched it with the rim of his own. "Sheriff, to a comfortable relationship."

"Association," she corrected, then drank. "Very nice," she approved. She let her eyes skim over him briefly. He wore casual slacks, impeccably tailored, with an open-collared cream-colored shirt that accented his lean torso. The candlelight picked up the deep tones of red in his hair. "You look more suited to your profession than when I first saw you," she commented.

"And you less to yours," he countered.

"Really?" Turning away, she wandered the tiny room. The small throw rug was worn thin in patches, the headboard of the bed scarred, the nightstand a bit unsteady. "How do you like the accommodations, Kincaid?"

"They'll do."

She laughed into her wine. "Wait until it gets hot."

"Isn't it?"

"Do the immortal words 'You ain't seen nothing yet' mean anything to you?"

He forced himself to keep his eyes from the movements of her body under the silk. "Want to see all the Hollywood riffraff melt away, Tory?"

Turning, she disconcerted him by giving him her dashing smile. "No, I'll wish you luck instead. After all, I invariably admire your finished product."

"If not what goes into making it."

"Perhaps not," she agreed. "What are you feeding me?"

He was silent for a moment, studying the eyes that laughed at him over the rim of a wineglass. "The menu is rather limited."

"Meat loaf?" she asked dubiously, knowing it was the hotel's specialty.

"God forbid. Chicken and dumplings."

Tory walked back to him. "In that case I'll stay." They sat, facing each other across the folding table. "Shall we get business out of the way, Kincaid, or will it interfere with your digestion?"

He laughed, then surprised her by reaching out to take one of her hands in both of his. "You're a hell of a woman, Tory. Why are you afraid to use my first name?"

She faltered a moment, but let her hand lay unresisting in his. Because it's too personal, she thought. "Afraid?" she countered.

"Reluctant?" he suggested, allowing his fingertip to trace the back of her hand.

"Immaterial." Gently she removed her hand from his. "I was told you'd be shooting here for about six weeks." She lifted the cover from her plate and set it aside. "Is that firm?"

"According to the guarantors," Phil muttered, taking another sip of wine.

"Guarantors?"

"Tyco, Inc., completion-bond company."

"Oh, yes." Tory toyed with her chicken. "I'd heard that was a new wave in Hollywood. They guarantee that the movie will be completed on time and within budget—or else they pay the overbudget costs. They can fire you, can't they?"

"Me, the producer, the stars, anyone," Phil agreed. "Practical."

"Stifling," he returned, and stabbed into his chicken.

"From your viewpoint, I imagine," Tory reflected. "Still, as a business, it makes sense. Creative people often have to be shown certain . . . boundaries. Such as," she continued, "the ones I outlined this morning."

"And boundaries often have to be flexible. Such as," he said with a smile, "some night scenes we'll be shooting. I'm going to need your cooperation. The townspeople are welcome to watch any phase of the shoot, as long as they don't interfere, interrupt, or get in the way. Also, some of the equipment being brought in is very expensive and very sensitive. We have security, but as sheriff, you may want to spread the word that it's off limits."

"Your equipment is your responsibility," she reminded him. "But I will issue a statement. Before you shoot your night scenes, you'll have to clear it through my office."

He gave her a long, hard look. "Why?"

"If you're planning on working in the middle of the night in the middle of town, I'll need prior confirmation. In that way I can keep disorder to a minimum."

"There'll be times I'll need the streets blocked off and cleared."

"Send me a memo," she said. "Dates, times. Friendly can't come to a stop to accommodate you."

"It's nearly there in any case."

"We don't have a fast lane." Irresistibly she sent him a grin. "As you discovered."

He gave her a mild glance. "I'd also like to use some of the locals for extras and walk-ons."

Tory rolled her eyes. "God, you are looking for trouble. Go ahead," she said with a shrug, "send out your casting call, but you'd better use everyone that answers it, one way or another."

As he'd already figured that one out for himself, Phil was unperturbed. "Interested?" he asked casually.

"Hmm?"

"Are you interested?"

Tory laughed as she held out her glass for more wine. "No."

Phil let the bottle hover a moment. "I'm serious, Tory. I'd like to put you on film."

"I haven't got the time or the inclination."

"You've got the looks and, I think, the talent."

She smiled, more amused than flattered. "Phil, I'm a lawyer. That's exactly what I want to be."

"Why?"

He saw immediately that the question had thrown her off balance. She stared at him a moment with the glass to her lips. "Because the law fascinates me," she said after a pause. "Because I respect it. Because I like to think that occasionally I have something to do with the process of justice. I worked hard to get into Harvard, and harder when I got there. It means something to me."

"Yet, you've given it up for six months."

"Not completely." She frowned at the steady flame of the candle. "Regardless, it's necessary. There'll still be cases to try when I go back."

"I'd like to see you in the courtroom," he murmured, watching the quiet light flicker in her eyes. "I bet you're fabulous."

"Outstanding," she agreed, smiling again. "The assistant D.A. hates me." She took another bite of chicken. "What about you? Why directing instead of acting?"

"It never appealed to me." Leaning back, Phil found himself curiously relaxed and stimulated. He felt he could look at her forever. Her fragrance, mixed with the scent of hot wax, was erotic, her voice soothing. "And I suppose I liked the idea of giving orders rather than taking them. With directing you can alter a scene, change a tone, set the pace for an entire story. An actor can only work with one character, no matter how complex it may be."

"You've never directed either of your parents." Tory let the words hang so that he could take them either as a statement or a question. When he smiled, the creases in his cheeks deepened so that she wondered how it would feel to run her fingers along them.

"No." He tipped more wine into his glass. "It might make quite a splash, don't you think? The three of us together on one film. Even though they've been divorced for over twenty-five years, they'd send the glossies into a frenzy."

"You could do two separate films," she pointed out.

"True." He pondered over it a moment. "If the right scripts came along . . ." Abruptly he shook his head. "I've thought of it, even been approached a couple of times, but I'm not sure it would be a wise move professionally or personally. They're quite a pair," he stated with a grin. "Temperamental, explosive, and probably two of the best dramatic actors in the last fifty years. Both of them wring the last drop of blood from a character."

"I've always admired them," Tory agreed. "Especially in the movies they made together. They put a lot of chemistry on the screen."

"And off it," Phil murmured. "It always amazed me that they managed to stay together for almost ten years. Neither of them had that kind of longevity in their other marriages. The problem was that they never stopped competing. It gave them the spark on the screen and a lot of problems at home. It's difficult to live with someone when you're afraid he or she might be just a little better than you are."

"But you're very fond of them, aren't you?" She watched his mobile brow lift in question. "It shows," she told him. "It's rather nice."

"Fond," he agreed. "Maybe a little wary. They're formidable people, together or separately. I grew up listening to lines being cued over breakfast and hearing producers torn to shreds at dinner. My father lived each role. If he was playing a psychotic, I could expect to find a crazed man in the bathroom."

"Obsession," Tory recalled, delighted. "1957."

"Very good," Phil approved. "Are you a fan?"

"Naturally. I got my first kiss watching Marshall Kincaid in *Endless Journey*." She gave a throaty laugh. "The movie was the more memorable of the two."

"You were in diapers when that movie was made," Phil calculated.

"Ever heard of the late show?"

"Young girls," he stated, "should be in bed at that hour."

Tory suppressed a laugh. Resting her elbows on the table, she set her chin on cupped hands. "And young boys?"

"Would stay out of trouble," he finished.

"The hell they would," Tory countered, chuckling. "As I recall, your . . . exploits started at a tender age. What was the name of that actress you were involved with when you were sixteen? She was in her twenties as I remember, and—"

"More wine?" Phil interrupted, filling her glass before she could answer.

"Then there was the daughter of that comedian."

"We were like cousins."

"Really?" Tory drew out the word with a doubtful look. "And the dancer . . . ah, Nicki Clark."

"Great moves," Phil remembered, then grinned at her. "You seem to be more up on my . . . exploits than I am. Did you spend all your free time at Harvard reading movie magazines?"

"My roommate did," Tory confessed. "She was a drama major. I see her on a commercial now and again. And then I knew someone in the business. Your name's dropped quite a bit at parties."

"The actor you dated."

"Total recall," Tory murmured, a bit uncomfortable. "You amaze me."

"Tool of the trade. What was his name?"

Tory picked up her wine, studying it for a moment. "Chad Billings."

"Billings?" Surprised and not altogether pleased, Phil frowned at her. "A second-rate leech, Tory. I wouldn't think him your style."

"No?" She shot him a direct look. "He was diverting and . . . educational."

"And married."

"Judgmental, Phil?" she countered, then gave a shrug. "He was in between victims at the time."

"Aptly put," Phil murmured. "If you got your view of the industry through him, I'm surprised you didn't put up roadblocks to keep us out."

"It was a thought," she told him, but smiled again. "I'm not a complete fool, you know."

But Phil continued to frown at her, studying her intensely. He was more upset at thinking of her with Billings than he should have been. "Did he hurt you?" he demanded abruptly.

Surprised, Tory stared at him. "No," she said slowly.

"Although I suppose he might have if I'd allowed it. We didn't see each other exclusively or for very long. I was in L.A. on a case at the time."

"Why Albuquerque?" Phil wondered aloud. "Lou was impressed with you, and he's not easily impressed. Why aren't you in some glass-and-leather office in New York?"

"I hate traffic." Tory sat back now, swirling the wine and relaxing. "And I don't rush."

"L.A.?"

"I don't play tennis."

He laughed, appreciating her more each moment. "I love the way you boil things down, Tory. What do you do when you're not upholding the law?"

"As I please, mostly. Sports and hobbies are too demanding." She tossed back her hair. "I like to sleep."

"You forget, I've seen you ride."

"That's different." The wine had mellowed her mood. She didn't notice that the candles were growing low and the hour late. "It relaxes me. Clears my head."

"Why do you live in a room in the hotel when you have a house right outside of town?" Her fingers tightened on the stem of the wineglass only slightly: He was an observant man.

"It's simpler."

Leave this one alone for a while, he warned himself. It's a very tender spot.

"And what do you do when you're not making a major statement on film?" she asked, forcing her hand to relax.

Phil accepted her change of subject without question. "Read scripts . . . watch movies."

"Go to parties," Tory added sagely.

"That too. It's all part of the game."

"Isn't it difficult sometimes, living in a town where so much is pretense? Even considering the business end of your profession, you have to deal with the lunacy, the make-believe, even the desperation. How do you separate the truth from the fantasy?"

"How do you in your profession?" he countered.

Tory thought for a moment, then nodded. "Touché." Rising, she wandered to the window. She pushed aside the shade, surprised to see that the sun had gone down. A few red streaks hovered over the horizon, but in the east the sky was dark. A few early stars were already out. Phil sat where he was, watched her, and wanted her.

"There's Merle making his rounds," Tory said with a smile in her voice. "He's got his official expression on. I imagine he's hoping to be discovered. If he can't be a tough lawman from the nineteenth century, he'd settle for playing one." A car pulled into town, stopping in front of the pool hall with a sharp squeal of brakes. "Oh God, it's the twins." She sighed, watching Merle turn and stride in their direction. "There's been no peace in town since that pair got their licenses. I suppose I'd better go down and see that they stay in line."

"Can't Merle handle a couple of kids?"

Tory's laugh was full of wicked appreciation. "You don't know the Kramers. There's Merle," she went on, "giving them basic lecture number twenty-two."

"Did they wash all of Hollister's windows?" Phil asked as he rose to join her.

Tory turned her head, surprised. "How did you know about that?"

"Tod told me." He peeked through the window, finding he wanted a look at the infamous twins. They

seemed harmless enough from a distance, and disconcertingly alike. "Which one's Zac?"

"Ah . . . on the right, I think. Maybe," she added
with a shake of her head. "Why?"

"'Zac Kramer don't hold with no woman sheriff,'"
he quoted.

Tory grinned up at him. "Is that so?"

"Just so." Hardly aware he did so, Phil reached for
her hair. "Obviously he's not a very perceptive boy."

"Perceptive enough to wash Mr. Hollister's windows," Tory corrected, amused by the memory. "And
to call me a foxy chick only under his breath when
he thought I couldn't hear. Of course, that could have
been Zeke."

"'Foxy chick'?" Phil repeated.

"Yes," Tory returned with mock hauteur. "'A *very*
foxy chick.' It was his ultimate compliment."

"Your head's easily turned," he decided. "What if I
told you that you had a face that belongs in a Raphael
painting?"

Tory's eyes lit with humor. "I'd say you're reaching."

"And hair," he said with a subtle change in his
voice. "Hair that reminds me of night . . . a hot summer night that keeps you awake, and thinking, and
wanting." He plunged both hands into it, letting his
fingers tangle. The shade snapped back into place, cutting them off from the outside.

"Phil," Tory began, unprepared for the suddenness
of desire that rose in both of them.

"And skin," he murmured, not even hearing her,
"that makes me think of satin sheets and tastes like
something forbidden." He touched his mouth to her
cheek, allowing the tip of his tongue to brush over her.
"Tory." She felt her name whisper along her skin and

thrilled to it. She had her hands curled tightly around his arms, but not in protest. "Do you know how often I've thought of you these past weeks?"

"No." She didn't want to resist. She wanted to feel that wild sweep of pleasure that came from the press of his mouth on hers. "No," she said again, and slid her arms around his neck.

"Too much," he murmured, then swore. "Too damn much." And his mouth took her waiting one.

The passion was immediate, frenetic. It ruled both of them. Each of them sought the mindless excitement they had known briefly weeks before. Tory had thought she had intensified the sensation in her mind as the days had passed. Now she realized she had lessened it. This sort of fervor couldn't be imagined or described. It had to be experienced. Everything inside her seemed to speed up—her blood, her heart, her brain. And all sensation, all emotion, seemed to be centered in her mouth. The taste of him exploded on her tongue, shooting through her until she was so full of him, she could no longer separate herself. With a moan she tilted her head back, inviting him to plunge deeper into her mouth. But he wanted more.

Her hair fell straight behind her, leaving her neck vulnerable. Surrendering to a desperate hunger, he savaged it with kisses. Tory made a sound that was mixed pain and pleasure. Her scent seemed focused there, heated by the pulse at her throat. It drove him nearer the edge. He dragged at the silk-covered buttons, impatient to find the hidden skin, the secret skin that had preyed on his mind. The groan sounded in his throat as he slipped his hand beneath the thin teddy and found her.

She was firm and slender enough to fit his palm.

Her heartbeat pounded against it. Tory turned her head, but only to urge him to give the neglected side of her neck attention. With her hands in his hair she pulled him back to her. His hands searched everywhere with a sort of wild reverence, exploring, lingering, possessing. She could feel his murmurs as his lips played over her skin, although she could barely hear them and understood them not at all. The room seemed to grow closer and hotter, so that she longed to be rid of her clothes and find relief . . . and delight.

Then he pulled her close so that their bodies pressed urgently. Their mouths met with fiery demand. It seemed the storm had just begun. Again and again they drew from each other until they were both breathless. Though he had fully intended to end the evening with Tory in his bed, Phil hadn't expected to be desperate. He hadn't known that all control could be so easily lost. The warm curves of a woman should bring easy pleasure, not this trembling pain. A kiss was a prelude, not an all-consuming force. He knew only that all of him, much more than his body, was crying out for her. Whatever was happening to him was beyond his power to stop. And she was the only answer he had.

"God, Tory." He took his mouth on a wild journey of her face, then returned to her lips. "Come to bed. For God's sake, come to bed. I want you."

She felt as though she were standing on the edge of a cliff. The plunge had never seemed more tempting—or more dangerous. It would be so easy, so easy, just to lean forward and fly. But the fall . . . She fought for sanity through a brain clouded with the knowledge of one man. It was much too soon to take the step.

"Phil." Shaken, she drew away from him to lean against the windowsill. "I . . . No," she managed, lifting both hands to her temples. He drew her back against him.

"Yes," he corrected, then crushed his lips to hers again. Her mouth yielded irresistibly. "You can't pretend you don't want me as much as I want you."

"No." She let her head rest on his shoulder a moment before she pushed out of his arms. "I can't," she agreed in a voice thickened with passion. "But I don't do everything I want. That's one of the basic differences between us."

His eyes flicked briefly down to the unbuttoned dress. "We also seem to have something important in common. This doesn't happen every time—between every man and woman."

"No." Carefully she began to do up her buttons. "It shouldn't have happened between us. I didn't intend it to."

"I did," he admitted. "But not quite this way."

Her eyes lifted to his. She understood perfectly. This had been more intense than either of them had bargained for. "It's going to be a long summer, Phil," she murmured.

"We're going to be together sooner or later, Tory. We both know it." He needed something to balance him. Going to the table, he poured out another glass of wine. He drank, drank again, then looked at her. "I have no intention of backing off."

She nodded, accepting. But she didn't like the way her hands were shaking. "I'm not ready."

"I can be a patient man when necessary." He wanted nothing more than to pull her to the bed and take what they both needed. Instead he took out a cigarette and reminded himself he was a civilized man.

Tory drew herself up straight. "Let's both concentrate on our jobs, shall we?" she said coolly. She wanted to get out, but she didn't want to retreat. "I'll see you around, Kincaid."

"Damn right you will," he murmured as she headed for the door.

She flicked the lock off, then turned to him with a half smile. "Keep out of trouble," she ordered, closing the door behind her.

CHAPTER 6

Phil sat beside the cameraman on the Tulip crane. "Boom up." At his order the crane operator took them seventeen feet above the town of Friendly. It was just dawn. He'd arranged to have everyone off the streets, although there was a crowd of onlookers behind the crane and equipment. All entrances to town had been blocked off on the off chance that someone might drive through. He wanted desolation and the tired beginning of a new day.

Glancing down, he saw that Bicks was checking the lighting and angles. Brutes, the big spotlights, were set to give daylight balance. He knew, to an inch, where he wanted the shadows to fall. For this shot Phil would act as assistant cameraman, pulling the focus himself.

Phil turned his attention back to the street. He knew what he wanted, and he wanted to capture it as the sun rose, with as much natural light as possible. He looked through the lens and set the shot himself. The crane was set on tracks. He would have the cameraman begin with a wide shot of the horizon and the rising

sun, then dolly back to take in the entire main street
of Friendly. No soft focus there, just harsh reality. He
wanted to pick up the dust on the storefront windows.
Satisfied with what he saw through the camera lens,
Phil marked the angle with tape, then nodded to his
assistant director.

"Quiet on the set."

"New Chance, scene three, take one."

"Roll it," Phil ordered, then waited. With his eyes
narrowed, he could visualize what his cameraman saw
through the lens. The light was good. Perfect. They'd
have to get it in three takes or less or else they'd have
to beef it up with gels and filters. That wasn't what he
wanted here. He felt the crane roll backward slowly on
cue. A straight shot, no panning right to left. They'd
take in the heart of the town in one long shot. Chipped
paint, sagging wood, torn screens. Later they'd cut in
the scene of the leading man walking in from the train
station. He was coming home, Phil mused, because
there was no place else to go. And he found it, exactly
as he had left it twenty years before.

"Cut." The noise on the ground started immediately. "I want another take. Same speed."

At the back of the crowd Tory watched. She wasn't
thrilled with being up at dawn. Both her sense of duty
and her curiosity had brought her. Phil had been perfectly clear about anyone peeking through windows
during this shot. He wanted emptiness. She told herself she'd come to keep her people out of mischief, but
when it was all said and done, she had wanted to see
Phil at work.

He was very commanding and totally at ease with
it, but, she reasoned as she stuck her hands in her
back pockets, it didn't seem so hard. Moving a little
to the side, she tried to see the scene she was imagin-

ing. The town looked tired, she decided, and a little reluctant to face the new day. Though the horizon was touched with golds and pinks, a gray haze lay over the street and buildings.

It was the first time he had shot anything there. For the past week he had been filming landscapes. Tory had stayed in Friendly, sending Merle out occasionally to check on things. It had kept him happy and had given Tory the distance she wanted. As her deputy came back brimming with reports and enthusiasm, she was kept abreast in any case.

But today the urge to see for herself had been too strong to resist. It had been several days—and several long nights—since their evening together. She had managed to keep herself busier than necessary in order to avoid him. But Tory wasn't a woman to avoid a problem for long. Phil Kincaid was still a problem.

Apparently satisfied, Phil ordered the operator to lower the crane. People buzzed around Tory like bees. A few children complained about being sent off to school. Spotting Tod, Tory smiled and waved him over.

"Isn't it neat?" he demanded the moment he was beside her. "I wanted to go up in it," he continued, indicating the crane, "but Mr. Kincaid said something about insurance. Steve let me see his camera though, even let me take some pictures. It's a thirty-five millimeter with all kinds of lenses."

"Steve?"

"The guy who was sitting next to Mr. Kincaid. He's the cameraman." Tod glanced over, watching Phil in a discussion with his cameraman and several members of the crew. "Isn't he something?"

"Steve?" Tory repeated, smiling at Tod's pleasure.

"Well, yeah, but I meant Mr. Kincaid." Shaking his head, he let out a long breath. "He's awful smart. You should hear some of the words he uses. And boy, when he says so, everybody jumps."

"Do they?" Tory murmured, frowning over at the man under discussion.

"You bet," Tod confirmed. "And I heard Mr. Bicks say to Steve that he'd rather work with Mr. Kincaid than anybody. He's a tough sonofa—" Catching himself, Tod broke off and flushed. "I mean, he said he was tough, but the best there was."

As she watched, Phil was pointing, using one hand and then the other as he outlined his needs for the next shot. It was very clear that he knew what he wanted and that he'd get it. She could study him now. He was too involved to notice her or the crowd of people who stared and mumbled behind the barrier of equipment.

He wore jeans and a pale blue T-shirt with scuffed sneakers. Hanging from his belt was a case that held sunglasses and another for a two-way radio. He was very intense, she noted, when working. There was none of the careless humor in his eyes. He talked quickly, punctuating the words with hand gestures. Once or twice he interrupted what he was saying to call out another order to the grips who were setting up light stands.

A perfectionist, she concluded, and realized it shouldn't surprise her. His movies projected the intimate care she was now seeing firsthand. A stocky man in a fielder's cap lumbered up to him, talking over an enormous wad of gum.

"That's Mr. Bicks," Tod murmured reverently. "The cinematographer. He's got two Oscars and owns part of a boxer."

Whatever he was saying, Phil listened carefully, then simply shook his head. Bicks argued another moment, shrugged, then gave Phil what appeared to be a solid punch on the shoulder before he walked away. A tough sonofabitch, Tory mused. Apparently so.

Turning to Tod, she mussed his hair absently. "You'd better get to school."

"Aw, but . . ."

She lifted her brow, effectively cutting off his excuse. "It's nearly time for summer vacation. They'll still be here."

He mumbled a protest, but she caught the look in his eye as he gazed up at her. Uh-oh, she thought, just as Phil had. Why hadn't she seen this coming? She was going to have to be careful to be gentle while pointing the boy in another direction. A teenage crush was nothing to smile at and brush away.

"I'll come by after school," he said, beaming up at her. Before she could respond, he was dashing off, leaving her gnawing on her bottom lip and worrying about him.

"Sheriff."

Tory whirled sharply and found herself facing Phil. He smiled slowly, setting the sunglasses in front of his eyes. It annoyed her that she had to strain to see his expression through the tinted glass. "Kincaid," she responded. "How's it going?"

"Good. Your people are very cooperative."

"And yours," she said. "So far."

He grinned at that. "We're expecting the cast this afternoon. The location manager's cleared it with you about parking the trailers and so forth?"

"She's very efficient," Tory agreed. "Are you getting what you want?"

He took a moment to answer. "With regard to the film, yes, so far." Casually he reached down to run a finger over her badge. "You've been busy the last few days."

"So have you."

"Not that busy. I've left messages for you."

"I know."

"When are you going to see me?"

She lifted both brows. "I'm seeing you right now." He took a step closer and cupped the back of her neck in his hand. "Phil—"

"Soon," he said quietly.

Though she could feel the texture of each of his fingers on the back of her neck, she gave him a cool look. "Kincaid, create your scenes on the other side of the camera. Accosting a peace officer will land you back in that cell. You'll find it difficult to direct from there."

"Oh, I'm going to accost you," he warned under his breath. "With or without that damn badge, Victoria. Think about it."

She didn't step back or remove his hand, although she knew several pair of curious eyes were on them. "I'll give it a few minutes," she promised dryly.

Only the tensing of his fingers on her neck revealed his annoyance. She thought he was about to release her and relaxed. His mouth was on hers so quickly, she could only stand in shock. Before she could think to push him away, he set her free. Her eyes were sharply green and furious when he grinned down at her.

"See you, Sheriff," he said cheerfully and sauntered back to his crew.

For the better part of the day Tory stayed in her office and fumed. Now and again Phil's voice carried through her open window as he called out instructions. She knew they were doing pans of the town and stayed away from the window. She had work to do, she reminded herself. And in any case she had no interest in the filming. It was understandable that the townspeople would stand around and gawk, but she had better things to do.

I should have hauled him in, she thought, scowling down at her legal pad. I should have hauled him in then and there. And she would have if it wouldn't have given him too much importance. He'd better watch his step, Tory decided. One wrong move and she was going to come down on him hard. She picked up her coffee and gulped it down with a grimace. It was cold. Swearing, she rose to pour a fresh cup.

Through the screen in the window she could see quite a bit of activity and hear a flood of conversation interrupted when the filming was in progress. It was past noon and hot as the devil. Phil had been working straight through for hours. With a grudging respect she admitted that he didn't take his job lightly. Going back to her desk, Tory concentrated on her own.

She hardly noticed that two hours had passed when Merle came bursting into the office. Hot, tired, and annoyed with having her concentration broken, she opened her mouth to snap at him, but he exploded with enthusiasm before she had the chance.

"Tory, they're here!"

"Terrific," she mumbled, turning to her notes again. "Who?"

"The actors. Came from the airport in limousines. Long, black limousines. There are a half dozen of those Winnebagos set up outside of town for dressing rooms and stuff. You should see inside them. They've got telephones and TVs and everything."

She lifted her head. "Been busy, Merle T.?" she asked languidly, but he was too excited to notice.

"Sam Dressier," he went on, pacing back and forth with a clatter of boots. "Sam Dressier, right here in Friendly. I guess I've seen every movie he's ever made. He shook my hand," he added, staring down at his own palm, awed. "Thought I was the sheriff." He sent Tory a quick look, "'Course I told him I was the deputy."

"Of course," she agreed, amused now. It was never possible for her to stay annoyed with Merle. "How'd he look?"

"Just like you'd think," he told her with a puzzled shake of his head. "All tanned and tough, with a diamond on his finger fit to blind you. Signed autographs for everybody who wanted one."

Unable to resist, Tory asked, "Did you get one?"

"Sure I did." He grinned and pulled out his ticket book. "It was the only thing I had handy."

"Very resourceful." She glanced at the bold signature Merle held out for her. At the other end of the page were some elegant looping lines. "Marlie Summers," Tory read. She recalled a film from the year before and the actress's pouting sexuality.

"She's about the prettiest thing I ever saw," Merle murmured.

Coming from anyone else, Tory would have given the remark no notice. In this case, however, her eyes shot up and locked on Merle's. What she saw evoked in her a feeling of distress similar to what she had experienced with Tod. "Really?" she said carefully.

"She's just a little thing," Merle continued, gazing down at the autograph. "All pink and blonde. Just like something in a store window. She's got big blue eyes and the longest lashes . . ." He trailed off, tucking the book back in his pocket.

Growing more disturbed, Tory told herself not to be silly. No Hollywood princess was going to look twice at Merle T. Johnson. "Well," she began casually, "I wonder what her part is."

"She's going to tell me all about it tonight," Merle stated, adjusting the brim of his hat.

"What?" It came out in a quick squeak.

Grinning, Merle gave his hat a final pat, then stroked his struggling mustache. "We've got a date." He strode out jauntily, leaving Tory staring with her mouth open.

"A date?" she asked the empty office. Before she could react, the phone beside her shrilled. Picking it up, she barked into it, "What is it?"

A bit flustered by the greeting, the mayor stammered. "Tory—Sheriff Ashton, this is Mayor Toomey."

"Yes, Bud." Her tone was still brisk as she stared at the door Merle had shut behind him.

"I'd like you to come over to the office, Sheriff. I have several members of the cast here." His voice rang with importance again. "Mr. Kincaid thought it might be a good idea for you to meet them."

"Members of the cast," she repeated, thinking of Marlie Summers. "I'd love to," she said dangerously, then hung up on the mayor's reply.

Her thoughts were dark as she crossed the street. No Hollywood tootsie was going to break Merle's heart while she was around. She was going to make that clear as soon as possible. She breezed into the hotel, giving several members of Phil's crew a potent stare as they loitered in the lobby. Bicks doffed his fielder's cap and grinned at her.

"Sheriff."

Tory sent him a mild glance and a nod as she sauntered through to the office. Behind her back he rolled his eyes to the ceiling, placing the cap over his heart. A few remarks were made about the advantages of breaking the law in Friendly while Tory disappeared into a side door.

The tiny office was packed, the window air-conditioning unit spitting hopefully. Eyes turned to her. Tory gave the group a brief scan. Marlie was sitting on the arm of Phil's chair, dressed in pink slacks and a frilled halter. Her enviable curves were displayed to perfection. Her hair was tousled appealingly around a piquant face accented with mink lashes and candy-pink lipstick. She looked younger than Tory had expected, almost like a high school girl ready to be taken out for an ice-cream soda. Tory met the baby-blue eyes directly, and with an expression that made Phil grin. He thought mistakenly that she might be a bit jealous.

"Sheriff." The mayor bustled over to her, prepared to act as host. "This is quite an honor for Friendly," he began, in his best politician's voice. "I'm sure you recognize Mr. Dressier."

Tory extended her hand to the man who approached her. "Sheriff." His voice was rich, the cadence mellow as he clasped her hand in both of his. She was a bit surprised to find them callused. "This is unexpected," he murmured while his eyes roamed her face thoroughly. "And delightful."

"Mr. Dressier, I admire your work." The smile was easy because the words were true.

"Sam, please." His brandy voice had only darkened attractively with age, losing none of its resonance. "We get to be a close little family on location shoots. Victoria, isn't it?"

"Yes." She found herself inclined to like him and gave him another smile.

"Bud, here, is making us all quite comfortable," he went on, clapping the mayor on the shoulder. "Will you join us in a drink?"

"Ginger ale's fine, Bud."

"The sheriff's on duty." Hearing Phil's voice, Tory

turned her head only, and glanced at him. "You'll find she takes her work very seriously." He touched Marlie's creamy bare shoulder. "Victoria Ashton, Marlie Summers."

"Sheriff." Marlie smiled her dazzling smile. The tiniest hint of a dimple peeked at the corner of her mouth. "Phil said you were unusual. It looks like he's right again."

"Really?" Accepting the cold drink Bud handed her, Tory assessed the actress over the rim. Marlie, accustomed to long looks and feminine coolness, met the stare straight on.

"Really," Marlie agreed. "I met your deputy a little while ago."

"So I heard."

So the wind blows in that direction, Marlie mused as she sipped from her own iced sangria. Sensing tension and wanting to keep things smooth, Bud hurried on with the rest of the introductions.

The cast ranged from ingenues to veterans—a girl Tory recognized from a few commercials; an ancient-looking man she remembered from the vague black-and-white movies on late-night television; a glitzy actor in his twenties, suited for heartthrobs and posters. Tory managed to be pleasant, stayed long enough to satisfy the mayor, then slipped away. She'd no more than stepped outside when she felt an arm on her shoulder.

"Don't you like parties, Sheriff?"

Taking her time, she turned to face Phil. "Not when I'm on duty." Though she knew he'd worked in the sun all day, he didn't look tired but exhilarated. His shirt was streaked with sweat, his hair curling damply over his ears, but there was no sign of fatigue on his face. It's the pressure that feeds him, she realized.

Again she was drawn to him, no less than when they had been alone in his room. "You've put in a long day," she murmured.

He caught her hair in his hand. "So have you. Why don't we go for a drive?"

Tory shook her head. "No, I have things to do." Wanting to steer away from the subject, she turned to what had been uppermost on her mind. "Your Marlie made quite an impression on Merle."

Phil gave a quick laugh. "Marlie usually does."

"Not on Merle," Tory said so seriously that he sobered.

"He's a big boy, Tory."

"A boy," she agreed significantly. "He's never seen anything like your friend in there. I won't let him get hurt."

Phil let out a deep breath. "Your duties as sheriff include advice to the lovelorn? Leave him alone," he ordered before she could retort. "You treat him as though he were a silly puppy who doesn't respond to training."

She took a step back at that. "No, I don't," she disagreed, sincerely shaken by the idea. "He's a sweet boy who—"

"Man," Phil corrected quietly. "He's a man, Tory. Cut the apron strings."

"I don't know what you're talking about," she snapped.

"You damn well do," he corrected. "You can't keep him under your wing the way you do with Tod."

"I've known Merle all my life," she said in a low voice. "Just keep Cotton Candy in line, Kincaid."

"Always so sure of yourself, aren't you?"

Her color drained instantly, alarmingly. For a moment Phil stared at her in speechless wonder. He'd never expected to see that kind of pain in her eyes. Instinctively he reached out for her. "Tory?"

"No." She lifted a hand to ward him off. "Just—leave me alone." Turning away, she walked across the street and climbed into her car. With an oath Phil started to go back into the hotel, then swore again and backtracked. Tory was already on her way north.

Her thoughts were in turmoil as she drove. Too much was happening. She squeezed her eyes shut briefly. Why should that throw her now? she wondered. She'd always been able to take things in stride, handle them at her own pace. Now she had a deep-seated urge just to keep driving, just to keep going. So many people wanted things from her, expected things. Including, she admitted, herself. It was all closing in suddenly. She needed someone to talk to. But the only one who had ever fit that job was gone.

God, she wasn't sure of herself. Why did everyone say so? Sometimes it was so hard to be responsible, to *feel* responsible. Tod, Merle, the mayor, the Kramers, Mr. Hollister. Her mother. She just wanted peace—enough time to work out what was happening in her own life. Her feelings for Phil were closing in on her. Pulling the car to a halt, Tory realized it was those feelings that were causing her—a woman who had always considered herself calm—to be tense. Piled on top of it were problems that had to come first. She'd learned that from her father.

Glancing up, she saw she had driven to the cemetery without even being aware of it. She let out a long breath, resting her forehead against the steering wheel. It was time she went there, time she came to terms with what she had closed her mind to since that night in the hospital. Climbing out of the car, Tory walked across the dry grass to her father's grave.

Odd that there'd been a breeze here, she mused, looking at the sky, the distant mountains, the long stretches of nothing. She looked at anything but what was at her feet. There should be some shade, she thought, and cupped her elbows in her palms. Someone should plant some trees. I should have brought some flowers, she thought suddenly, then looked down.

WILLIAM H. ASHTON

She hadn't seen the gravestone before—hadn't been back to the cemetery since the day of the funeral. Now a quiet moan slipped through her lips. "Oh, Dad."

It isn't right, she thought with a furious shake of her head. It just isn't right. How can he be down there in the dark when he always loved the sun? "Oh, no," she murmured again. I don't know what to do, she thought silently, pleading with him. I don't know how to deal with it all. I still need you. Pressing a palm on her forehead, she fought back tears.

Phil pulled up behind her car, then got out quietly. She looked very alone and lost standing among the headstones. His first instinct was to go to her, but he suppressed it. This was private for her. Her father, he thought, looking toward the grave at which Tory stared. He stood by a low wrought-iron gate at the edge of the cemetery and waited.

There was so much she needed to talk about, so much she still needed to say. But there was no more time. He'd been taken too suddenly. Unfair, she thought again on a wave of desolate fury. He had been so young and so good.

"I miss you so much," she whispered. "All those long talks and quiet evenings on the porch. You'd smoke those awful cigars outside so that the smell wouldn't get in the curtains and irritate Mother. I was always so proud of you. This badge doesn't suit me," she continued softly, lifting her hand to it. "It's the law books and the courtroom that I understand. I don't want to make a mistake while I'm wearing it, because it's yours." Her fingers tightened around it. All at once she felt painfully alone, helpless, empty. Even the anger had slipped away unnoticed. And yet the acceptance she tried to feel was blocked behind a grief she refused to release. If she cried, didn't it mean she'd taken the first step away?

Wearily she stared down at the name carved into the granite. "I don't want you to be dead," she whispered. "And I hate it because I can't change it."

When she turned away from the grave, her face was grim. She walked slowly but was halfway across the small cemetery before she saw Phil. Tory stopped and stared at him. Her mind went blank, leaving her with only feelings. He went to her.

For a moment they stood face-to-face. He saw her lips tremble open as if she were about to speak, but she only shook her head helplessly. Without a word he gathered her close. The shock of grief that hit her was stronger than anything that had come before. She trembled first, then clutched at him.

"Oh, Phil, I can't bear it." Burying her face against his shoulder, Tory wept for the first time since her father's death.

In silence he held her, overwhelmed with a tenderness he'd felt for no one before. Her sobbing was raw and passionate. He stroked her hair, offering comfort without words. Her grief poured out in waves that seemed to stagger her and made him hurt for her to a degree that was oddly intimate. He thought he could feel what she felt, and held her tighter, waiting for the first throes to pass.

At length her weeping quieted, lessening to trembles that were somehow more poignant than the passion. She kept her face pressed against his shoulder, relying on his strength when her own evaporated. Light-headed and curiously relieved, she allowed him to lead her to a small stone bench. He kept her close to his side when they sat, his arm protectively around her.

"Can you talk about it?" he asked softly.

Tory let out a long, shuddering sigh. From where they sat she could see the headstone clearly. "I loved him," she murmured. "My mother says too much." Her throat felt dry and abused when she swallowed. "He was everything good. He taught me not just right and wrong but all the shades in between." Closing her eyes, she let her head rest on Phil's shoulder. "He always knew the right thing. It was something innate and effortless. People knew they could depend on him, that he'd make it right. I depended on him, even in college, in Albuquerque—I knew he was there if I needed him."

He kissed her temple in a gesture of simple understanding. "How did he die?"

Feeling a shudder run through her, Phil drew her closer still. "He had a massive stroke. There was no warning. He'd never even been sick that I can remember. When I got here, he was in a coma. Everything . . ." She faltered, searching for the strength to continue. With his free hand Phil covered hers. "Everything seemed to go wrong at once. His heart just . . . stopped." She ended in a whisper, lacing her fingers through his. "They put him on a respirator. For weeks there was nothing but that damn machine. Then my mother told them to turn it off."

Phil let the silence grow, following her gaze toward the headstone. "It must have been hard for her."

"No." The word was low and flat. "She never wavered, never cried. My mother's a very decisive woman," she added bitterly. "And she made the decision alone. She told me after it was already done."

"Tory." Phil turned her to face him. She looked pale, bright-eyed, and achingly weary. Something seemed to tear inside him. "I can't tell you the right or wrong of it, because there really isn't any. But I do know there comes a time when everyone has to face something that seems impossible to accept."

"If only I could have seen it was done for love and not . . . expediency." Shutting her eyes, she shook her head. "Hold me again." He drew her gently into his arms. "That last night at the hospital was so ugly between my mother and me. He would have hated that. I couldn't stop it," she said with a sigh. "I still can't."

"Time." He kissed the top of her head. "I know how trite that sounds, but there's nothing else but time."

She remained silent, accepting his comfort, drawing strength from it. If she had been able to think logically, Tory would have found it inconsistent with their relationship thus far that she could share her intimate feelings with him. At the moment she trusted Phil implicitly.

"Once in a while, back there," she murmured, "I panic."

It surprised him enough to draw her back and study her face again. "You?"

"Everyone thinks because I'm Will Ashton's daughter, I'll take care of whatever comes up. There're so many variables to right and wrong."

"You're very good at your job."

"I'm a good lawyer," she began.

"And a good sheriff," he interrupted. Tilting her chin up, he smiled at her. "That's from someone who's been on the wrong side of your bars." Gently he brushed the hair from her cheeks. They were warm and still damp. "And don't expect to hear me say it in public."

Laughing, she pressed her cheek to his. "Phil, you can be a very nice man."

"Surprised?"

"Maybe," she murmured. With a sigh she gave him one last squeeze, then drew away. "I've got work to do."

He stopped her from rising by taking her hands again. "Tory, do you know how little space you give yourself?"

"Yes." She disconcerted him by bringing his hand to her lips. "These six months are for him. It's very important to me."

Standing as she did, Phil cupped her face in his hands. She seemed to him very fragile, very vulnerable, suddenly. His need to look out for her was strong. "Let me drive you back. We can send someone for your car."

"No, I'm all right. Better." She brushed her lips over his. "I appreciate this. There hasn't been anyone I could talk to."

His eyes became very intense. "Would you come to me if you needed me?"

She didn't answer immediately, knowing the question was more complex than the simple words. "I don't know," she said at length.

Phil let her go, then watched her walk away.

CHAPTER 7

The camera came in tight on Sam and Marlie. Phil wanted the contrast of youth and age, of dissatisfaction and acceptance. It was a key scene, loaded with tension and restrained sexuality. They were using Hernandez's Bar, where the character Marlie portrayed worked as a waitress. Phil had made almost no alterations in the room. The bar was scarred, the mirror behind it cracked near the bottom. It smelled of sweat and stale liquor. He intended to transmit the scent itself onto film.

The windows were covered with neutral-density paper to block off the stream of the sun. It trapped the stale air in the room. The lights were almost unbearably hot, so that he needed no assistance from makeup to add beads of sweat to Sam's face. It was the sixth take, and the mood was growing edgy.

Sam blew his lines and swore ripely.

"Cut." Struggling with his temper, Phil wiped his forearm over his brow. With some actors a few furious words worked wonders. With Dressler, Phil knew, they would only cause more delays.

"Look, Phil"—Sam tore off the battered Stetson he wore and tossed it aside—"this isn't working."

"I know. Cut the lights," he ordered. "Get Mr. Dressler a beer." He addressed this to the man he had hired to see to Sam's needs on the location shoot. The individual attention had been Phil's way of handling Dressler and thus far had had its benefits. "Sit down for a while, Sam," he suggested. "We'll cool off." He waited until Sam was seated at a rear table with a portable fan and a beer before he plucked a can from the cooler himself.

"Hot work," Marlie commented, leaning against the bar.

Glancing over, Phil noted the line of sweat that ran down the front of her snug blouse. He passed her the can of beer. "You're doing fine."

"It's a hell of a part," she said before she took a deep drink. "I've been waiting for one like this for a long time."

"The next take," Phil began, narrowing his eyes, "when you say the bit about sweat and dust, I want you to grab his shirt and pull him to you."

Marlie thought it over, then set the can on the bar. "Like this . . . ? *There's nothing*," she spat out, grabbing Phil's damp shirt, *"nothing in this town but sweat and dust."* She put her other hand to his shirt and pulled him closer. *"Even the dreams have dust on them."*

"Good."

Marlie flashed a smile before she picked up the beer again. "Better warn Sam," she suggested, offering Phil the can. "He doesn't like improvising."

"Hey, Phil." Phil glanced over to see Steve with his hand on the doorknob. "That kid's outside with the sheriff. Wants to know if they can watch."

Phil took a long, slow drink. "They can sit in the

back of the room." His eyes met Tory's as she entered.
It had been two days since their meeting in the cemetery. Since then there had been no opportunity—or
she'd seen to it that there'd been none—for any private
conversation. She met the look, nodded to him, then
urged Tod back to a rear table.

"The law of the land," Marlie murmured, causing
Phil to look at her in question. "She's quite a woman,
isn't she?"

"Yes."

Marlie grinned before she commandeered the beer
again. "Merle thinks she's the greatest thing to come
along since sliced bread."

Phil pulled out a cigarette. "You're seeing quite a
bit of the deputy, aren't you? Doesn't seem your style."

"He's a nice guy," she said simply, then laughed.
"His boss would like me run out of town on a rail."

"She's protective."

With an unintelligible murmur that could have meant
anything, Marlie ran her fingers through her disordered
cap of curls. "At first I thought she had something
going with him." In response to Phil's quick laugh she
lifted a thin, penciled brow. "Of course, that was before I saw the way you looked at her." It was her turn
to laugh when Phil's expression became aloof. "Damn,
Phil, you can look like your father sometimes." After
handing him the empty can of beer, she turned away.
"Makeup!" she demanded.

"Those are 4Ks," Tod was telling Tory, pointing to
lights. "They have to put that stuff over the windows
so the sun doesn't screw things up. On an inside shoot
like this, they have to have something like 175-foot
candles."

"You're getting pretty technical, aren't you?"

Tod shifted a bit in his chair, but his eyes were

excited when they met Tory's. "Mr. Kincaid had them develop the film I shot in the portable lab. He said it was good. He said there were schools I could go to to learn about cinematography."

She cast a look in Phil's direction, watching him discuss something in undertones with Steve. "You're spending quite a lot of time with him," she commented.

"Well, when he's not busy . . . He doesn't mind."

"No, I'm sure he doesn't." She gave his hand a squeeze.

Tod returned the pressure boldly. "I'd rather spend time with you," he murmured.

Tory glanced down at their joined hands, wishing she knew how to begin. "Tod . . ."

"Quiet on the set!"

With a sigh Tory turned her attention to the scene in front of the bar. She'd come because Tod had been so pitifully eager that she share his enthusiasm. And she felt it was good for him to take such an avid interest in the technical aspects of the production. Unobtrusively she had kept her eye on him over the past days, watching him with members of the film crew. Thus far, no one appeared to object to his presence or his questions. In fact, Tory mused, he was becoming a kind of mascot. More and more his conversations were accented with the jargon of the industry. His mind seemed to soak up the terms, and his understanding was almost intuitive. He didn't appear to be interested in the glamorous end of it.

And what was so glamorous about it? she asked herself. The room was airless and steaming. It smelled, none too pleasantly, of old beer. The lights had the already unmerciful temperature rising. The two people in position by the bar were circled by equipment. How could they be so intense with each other, she wondered, when lights and cameras were all but on top of them? Yet, despite herself, Tory became engrossed with the drama of the scene.

Marlie's character was tormenting Sam's, ridiculing him for coming back a loser, taunting him. But somehow a rather abrasive strength came through in her character. She seemed a woman trapped by circumstances who was determined to fight her way out. Somehow she made the differences in their ages inconsequential. As the scene unfolded, an objective viewer would develop a respect for her, perhaps a cautious sympathy. Before long the viewer would be rooting for her. Tory wondered if Dressler realized, for all his reputation and skill, who would be the real star of this scene.

She's very good, Tory admitted silently. Marlie Summers wasn't the pampered, glittery Tinseltown cutie Tory had been ready to believe her to be. Tory recognized strength when she saw it. Marlie infused grit and vulnerability into the character that was instantly admirable. And the sweat, Tory continued, was her own.

"Cut!" Phil's voice jolted her in her chair. "That's it." Tory saw Marlie exhale a long breath. She wondered if there was some similarity in finishing a tense scene such as that one and winding up a difficult cross-examination. She decided that the emotion might be very much the same.

"Let's get some reaction shots, Marlie." Painstakingly he arranged for the change in angles and lighting. When the camera was in position, he checked through the lens himself, repositioned Marlie, then checked again. "Roll it. . . . Cue."

They worked for another thirty minutes, perfecting the shot. It was more than creativity, more than talent. The nuts and bolts end of the filming were tough, technical, and wearily repetitious. No one complained, no one questioned, when told to change or to do over. There was an unspoken bond: the film. Perhaps, she reflected, it was because they knew it would outlast all of them. Their small slice of immortality. Tory found herself developing a respect for these people who took such an intense pride in their work.

"Cut. That's a wrap." Tory could almost feel the communal sigh of relief. "Set up for scene fifty-three in . . ." Phil checked his watch. "Two hours." The moment the lights shut down, the temperature dropped.

"I'm going to see what Mr. Bicks is doing," Tod announced, scrambling up. Tory remained sitting where she was a moment, watching Phil answer questions and give instructions. He never stops, she realized. One might be an actor, another a lighting expert or a cinematographer, but he touches every aspect. Rich and privileged, yes, she reflected, but not afraid of hard work.

"Sheriff."

Tory turned her head to see Marlie standing beside her. "Ms. Summers. You were very impressive."

"Thanks." Without waiting for an invitation, Marlie took a chair. "What I need now is a three-hour shower." She took a long pull from the glass of ice water she held in her hand as the two women studied each other in silence. "You've got an incredible face," Marlie said at length. "If I'd had one like that, I wouldn't have had to fight for a part with some meat on it. Mine's like a sugarplum."

Tory found herself laughing. Leaning back, she hooked her arm over the back of her chair. "Ms. Summers, as sheriff, I should warn you that stealing's a crime. You stole that scene from Sam very smoothly."

Tilting her head, Marlie studied her from a new angle. "You're very sharp."

"On occasion."

"I can see why Merle thinks you hold the answer to the mysteries of the universe."

Tory sent her a long, cool look. "Merle is a very naive, very vulnerable young man."

"Yes." Marlie set down her glass. "I like him." They gave each other another measuring look. "Look, let me ask you something, from one attractive woman to another. Did you ever find it pleasant to be with a man who liked to talk to you, to listen to you?"

"Yes, of course." Tory frowned. "Perhaps it's that I can't imagine what Merle would say to interest you."

Marlie gave a quick laugh, then cupped her chin on her palm. "You're too used to him. I've been scrambling my way up the ladder since I was eighteen. There's nothing I want more than to be on top. Along the way, I've met a lot of men. Merle's different."

"If he falls in love with you, he'll be hurt," Tory pointed out. "I've looked out for him on and off since we were kids."

Marlie paused a moment. Idly she drew patterns through the condensation on the outside of her water glass. "He's not going to fall in love with me," she said slowly. "Not really. We're just giving each other a bit of the other's world for a few weeks. When it's over, we'll both have something nice to remember." She glanced over her shoulder and spotted Phil. "We all need someone now and again, don't we, Sheriff?"

Tory followed the direction of Marlie's gaze. At that moment Phil's eyes lifted to hers. "Yes," she murmured, watching him steadily. "I suppose we do."

"I'm going to get that shower now." Marlie rose. "He's a good man," she added. Tory looked back at her, knowing who she referred to now.

"Yes, I think you're right." Deep in thought, Tory

sat a moment longer. Then, standing, she glanced around for Tod.

"Tory." Phil laid a hand on her arm. "How are you?"

"Fine." She smiled, letting him know she hadn't forgotten the last time they had been together. "You're tougher than I thought, Kincaid, working in this oven all day."

He grinned. "That, assuredly, is a compliment."

"Don't let it go to your head. You're sweating like a pig."

"Really," he said dryly. "I hadn't noticed."

She spotted a towel hung over the back of a chair and plucked it up. "You know," she said as she wiped off his face, "I imagined directors would do more delegating than you do."

"My film," he said simply, stirred by the way she brushed the cloth over his face. "Tory." He captured her free hand. "I want to see you—alone."

She dropped the towel back on the table. "Your film," she reminded him. "And there's something I have to do." Her eyes darted past him, again in search of Tod.

"Tonight," he insisted. He'd gone beyond the point of patience. "Take the evening off, Tory."

She brought her eyes back to his. She'd gone beyond the point of excuses. "If I can," she agreed. "There's a place I know," she added with a slow smile. "South of town, about a mile. We used it as a swimming hole when I was a kid. You can't miss it—it's the only water around."

"Sunset?" He would have lifted her hand to his lips, but she drew it away.

"I can't promise." Before he could say anything else, she stepped past him, then called for Tod.

Even as she drew the boy back outside, he was expounding. "Tory, it's great, isn't it? About the greatest thing to happen in town in forever! If I could, I'd go with them when they leave." He sent her a look from under his tumbled hair. "Wouldn't you like to go, Tory?"

"To Hollywood?" she replied lightly. "Oh, I don't think it's my style. Besides, I'll be going back to Albuquerque soon."

"I want to come with you," he blurted out.

They were just outside her office door. Tory turned and looked down at him. Unable to resist, she placed her hand on his cheek. "Tod," she said softly.

"I love you, Tory," he began quickly. "I could—"

"Tod, come inside." For days she had been working out what she would say to him and how to say it. Now, as they walked together into her office, she felt completely inadequate. Carefully she sat on the edge of her desk and faced him. "Tod—" She broke off and shook her head. "Oh, I wish I were smarter."

"You're the smartest person I know," he said swiftly. "And so beautiful, and I love you, Tory, more than anything."

Her heart reached out for him even as she took his hands. "I love you, too, Tod." As he started to speak she shook her head again. "But there are different kinds of love, different ways of feeling."

"I only know how I feel about you." His eyes were very intense and just above hers as she sat on the desk. Phil had been right, she realized. He wasn't quite a child.

"Tod, I know this won't be easy for you to understand. Sometimes people aren't right for each other."

"Just because I'm younger," he began heatedly.

"That's part of it," Tory agreed, keeping her voice quiet. "It's hard to accept, when you feel like a man, that you're still a boy. There's so much you have to experience yet, and to learn."

"But when I do . . ." he began.

"When you do," she interrupted, "you won't feel the same way about me."

"Yes, I will!" he insisted. He surprised both of them by grabbing her arms. "It won't change because I don't want it to. And I'll wait if I have to. I love you, Tory."

"I know you do. I know it's very real." She lifted her hands to cover his. "Age doesn't mean anything to the heart, Tod. You're very special to me, a very important part of my life."

"But you don't love me." The words trembled out with anger and frustration.

"Not in the way you mean." She kept her hands firm on his when he would have jerked away.

"You think it's funny."

"No," she said sharply, rising. "No, I think it's lovely. And I wish things could be different because I know the kind of man you'll be. It hurts—for me too."

He was breathing quickly, struggling with tears and a sharp sense of betrayal. "You don't understand," he accused, pulling away from her. "You don't care."

"I do. Tod, please—"

"No." He stopped her with one ravaged look. "You don't." With a dignity that tore at Tory's heart, he walked out of the office.

She leaned back against the desk, overcome by a sense of failure.

The sun was just setting when Tory dropped down on the short, prickly grass by the water. Pulling her knees to her chest, she watched the flaming globe sink toward the horizon. There was an intensity of color against the darkening blue of the sky. Nothing soft or mellow. It was a vivid and demanding prelude to night.

Tory watched the sky with mixed emotions. The day as a whole was the kind she would have liked to wrap up and ship off to oblivion. The situation with Tod had left her emotionally wrung out and edgy. As a result she had handled a couple of routine calls with less finesse than was her habit. She'd even managed to snarl at Merle before she had gone off duty. Glancing down at the badge on her breast, she considered tossing it into the water.

A beautiful mess you've made of things, Sheriff, she told herself. Ah, the hell with it, she decided, resting her chin on her knees. She was taking the night off. Tomorrow she would straighten everything out, one disaster at a time.

The trouble was, she thought with a half smile, she'd forgotten the art of relaxation over the past few weeks. It was time to reacquaint herself with laziness. Lying back, Tory shut her eyes and went instantly to sleep.

Drifting slowly awake with the feather-light touch of fingers on her cheek, Tory gave a sleepy sigh and debated whether she should open her eyes. There was another touch—a tracing of her lips this time. Enjoying the sensation, she made a quiet sound of pleasure and let her lashes flutter up.

The light was dim, deep, deep dusk. Her eyes focused gradually on the sky above her. No clouds, no stars, just a mellow expanse of blue. Taking a deep breath, she lifted her arms to stretch. Her hand was captured and kissed. Tory turned her head and saw Phil sitting beside her.

"Hello."

"Watching you wake up is enough to drive a man crazy," he murmured, keeping her hand in his. "You're sexier sleeping than most women are wide awake."

She gave a lazy laugh. "Sleeping's always been one of my best things. Have you been here long?"

"Not long. The filming ran a bit over schedule." He flexed his back muscles, then smiled down at her. "How was your day?"

"Rotten." Tory blew out a breath and struggled to sit up. "I talked with Tod this afternoon. I didn't handle it well. Damn." Tory rested her forehead on her knees again. "I didn't want to hurt that boy."

"Tory"—Phil stroked a hand down her hair—"there was no way he wouldn't be hurt some. Kids are resilient. He'll bounce back."

"I know." She turned her head to look at him, keeping her cheeks on her knees. "But he's so fragile. Love's fragile, isn't it? So easily shattered. I suppose it's best that he hate me for a while."

"He won't," Phil disagreed. "You mean too much to him. After a while his feelings will slip into perspective. I imagine he'll always think of you as his first real love."

"It makes me feel very special, but I don't think I made him believe that. Anyway," she continued, "after I'd made a mess out of that, I snarled at one of the town fathers, bit off the head of a rancher, and took a few swipes at Merle." She swore with the expertise he had admired before. "Sitting here, I knew I was in danger of having a major pity party, so I went to sleep instead."

"Wise choice. I came near to choking my overseer."

"Overseer? Oh, the guarantor." Tory laughed, shaking back her hair. "So we both had a lovely day."

"Let's drink to it." Phil picked up a bottle of champagne from beside him.

"Well, how about that." Tory glanced at the label and pursed her lips. "You always go first class, Kincaid."

"Absolutely," he agreed, opening the bottle with a pop and fizz. He poured the brimming wine into a glass. Tory took it, watching the bubbles explode as he filled his own. "To the end of the day."

"To the end of the day!" she agreed, clinking her glass against his. The ice-cold champagne ran excitedly over her tongue. "Nice," she murmured, shutting her eyes and savoring. "Very nice."

They drank in companionable silence as the darkness deepened. Overhead a few stars flickered hesitantly while the moon started its slow rise. The night was as hot and dry as the afternoon and completely still. There wasn't even a whisper of breeze to ripple the water. Phil leaned back on an elbow, studying Tory's profile.

"What are you thinking?"

"That I'm glad I took the night off." Smiling, she turned her head so she faced him fully. The pale light of the moon fell over her features, accenting them.

"Good God, Tory," he breathed. "I've got to get that face on film."

She threw back her head and laughed with a freedom she hadn't felt in days. "So take a home movie, Kincaid."

"Would you let me?" he countered immediately.

She merely filled both glasses again. "You're obsessed," she told him.

"More than's comfortable, yes," he murmured. He sipped, enjoying the taste but thinking of her. "I wasn't sure you'd come."

"Neither was I." She studied the wine in her glass with apparent concentration. "Another glass of this and I might admit I enjoy being with you."

"We've half a bottle left."

Tory lifted one shoulder in a shrug before she

drank again. "One step at a time," she told him. "But then," she murmured, "I suppose we've come a few steps already, haven't we?"

"A few." His fingers ran over the back of her hand. "Does it worry you?"

She gave a quick, rueful laugh. "More than's comfortable, yes."

Sitting up, he draped a casual arm around her shoulders. "I like the night best. I have the chance to think." He sensed her complete relaxation, feeling a pleasant stir as she let her head rest on his shoulder. "During the day, with all the pressure, the demands, when I think, I think on my feet."

"That's funny." She lifted a hand across her body to lace her fingers with his. "In Albuquerque I did some of my best planning in bed the night before a court date. It's easier to let things come and go in your head at night." Tilting her face, Tory brushed his lips with hers. "I do enjoy being with you."

He returned the kiss, but with equal lightness. "I didn't need the champagne?"

"Well . . . it didn't hurt." When he chuckled, she settled her head in the crook of his shoulder again. It felt right there, as if it belonged. "I've always loved this spot," Tory said quietly. "Water's precious around here, and this has always been like a little mirage. It's not very big, but it's pretty deep in places. The townspeople enjoy calling it a lake." She laughed suddenly. "When we were kids, we'd troop out here sometimes on an unbearably hot day. We'd strip and jump in. Of course, it was frowned on when we were teenagers, but we still managed."

"Our decadent youth."

"Good, clean fun, Kincaid," she disagreed.

"Oh, yeah? Why don't you show me?"

Tory turned to him with a half smile. When he only lifted a brow in challenge, she grinned. A small pulse of excitement beat deep inside her. "You're on." Pushing him away, she tugged off her shoes. "The name of the game is to get in first."

As he stripped off his shirt it occurred to him that he'd never seen her move quickly before. He was still pulling off his shoes when she was naked and racing for the water. The moonlight danced over her skin, over the hair that streamed behind her back, causing him to stop and stare after her. She was even more exquisite than he had imagined. Then she was splashing up to her waist and diving under. Shaking himself out of the trance, Phil stripped and followed her.

The water was beautifully cool. It shocked his heated skin on contact, then caressed it. Phil gave a moan of pure pleasure as he sank to his shoulders. The small swimming hole in the middle of nowhere gave him just as much relief as his custom-made pool. More, he realized, glancing around for Tory. She surfaced, face lifted, hair slicked back. The moonlight caught the glisten of water on her face. A naiad, he thought. She opened her eyes. They glimmered green, like a cat's.

"You're slow, Kincaid."

He struggled against an almost painful flood of desire. This wasn't the moment to rush. They both knew this was their time, and there were hours yet to fill. "I've never seen you move fast before," he commented, treading water.

"I save it up." The bottom was just below her toes. Tory kicked lazily to keep afloat. "Conserving energy is one of my personal campaigns."

"I guess that means you don't want to race."

She gave him a long look. "You've got to be kidding."

"Guess you wouldn't be too hard to beat," he considered. "Skinny," he added.

"I am not." Tory put the heel of her hand into the water, sending a spray into his face.

"Couple of months in a good gym might build you up a bit." He smiled, calmly wiping the water from his eyes.

"I'm built up just fine," she returned. "Is this amateur psychology, Kincaid?"

"Did it work?" he countered.

In answer she twisted and struck out, kicking up a curtain of water into his face as she headed for the far side of the pool. Phil grinned, observing that she could move like lightning when she put her mind to it, then started after her.

She beat him by two full strokes, then waited, laughing, while she shook back her hair. "Better keep up your membership to that gym, Kincaid."

"You cheated," he pointed out.

"I won. That's what counts."

He lifted a brow, amused and intrigued that she wasn't even winded. Apparently her statement about strong energy was perfectly true. "And that from an officer of the law."

"I'm not wearing my badge."

"I noticed."

Tory laughed again, moving out in a gentle sidestroke toward the middle of the pool. "I guess you're in pretty good shape . . . for a Hollywood director."

"Is that so?" He swam alongside of her, matching her languid movements.

"You don't have a paunch—yet," she added, grinning.

Gently but firmly, Phil pushed her head under. "So you want to play dirty," she murmured when she surfaced. In a quick move she had his legs scissored between hers, then gave his chest a firm shove. Off guard, Phil went over backward and submerged. He came up, giving his head a toss to free his eyes of dripping hair. Tory was already a few yards away, treading water and chuckling.

"Basic Self-Defense 101," she informed him. "Though you have to make allowances for buoyancy in the water."

This time Phil put more effort into his strokes. Before Tory had reached the other side, he had a firm grip on her ankle. With a tug he took her under the water and back to him. Sputtering, she found herself caught in his arms.

"Want to try a few free throws?" he invited.

A cautious woman, Tory measured her opponent and the odds. "I'll pass. Water isn't my element."

Her arms were trapped between their bodies, but when she tried to free them, he only brought her closer. His smile faded into a look of understanding. She felt her heart begin a slow, dull thud.

He took her mouth with infinite care, wanting to savor the moment. Her lips were wet and cool. With no hesitation her tongue sought his. The kiss deepened slowly, luxuriously while he supported her, keeping her feet just above the sandy bottom. The feeling of weightlessness aroused her, and she allowed herself to float, holding on to him as though he were an anchor. Their lips warmed from an intimate heat before they began to search for new tastes.

Without hurry they roamed each other's faces, running moist kisses over moist skin. With quiet whispers the water lapped around them as they shifted and searched.

Finding her arms free at last, Tory wrapped them about his neck, pressing her body against his. She heard Phil suck in his breath at the contact, felt the shudder race through him before his mouth crushed down on hers. The time had passed for slow loving. Passion too long suppressed exploded as mouth sought eager mouth. Keeping one arm firm at her waist, he began to explore her as he had longed to do. His fingers slid over her wet skin.

Tory moved against him, weakening them both so that they submerged, locked together. Streaming wet, they surfaced with their lips still fused, then gasped for air. Her hands ran over him, drawing him closer, then away, to seek more of him. Unable to bear the hunger, she thrust her fingers into his hair and pulled his lips back to hers. With a sudden violence he bent her back until her hair streamed behind her on the surface of the water. His mouth rushed over her face, refusing her efforts to halt it with hers while he found her breast with his palm.

The throaty moan that wrenched from her evoked a new wave of passion. Phil lifted her so he could draw her hot, wet nipple into his mouth. His tongue tormented them both until her hands fell into the pool in a submission he hadn't expected. Drunk on power, he took his mouth over her trembling skin, down to where the water separated him from her. Frustrated with the barrier, he let his mouth race up again to her breast until Tory clutched at his shoulders, shuddering.

Her head fell back as he lowered her so that her neck was vulnerable and glistening in the moonlight.

He kissed it hungrily, hearing her cry with anguished delight.

Cool, cool water, but she was so hot that his legs nearly buckled at the feel of her. Tory was beyond all but dark, vivid sensations. To her the water felt steamy, heated by her own body. Her breathing seemed to echo in the empty night, then shudder back to her. She would have shouted for him to take her, but his name would only come as a gasp through her lips. She couldn't bear it; the need was unreasonable. With a strength conceived in passion she locked her legs tightly around his waist and lowered herself to him.

They swayed for a moment, equally stunned. Then he gripped her legs, letting her take him on a wild, impossible journey. There was a rushing, like the sound of the wind inside her head. Trembling, they slid down into the water.

With some vague recollection of where they were, Phil caught Tory against him again. "We'd better get out of here," he managed. "We'll drown."

Tory let her head fall on his shoulder. "I don't mind."

With a low, shaky laugh, Phil lifted her into his arms and carried her from the pond.

CHAPTER 8

He laid her down, then dropped on his back on the grass beside her. For some time the only sound in the night was their mixed breathing. The stars were brilliant now, the moon nearly full. Both of them stared up.

"You were saying something," Phil began in a voice that still wasn't steady, "about water not being your element."

Tory gave a choke of laughter that turned into a bubble, then a burst of pure appreciation. "I guess I could be wrong."

Phil closed his eyes, the better to enjoy the heavy weakness that flowed through his system.

Tory sighed and stretched. "That was wonderful."

He drew her closer against his side. "Cold?"

"No."

"This grass—"

"Terrible, isn't it?" With another laugh Tory twisted so that she lay over his chest. Her wet skin slid over his. Lazily he ran a hand down the length of her back as she smiled back at him. Her hair was slicked close to her head, her skin as pale and exquisite as marble in the moonlight. A few small drops of water clung to her lashes.

"You're beautiful when you're wet," he told her, drawing her down for a slow, lingering kiss.

"So are you." When he grinned, she ran both thumbs from his jaw to his cheekbones. "I like your face," she decided, tilting her head as she studied it. "That aristocratic bone structure you get from your father. It's no wonder he was so effective playing those swashbuckling roles early in his career." She narrowed her eyes as if seeking a different perspective. "Of course," she continued thoughtfully, "I rather like it when yours takes on that aloof expression."

"Aloof?" He shifted a bit as the grass scratched his bare skin.

"You do it very well. Your eyes have a terrific way of saying 'I beg your pardon' and meaning 'Go to hell.' I've noticed it, especially when you talk to that short man with the little glasses."

"Tremaine," Phil muttered. "Associate producer and general pain in the neck."

Tory chuckled and kissed his chin. "Don't like anyone else's hands on your movie, do you?"

"I'm very selfish with what belongs to me." He took her mouth again with more fervor than he had intended. As the kiss lengthened and deepened he gave a quick sound of pleasure and pressed her closer. When their lips parted, their eyes met. Both of them knew they were heading for dangerous ground. Both of them treaded carefully. Tory lowered her head to his chest, trying to think logically.

"I suppose we knew this was going to happen sooner or later."

"I suppose we did."

She caught her bottom lip between her teeth a moment. "The important thing is not to let it get complicated."

"No." He frowned up at the stars. "We both want to avoid complications."

"In a few weeks we'll both be leaving town." They were unaware that they had tightened their holds on the other. "I have to pick up my caseload again."

"I have to finish the studio scenes," he murmured.

"It's a good thing we understand each other right from the beginning." She closed her eyes, drawing in his scent as though she were afraid she might forget it. "We can be together like this, knowing no one will be hurt when it's over."

"Yeah."

They lay in silence, dealing with a mutual and unstated sense of depression and loss. We're adults, Tory thought, struggling against the mood. Attracted to each other. It isn't any more than that. Can't be any more than that. But she wasn't as sure of herself as she wanted to be.

"Well," she said brightly, lifting her head again. "So tell me how the filming's going? That scene today seemed to click perfectly."

Phil forced himself to match her mood, ignoring the doubts forming in his own head. "You came in on the last take," he said dryly. "It was like pulling teeth."

Tory reached across him for the bottle of champagne. The glass was covered with beads of sweat. "It looked to me like Marlie Summers came out on top," she commented as she poured.

"She's very good."

Resting her arm on his chest, Tory drank. The wine still fizzled cold. "Yes, I thought so, too, but I wish she'd steer away from Merle."

"Worried about his virtue, Tory?" he asked dryly.

She shot him an annoyed look. "He's going to get hurt."

"Why?" he countered. "Because a beautiful woman's interested enough to spend some time with him? Now, look," he continued before she could retort, "you have your own view of him. It's possible someone else might have another."

Frowning, she drank again. "How's he going to feel when she leaves?"

"That's something he'll have to deal with," Phil said quietly. "He already knows she's going to."

Again their eyes met in quick, almost frightened recognition. Tory looked away to study the remaining wine in her glass. It was different, she told herself. She and Phil both had certain priorities. When they parted, it would be without regret or pain. It had to be.

"It might not be easy to accept," she murmured, wanting to believe she still spoke of Merle.

"On either side," he replied after a long pause.

Tory turned her head to find his eyes on hers, light and clear and very intense. The ground was getting shaky again. "I suppose it'll work out for the best . . . for everyone." Determined to lighten the mood, she smiled down at him. "You know, the whole town's excited about those scenes you're shooting with them as extras. The Kramer twins haven't gotten out of line for an entire week."

"One of them asked me if he could have a close-up."

"Which one?"

"Who the hell can tell?" Phil demanded. "This one tried to hustle a date with Marlie."

Tory laughed, pressing the back of her wrist to her mouth to hold in a swallow of champagne. "Had to be

Zac. He's impossible. Are you going to give him his close-up?"

"I'll give him a swift kick in the pants if he messes around the crane again," Phil returned.

"Uh-oh, I didn't hear about that."

Phil shrugged. "It didn't seem necessary to call the law on him."

"Tempting as it might be," she returned. "I wouldn't have thrown him in the penitentiary. Handling the Kramers has become an art."

"I had one of my security guards put the fear of God into him," Phil told her easily. "It seemed to do the trick."

"Listen, Phil, if any of my people need restraining, I expect to be informed."

With a sigh, he plucked the glass from her hand, tossed it aside, then rolled on top of her. "You've got the night off, Sheriff. We're not going to talk about it."

"Really." Her arms were already linked around his neck. "Just what are we going to talk about, then?"

"Not a damn thing," he muttered and pressed his mouth to hers.

Her response was a muffled sound of agreement. He could taste the champagne on her tongue and lingered over it. The heat of the night had already dried their skin, but he ran his hands through the cool dampness of her hair. He could feel her nipples harden against the pressure of his chest. This time, he thought, there would be no desperation. He could enjoy her slowly— the long, lean lines of her body, the silken texture of her skin, the varied, heady tastes of her.

From the wine-flavored lips he took an unhurried journey to the warmer taste of her throat. But his hands were already roaming demandingly. Tory moved under

him with uncontrollable urgency as his thumb found
the peak of her breast, intensifying her pleasure. To his
amazement Phil found he could have taken her immediately. He banked the need. There was still so much
of her to learn of, so much to experience. Allowing
the tip of his tongue to skim along her skin, he moved
down to her breast.

Tory arched, pressing him down. His slow, teasing
kisses made her moan in delighted frustration. Beneath
the swell of her breast, his mouth lingered to send
shivers and more shivers of pleasure through her. His
tongue flicked lazily over her nipple, then retreated to
soft flesh. She moaned his name, urging him back. He
circled slowly, mouth on one breast, palm on the other,
thrilling to her mindless murmurs and convulsive
movements beneath him. Taking exquisite care, he
captured a straining peak between his teeth. Leaving it
moist and wanting, he journeyed to her other breast to
savor, to linger, then to devour.

His hands had moved lower, so that desire throbbed
over her at so many points, she was delirious for ful-
fillment. Anxious to discover all she could about his
body, Tory ran her fingertips over the taut muscles of
his shoulders, down the strong back. Through a haze
of sensation she felt him shudder at her touch. With
delicious slowness she skimmed her fingers up his rib
cage. She heard him groan before his teeth nipped into
her tender flesh. Open and hungry, his mouth came
swiftly back to hers.

When she reached for him, he drew in a sharp
breath at the contact. Burying his face in her neck,
Phil felt himself drowning in pleasure. The need grew
huge, but again he refused it.

"Not yet," he murmured to himself and to her.
"Not yet."

He passed down the valley between her breasts, wallowing in the hot scent that clung to her skin. Her stomach quivered under his lips. Tory no longer felt the rough carpet of grass under her back, only Phil's seeking mouth and caressing hands. His mouth slipped lower and she moaned, arching—willing, wanting. His tongue was quick and greedy, shooting pleasure from the core of her out even to her fingertips. Her body was heavy with it, her head light. He brought her to a shuddering crest, but relentlessly allowed no time for recovery. His fingers sought her even as his mouth found fresh delight in the taste of her thigh.

She shook her head, unable to believe she could be so helpless. Her fingers clutched at the dry grass while her lips responded to the dizzying pace he set. Her skin was damp again, quivering in the hot night air. Again and again he drove her up, never letting her settle, never allowing her complete release.

"Phil," she moaned between harsh, shallow breaths. "I need . . ."

He'd driven himself to the verge of madness. His body throbbed in one solid ache for her. Wildly he took his mouth on a frantic journey up her body. "What?" he demanded. "What do you need?"

"You," she breathed, no longer aware of words or meanings. "You."

With a groan of triumph he thrust into her, catapulting them both closer to what they insisted on denying.

She'd warned him about the heat. Still, Phil found himself cursing the unrelenting sun as he set up for another outdoor shot. The grips had set up stands with butterflies—long black pieces of cloth—to give shade between takes. The cameraman stood under a huge orange-and-white umbrella and sweated profusely. The actors at least could spend a few moments in the shade provided while Phil worked almost exclusively in the streaming sun, checking angles, lighting, shadows. Reflectors were used to bounce the sunlight and carbon arcs balanced the back lighting. A gaffer, stripped to the waist, adjusted a final piece of blue gel over a bulb. The harsh, glaring day was precisely what Phil wanted, but it didn't make the work any more pleasant.

Forcing down more salt tablets, he ordered the next take. Oddly, Dressler seemed to have adjusted to the heat more easily than the younger members of the cast and crew. Or, Phil mused as he watched him come slowly down the street with the fledgling actor who played his alter ego, he's determined not to be outdone. As time went on, he became more competitive—and the more competitive he became, particularly with Marlie, the more Phil was able to draw out of him.

Yeah, Phil thought as Dressler turned to the younger actor with a look of world-weariness. He ran through his dialogue slowly, keeping the pace just short of dragging. He was a man giving advice reluctantly, without any confidence that it was viable or would be listened to in any case. He talked almost to himself. For a moment Phil forgot his own discomfort in simple admiration for a pro who had found the heart of his character. He was growing old and didn't give a damn—wanted to be left alone, but had no hope that his wishes would be respected. Once he had found his moment of glory, then had lost it. He saw himself in the younger man and felt a bitter pity. Ultimately he turned and walked slowly away. The camera stayed on him for a silent thirty seconds.

"Cut. Perfect," Phil announced in a rare show of unconditional approval. "Lunch," he said dropping a hand on the younger actor's shoulder. "Get out of the sun for a while. I'll need you for reaction shots in thirty minutes." He walked over to meet Sam. "That was a hell of a job."

Grinning, Sam swiped at his brow. "Somebody's got to show these kids how it's done. That love scene with Marlie's going to be interesting," he added a bit ruefully. "I keep remembering she's my daughter's age."

"That should keep you in character."

Sam laughed, running his fingers through his thick salt-and-pepper hair. "Well, the girl's a pro," he said after a moment. "This movie's going to shoot her into the fast lane quick." He sent Phil a long, steady look. "And you and I," he added, "are going to win each other an Oscar." When Phil only lifted a brow, Sam slapped him on the back. "Don't give me that look, boy," he said, amused. "You're talking to one who's been passed over a few times himself. You can be lofty and say awards don't mean a damn . . . but they do." Again his eyes met Phil's. "I want this one just as much as you do." He ran a hand over his stomach. "Now I'm going to get myself a beer and put my feet up."

He sauntered off, leaving Phil looking after him. He didn't want to admit, even to himself, that he desired his profession's ultimate accolade. In a few short words Dressler had boiled it all down. Yes, he wanted to direct outstanding films—critically and financially successful, lasting, important. But he wanted that little gold statue. With a wry grin Phil swiped at his brow with his forearm. It seemed that the need to win, and to be acknowledged, didn't fade with years. Dressler had been in the business longer than Phil had been alive; yet, he was still waiting for the pot at the end of the rainbow. Phil adjusted his sunglasses, admitting he wasn't willing to wait thirty-five years.

"Hey, Phil." Bicks lumbered over to him, mopping his face. "Look, you've got to do something about that woman."

Phil pulled out a cigarette. "Which?"

"That sheriff." Bicks popped another piece of gum into his mouth. "Great looker," he added. "Got a way of walking that makes a man home right in on her . . ." He trailed off, observing the look in Phil's eyes. "Just an observation," he muttered.

"What do you expect me to do about the way Sheriff Ashton walks, Bicks?"

Catching the amusement in Phil's tone, Bicks grinned. "Nothing, please. A man's got to have something pleasant to look at in this place. But damn it, Phil, she gave me a ticket and slapped a two-hundred-and-fifty-dollar fine on me."

Phil pushed his glasses up on his head with a weary sigh. He'd wanted to catch a quick shower before resuming the shoot. "What for?"

"Littering."

"Littering?" Phil repeated over a snort of laughter.

"Two hundred and fifty bucks for dropping gum wrappers in the street," Bicks returned, not seeing the humor. "Wouldn't listen to reason either. I'd have picked 'em up and apologized. Two hundred and fifty bucks for a gum wrapper, Phil. Jeez."

"All right, all right, I'll talk to her." After checking his watch, Phil started up the street. "Set up for the next scene in twenty minutes."

Tory sat with her feet propped up on the desk as she struggled to decipher Merle's report on a feud between two neighboring ranches. It seemed that a dispute over a line of fence was becoming more heated. It was going to require her attention. So was the letter she had just received from one of her clients in Albuquerque. When

Phil walked in, she glanced up from the scrawled pad and smiled.

"You look hot," she commented.

"Am hot," he countered, giving the squeaking fan above their heads a glance. "Why don't you get that thing fixed?"

"And spoil the atmosphere?"

Phil stepped over the sleeping dog, taking a seat on the corner of her desk. "We're going to be shooting one of the scenes with the townspeople milling around later. Are you going to watch?"

"Sure."

"Want to do a cameo?" he asked with a grin.

"No, thanks."

Leaning over, he pressed his lips to hers. "Dinner in my room tonight?"

Tory smiled. "You still have those candles?"

"All you want," he agreed.

"You talked me into it," she murmured, drawing his face back for a second kiss.

"Tory, if I brought a camera out to your ranch one day, would you let me film you riding that palomino?"

"Phil, for heaven's sake—"

"Home movies?" he interrupted, twirling her hair around his finger.

She gave a capitulating sigh. "If it's important to you."

"It is." He straightened, checked his watch, then pulled out a cigarette. "Listen, Tory, Bicks tells me you fined him for littering."

"That's right." The phone rang, and Phil waited while she took the call. After a moment he realized her tone was slightly different. With interest he listened to the legal jargon roll off her tongue. It must be Albuquerque, he realized. He watched her carefully, discovering this was a part of her life he knew nothing of. She'd be tough in court, he mused. There was an intensity under that languid exterior that slipped out at unexpected moments. And what did she do after a day in court or a day in the office?

There'd be men, he thought, instantly disliking the image. A woman like Tory would only spend evenings alone, nights alone, if she chose to. He looked away, taking a deep drag on his cigarette. He couldn't start thinking along those lines, he reminded himself. They were both free agents. That was the first rule.

"Phil?"

He turned back to see that she had replaced the receiver. "What?"

"You were saying?"

"Ah . . ." He struggled to remember the point of his visit "Bicks," he continued.

"Yes, what about him?"

"A two-hundred-and-fifty-dollar fine for littering," Phil stated, not quite erasing the frown that had formed between his brows.

"Yes, that's the amount of the fine."

"Tory, be reasonable."

Her brow lifted. "Reasonable, Kincaid?"

Her use of his surname told him what level they were dealing on. "It's certainly extreme for a gum wrapper."

"We don't vary the fine according to the style of trash," she replied with an easy shrug. "A tin of caviar would have cost him the same amount."

Goaded, Phil rose. "Listen, Sheriff—"

"And while we're on the subject," she interrupted, "you can tell your people that if they don't start picking up after themselves more carefully, they're all going to be slapped with fines." She gave him a mild smile. "Let's keep Friendly clean, Kincaid."

He took a slow drag. "You're not going to hassle my people."

"You're not going to litter my town."

He swore, coming around the desk when the door opened. Pleased to see Tod, Tory swung her legs to the floor and started to stand. It was then that she saw the dull bruise on the side of his face. Fury swept through her so quickly, she was forced to clench her hands into fists to control it. Slowly she walked to him and took his face in her hands.

"How did you get this?"

He shrugged, avoiding her eyes. "It's nothing."

Fighting for calm, Tory lifted his hands, examining the knuckles carefully. There was no sign that he'd been fighting. "Your father?"

He shook his head briskly. "I came to do the sweeping up," he told her and tried to move away.

Tory took him firmly by the shoulders. "Tod, look at me."

Reluctantly he lifted his eyes. "I've still got five dollars to work off," he said tightly.

"Did your father put this bruise on your face?" she demanded. When he started to drop his eyes again, she gave him a quick shake. "You answer me."

"He was just mad because—" He broke off, observing the rage that lit her face. Instinctively he cringed away from it. Tory set him aside and started for the door.

"Where are you going?" Moving quickly, Phil was at the door with her, his hand over hers on the knob.

"To see Swanson."

"No!" They both turned to see Tod standing rigid

in the center of the room. "No, you can't. He won't like it. He'll get awful mad at you."

"I'm going to talk to your father, Tod," Tory said in a careful voice, "to explain to him why it's wrong for him to hurt you this way."

"Only when he loses his temper." Tod dashed across the room to grab her free hand. "He's not a bad man. I don't want you to put him in jail."

Though her anger was lethal, Tory gave Tod's hand a reassuring squeeze. "I'm just going to talk to him, Tod."

"He'll be crazy mad if you do, Tory. I don't want him to hurt you either."

"He won't, don't worry." She smiled, seeing by the expression in Tod's eyes that she'd already been forgiven. "Go get the broom now. I'll be back soon."

"Tory, please . . ."

"Go on," she said firmly.

Phil waited until the boy had disappeared into the back room. "You're not going."

Tory sent him a long look, then pulled open the door. Phil spun her around as she stepped outside. "I said you're not going."

"You're interfering with the law, Kincaid."

"The hell with that!" Infuriated, Phil pushed her back against the wall. "You're crazy if you think I'm going to let you go out there."

"You don't *let* me do anything," she reminded him. "I'm sworn to protect the people under my jurisdiction. Tod Swanson is one of my people."

"A man who punches a kid isn't going to hesitate to take a swing at you just because you've got that little piece of tin on your shirt."

Because her anger was racing, Tory forced herself

to speak calmly. "What do you suggest I do? Ignore what I just saw?"

Frustrated by the image of Tod's thin face, Phil swore. "I'll go."

"You have no right." She met his eyes squarely. "You're not the law, and what's more, you're an outsider."

"Send Merle."

"Don't you hold with no woman sheriff, Kincaid?"

"Damn it, Tory." He shook her, half in fear, half in frustration. "This isn't a joke."

"No, it's not," she said seriously. "It's my job. Now, let go of me, Phil."

Furious, Phil complied, then watched her stride to her car. "Tory," he called after her, "if he puts a hand on you, I'll kill him."

She slipped into the car, driving off without looking back.

Tory took the short drive slowly, wanting to get her emotions under control before she confronted Swanson. She had to be objective, she thought, as her knuckles whitened on the steering wheel. But first she had to be calm. It wasn't possible to do what she needed to do in anger, or to let Phil's feelings upset her. To live up to the badge on her shirt, she had to set all that aside.

She wasn't physically afraid, not because she was foolishly brave, but because when she saw a blatant injustice, Tory forgot everything but the necessity of making it right. As she took the left fork toward the Swanson ranch, however, she had her first stirring of self-doubt.

What if she mishandled the situation? she thought in sudden panic. What if her meeting with Swanson only made more trouble for the boy? The memory of Tod's terrified face brought on a quick queasiness that she fought down. No, she wasn't going to mishandle it, she told herself firmly as the house came into view. She was going to confront Swanson and at the very least set the wheels in motion for making things right. Tory's belief that all things could be set right with patience, through the law, had been indoctrinated in childhood. She knew and accepted no other way.

She pulled up behind Swanson's battered pickup, then climbed out of the sheriff's car. Instantly a dog who had been sleeping on the porch sent out angry, warning barks. Tory eyed him a moment, wary, then saw that he came no farther than the edge of the sagging porch. He looked as old and unkempt as the house itself.

Taking a quick look around, Tory felt a stir of pity for Tod. This was borderline poverty. She, too, had grown up where a tightened belt was often a rule, but between her mother's penchant for neatness and the hard work of both her parents, their small ranch had always had a homey charm. This place, on the other hand, looked desolate and hopeless. The grass grew wild, long overdue for trimming. There were no brightening spots of color from flowers or potted plants. The house itself was frame, the paint faded down to the wood in places. There was no chair on the porch, no sign that anyone had the time or inclination to sit and appreciate the view.

No one came to the door in response to the dog's barking. Tory debated calling out from where she stood or taking a chance with the mangy mutt. A shout came from the rear of the house with a curse and an order to shut up. The dog obeyed, satisfying himself with low growls as Tory headed in the direction of the voice.

She spotted Swanson working on the fence of an empty corral. The back of his shirt was wet with sweat, while his hat was pulled low to shade his face. He was a short, stocky man with the strong shoulders of a laborer. Thinking of Tod's build, Tory decided he had inherited it, and perhaps his temperament, from his mother.

"Mr. Swanson?"

His head jerked up. He had been replacing a board on the fence; the hand that swung the hammer paused on the downswing. Seeing his face, Tory decided he had the rough, lined face of a man constantly fighting the odds of the elements. He narrowed his eyes; they passed briefly over her badge.

"Sheriff," he said briefly, then gave the nail a final whack. He cared little for women who interfered in a man's work.

"I'd like to talk to you, Mr. Swanson."

"Yeah?" He pulled another nail out of an old coffee can. "What about?"

"Tod." Tory waited until he had hammered the nail into the warped board.

"That boy in trouble?"

"Apparently," she said mildly. She told herself to overlook his rudeness as he turned his back to take out another nail.

"I handle my own," he said briefly. "What's he done?"

"He hasn't done anything, Mr. Swanson."

"Either he's in trouble or he's not." Swanson placed another nail in position and beat it into the wood. The sound echoed in the still air. From somewhere to the right, Tory heard the lazy moo of a cow. "I ain't got time for conversation, Sheriff."

"He's in trouble, Mr. Swanson," she returned levelly. "And you'll talk to me here or in my office."

The tone had him taking another look and measuring her again. "What do you want?"

"I want to talk to you about the bruise on your son's face." She glanced down at the meaty hands, noting that the knuckles around the hammer whitened.

"You've got no business with my boy."

"Tod's a minor," she countered. "He's very much my business."

"I'm his father."

"And as such, you are not entitled to physically or emotionally abuse your child."

"I don't know what the hell you're talking about." The color in his sun-reddened face deepened angrily. Tory's eyes remained calm and direct.

"I'm well aware that you've beaten the boy before," she said coolly. "There are very strict laws to protect a child against this kind of treatment. If they're unknown to you, you might want to consult an attorney."

"I don't need no damn lawyer," he began, gesturing at Tory with the hammer as his voice rose.

"You will if you point that thing at me again," she told him quietly. "Attempted assault on a peace officer is a very serious crime."

Swanson looked down at the hammer, then dropped it disgustedly to the ground. "I don't assault women," he muttered.

"Just children?"

He sent her a furious glance from eyes that watered against the sun. "I got a right to discipline my own. I got a ranch to run here." A gesture with his muscular arm took in his pitiful plot of land. "Every time I turn around, that boy's off somewheres."

"Your reasons don't concern me. The results do."

With rage burning on his face, he took a step toward her. Tory held her ground. "You just get back in your car and get out. I don't need nobody coming out here telling me how to raise my boy."

Tory kept her eyes on his, although she was well aware his hands had clenched into fists. "I can start proceedings to make Tod a ward of the court."

"You can't take my boy from me."

Tory lifted a brow. "Can't I?"

"I got rights," he blustered.

"So does Tod."

He swallowed, then turned back to pick up his hammer and nails. "You ain't taking my boy."

Something in his eyes before he had turned made Tory pause. Justice, she reminded herself, was individual. "He wouldn't want me to," she said in a quieter tone. "He told me you were a good man and asked me not to put you in jail. You bruise his face, but he doesn't stop loving you."

She watched Swanson's back muscles tighten. Abruptly he flung the hammer and the can away. Nails scattered in the wild grass. "I didn't mean to hit him like that," he said with a wrench in his voice that kept Tory silent. "Damn boy should've fixed this fence like I told him." He ran his hands over his face. "I didn't mean to hit him like that. Look at this place," he muttered, gripping the top rail of the fence. "Takes every minute just to keep it up and scrape by, never amount to anything. But it's all I got. All I hear from Tod is how he wants to go off to school, how he wants this and that, just like—"

"His brother?" Tory ventured.

Swanson turned his head slowly, and his face was set. "I ain't going to talk about that."

"Mr. Swanson, I know something about what it takes to keep up a place like this. But your frustrations and your anger are no excuse for misusing your boy."

He turned away again, the muscles in his jaw tightening. "He's gotta learn."

"And your way of teaching him is to use your fists?"

"I tell you I didn't mean to hit him." Furious, he whirled back to her. "I don't mean to take a fist to him the way my father done to me. I know it ain't right, but when he pushes me—" He broke off again, angry with himself for telling his business to an outsider. "I ain't going to hit him anymore," he muttered.

"But you've told yourself that before, haven't you?" Tory countered. "And meant it, I'm sure." She took a deep breath, as he only stared at her. "Mr. Swanson, you're not the only parent who has a problem with control. There are groups and organizations designed to help you and your family."

"I'm not talking to any psychiatrists and do-gooders."

"There are ordinary people, exactly like yourself, who talk and help each other."

"I ain't telling strangers my business. I can handle my own."

"No, Mr. Swanson, you can't." For a moment Tory wished helplessly that there was an easy answer. "You don't have too many choices. You can drive Tod away, like you did your first boy." Tory stood firm as he whirled like a bull. "Or," she continued calmly, "you can seek help, the kind of help that will justify your son's love for you. Perhaps your first decision is what comes first, your pride or your boy."

Swanson stared out over the empty corral. "It would kill his mother if he took off too."

"I have a number you can call, Mr. Swanson. Someone who'll talk to you, who'll listen. I'll give it to Tod."

His only acknowledgment was a shrug. She waited a moment, praying her judgment was right. "I don't like ultimatums," she continued. "But I'll expect to see Tod daily. If he doesn't come to town, I'll come here. Mr. Swanson, if there's a mark on that boy, I'll slap a warrant on you and take Tod into custody."

He twisted his head to look at her again. Slowly, measuringly, he nodded. "You've got a lot of your father in you, Sheriff."

Automatically Tory's hand rose to her badge. She smiled for the first time. "Thanks." Turning, she walked away. Not until she was out of sight did she allow herself the luxury of wiping her sweaty palms on the thighs of her jeans.

CHAPTER 9

Tory was stopped at the edge of town by a barricade. Killing the engine, she stepped out of the car as one of Phil's security men approached her.

"Sorry, Sheriff, you can't use the main street. They're filming."

With a shrug Tory leaned back on the hood of her car. "It's all right. I'll wait."

The anger that had driven her out to the Swanson ranch was gone. Now Tory appreciated the time to rest and think. From her vantage point she could see the film crew and the townspeople who were making their debut as extras. She watched Hollister walk across the street in back of two actors exchanging lines in the scene. It made Tory smile, thinking how Hollister would brag about this moment of glory for years to come. There were a dozen people she knew, milling on the streets or waiting for their opportunity to mill. Phil cut the filming, running through take after take. Even with the distance Tory could sense he was frustrated. She frowned, wondering if their next encounter would turn into a battle. She couldn't back down, knowing that she had done the right thing—essentially the only thing.

Their time together was to be very brief, she mused. She didn't want it plagued by arguments and tension. But until he accepted the demands and responsibilities of her job, tension was inevitable. It had already become very important to Tory that the weeks ahead be un-marred. Perhaps, she admitted thoughtfully, too important. It was becoming more difficult for her to be perfectly logical when she thought of Phil. And since the night before, the future had become blurred and distant. There seemed to be only the overwhelming present.

She couldn't afford that, Tory reminded herself. That wasn't what either one of them had bargained for. She shifted her shoulders as her shirt grew hot and damp against her back. There was the summer, and just the summer, before they both went their separate ways. It was, of course, what each of them wanted.

"Sheriff . . . ah, Sheriff Ashton?"

Disoriented, Tory shook her head and stared at the man beside her. "What—? Yes?"

The security guard held out a chilled can of soda. "Thought you could use this."

"Oh, yeah, thanks." She pulled the tab, letting the air out in a hiss. "Do you think they'll be much longer?"

"Nah." He lifted his own can to drink half of it down without a breath. "They've been working on this one scene over an hour now."

Gratefully, Tory let the icy drink slide down her dry throat. "Tell me, Mr.—"

"Benson, Chuck Benson, ma'am."

"Mr. Benson," Tory continued, giving him an easy smile. "Have you had any trouble with any of the townspeople?"

"Nothing to speak of," he said as he settled beside her against the hood. "Couple of kids—those twins."

"Oh, yes," Tory murmured knowingly.

"Only tried to con me into letting them on the crane." He gave an indulgent laugh, rubbing the cold can over his forehead to cool it. "I've got a couple teenagers of my own," he explained.

"I'm sure you handled them, Mr. Benson." Tory flashed him a dashing smile that lifted his blood pressure a few degrees. "Still, I'd appreciate hearing about it if anyone in town gets out of line—particularly the Kramer twins."

Benson chuckled. "I guess those two keep you busy."

"Sometimes they're a full-time job all by themselves." Tory rested a foot on the bumper and settled herself more comfortably. "So tell me, how old are your kids?"

By the time Phil had finished shooting the scene, he'd had his fill of amateurs for the day. He'd managed, with a good deal of self-control, to hold on to his patience and speak to each one of his extras before he dismissed them. He wanted to shoot one more scene before they wrapped up for the day, so he issued instructions immediately. It would take an hour to set up, and with luck they'd have the film in the can before they lost the light.

The beeper at his hip sounded, distracting him. Impatiently, Phil drew out the walkie-talkie. "Yeah, Kincaid."

"Benson. I've got the sheriff here. All right to let her through now?"

Automatically, Phil looked toward the edge of town.

He spotted Tory leaning lazily against the hood, drinking from a can. He felt twin surges of relief and annoyance. "Let her in," he ordered briefly, then shoved the radio back in place. Now that he knew she was perfectly safe, Phil had a perverse desire to strangle her. He waited until she had parked in front of the sheriff's office and walked up the street to meet her. Before he was halfway there, Tod burst out of the door.

"Sheriff!" He teetered at the edge of the sidewalk, as if unsure of whether to advance any farther.

Tory stepped up and ran a fingertip down the bruise on his cheek. "Everything's fine, Tod."

"You didn't . . ." He moistened his lips. "You didn't arrest him?"

She rested her arms on his shoulders. "No." Tory felt his shuddering sigh.

"He didn't get mad at you or . . ." He trailed off again and looked at her helplessly.

"No, we just talked. He knows he's wrong to hurt you, Tod. He wants to stop."

"I was scared when you went, but Mr. Kincaid said you knew what you were doing and that everything would be all right."

"Did he?" Tory turned her head as Phil stepped beside her. The look held a long and not quite comfortable moment. "Well, he was right." Turning back to Tod, she gave his shoulders a quick squeeze. "Come inside a minute. There's a number I want you to give to your father. Want a cup of coffee, Kincaid?"

"All right."

Together, they walked into Tory's office. She went directly to her desk, pulling out a smart leather-bound address book that looked absurdly out of place. After flipping through it, she wrote a name and phone number on a pad, then ripped off the sheet. "This number is for your whole family," she said as she handed Tod the paper. "Go home and talk to your father, Tod. He needs to understand that you love him."

He folded the sheet before slipping it into his back pocket. Shifting from foot to foot, he stared down at the cluttered surface of her desk. "Thanks. Ah . . . I'm sorry about the things I said before." Coloring a bit, he glanced at Phil. "You know," he murmured, lowering his gaze to the desk again.

"Don't be sorry, Tod." She laid a hand over his until he met her eyes. "Okay?" she said, and smiled.

"Yeah, okay." He blushed again, but drew up his courage. Giving Tory a swift kiss on the cheek, he darted for the door.

With a low laugh she touched the spot where his lips had brushed. "I swear," she murmured, "if he were fifteen years older . . ." Phil grabbed both her arms.

"Are you really all right?"

"Don't I look all right?" she countered.

"Damn it, Tory!"

"Phil." Taking his face in her hands, she gave him a hard, brief kiss. "You had no reason to worry. Didn't you tell Tod that I knew what I was doing?"

"The kid was terrified." And so was I, he thought as he pulled her into his arms. "What happened out there?" he demanded.

"We talked," Tory said simply. "He's a very troubled man. I wanted to hate him and couldn't. I'm counting on him calling that number."

"What would you have done if he'd gotten violent?"

"I would have handled it," she told him, drawing away a bit. "It's my job."

"You can't—"

"Phil," Tory cut him off quickly and firmly. "I don't

tell you how to set a scene. Don't tell me how to run my town."

"It's not the same thing and you know it." He gave her an angry shake. "Nobody takes a swing at me when I do a retake."

"How about a frustrated actor?"

His eyes darkened. "Tory, you can't make a joke out of this."

"Better a joke than an argument," she countered. "I don't want to fight with you. Phil, don't focus on something like this. It isn't good for us."

He bit off a furious retort, then strode away to stare out the window. Nothing seemed as simple as it had been since the first time he'd walked into that cramped little room. "It's hard," he murmured. "I care."

Tory stared at his back while a range of emotions swept through her. Her heart wasn't listening to the strict common sense she had imposed on it. No longer sure what she wanted, she suppressed the urge to go to him and be held again. "I know," she said at length. "I care too."

He turned slowly. They looked at each other as they had once before, when there were bars between them—a bit warily. For a long moment there was only the sound of the whining fan and the mumble of conversation outside. "I have to get back," he told her, carefully slipping his hands in his pockets. The need to touch her was too strong. "Dinner?"

"Sure." She smiled but found it wasn't as easy to tilt her lips up as it should have been. "It'll have to be a little later—around eight?"

"That's fine. I'll see you then."

"Okay." She waited until the door had closed behind him before she sat at her desk. Her legs were weak. Leaning her head on her hand, she let out a long breath.

Oh, boy, she thought. Oh, boy. The ground was a lot shakier than she had anticipated. But she couldn't be falling in love with him, she reassured herself. Not that. Everything was intensified because of the emotional whirlwind of the past couple of days. She wasn't ready for the commitments and obligations of being in love, and that was all there was to it. Rising, she plugged in the coffeepot. She'd feel more like herself if she had a cup of coffee and got down to work.

Phil spent more time than he should have in the shower. It had been a very long, very rough twelve-hour day. He was accustomed to impossible hours and impossible demands in his job. Characteristically he took them in stride. Not this time.

The hot water and steam weren't drawing out the tension in his body. It had been there from the moment when Tory had driven off to the Swanson ranch, then had inexplicably increased during their brief conversation in her office. Because he was a man who always dealt well with tension, he was annoyed that he wasn't doing so this time.

He shut his eyes, letting the water flood over his head. She'd been perfectly right, he mused, about his having no say in her work. For that matter he had no say in any aspect of her life. There were no strings on their relationship. And he didn't want them any more than Tory did. He'd never had this problem in a relationship before. Problem? he mused, pushing wet hair out of his eyes. A perspective problem, he decided. What was necessary was to put his relationship with Tory back in perspective.

And who better to do that than a director, he thought wryly, then switched off the shower with a jerk of the wrist. He was simply letting too much emotion leak into the scene. Take two, he decided, grabbing a towel. Somehow he'd forgotten a very few basic, very vital rules. Keep it simple, keep it light, he reminded himself. Certainly someone with his background and experience was too smart to look for complications. What was between him and Tory was completely elemental and without strain, because they both wanted to keep it that way.

That was one of the things that had attracted him to her in the first place, Phil remembered. Hooking a towel loosely around his waist, he grabbed another to rub his hair dry. She wasn't a woman who expected a commitment, who looked for a permanent bond like love or marriage. Those were two things they were both definitely too smart to get mixed up with. In the steam-hazed mirror Phil caught the flicker of doubt in his own eyes.

Oh, no, he told himself, absolutely not. He wasn't in love with her. It was out of the question. He cared, naturally: She was a very special woman—strong, beautiful, intelligent, independent. And she had a great deal of simple sweetness that surfaced unexpectedly. It was that one quality that kept a man constantly off balance. So he cared about her, Phil mused, letting the second towel fall to the floor. He could even admit that he felt closer to her than to many people he'd known for years. There was nothing unusual about that. They had something in common that clicked—an odd sort of friendship, he decided. That was safe enough. It was only because he'd been worried about her that he'd allowed things to get out of proportion for a time.

But he was frowning abstractedly at his reflection when he heard the knock on the door.

"Who is it?"

"Room service."

The frown turned into a grin instantly as he recognized Tory's voice.

"Well, hi." Tory gave him a look that was both encompassing and lazy when he opened the door. "You're a little late for your reservation, Kincaid."

He stepped aside to allow her to enter with a large tray. "I lost track of time in the shower. Is that our dinner?"

"Bud phoned me." Tory set the tray on the card table they'd used before. "He said you'd ordered dinner for eight but didn't answer your phone. Since I was starving, I decided to expedite matters." Slipping her arms around his waist, she ran her hands up his warm, damp back. "Ummm, you're tense," she murmured, enjoying the way his hair curled chaotically around his face. "Rough day?"

"And then some," he agreed before he kissed her.

He smelled clean—of soap and shampoo—yet, Tory found the scent as arousing as the darker musky fragrance she associated with him. Her hunger for food faded as quickly as her hunger for him rose. Pressing closer, she demanded more. His arms tightened; his muscles grew taut. He was losing himself in her again, and found no power to control it.

"You really are tense," Tory said against his mouth. "Lie down."

He gave a half chuckle, nibbling on her bottom lip. "You work fast."

"I'll rub your back," she informed him as she drew away. "You can tell me all the frustrating things those nasty actors did today while you were striving to be brilliant."

"Let me show you how we deal with smart alecks on the coast," Phil suggested.

"On the bed, Kincaid."

"Well . . ." He grinned. "If you insist."

"On your stomach," she stated when he started to pull her with him.

Deciding that being pampered might have its advantages, he complied. "I've got a bottle of wine in the cooler." He sighed as he stretched out full length. "It's a hell of a place to keep a fifty-year-old Burgundy."

"Don't be a snob," Tory warned, sitting beside him. "You must have worked ten or twelve hours today," she began. "Did you get much accomplished?"

"Not as much as we should have." He gave a quiet groan of pleasure as she began to knead the muscles in his shoulders. "That's wonderful."

"The guys in the massage parlor always asked for Tory."

His head came up. "What?"

"Just wanted to see if you were paying attention. Down, Kincaid." She chuckled softly, working down his arms. "Were there technical problems or temperament ones?"

"Both," he answered, settling again. He found closing his eyes was a sensuous luxury. "Had some damaged dichroics. With luck the new ones'll get here tomorrow. Most of the foul-ups came during the crowd scene. Your people like to grin into the camera," he said dryly. "I expected one of them to wave any minute."

"That's showbiz," Tory concluded as she shifted to her knees. She hiked her dress up a bit for more freedom. Opening his eyes, Phil was treated to a view of thigh. "I wouldn't be surprised if the town council elected to build a theater in Friendly just to show your movie. Think of the boon to the industry."

"Merle walked across the street like he's sat on a horse for three weeks." Because her fingers were working miracles over his back muscles, Phil shut his eyes again.

"Merle's still seeing Marlie Summers."

"Tory."

"Just making conversation," she said lightly but dug a bit harder than necessary into his shoulder blades.

"Ouch!"

"Toughen up, Kincaid." With a laugh she placed a loud, smacking kiss in the center of his back. "You're not behind schedule, are you?"

"No. With all the hazards of shooting on location, we're doing very well. Another four weeks should wrap it up."

They were both silent for a moment unexpectedly depressed. "Well, then," Tory said briskly, "you shouldn't have to worry about the guarantor."

"He'll be hanging over my shoulder until the film's in the can," Phil muttered. "There's a spot just to the right . . . oh, yeah," he murmured as her fingers zeroed in on it.

"Too bad you don't have any of those nifty oils and lotions," she commented. In a fluid movement Tory straddled him, the better to apply pressure. "You're a disappointment, Kincaid. I'd have thought all you Hollywood types would carry a supply of that kind of thing."

"Mmmm." He would have retorted in kind, but his mind was beginning to float. Her fingers were cool and sure as they pressed on the small of his back just above the line of the towel. Her legs, clad in thin stockings, brushed his sides, arousing him with each time she flexed. The scent of her shampoo tickled his nostrils as she leaned up to knead his shoulders again. Though the sheet was warm—almost too warm—beneath him, he couldn't summon the energy to move. As the sun was setting, the light shifted, dimming. The room was filled with a golden haze that suited his mood. He could hear the rumble of a car on the street below, then only the sound of Tory's light, even breathing above him. His muscles were relaxed and limber, but he didn't consider telling her to stop. He'd forgotten completely about the dinner growing cold on the table behind them.

Tory continued to run her hands along his back, thinking him asleep. He had a beautiful body, she mused, hard and tanned and disciplined. The muscles in his back were supple and strong. For a moment she simply enjoyed exploring him. When she shifted lower, the skirt of her dress rode up high on her thighs. With a little sound of annoyance she unzipped the dress and pulled it over her head. She could move with more freedom in her sheer teddy.

His waist was trim. She allowed her hands to slide over it, approving its firmness. Before their lovemaking had been so urgent, and she had been completely under his command. Now she enjoyed learning the lines and planes of his body. Down the narrow hips, over the brief swatch of towel, to his thighs. There were muscles there, too, she discovered, hardened by hours of standing, tennis, swimming. The light mat of hair over his skin made her feel intensely feminine. She massaged his calves, then couldn't resist the urge to place a light kiss on the back of his knee. Phil's blood began to heat in a body too drugged with pleasure to move. It gave her a curiously warm feeling to rub his feet.

He worked much harder than she'd initially given him credit for, she mused as she roamed slowly back up his legs. He spent hours in the sun, on his feet, going over and over the same shot until he'd reached the perfection he strove for. And she had come to know that the film was never far from his thoughts, even during his free hours. Phillip Kincaid, she thought with a gentle smile, was a very impressive man—with much more depth than the glossy playboy the press loved to tattle on. He'd earned her respect during the time he'd been in Friendly, and she was growing uncomfortably certain he'd earned something more complex. She wouldn't think of it now. Perhaps she would have no choice but to think of it after he'd gone. But for now, he was here. That was enough.

With a sigh she bent low over his back to lay her cheek on his shoulder. The need for him had crept into her while she was unaware. Her pulse was pounding, and a thick warmth, like heated honey, seemed to flow through her veins.

"Phil." She moved her mouth to his ear. Her tongue traced it, slipping inside to arouse him to wakefulness. She heard his quiet groan as her heart began to beat jerkily. With her teeth she pulled and tugged on the lobe, then moved to experiment with the sensitive area just below. "I want you," she murmured. Quickly she began to take her lips over him with the same thorough care as her fingers.

He seemed so pliant as she roamed over him that when a strong arm reached out to pull her down, it took her breath away. Before she could recover it, his mouth was on hers. His lips were soft and warm, but the kiss was bruisingly potent. His tongue went deep to make an avid search of moist recesses as his weight pressed her into the mattress. He took a quick, hungry journey across her face before he looked down at her. There was nothing sleepy in his expression. The look alone had her breath trembling.

"My turn," he whispered.

With nimble fingers he loosened the range of tiny buttons down the front of her teddy. His lips followed, to send a trail of fire along the newly exposed skin. The plunge of the V stopped just below her navel. He lingered there, savoring the soft, honey-hued flesh. Tory felt herself swept through a hurricane of sensation to the heavy, waiting air of the storm's eye. Phil's hands cupped her upper thighs, his thumbs pressing insistently where the thin silk rose high. Expertly he unhooked her stockings, drawing them off slowly, his mouth hurrying to taste. Tory moaned, bending her leg to help him as torment and pleasure tangled.

For one heady moment his tongue lingered at the top of her thigh. With his tongue he gently slipped beneath the silk, making her arch in anticipation. His breath shot through the material into the core of her. But he left her moist and aching to come greedily back to her mouth. Tory met the kiss ardently, dragging him closer. She felt his body pound and pulse against hers with a need no greater than her own. He found her full bottom lip irresistible and nibbled and sucked gently. Tory knew a passion so concentrated and volatile, she struggled under him to find the ultimate release.

"Here," he whispered, moving down to the spot on her neck that always drew him. "You taste like no one else," he murmured. Her flavor seemed to tremble on the tip of his tongue. With a groan he let his voracious appetite take over.

Her breasts were hard, waiting for him. Slowly he moistened the tips with his tongue, listening to her shuddering breathing as he journeyed from one to the other—teasing, circling, nibbling, until her movements beneath him were abandoned and desperate. Passion built to a delicious peak until he drew her, hot and moist, into his mouth to suckle ravenously. She wasn't aware when he slipped the teddy down her shoulders, down her body, until she was naked to the waist. The last lights of the sun poured into the room like a dark red mist. It gave her skin an exotic cast that aroused him further. He drew the silk lower and still lower, until it was lost in the tangle of sheets.

Desperate, Tory reached for him. She heard Phil's sharp intake of breath as she touched him, felt the sudden, convulsive shudder. She wanted him now with an intensity too strong to deny.

"More," he breathed, but was unable to resist as she drew him closer.

"Now," she murmured, arching her hips to receive him.

Exhausted, they lay in silence as the first fingers of moonlight flickered into the room. He knew he should move—his full weight pushed Tory deep into the mattress. But they felt so right, flesh to flesh, his mouth nestled comfortably against her breast. Her fingers were in his hair, tangling and stroking with a sleepy gentleness. Time crept by easily—seconds to minutes without words or the need for them. He could hear her heartbeat gradually slow and level. Lazily he flicked his tongue over a still-erect nipple and felt it harden even more.

"Phil," she moaned in weak protest.

He laughed quietly, enormously pleased that he could move her so effortlessly. "Tired?" he asked, nibbling a moment longer.

"Yes." She gave a low groan as he began to toy with her other breast. "Phil, I can't."

Ignoring her, he brought his mouth to hers for long, slow kisses while his hands continued to stroke. He had intended only to kiss her before taking his weight from her. Her lips were unbearably soft and giving. Her breath shuddered into him, rebuilding his passion with dizzying speed. Tory told herself it wasn't possible as sleepy desire became a torrent of fresh need.

Phil found new delight in the lines of her body, in the heady, just-loved flavor of her skin. A softly glowing spark rekindled a flame. "I want a retake," he murmured.

He took her swiftly, leaving them both staggered and damp and clinging in a room speckled with moonlight.

How do you feel?" Phil murmured later. She was close to his side, one arm flung over his chest.

"Astonished."

He laughed, kissing her temple. "So do I. I guess our dinner got cold."

"Mmm. What was it?"

"I don't remember."

Tory yawned and snuggled against him. "That's always better cold anyway." She knew with very little effort she could sleep for a week.

"Not hungry?"

She considered a moment. "Is it something you have to chew?"

He grinned into the darkness. "Probably."

"Uh-uh." She arched like a contented cat when he ran a hand down her back. "Do you have to get up early?"

"Six."

Groaning, she shut her eyes firmly. "You're ruining your mystique," she told him. "Hollywood Casanovas don't get up at six."

He gave a snort of laughter. "They do if they've got a film to direct."

"I suppose when you leave, you'll still have a lot of work to do before the film's finished."

His frown mirrored hers, although neither was aware of it. "There's still a lot to be shot in the studio, then the editing . . . I wish there was more time."

She knew what he meant and schooled her voice carefully. "We both knew. I'll only be in town a few weeks longer than you," she added. "I've got a lot of work to catch up on in Albuquerque."

"It's lucky we're both comfortable with the way things are." Phil stared up at the ceiling while his fingers continued to tangle in her hair. "If we'd fallen in love, it would be an impossible situation."

"Yes," Tory murmured, opening her eyes to the darkness. "Neither of us has the time for impossible situations."

CHAPTER 10

Tory pulled up in front of the ranch house. Her mother's geraniums were doing beautifully. White-and-pink plants had been systematically placed between the more common red. The result was an organized, well-tended blanket of color. Tory noted that the tear in the window screen had been mended. As always, a few articles of clothing hung on the line at the side of the house. She dreaded going in.

It was an obligation she never shirked but never did easily. At least once a week she drove out to spend a strained half hour with her mother. Only twice since the film crew had come to Friendly had her mother made the trip into town. Both times she had dropped into Tory's office, but the visits had been brief and uncomfortable for both women. Time was not bridging the gap, only widening it.

Normally, Tory confined her trips to the ranch to Sunday afternoons. This time, however, she had driven out a day early in order to placate Phil. The thought caused her to smile. He'd finally pressured her into agreeing to his "home movies." When he had wound up the morning's shoot in town, he would bring out one of the backup video cameras. Though she could hardly see why it was so vital to him to put her on film, Tory decided it wouldn't do any harm. And, she thought wryly, he wasn't going to stop bringing it up until she agreed. So let him have his fun, she concluded as she slipped from the car. She'd enjoy the ride.

From the corral the palomino whinnied fussily. He pawed the ground and pranced as Tory watched him. He knew, seeing Tory, that there was a carrot or apple in it for him, as well as a bracing ride. They were both aware that he could jump the fence easily if he grew impatient enough. As he reared, showing off for her, Tory laughed.

"Simmer down, Justice. You're going to be in the movies." She hesitated a moment. It would be so easy to go to the horse, pamper him a bit in return for his unflagging affection. There were no complications or undercurrents there. Her eyes drifted back to the house. With a sigh she started up the walk.

Upon entering, Tory caught the faint whiff of bee's wax and lemon and knew her mother had recently polished the floors. She remembered the electric buffer her father had brought home one day. Helen had been as thrilled as if he'd brought her diamonds. The windows glittered in the sun without a streak or speck.

How does she do it? Tory wondered, gazing around the spick-and-span room. How does she stand spending each and every day chasing dust? Could it really be all she wants out of life?

As far back as she could remember, she could recall her mother wanting nothing more than to change slipcovers or curtains. It was difficult for a woman who always looked for angles and alternatives to understand such placid acceptance. Perhaps it would have been easier if the daughter had understood the mother, or the mother the daughter. With a frustrated shake of her head she wandered to the kitchen, expecting to find Helen fussing at the stove.

The room was empty. The appliances winked, white and gleaming, in the strong sunlight. The scent of fresh-baked bread hovered enticingly in the air. Whom did she bake it for? Tory demanded of herself, angry without knowing why. There was no one there to appreciate it now—no one to break off a hunk and grin as he was scolded. Damn it, didn't she know that everything was different now? Whirling away, Tory strode out of the room.

The house was too quiet, she realized. Helen was certainly there. The tired little compact was in its habitual place at the side of the house. It occurred to Tory that her mother might be in one of the outbuildings. But then, why hadn't she come out when she heard the car drive up? Vaguely disturbed, Tory glanced up the stairs. She opened her mouth to call, then stopped. Something impelled her to move quietly up the steps.

At the landing she paused, catching some faint sound coming from the end of the hall. Still moving softly, Tory walked down to the doorway of her parents' bedroom. The door was only half closed. Pushing it open, Tory stepped inside.

Helen sat on the bed in a crisp yellow housedress. Her blonde hair was caught back in a matching kerchief. Held tight in her hands was one of Tory's father's work shirts. It was a faded blue, frayed at the cuffs. Tory remembered it as his favorite, one that Helen had claimed was fit only for a dust rag. Now she clutched it to her breast, rocking gently and weeping with such quiet despair that Tory could only stare.

She'd never seen her mother cry. It had been her father whose eyes had misted during her high school and college graduations. It had been he who had wept with her when the dog she had raised from a puppy had died. Her mother had faced joy and sadness with equal restraint. But there was no restraint in the woman Tory saw now. This was a woman in the depths of grief, blind and deaf to all but her own mourning.

All anger, all resentment, all sense of distance, vanished in one illuminating moment. Tory felt her heart fill with sympathy, her throat burn from her own grief.

"Mother."

Helen's head jerked up. Her eyes were glazed and confused as they focused on Tory. She shook her head as if in denial, then struggled to choke back the sobs.

"No, don't." Tory rushed to her, gathering her close. "Don't shut me out."

Helen went rigid in an attempt at composure, but Tory only held her tighter. Abruptly, Helen collapsed, dropping her head on her daughter's shoulder and weeping without restraint. "Oh, Tory, Tory, why couldn't it have been me?" With the shirt caught between them, Helen accepted the comfort of her daughter's strong arms. "Not Will, never Will. It should have been me."

"No, don't say that." Hot tears coursed down her face. "You mustn't think that way. Dad wouldn't want you to."

"All those weeks, those horrible weeks, in the hospital I prayed and prayed for a miracle." She gripped Tory tighter, as if she needed something solid to hang on to. "They said no hope. No hope. Oh, God, I wanted to scream. He couldn't die without me . . . not without me. That last night in the hospital before . . . I went into his room. I begged him to show them they were wrong, to come back. He was gone." She moaned and would have slid down if Tory hadn't held her close. "He'd already left me. I couldn't leave him lying there with that machine. I couldn't do that, not to Will. Not to my Will."

"Oh, Mother." They rocked together, heads on each other's shoulders. "I'm so sorry. I didn't know—I didn't think . . . I'm so sorry."

Helen breathed a long, shuddering sigh as her sobs quieted. "I didn't know how to tell you or how to explain. I'm not good at letting my feelings out. I knew how much you loved your father," she continued. "But I was too angry to reach out. I suppose I wanted you to lash out at me. It made it easier to be strong, even though I knew I hurt you more."

"That doesn't matter now."

"Tory—"

"No, it doesn't." Tory drew her mother back, looking into her tear-ravaged eyes. "Neither of us tried to understand the other that night. We were both wrong. I think we've both paid for it enough now."

"I loved him so much." Helen swallowed the tremor in her voice and stared down at the crumpled shirt still in her hand. "It doesn't seem possible that he won't walk through the door again."

"I know. Every time I come in the house, I still look for him."

"You're so like him." Hesitantly, Helen reached up to touch her cheek. "There's been times it's been hard for me even to look at you. You were always his more than mine when you were growing up. My fault," she added before Tory could speak. "I was always a little awed by you."

"Awed?" Tory managed to smile.

"You were so smart, so quick, so demanding. I always wondered how much I had to do with the forming of you. Tory"—she took her hands, staring down at them a moment—"I never tried very hard to get close to you. It's not my way."

"I know."

"It didn't mean that I didn't love you."

She squeezed Helen's hands. "I know that too. But it was always him we looked at first."

"Yes." Helen ran a palm over the crumpled shirt. "I thought I was coping very well," she said softly. "I was going to clean out the closet. I found this, and . . . He loved it so. You can still see the little holes where he'd pin his badge."

"Mother, it's time you got out of the house a bit, starting seeing people again." When Helen started to shake her head, Tory gripped her hands tighter. "Living again."

Helen glanced around the tidy room with a baffled smile. "This is all I know how to do. All these years . . ."

"When I go back to Albuquerque, why don't you come stay with me awhile? You've never been over."

"Oh, Tory, I don't know."

"Think about it," she suggested, not wanting to push. "You might enjoy watching your daughter rip a witness apart in cross-examination."

Helen laughed, brushing the lingering tears briskly away. "I might at that. Would you be offended if I said sometimes I worry about you being alone—not having someone like your father to come home to?"

"No." The sudden flash of loneliness disturbed her far more than the words. "Everyone needs something different."

"Everyone needs someone, Tory," Helen corrected gently. "Even you."

Tory's eyes locked on her mother's a moment, then dropped away. "Yes, I know. But sometimes the someone—" She broke off, distressed by the way her thoughts had centered on Phil. "There's time for that," she said briskly. "I still have a lot of obligations, a lot of things I want to do, before I commit myself . . . to anyone."

There was enough anxiety in Tory's voice to tell Helen that "anyone" had a name. Feeling it was too soon to offer advice, she merely patted Tory's hand. "Don't wait too long," she said simply. "Life has a habit of moving quickly." Rising, she went to the closet again. The need to be busy was too ingrained to allow her to sit for long. "I didn't expect you today. Are you going to ride?"

"Yes." Tory pressed a hand down on her father's shirt before she stood. "Actually I'm humoring the director of the film being shot in town." Wandering to the window, she looked down to see Justice pacing the corral restlessly. "He has this obsession with getting me on film. I flatly refused to be an extra in his production, but I finally agreed to let him shoot some while I rode Justice."

"He must be very persuasive," Helen commented.

Tory gave a quick laugh. "Oh, he's that all right."

"That's Marshall Kincaid's son," Helen stated, remembering. "Does he favor his father?"

With a smile Tory thought that her mother would be more interested in the actor than the director. "Yes, actually he does. The same rather aristocratic bone structure and cool blue eyes." Tory saw the car kicking up dust on the road leading to the ranch. "He's coming now, if you'd like to meet him."

"Oh, I . . ." Helen pressed her fingers under her eyes. "I don't think I'm really presentable right now, Tory."

"All right," she said as she started toward the door. In the doorway she hesitated a moment. "Will you be all right now?"

"Yes, yes, I'm fine. Tory . . ." She crossed the room to give her daughter's cheek a brief kiss. Tory's eyes widened in surprise at the uncharacteristic gesture. "I'm glad we talked. Really very glad."

Phil again stopped his car beside the corral. The horse pranced over to hang his head over the fence, waiting for attention. Leaving the camera in the backseat, Phil walked over to pat the strong golden neck. He found the palomino avidly nuzzling at his pockets.

"Hey!" With a half laugh he stepped out of range.

"He's looking for this." Holding a carrot in her hand, Tory came down the steps.

"Your friend should be arrested for pickpocketing," Phil commented as Tory drew closer. His smile of greeting faded instantly. "Tory . . ." He took her shoulders, studying her face. "You've been crying," he said in an odd voice.

"I'm fine." Turning, she held out the carrot, letting the horse pluck it from her hand.

"What's wrong?" he insisted, pulling her back to him again. "What happened?"

"It was my mother."

"Is she ill?" he demanded quickly.

"No." Touched by the concern in his voice, Tory smiled. "We talked," she told him, then let out a long sigh. "We really talked, probably for the first time in twenty-seven years."

There was something fragile in the look as she lifted her eyes to his. He felt much as he had the day in the cemetery—protective and strong. Wordlessly he drew her into the circle of his arms. "Are you okay?"

"Yes, I'm fine." She closed her eyes as her head rested against his shoulder. "Really fine. It's going to be so much easier now."

"I'm glad." Tilting her face to his, he kissed her softly. "If you don't feel like doing this today—"

"No you don't, Kincaid," she said with a quick grin. "You claimed you were going to immortalize me, so get on with it."

"Go fix your face first, then." He pinched her chin. "I'll set things up."

She turned away to comply but called back over her shoulder. "There's not going to be any of that 'Take two' business. You'll have to get it right the first time."

He enjoyed her hoot of laughter before he reached into the car for the camera and recorder.

Later, Tory scowled at the apparatus. "You said film," she reminded him. "You didn't say anything about sound."

"It's tape," he corrected, expertly framing her. "Just saddle the horse."

"You're arrogant as hell when you play movies, Kincaid." Without fuss Tory slipped the bit into the palomino's mouth. Her movements were competent as she hefted the saddle onto the horse's back. She was a natural, he decided. No nerves, no exaggerated gestures for the benefit of the camera. He wanted her to talk again. Slowly he circled around for a new angle. "Going to have dinner with me tonight?"

"I don't know," Tory considered as she tightened the cinches. "That cold steak you fed me last night wasn't very appetizing."

"Tonight I'll order cold cuts and beer," he suggested. "That way it won't matter when we get to it."

Tory sent him a grin over her shoulder. "It's a deal."

"You're a cheap date, Sheriff."

"Uh-uh," she disagreed, turning to him while she wrapped a companionable arm around the horse's neck. "I'm expecting another bottle of that French champagne very soon. Why don't you let me play with the camera now and you can stand next to the horse?"

"Mount up."

Tory lifted a brow. "You're one tough cookie, Kincaid." Grasping the saddle horn, Tory swung into the saddle in one lazy movement. "And now?"

"Head out, the direction you took the first time I saw you ride. Not too far," he added. "When you come back, keep it at a gallop. Don't pay any attention to the camera. Just ride."

"You're the boss," she said agreeably. "For the moment." With a kick of her heels Tory sent the palomino west at a run.

She felt the exhilaration instantly. The horse wanted speed, so Tory let him have his head as the hot air whipped at her face and hair. As before, she headed toward the mountains. There was no need to escape this time, but only a pleasure in moving fast. The power and strength below her tested her skill.

Zooming in on her, Phil thought she rode with understated flair. No flash, just confidence. Her body hardly seemed to move as the horse pounded up dust. It almost seemed as though the horse led her, but something in the way she sat, in the way her face was lifted, showed her complete control.

When she turned, the horse danced in place a moment, still anxious to run. He tossed his head, lifting his front feet off the ground in challenge. Over the still, silent air, Phil heard Tory laugh. The sound of it sent shivers down his spine.

Magnificent, he thought, zooming in on her as close as the lens would allow. She was absolutely magnificent. She wasn't looking toward him. Obviously she had no thoughts about the camera focused on her. Her face was lifted to the sun and the sky as she controlled the feisty horse with apparent ease. When she headed back, she started at a loping gallop that built in speed.

The palomino's legs gathered and stretched, sending up a plume of dirt in their wake. Behind them was a barren land of little more than rock and earth with the mountains harsh in the distance. She was Eve, Phil thought. The only woman. And if this Eve's paradise was hard and desolate, she ruled it in her own style.

Once, as if remembering he was there, Tory looked over, full into the camera. With her face nearly filling the lens, she smiled. Phil felt his palms go damp. If a man had a woman like that, he realized abruptly, he'd need nothing and no one else. The only woman, he thought again, then shook his head as if to clear it.

With a quick command and a tug on the reins, Tory brought the horse to a stop. Automatically she leaned forward to pat his neck. "Well, Hollywood?" she said lazily.

Knowing he wasn't yet in complete control, Phil kept the camera trained on her. "Is that the best you can do?"

She tossed her hair behind her head. "What did you have in mind?"

"No fancy tricks?" he asked, moving around the horse to vary the angle.

Tory looked down on him with tolerant amusement. "If you want to see someone stand on one foot in the saddle, go to the circus."

"We could set up a couple of small jumps—if you can handle it."

As she ruffled the palomino's blond mane, she gave a snort of laughter. "I thought you wanted me to ride, not win a blue ribbon." Grinning, she turned the horse around. "But okay," she said obligingly. At an easy lope she went for the corral fence. The horse took the four feet in a long, powerful glide. "Will that do?" she asked as she doubled back and rode past.

"Again," Phil demanded, going down on one knee. With a shrug Tory took the horse over the fence again. Lowering his camera for the first time, Phil shaded his eyes and looked up at her. "If he can do that, how do you keep him in?"

"He knows a good thing when he's got it," Tory stated, letting the palomino prance a bit while she rubbed his neck. "He's just showing off for the camera. Is that a wrap, Kincaid?"

Lifting the camera again, he aimed it at her. "Is that all you can do?"

"Well . . ." Tory considered a moment, then sent him a slow smile. "How about this?" Keeping one hand loosely on the reins, she started to unbutton her blouse.

"I like it."

After three buttons she paused, catching her tongue between her teeth. "I don't want you to lose your G rating," she decided. Swinging a leg over the saddle, she slid to the ground.

"This is a private film," he reminded her. "The censors'll never see it."

She laughed but shook her head. "Fade out," she suggested, loosening the horse's girth. "Put your toy away, Kincaid," she told him as he circled around the horse, still taping.

"Look at me a minute." With a half smile Tory complied. "God, that face," he muttered. "One way or the other, I'm going to get it on the screen."

"Forget it." Tory lifted the saddle to balance it on the fence. "Unless you start videotaping court cases."

"I can be persistent."

"I can be stubborn," she countered. At her command the palomino trotted back into the corral.

After loading the equipment back in the car, Phil turned to gather Tory in his arms. Without a word their mouths met in long, mutual pleasure. "If there was a way," he murmured as he buried his face in her hair, "to have a few days away from here, alone . . ."

Tory shut her eyes, feeling the stir . . . and the ache. "Obligations, Phil," she said quietly. "We both have a job to do."

He wanted to say the hell with it but knew he couldn't. Along with the obligations was the agreement they had made at the outset. "If I called you in Albuquerque, would you see me?"

She hesitated. It was something she wanted and feared. "Yes." She realized abruptly that she was suffering. For a moment she stood still, absorbing the unexpected sensation. "Phil, kiss me again."

She found his mouth quickly to let the heat and pleasure of the kiss dull the pain. There were still a few precious weeks left, she told herself as she wrapped her arms tighter around him. There was still time before . . . with a moan she pressed urgently against him, willing her mind to go blank. There was a sigh, then a tremble, before she rested her head against his shoulder. "I have to put the tack away," she murmured. It was tempting to stay just as she was, held close, with her blood just beginning to swim. Taking a long breath, she drew away from him and smiled. "Why don't you be macho and carry the saddle?"

"Directors don't haul equipment," he told her as he tried to pull her back to him.

"Heave it up, Kincaid." Tory swung the reins over her shoulder. "You've got some great muscles."

"Yeah?" Grinning, he lifted the saddle and followed her toward the barn. Bicks was right, Phil mused, watching her walk. She had a way of moving that drove men mad.

The barn door creaked in protest when Tory pulled it open. "Over here." She moved across the concrete floor to hang the reins on a peg.

Phil set down the saddle, then turned. The place was large, high-ceilinged, and refreshingly cool. "No animals?" he asked, wandering to an empty stall.

"My mother keeps a few head of cattle," Tory explained as she joined him. "They're grazing. We had more horses, but she doesn't ride much." Tory lifted a shoulder. "Justice has the place mostly to himself."

"I've never been in a barn."

"A deprived child."

He sent her a mild glance over his shoulder as he roamed. "I don't think I expected it to be so clean."

Tory's laugh echoed. "My mother has a vendetta against dirt," she told him. Oddly, she felt amusement now rather than resentment. It was a clean feeling. "I think she'd have put curtains on the windows in the loft if my father had let her."

Phil found the ladder and tested its sturdiness. "What's up there?"

"Hay," Tory said dryly. "Ever seen hay?"

"Don't be smug," he warned before he started to climb. Finding his fascination rather sweet, Tory

exerted the energy to go up with him. "The view's incredible." Standing beside the side opening, he could
see for miles. The town of Friendly looked almost neat
and tidy with the distance.

"I used to come up here a lot." Tucking her hands
in her back pockets, Tory looked over his shoulder.

"What did you do?"

"Watch the world go by," she said, nodding toward
Friendly. "Or sleep."

He laughed, turning back to her. "You're the only
person I know who can turn sleeping into an art."

"I've dedicated quite a bit of my life to it." She took
his hand to draw him away.

Instead he pulled her into a dim corner. "There's
something I've always wanted to do in a hayloft."

With a laugh Tory stepped away. "Phil, my mother's
in the house."

"She's not here," he pointed out. He hooked a hand
in the low V where she had loosened her blouse. A
hard tug had her stumbling against him.

"Phil—"

"It must have been carrying that saddle," he mused,
giving her a gentle push that had her falling backward
into a pile of hay.

"Now, wait a minute . . ." she began, and struggled
up on her elbows.

"And the primitive surroundings," he added as he
pressed her body back with his own. "If I were directing this scene, it would start like this." He took her
mouth in a hot, urgent kiss that turned her protest into
a moan. "The lighting would be set so that it seemed
one shaft of sunlight was slanting down across here."
With a fingertip he traced from her right ear, across
her throat, to the hollow between her breasts. "Everything else would be a dull gold, like your skin."

She had her hands pressed against his shoulders, holding him off, although her heart was beating thickly. "Phil, this isn't the time."

He placed two light kisses at either corner of her mouth. He found it curiously exciting to have to persuade her. Light as a breeze, his hand slipped under her blouse until his fingers found her breast. The peak was already taut. At his touch her eyes lost focus and darkened. The hands at his shoulders lost their resistance and clutched at him. "You're so sensitive," he murmured, watching the change in her face. "It drives me crazy to know when I touch you like this, your bones turn to water and you're completely mine."

Letting his fingers fondle and stroke, he lowered his mouth to nibble gently at her yielding lips. *Strong, self-sufficient, decisive.* Those were words he would have used to describe her. Yet, he knew, when they were together like this, he had the power to mold her. Even now, as she lifted them to his face to urge him closer, he felt the weakness come over him in thick waves. It was both frightening and irresistible.

She could have asked anything of him, and he would have been unable to deny her. Even his thoughts could no longer be considered his own when she was so intimately entwined in them. The fingers that loosened the rest of her buttons weren't steady. He should have been used to her by now, he told himself as he sought the tender skin of her neck almost savagely. It shouldn't be so intense every time he began to make love to her. Each time he told himself the desperation would fade; yet, it only returned—doubled, tripled, until he was completely lost in her.

There was only her now, over the clean, country

smell of hay. Her subtly alluring fragrance was a
contrast too exciting to bear. She was murmuring to
him as she drew his shirt over his head. The sound
of her voice seemed to pulse through his system. The
sun shot through the window to beat on his bare back,
but he only felt the cool stroking of her fingers as she
urged him down until they were flesh to flesh.

His mouth devoured hers as he tugged the jeans
over her hips. Greedily he moved to her throat, her
shoulders, her breasts, ravenous for each separate
taste. His mouth ranged over her, his tongue moistening, savoring, as her skin heated. She was naked but
for the brief swatch riding low on her hips. He hooked
his fingers beneath it, tormenting them both by lowering it fraction by fraction while his lips followed the
progress.

The pleasure grew unmanageable. He began the
wild journey back up her body, his fingers fumbling
with the snap of his jeans until Tory's brushed them
impatiently away.

She undressed him swiftly, while her own mouth
streaked over his skin. The sudden change from pli-
ancy to command left him stunned. Then she was on
top of him, straddling him while her lips and teeth
performed dark magic at the pulse in his throat. Beyond reason, he grasped her hips, lifting her. Tory gave
a quick cry as they joined. In delight her head flung
back as she let this new exhilaration rule her. Her skin
was shiny with dampness when she crested. Delirious,
she started to slide toward him, but he rolled her over,
crushing her beneath him as he took her to a second
peak, higher than the first.

As they lay, damp flesh to damp flesh, their breaths
shuddering, she knew a contentment so fulfilling, it

brought the sting of tears to her eyes. Hurriedly blinking them away, Tory kissed the curve of his shoulder.

"I guess there's more to do in a hayloft than sleep."

Phil chuckled. Rolling onto his back, he drew her against his side to steal a few more moments alone with her.

CHAPTER 11

One of the final scenes to be filmed was a tense night sequence outside Hernandez's Bar. Phil had opted to shoot at night with a low light level rather than film during the day with filters. It would give the actors more of a sense of the ambience and keep the gritty realism in the finished product. It was a scene fraught with emotion that would lose everything if overplayed. From the beginning nothing seemed to go right.

Twice the sound equipment broke down, causing lengthy delays. A seasoned supporting actress blew her lines repeatedly and strode off the set, cursing herself. A defective bulb exploded, scattering shards of glass that had to be painstakingly picked up. For the first time since the shooting began, Phil had to deal with a keyed-up, uncooperative Marlie.

"Okay," he said, taking her by the arm to draw her away. "What the hell's wrong with you?"

"I can't get it right," she said furiously. With her hands on her hips she strode a few paces away and kicked at the dirt. "Damn it, Phil, it just doesn't *feel* right."

"Look, we've been at this over two hours. Everybody's a little fed up." His own patience was hanging on by a thread. In two days at the most, he'd have no choice but to head back to California. He should have been pleased that the bulk of the filming was done— that the rushes were excellent. Instead he was tense, irritable, and looking for someone to vent his temper on. "Just pull yourself together," he told Marlie curtly. "And get it done."

"Now, just a damn minute!" Firing up instantly, Marlie let her own frustration pour out in temper. "I've put up with your countless retakes, with that stinking, sweaty bar and this godforsaken town because this script is gold. I've let you work me like a horse because I need you. This part is my ticket into the big leagues and I know it right down to the gut."

"You want the ticket," Phil tossed back, "you pay the price."

"I've paid my dues," she told him furiously. A couple of heads turned idly in their direction, but no one ventured over. "I don't have to take your lousy temper on the set because you've got personal problems."

He measured her with narrowed eyes. "You have to take exactly what I give you."

"I'll tell you something, Kincaid"—she poked a small finger into his chest—"I don't have to take anything, because I'm every bit as important to this movie as you are, and we both know it. It doesn't mean a damn who's getting top billing. Kate Lohman's the key to this picture, and I'm Kate Lohman. Don't you forget it, and don't throw your weight around with me."

When she turned to stride off, Phil grabbed her arm, jerking her back. His eyes had iced. The fingers on her arm were hard. Looking down at her set face, he felt temper fade into admiration. "Damn you, Marlie," he said quietly, "you know how to stay in character, don't you?"

"I know this one inside out," she returned. The stiffness went out of her stance.

"Okay, what doesn't feel right?"

The corners of her mouth curved up. "I wanted to work with you," she began, "because you're the best out there these days. I didn't expect to like you. All right," she continued, abruptly professional, "when Sam follows me out of the bar, grabs me, finally losing control, he's furious. Everything he's held in comes pouring out. His dialogue's hard."

"You haven't been off his back since he came into town," Phil reminded her, running over the scene in his mind. "Now he's had enough. After the scene he's going to take you back to your room and make love. You win."

"Do I?" Marlie countered. "My character is a tough lady. She's got reason to be. She's got enough vulnerabilities to keep the audience from despising her, but she's no pushover."

"So?"

"So he comes after me, he calls me a tramp—a cold, money-grabbing whore, among other things— and my response is to take it, damp-eyed and shocked."

Phil considered, a small smile growing. "What would you do?"

"I'd punch the jerk in the mouth."

His laugh echoed down the street. "Yeah, I guess you would at that."

"Tears, maybe," Marlie went on, tasting victory, "but anger too. She's becoming very close to what he's accusing her of. And she hates it—and him, for making it matter."

Phil nodded, his mind already plotting the changes

and the angles. Frowning, he called Sam over and outlined the change.

"Can you pull this off without busting my caps?"
Sam demanded of Marlie.

She grinned. "Maybe."

"After she hits you," Phil interrupted, "I want dead
silence for a good ten seconds. You wipe your mouth
with the back of your hand, slow, but don't break the
eye contact. Let's set it up from where Marlie walks
out of the bar. Bicks!" He left the actors to give his
cinematographer a rundown.

"*Quiet. . . . Places. . . . Roll. . . .*" Standing by the
cameraman's shoulder, Phil watched the scene unfold. The adrenaline was pumping now. He could see
it in Marlie's eyes, in the set of her body, as she burst
out the door of the bar onto the sidewalk. When Sam
grabbed her, instead of merely being whirled around,
she turned on him. The mood seemed to fire into him
as well, as his lines became harsher, more emotional.
Before there had been nothing in the scene but the
man's anger; now there was the woman's too. Now
the underlying sexuality was there. When she hit him,
it seemed everyone on the set held their breath. The
gesture was completely unexpected and, Phil mused
as the silence trembled, completely in character. He
could almost feel Sam's desire to strike her back, and
his inability to do so. She challenged him to, while her
throat moved gently with a nervous swallow. He wiped
his mouth, never taking his eyes from hers.

"Cut!" Phil swore jubilantly as he walked over and
grabbed Marlie by the shoulders. He kissed her, hard.
"Fantastic," he said, then kissed her again. "Fantastic."
Looking up, he grinned at Sam.

"Don't try that on me," Sam warned, nursing his
lower lip. "She packs a hell of a punch." He gave her

a rueful glance. "Ever heard about pulling right before you make contact?" he asked. "Showbiz, you know."

"I got carried away."

"I nearly slugged you."

"I know." Laughing, she pushed her hair back with both hands.

"Okay, let's take it from there." Phil moved back to the cameraman. "Places."

"Can't we take it from right before the punch?" Marlie asked with a grin for Sam. "It would sort of give me a roll into the rest of the scene."

"Stand-in!" Sam called.

In her office Tory read over with care a long, detailed letter from an opposing attorney. The tone was very clear through the legal terms and flowery style. The case was going through litigation, she thought with a frown. It might take two months or more, she mused, but this suit wasn't going to be settled out of court. Though normally she would have wanted to come to terms without a trial, she began to feel a tiny flutter of excitement. She'd been away from her own work for too long. She would be back in Albuquerque in a month. Tory discovered she wanted—needed—something complicated and time-consuming on her return.

Adjustments, she decided as she tried to concentrate on the words in the letter. There were going to be adjustments to be made when she left Friendly this time. When she left Phil. No, she corrected, catching the bridge of her nose between her thumb and forefinger. He was leaving first—tomorrow, the day after. It was uncomfortably easy to see the hole that was already taking shape in her life. Tory reminded herself that she wasn't allowed to think of it. The rules had been made plain at the outset—by both of them. If things had begun to change for her, she simply had to backpedal a bit and reaffirm her priorities. *Her* work, *her* career, *her* life. At that moment the singular possessive pronoun never sounded more empty. Shaking her head, Tory began to read the letter from the beginning a second time.

Merle paced the office, casting quick glances at Tory from time to time. He'd made arrangements for Marlie to meet him there after her work was finished. What he hadn't expected was for Tory to be glued to her desk all evening. No expert with subtleties, Merle had no idea how to move his boss along and have the office to himself. He peeked out the window, noting that the floodlights up the street were being shut off. Shuffling his feet and clearing his throat, he turned back to Tory.

"Guess you must be getting tired," he ventured.

"Hmmm."

"Things are pretty quiet tonight," he tried again, fussing with the buttons on his shirt.

"Um-hmm." Tory began to make notations on her yellow pad.

Merle lifted his eyes to the ceiling. Maybe the direct approach would do it, he decided. "Why don't you knock off and go home."

Tory continued to write. "Trying to get rid of me, Merle T.?"

"Well, no, ah . . ." He looked down at the dusty tips of his shoes. Women never got any easier to handle.

"Got a date?" she asked mildly as she continued to draft out her answer to the letter.

"Sort of . . . well, yeah," he said with more confidence.

"Go ahead, then."

"But—" He broke off, stuffing his hands in his pockets.

Tory looked up and studied him. The mustache, she noted, had grown in respectability. It wasn't exactly a prizewinner, but it added maturity to a face she'd always thought resembled a teddy bear's. He still slouched, and even as she studied him, color seeped into his cheeks. But he didn't look away as he once would have done. His eyes stayed on hers so that she could easily read both frustration and embarrassment. The old affection stirred in her.

"Marlie?" she asked gently.

"Yeah." He straightened his shoulders a bit.

"How are you going to feel when she leaves?"

With a shrug Merle glanced toward the window again. "I guess I'll miss her. She's a terrific lady."

The tone caused Tory to give his profile a puzzled look. There was no misery in it, just casual acceptance. With a light laugh she stared back at her notes. Odd, she thought, it seemed their reactions had gotten reversed somewhere along the line. "You don't have to stay, Merle," she said lightly. "If you'd planned to have a late supper or—"

"We did," he interrupted. "Here."

Tory looked up again. "Oh, I see." She couldn't quite control the smile. "Looks like I'm in the way."

Uncomfortable, he shuffled again. "Aw, Tory."

"It's okay." Rising, she exaggerated her accommodating tone. "I know when I'm not wanted. I'll just go back to my room and work on this all by myself."

Merle struggled with loyalty and selfishness while Tory gathered her papers. "You could have supper with us," he suggested gallantly.

Letting the papers drop, Tory skirted the desk.

With her hands on his shoulders, she kissed both of his cheeks. "Merle T.," she said softly, "you're a jewel."

Pleased, he grinned as the door opened behind them. "Just like I told you, Phil," Marlie stated as they entered. "Beautiful women can't keep away from him. You'll have to stand in line, Sheriff," she continued, walking over to hook her arm through Merle's. "I've got first dibs tonight."

"Why don't I get her out of your way?" Phil suggested. "It's the least I can do after that last scene."

"The man is totally unselfish," Marlie confided to Tory. "No sacrifice is too great for his people."

With a snort Tory turned back to her desk. "I might let him buy me a drink," she considered while slipping her papers into a small leather case. When he sat on the corner of her desk, she cast him a look. "And dinner," she added.

"I might be able to come up with some cold cuts," he murmured.

Tory's low, appreciative laugh was interrupted by the phone. "Sheriff's office." Her sigh was automatic as she listened to the excited voice on the other end. "Yes, Mr. Potts." Merle groaned, but she ignored him. "I see. What kind of noise?" Tory waited while the old man jabbered in her ear. "Are your doors and windows locked? No, Mr. Potts, I don't want you going outside with your shotgun. Yes, I realize a man has to protect his property." A sarcastic sound from Merle earned him a mild glare. "Let me handle it. I'll be there in ten minutes. No, I'll be quiet, just sit tight."

"Sheep thieves," Merle muttered as Tory hung up.

"Burglars," she corrected, opening the top drawer of her desk.

"Just what do you think you're going to do with that?" Phil demanded as he saw Tory pull out the gun.

"Absolutely nothing, I hope." Coolly she began to load it.

"Then why are you—? Wait a minute," he interrupted himself, rising. "Do you mean that damn thing wasn't loaded?"

"Of course not." Tory slipped in the last bullet. "Nobody with sense keeps a loaded gun in an unlocked drawer."

"You got me into that cell with an empty gun?"

She sent him a lazy smile as she strapped on a holster. "You were so cute, Kincaid."

Ignoring amusement, he took a step toward her. "What would you have done if I hadn't backed down?"

"The odds were in my favor," she reminded him. "But I'd have thought of something. Merle, keep an eye on things until I get back."

"Wasting your time."

"Just part of the job."

"If you're wasting your time," Phil began as he stopped her at the door, "why are you taking that gun?"

"It looks so impressive," Tory told him as she walked outside.

"Tory, you're not going out to some sheep ranch with a gun at your hip like some modern-day Belle Starr."

"She was on the wrong side," she reminded him.

"Tory, I mean it!" Infuriated, Phil stepped in front of the car to block her way.

"Look, I said I'd be there in ten minutes. I'm going to have to drive like a maniac as it is."

He didn't budge. "What if there is someone out there?"

"That's exactly why I'm going."

When she reached for the door handle, he put his hand firmly over hers. "I'm going with you."

"Phil, I don't have time."

"I'm going."

Narrowing her eyes, she studied his face. There was no arguing with that expression, she concluded. "Okay, you're temporarily deputized. Get in and do what you're told."

Phil lifted a brow at her tone. The thought of her going out to some secluded ranch with only a gun for company had him swallowing his pride. He slid across to the passenger seat. "Don't I get a badge?" he asked as Tory started the engine.

"Use your imagination," she advised.

Tory's speed was sedate until they reached the town limits. Once the buildings were left behind, Phil watched the climbing speedometer with growing trepidation. Her hands were relaxed and competent on the wheel. The open window caused her hair to fly wildly, but her expression was calm.

She doesn't think there's anything to this, he decided as he watched the scenery whiz by. But if she did, his thoughts continued, she'd be doing exactly the same thing. The knowledge gave him a small thrill of fear. The neat black holster at her side hid an ugly, very real weapon. She had no business chasing burglars or carrying guns. She had no business taking the remotest chance with her own well-being. He cursed the phone call that had made it all too clear just how potentially dangerous her position in Friendly was. It had been simpler to think of her as a kind of figurehead, a referee for small-town squabbles. The late-night call and the gun changed everything.

"What will you do if you have to use that thing?" he demanded suddenly.

Without turning, Tory knew where his thoughts centered. "I'll deal with that when the time comes."

"When's your term up here?"

Tory took her eyes from the road for a brief two seconds. Phil was looking straight ahead. "Three weeks."

"You're better off in Albuquerque," he muttered. *Safer* was the word heard but not said. Tory recalled the time a client had nearly strangled her in his cell before the guards had pulled him off. She decided it was best unmentioned. Hardly slackening the car's speed, she took a right turn onto a narrow, rut-filled dirt road. Phil swore as the jolting threw him against the door.

"You should have strapped in," she told him carelessly.

His response was rude and brief.

The tiny ranch house had every light blazing. Tory pulled up in front of it with a quick squeal of brakes.

"Think you missed any?" Phil asked her mildly as he rubbed the shoulder that had collided with the door.

"I'll catch them on the way back." Before he could retort, Tory was out of the car and striding up the porch steps. She knocked briskly, calling out to identify herself. When Phil joined her on the porch, the door opened a crack. "Mr. Potts," she began.

"Who's he?" the old man demanded through the crack in the door.

"New deputy," Tory said glibly. "We'll check the grounds and the outside of the house now."

Potts opened the door a bit more, revealing an ancient, craggy face and a shiny black shotgun. "I heard them in the bushes."

"We'll take care of it, Mr. Potts." She put her hands on the butt of his gun. "Why don't you let me have this for now?"

Unwilling, Potts held firm. "I gotta have protection."

"Yes, but they're not in the house," she reminded him gently. "I could really use this out here."

He hesitated, then slackened his grip. "Both barrels," he told her, then slammed the door. Tory heard the triple locks click into place.

"That is not your average jolly old man," Phil commented.

Tory took the two shells out of the shotgun. "Alone too long," she said simply. "Let's take a look around."

"Go get 'em, big guy."

Tory barely controlled a laugh. "Just keep out of the way, Kincaid."

Whether she considered it a false alarm or not, Phil noted that Tory was very thorough. With the empty shotgun in one hand and a flashlight in the other, she checked every door and window on the dilapidated ranch house. Watching her, he walked into a pile of empty paint cans, sending them clattering. When he swore, Tory turned her head to look at him.

"You move like a cat, Kincaid," she said admiringly.

"The man's got junk piled everywhere," he retorted. "A burglar doesn't have a chance."

Tory smothered a chuckle and moved on. They circled the house, making their way through Potts's obstacle course of old car parts, warped lumber, and rusted tools. Satisfied that no one had attempted to break into the house for at least twenty-five years, Tory widened her circle to check the ground.

"Waste of time," Phil muttered, echoing Merle.

"Then let's waste it properly." Tory shone her light on the uneven grass as they continued to walk. Resigned, Phil kept to her side. There were better ways, he was thinking, to spend a warm summer night. And the moon was full. Pure white, he observed as he gazed up at it. Cool and full and promising. He wanted to make love to her under it, in the still, hot air with nothing and no one around for miles. The desire came suddenly, intensely, washing over him with a wave of possession that left him baffled.

"Tory," he murmured, placing a hand on her shoulder.

"Ssh!"

The order was sharp. He felt her stiffen under his hand. Her eyes were trained on a dry, dying bush directly in front of them. Even as he opened his mouth to say something impatient, Phil saw the movement. His fingers tightened on Tory's shoulder as he automatically stepped forward. The protective gesture was instinctive and so natural neither of them noticed it. He never thought: This is my woman, and I'll do anything to keep her from harm; he simply reacted. With his body as a shield for hers, they watched the bush in silence.

There was a slight sound, hardly a whisper on the air, but Tory felt the back of her neck prickle. The dry leaves of the bush cracked quietly with some movement. She reached in her pocket for the two shells, then reloaded the shotgun. The moonlight bounced off the oiled metal. Her hands were rock steady. Phil was poised, ready to lunge as Tory aimed the gun at the moon and fired both barrels. The sound split the silence like an axe.

With a terrified bleat, the sheep that had been grazing lazily behind the bush scrambled for safety. Without a word Phil and Tory watched the dirty white blob run wildly into the night.

"Another desperate criminal on the run from the law," Tory said dryly.

Phil burst into relieved laughter. He felt each separate muscle in his body relax. "I'd say 'on the lamb.'"

"I was hoping you wouldn't." Because the hand

holding the gun was shaking, Tory lowered it to her side. She swallowed; her throat was dry. "Well, let's go tell Potts his home and hearth are safe. Then we can go have that drink."

Phil laid his hands on her shoulders, looking down on her face in the moonlight. "Are you all right?"

"Sure."

"You're trembling."

"That's you," she countered, smiling at him.

Phil slid his hand down to her wrist to feel the race of her pulse. "Scared the hell out of you," he said softly.

Tory's eyes didn't waver. "Yeah." She was able to smile again, this time with more feeling. "How about you?"

"Me too." Laughing, he gave her a light kiss. "I'm not going to need that badge after all." And I'm not going to feel safe, he added silently, until you take yours off for the last time.

"Oh, I don't know, Kincaid." Tory led the way back with the beam of her flashlight. "First night on the job and you flushed out a sheep."

"Just give the crazy old man his gun and let's get out of here."

It took ten minutes of Tory's diplomacy to convince Potts that everything was under control. Mollified more by the fact that Tory had used his gun than the information that his intruder was one of his own flock, he locked himself in again. After contacting Merle on the radio, she headed back to town at an easy speed.

"I guess I could consider this a fitting climax to my sojourn to Friendly," Phil commented. "Danger and excitement on the last night in town."

Tory's fingers tightened on the wheel, but she managed to keep the speed steady. "You're leaving tomorrow."

He listened for regret in the statement but heard none. Striving to match her tone, he continued to stare out the window. "We finished up tonight, a day ahead of schedule. I'll head out with the film crew tomorrow. I want to be there when Huffman sees the film."

"Of course." The pain rammed into her, dazzlingly physical. It took concentrated control to keep from moaning with it. "You've still quite a lot of work to do before it's finished, I suppose."

"The studio scenes," he agreed, struggling to ignore twin feelings of panic and desolation. "The editing, the mixing . . . I guess your schedule's going to be pretty tight when you get back to Albuquerque."

"It looks that way." Tory stared at the beams of the headlights. A long straight road, no curves, no hills. No end. She bit the inside of her lip hard before she trusted herself to continue. "I'm thinking about hiring a new law clerk."

"That's probably a good idea." He told himself that the crawling emptiness in his stomach was due to a lack of food. "I don't imagine your caseload's going to get any smaller."

"No, it should take me six months of concentrated work to get it under control again. You'll probably start on a new film the minute this one's finished."

"It's being cast now," he murmured. "I'm going to produce it too."

Tory smiled. "No guarantors?"

Phil answered the smile. "We'll see."

They drove for another half mile in silence. Slowing down, Tory pulled off onto a small dirt road and stopped. Phil took a quick glance around at nothing in particular, then turned to her. "What are we doing?"

"Parking." She scooted from under the steering wheel, winding her arms around his neck.

"Isn't there some legality about using an official car for illicit purposes?" His mouth was already seeking hers, craving.

"I'll pay the fine in the morning." She silenced his chuckle with a deep, desperate kiss.

As if by mutual consent, they went slowly. All pleasure, all desire, was concentrated in tastes. Lips, teeth, and tongues brought shuddering arousal, urging them to hurry. But they would satisfy needs with mouths only first. Her lips were silkily yielding even as they met and increased his demand. Wild, crazy desires whipped through him, but her mouth held him prisoner. He touched her nowhere else. This taste—spiced honey, this texture—heated satin—would live with him always.

Tory let her lips roam his face. She knew each crease, each angle, each slope, more intimately than she knew her own features. With her eyes closed she could see him perfectly, and knew she had only to close her eyes again, in a year, in ten years, to have the same vivid picture. The skin on his neck was damp, making the flavor intensify as her tongue glided over it. Without thinking, she ran her fingers down his shirt, nimbly loosening buttons. When his chest was vulnerable, she spread both palms over it to feel his quick shudder. Then she brought her mouth, lazily, invitingly, back to his.

Her fingertips sent a path of ice, a path of fire, over his naked skin. Her mouth was drawing him in until his head swam. His labored breathing whispered on the night air. Wanting her closer, he shifted, cursed the cramped confines of the car, then dragged her across his lap. Lifting her to him, he buried his face against the side of her neck. He fed there, starving for her until she moaned and brought his hand to rest on her breast. With torturous slowness he undid the series of buttons, allowing his fingertips to trail along her skin as it was painstakingly exposed. He let the tips of his fingers bring her to desperation.

The insistent brush of his thumb over the point of her breast released a shaft of exquisite pain so sharp, she cried out with it, dragging him closer. Open and hungry, her mouth fixed on his while she fretted to touch more of him. Their position made it impossible, but her body was his. He ran his hands over it, feeling her skin jump as he roamed to the waistband of her jeans. Loosening them, he slid his hand down to warm, moist secrets. His mouth crushed hers as he drank in her moan.

Tory struggled, maddened by the restrictions, wild with desire, as his fingers aroused her beyond belief. He kept her trapped against him, knowing once she touched him that his control would shatter. This night, he thought, this final night, would last until there was no tomorrow.

When she crested, he rose with her, half delirious. No woman was so soft, no woman was so responsive. His heart pounded, one separate pain after another, as he drove her up again.

Her struggles ceased. Compliance replaced them. Tory lay shuddering in a cocoon of unrivaled sensations. She was his. Though her mind was unaware of the total gift of self, her body knew. She'd been his, perhaps from the first, perhaps only for that moment, but there would never be any turning back. Love swamped her; desire sated her. There was nothing left but the need to possess, to be possessed, by one man. In that instant she conceded her privacy.

The change in her had something racing through him. Phil couldn't question, couldn't analyze. He knew only that they must come together now—now, while there was something magic shimmering. It had nothing to do with the moonlight beaming into the car or the eerie silence surrounding them. It concerned only them and the secret that had grown despite protests. He didn't think, he didn't deny. With a sudden madness he tugged on her clothes and his own. Speed was foremost in his mind. He had to hurry before whatever trembled in the tiny confines was lost. Then her body was beneath his, fused to his, eager, asking.

He took her on the seat of the car like a passionate teenager. He felt like a man who had been given something precious, and as yet unrecognizable.

CHAPTER 12

A long sleepy time. Moonlight on the back of closed lids . . . night air over naked skin. The deep, deep silence of solitude by the whispering breathing of intimacy.

Tory floated in that luxurious plane between sleep and wakefulness—on her side, on the narrow front seat, with her body fitted closely against Phil's. Their legs were tangled, their arms around each other, as much for support as need. With his mouth near her ear, his warm breath skipped along her skin.

There were two marginally comfortable beds back at the hotel. They could have chosen either of them for their last night together, but they had stayed where they were, on a rough vinyl seat, on a dark road, as the night grew older. There they were alone completely. Morning still seemed very far away.

A hawk cried out as it drove toward earth. Some small animal screamed in the brush. Tory's lids fluttered up to find Phil's eyes open and on hers. In the moonlight his irises were very pale. Needing no words, perhaps wanting none, Tory lifted her mouth to his. They made love again, quietly, slowly, with more tenderness than either was accustomed to.

So they dozed again, unwilling to admit that the night was slipping away from them. When Tory awoke, there was a faint lessening in the darkness—not light, but the texture that meant morning was close.

A few more hours, she thought, gazing at the sky through the far window as she lay beside him. When the sun came up, it would be over. Now his body was warm against hers. He slept lightly, she knew. She had only to shift or murmur his name and he would awaken. She remained still. For a few more precious moments she wanted the simple unity that came from having him sleep at her side. There would be no stopping the sun from rising in the east—or stopping her lover from going west. It was up to her to accept the second as easily as she accepted the first. Closing her eyes, she willed herself to be strong. Phil stirred, dreaming.

He walked through his house in the hills, purposely, from room to room, looking, searching, for what was vague to him; but time after time he turned away, frustrated. Room after room after room. Everything was familiar: the colors, the furniture, even small personal objects that identified his home, his belongings. Something was missing. Stolen, lost? The house echoed emptily around him as he continued to search for something vital and unknown. The emotions of the man in the dream communicated themselves to the man dreaming. He felt the helplessness, the anger and the panic.

Hearing him murmur her name, Tory shifted yet closer. Phil shot awake, disoriented. The dream slipped into some corner of his mind that he couldn't reach.

"It's nearly morning," she said quietly.

A bit dazed, struggling to remember what he had dreamed that had left him feeling so empty, Phil looked at the sky. It was lightening. The first pale pinks bloomed at the horizon. For a moment they watched in silence as the day crept closer, stealing their night.

"Make love to me again," Tory whispered. "Once more, before morning."

He could see the quiet need in her eyes, the dark smudges beneath that told of patchy sleep, the soft glow that spoke clearly of a night of loving. He held the picture in his mind a moment, wanting to be certain he wouldn't lose it when time had dimmed other memories. He lowered his mouth to hers in bittersweet good-bye.

The sky paled to blue. The horizon erupted with color. The gold grew molten and scarlet bled into it as dawn came up. They loved intensely one final time. As morning came they lost themselves in each other, pretending it was still night. Where he touched, she trembled. Where she kissed, his skin hummed until they could no longer deny the need. The sun had full claim when they came together, so that the light streamed without mercy. Saying little, they dressed, then drove back to town.

When Tory stopped in front of the hotel, she felt she was in complete control again. No regrets, she reminded herself, as she turned off the ignition. We've just come to the fork in the road. We knew it was there when we started. Turning, she smiled at Phil.

"We're liable to be a bit stiff today."

Grinning, he leaned over and kissed her chin. "It was worth it."

"Remember that when you're moaning for a hot

bath on your way back to L.A." Tory slid from the car. When she stepped up on the sidewalk, Phil took her hand. The contact threatened her control before she snapped it back into place.

"I'm going to be thinking of you," he murmured as they stepped into the tiny lobby.

"You'll be busy." She let her hand slide on the banister as they mounted the stairs.

"Not that busy." Phil turned her to him when they reached the top landing. "Not that busy, Tory," he said again.

Her courtroom experience came to her aid. Trembling inside, Tory managed an easy smile. "I'm glad. I'll think of you too." *Too often, too much. Too painful.*

"If I call you—"

"I'm in the book," she interrupted. Play it light, she ordered herself. The way it was supposed to be, before . . . "Keep out of trouble, Kincaid," she told him as she slipped her room key into its lock.

"Tory."

He stepped closer, but she barred the way into the room. "I'll say good-bye now." With another smile she rested a hand on his cheek. "It'll be simpler, and I think I'd better catch a couple hours' sleep before I go into the office."

Phil took a long, thorough study of her face. Her eyes were direct, her smile easy. Apparently there was nothing left to say. "If that's what you want."

Tory nodded, not fully trusting herself. "Be happy, Phil," she managed before she disappeared into her room. Very carefully Tory turned the lock before she walked to the bed. Lying down, she curled into a ball and wept, and wept, and wept.

It was past noon when Tory awoke. Her head was pounding. Dragging herself to the bathroom, she studied herself objectively in the mirror over the sink. Terrible, she decided without emotion. The headache had taken the color from her cheeks, and her eyes were swollen and red from tears. Dispassionately, Tory ran the water until it was icy cold, then splashed her face with it. When her skin was numb, she stripped and stepped under the shower.

She decided against aspirin. The pills would dull the pain, and the pain made it difficult to think. Thinking was the last thing she felt she needed to do at the moment; Phil was gone, back to his own life. She would go on with hers. The fact that she had fallen in love with him over her own better judgment was simply her hard luck. In a few days she would be able to cope with it easily enough. Like hell you will, she berated herself as she dried her skin with a rough towel. You fell hard, and some bruises take years to heal . . . if ever.

Wasn't it ironic, she mused as she went back into the bedroom to dress. Victoria L. Ashton, Attorney at Law, dedicated to straightening out other people's lives, had just made a beautiful mess of her own. And yet, there hadn't been any options. A deal was a deal.

Phil, she said silently, I've decided to change our contract. Circumstances have altered, and I'm in love with you. I propose we include certain things like commitment and reciprocal affection into our arrangement, with options for additions such as marriage and children, should both parties find it agreeable.

She gave a short laugh and pulled on a fresh shirt. Of course, she could merely have clung to him, tearfully begging him not to leave her. What man wouldn't love to find himself confronted with a hysterical woman who won't let go?

Better this way, she reminded herself, tugging on

jeans. Much better to have a clean, civilized break. Aloud, she said something potent about being civilized as she pinned on her badge. The one thing she had firmly decided during her crying jag was that it was time for her to leave Friendly. Merle could handle the responsibilities of the office for the next few weeks without too much trouble. She had come to terms with her father's death, with her mother. She felt confident that she'd helped in Tod's family situation. Merle had grown up a bit. All in all, Tory felt she wasn't needed any longer. In Albuquerque she could put her own life in motion again. She needed that if she wasn't going to spend three weeks wallowing in self-pity and despair. At least, she decided, it was something she could start on. Naturally she would have to talk to the mayor and officially resign. There would be a visit to her mother. If she spent a day briefing Merle, she should be able to leave before the end of the week.

Her own rooms, Tory thought, trying to work up some excitement. The work she was trained for—a meaty court case that would take weeks of preparation and a furnace of energy. She felt suddenly that she had a surplus of it and nowhere to go. Back in the bath, she applied a careful layer of makeup to disguise the effects of tears, then brushed her hair dry. The first step was the mayor. There was no point putting it off.

It took thirty minutes for Tory to convince the mayor she was serious and another fifteen to assure him that Merle was capable of handling the job of acting sheriff until the election.

"You know, Tory," Bud said when he saw her mind was made up, "we're going to be sorry to lose you. I guess we all kept hoping you'd change your mind and run. You've been a good sheriff, I guess you come by it naturally."

"I appreciate that—really." Touched, Tory took the hand he offered her. "Pat Rowe and Nick Merriweather are both fair men. Whoever wins, the town's in good hands. In a few years Merle will make you a fine sheriff."

"If you ever change your mind . . ." Bud trailed off wanting to leave the door open.

"Thanks, but my niche in the law isn't in enforcement. I have to get back to my practice."

"I know, I know." He sighed, capitulating. "You've done more than we had a right to expect."

"I did what I wanted to do," she corrected.

"I guess things will be quiet for a while, especially with the movie people gone." He gave a regretful glance toward the window. Excitement, he mused, wasn't meant for Friendly. "Come by and see me before you leave town."

Outside, the first thing Tory noticed was the absence of the movie crew. There were no vans, no sets, no lights or packets of people. Friendly had settled back into its yawning pace as though there had never been a ripple. Someone had written some graffiti in the dust on the window of the post office. A car puttered into town and stopped in front of the hardware store. Tory started to cross the street, but stopped in the center when she was hailed. Shielding her eyes, she watched Tod race toward her.

"Sheriff, I've been looking for you."

"Is something wrong?"

"No." He grinned the quick-spreading grin that transformed his thin face. "It's real good, I wanted you to know. My dad . . . well, we've been talking, you know, and we even drove out to see those people you told us about."

"How'd it go?"

"We're going to go back—my mom too."

"I'm happy for you." Tory brushed her knuckles over his cheek. "It's going to take time, Tod. You'll all have to work together."

"I know, but . . ." He looked up at her, his eyes wide and thrilled. "He really loves me. I never thought he did. And my mom, she wondered if you could come out to the house sometime. She wants to thank you."

"There isn't any need for that."

"She wants to."

"I'll try." Tory hesitated, finding that this good-bye would be more difficult than most. "I'm going away in a couple of days."

His elated expression faded. "For good?"

"My mother lives here," she reminded him. "My father's buried here. I'll come back from time to time."

"But not to stay."

"No," Tory said softly. "Not to stay."

Tod lowered his gaze to the ground. "I knew you'd leave. I guess I was pretty stupid that day in your office when I . . ." He trailed off with a shrug and continued to stare at the ground.

"I didn't think you were stupid. It meant a lot to me." Tory put out a hand to lift his face. "*Means* a lot to me."

Tod moistened his lips. "I guess I still love you—if you don't mind."

"Oh." Tory felt the tears spring to her eyes and pulled him into her arms. "I'm going to miss you like crazy. Would you think I was stupid if I said I wish I were a fourteen-year-old girl?"

Grinning, he drew away. Nothing she could have said could have pleased him more. "I guess if you were, I could kiss you good-bye."

With a laugh Tory brushed a light kiss on his lips.

"Go on, get out of here," she ordered unsteadily. "Nothing undermines the confidence of a town more than having its sheriff crying in the middle of the street."

Feeling incredibly mature, Tod dashed away. Turning, he ran backward for a moment. "Will you write sometime?"

"Yes, yes, I'll write." Tory watched him streak off at top speed. Her smile lost some of its sparkle. She was losing, she discovered, quite a bit in one day. Briskly shaking off the mood, she turned in the direction of her office. She was still a yard away when Merle strolled out.

"Hey," he said foolishly, glancing from her, then back at the door he'd just closed.

"Hey yourself," she returned. "You just got yourself a promotion, Merle T."

"Tory, there's—Huh?"

"Incredibly articulate," she replied with a fresh smile. "I'm resigning. You'll be acting sheriff until the election."

"Resigning?" He gave her a completely baffled look. "But you—" He broke off, shaking his head at the door again. "How come?"

"I need to get back to my practice. Anyway"—she stepped up on the sidewalk—"it shouldn't take long for me to fill you in on the procedure. You already know just about everything. Come on inside and we'll get started."

"Tory." In an uncharacteristic gesture he took her arm and stopped her. Shrewdly direct, his eyes locked on hers. "Are you upset about something?"

Merle was definitely growing up, Tory concluded. "I just saw Tod." It was part of the truth, and all she would discuss. "That kid gets to me."

His answer was a slow nod, but he didn't release

her arm. "I guess you know the movie people left late this morning."

"Yes, I know." Hearing her own clipped response, Tory took a mental step back. "I don't suppose it was easy for you to say good-bye to Marlie," she said more gently.

"I'll miss her some," he admitted, still watching Tory critically. "We had fun together."

His words were so calm that Tory tilted her head as she studied him. "I was afraid you'd fallen in love with her."

"In love with her?" He let out a hoot of laughter. "Shoot, I ain't ready for that. No way."

"Sometimes being ready doesn't make any difference," Tory muttered. "Well," she said more briskly, "since you're not crying in your beer, why don't we go over some things? I'd like to be in Albuquerque before the end of the week."

"Ah . . . yeah, sure." Merle glanced around the empty street. "I gotta talk to somebody first over at, um . . . the hotel," he announced. "Be right back."

Tory shot him an exasperated glance as he loped across the street. "Well," she murmured, "some things never change." Deciding she could spend the time packing her books and papers, Tory walked into the office.

Seated at her desk, casually examining the .45, was Phil Kincaid. She stopped dead, gaping at him. "Sheriff," he said mildly, giving the barrel an idle spin.

"Phil." She found her voice, barely. "What are you doing here?"

He didn't rise but propped his feet up on the desk instead. "I forgot something. Did you know you didn't unload this thing last night?"

She didn't even glance at the gun but stood rooted to the spot. "I thought you'd left hours ago."

"Did you?" He gave her a long, steady look. The cold water and makeup had helped, but he knew her face intimately. "I did," he agreed after a moment. "I came back."

"Oh." So now she would have to deal with the good-bye a second time. Tory ignored the ache in her stomach and smiled. "What did you forget?"

"I owe you something," he said softly. The gesture with the gun was very subtle but clear enough.

Only partially amused, Tory lifted a brow. "Let's call it even," she suggested. Wanting to busy her hands, she went to the shelf near the desk to draw out her books.

"No," he said mildly. "I don't think so. Turn around, Sheriff."

Annoyance was the least painful of her emotions, so Tory let it out. "Look, Phil—"

"In the cell," he interrupted. "I can recommend the first one."

"You're out of your mind." With a thud she dropped the books. "If that thing's loaded, you could hurt someone."

"I have some things to say to you," he continued calmly. "In there." Again he gestured toward the cell.

Her hands went to her hips. "All right, Kincaid, I'm still sheriff here. The penalty for armed assault on a peace officer—"

"Shut up and get in," Phil ordered.

"You can take that gun," Tory began dangerously, "and—"

Her suggestion was cut off when Phil grabbed her arm and hauled her into a cell. Stepping in with her, he pulled the door shut with a shattering clang.

"You *idiot!*" Impotently, Tory gave the locked door a furious jerk. "Now just how the hell are we supposed to get out?"

Phil settled comfortably on the bunk, propped on one elbow, with the gun lowered toward the floor. It was just as empty as it had been when Tory had bluffed him. "I haven't anyplace better to go."

Fists on hips, Tory whirled. "Just what is this all about, Kincaid?" she demanded. "You're supposed to be halfway to L.A. Instead you're propped up at my desk. Instead of a reasonable explanation, you throw that gun around like some two-bit hood—"

"I thought I did it with such finesse," he complained, frowning at the object under discussion. "Of course, I'd rather have a piece with a bit more style." He grinned up at her. "Pearl handle, maybe."

"Do you have to behave like such a fool?"

"I suppose."

"When this is over, you're going to find yourself locked up for months. Years, if I can manage it," she added, turning to tug uselessly on the bars again.

"That won't work," he told her amiably. "I shook them like crazy a few months ago."

Ignoring him, Tory stalked to the window. Not a soul on the street. She debated swallowing her pride and calling out. It would look terrific, she thought grimly, to have the sheriff shouting to be let out of one of her own cells. If she waited for Merle, at least she could make him swear to secrecy.

"All right, Kincaid," she said between her teeth. "Let's have it. Why are you here and why the devil are we locked in the cell?"

He glanced down at the gun again, then set it on the edge of the bunk. Automatically, Tory judged the distance. "Because," and his voice had altered enough to lure her eyes to his, "I found myself in an impossible situation."

At those words Tory felt her heart come to a stop, then begin again at a furious rate. Cautiously she warned herself not to read anything into the statement. True, she remembered his use of the phrase when talking about love, but it didn't follow that he meant the same thing now.

"Oh?" she managed, and praised herself for a brilliant response.

"*'Oh?'*" Phil pushed himself off the bunk in a quick move. "Is that all you can say? I got twenty miles out of town," he went on in sudden fury. "I told myself that was it. You wanted—I wanted—a simple transient relationship. No complications. We'd enjoyed each other—it was over."

Tory swallowed. "Yes, we'd agreed—"

"The hell with what we agreed." Phil grabbed her shoulders, shaking her until her mouth dropped open in shock. "It got complicated. It got very, very complicated." Releasing her abruptly, he began to pace the cell he had locked them both into.

"Twenty miles out of town," he repeated, "and I couldn't make it. Even last night I told myself it was all for the best. You'd go your way, I'd go mine. We'd both have some great memories." He turned to her then; although his voice lowered, it was no calmer. "Damn it, Tory, I want more than memories of you. I need more. You didn't want this to happen, I know that." Agitated, he ran a hand through his hair, while she said nothing. "I didn't want it, either, or thought I didn't. I'm not sure anymore. It might have been the first minute I walked in here, or that day at the cemetery. It might have been that night at the lake or a hundred other times. I don't know when it happened, why it happened." He shook his head as though it was a problem he'd struggled with and ultimately given up on. "I only know I love you. And God knows I can't leave you. I tried—I can't."

With a shuddering sigh Tory walked back to the bars and rested her head against them. The headache she had awoken with was now a whirling dizziness. A minute, she told herself. I just need a minute to take it in.

"I know you've got a life in Albuquerque," Phil continued, fighting against the fluttering panic in his stomach. "I know you've got a career that's important to you. It isn't something I'm asking you to choose between. There are ways to balance things if people want to badly enough. I broke the rules. I'm willing to make the adjustments."

"Adjustments . . ." Tory managed before she turned back to him.

"I can live in Albuquerque," he told her as he crossed the cell. "That won't stop me from making movies."

"The studio—"

"I'll buy a plane and commute," he said quickly. "It's been done before."

"A plane." With a little laugh she walked away, dragging a hand through her hair. "A plane."

"Yes, damn it, a plane." Her reaction was nothing that he had expected. The panic grew. "You didn't want me to go," he began in defense, in fury. "You've been crying. I can tell."

A bit steadier, Tory faced him again. "Yes, I cried. No, I didn't want you to go. Still, I thought it was best for both of us."

"Why?"

"It wouldn't be easy, juggling two careers and one relationship."

"Marriage," he corrected firmly. "Marriage, Tory. The whole ball of wax. Kids too. I want you to have my children." He saw the change in her eyes—shock, fear? Unable to identify it, Phil went to her again. "I said I love you." Again he took her by the shoulders. This time he didn't shake her but held her almost tentatively. "I have to know what you feel for me."

She spent a moment simply looking into his eyes. Loved her? Yes, she realized with something like a jolt. She could see it. It was real. And more, he was hurting because he wasn't sure. Doubts melted away. "I've been in an impossible situation, I think, from the first moment Merle hauled you in here."

She felt his fingers tense, then relax again. "Are you sure?" he asked, fighting the need to drag her against him.

"That I'm in love with you?" For the first time a ghost of a smile hovered around her mouth. "Sure enough that I nearly died when I thought you were leaving me. Sure enough that I was going to let you go because I'm just as stupid as you are."

His hands dove into her hair. "Stupid?" he repeated, drawing her closer.

"'He needs his own life. We agreed not to complicate things. He'd hate it if I begged him to stay.'" She smiled more fully. "Sound familiar?"

"With a slight change in the personal pronoun." Phil pulled her close just to hold her. *Mine*, they thought simultaneously, then clung. "Ah, Tory, last night was so wonderful—and so terrible."

"I know, thinking it was the last time." She drew back only enough so their mouths could meet. "I've been giving some thought to it for a while," she murmured, then lost the trend of thought as they kissed again.

"To what?"

"To . . . oh, to moving to the coast."

Framing her face with his hands, Phil tilted it to his. "You don't have to do that. I told you, I can—"

"Buy a plane," she finished on a laugh. "And I'm sure you can. But I have given some thought lately to moving on. Why not California?"

"We'll work that out."

"Eventually," she agreed, drawing his mouth back to hers.

"Tory." He held her off a moment, his eyes serious again. "Are you going to marry me?"

She considered a moment, letting her fingers twine in his hair. "It might be wise," she decided, "since we're going to have those kids."

"When?"

"It takes nine months," she reminded him.

"Marriage," he corrected, nipping her bottom lip.

"Well, after you've served your sentence . . . about three months."

"Sentence?"

"Illegal use of a handgun, accosting a peace officer, improper use of a correctional facility . . ." She shrugged, giving him her dashing grin. "Time off for good behavior, you should be out in no time. Remember, I'm still sheriff here, Kincaid."

"The hell you are." Pulling the badge from her blouse, he tossed it through the bars of the window. "Besides, you'll never make it stick."

THE FIRST IN A BRAND NEW TRILOGY
from the *New York Times* bestselling author

NORA ROBERTS

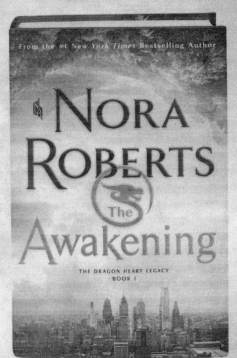

From the #1 New York Times Bestselling Author

NORA ROBERTS

The
Awakening

THE DRAGON HEART LEGACY
BOOK I

Where parallel worlds clash over
the struggle between good and evil

AVAILABLE WHEREVER BOOKS ARE SOLD